zodiac AWAKENING
Book One

Drew Smith

2nd Edition

Drew Smith

All rights reserved. No part of this publication may be reproduced or transmitted by any means, electronic, mechanical, photocopying or otherwise, without prior permission of the publisher and author.

Copyright © Drew Smith 2017
Cover illustrations by Jon Merchant © 2017

For more information regarding sales, events, and the community follow along on Facebook.com/ZodiacAwakening
Or follow us on Twitter: @DrewJTSmith

ISBN: 9781979566742

Chapter One: A Hero in Darkness

The darkness seemed to take over the sky, and the night seemed still. The wind whistled gently as it passed through the dark forests that surrounded Ruben. A fire blazed under the red moonlit night in front of him and roared like a hundred raging boars. He was a young man dressed in brown clothes like rags, and brown hair to match. He had a strong build. He was a farmer like his father after all.
Ruben stared into the night sky at the moon that never seemed to move and smiled as he daydreamed. Ruben thought that it was the most beautiful thing in the world. He often dreamed that a brighter moon would appear to make his world seem more alive, one that would light the darkness around him to show him the way to a better place, and he didn't mean the blue moon of the day, but something brighter. Ruben sat quietly by the fire and only snapped out of his daydream when the charred logs began to collapse. Ruben waited for his father to return with the firewood from the farm cellar. The farm was quite the walk north of the cliffs and it would still be sometime before he returned. His father was a strong man with pale blue skin and dark blue hair. He did most of the footwork at night, to stay alert while wild demons plagued the area near their home.

They had a new neighbour that settled in the woods to the east. An old demon by the name of Hector. There were many stories of him from his youth that Ruben had heard. They say he was a great demon swordsman. A hunter of humans, and killer of the wild demons. Ruben's father told him to never go off their farm, or even past the tree line of the farm for that matter. His father also told Ruben to never approach Hector under any circumstances. Ruben was a human boy after all, and the demon Hector would surely kill him on sight. Ruben thought it would be crazy to go that far from the farm for any reason anyway. Shortly after Hector had settled into the land beside their farm, a human girl began showing up when Rubens father wasn't around. Her name was Scarlette, and she was a beautiful young woman with long pink hair and bright blue eyes. She was a year older than Ruben but seemed so wise for her age. Scarlette was very mysterious in her ways, and she always came when the red moon was covered by the clouds. Ruben often thought she was brave for moving through the night alone, for a human anyway.

Ruben turned back to the red moon and continued to stare. His mind fluttering from thought to thought, and had caused him to forget to watch his surroundings.

"Ruben," whispered Scarlette quietly from the bushes. Scarlette was the only one that called him Ruben, but then again he had no one else other than his father who called him by Ben.

"Scarlette you nearly gave me a heart attack!" Ruben blurted out quickly.

"At your age? Ruben, that's impossible." Scarlette whispered with a laugh. She stood close to Ruben with a small grin as if happy to see him, but almost upset with him too.

"Are you sure Scarlette? Father says it can happen to anybody." Ruben smiled as if he was sure.

"Sure Ruben, and only if you don't watch what you eat, but you're a fit looking lad are you not?" Scarlette laughed once again.

"Wow, you really sound like my father there Scarlette. I'm sure of it. He says that on the fields almost every day when I get tired, and he says those exact words." Scarlette turned her eyes to the fire.

"Is your father coming back anytime soon?" She muttered.

A breeze came through the forest brushing trees against each other fiercely for a moment. Ruben looked up from the fire, and toward the farm in the north.

"He went back to the farm for more firewood. We haven't had time to restock. It is harvest season after all."

"I see. Ruben... What is it that you want?" Scarlette asked as she glared at him.

"What do I want? What do you mean?"

"I mean what do you want out of life? Are you happy working on a farm you can never leave? Do you not feel like you are meant for something else?

Something more?" She looked up to the sky with her eyes locked on the moon.

"I suppose... I have always wanted to help people. Sometimes I feel... Incomplete..." He replied.

"Incomplete? What do you mean?" Scarlette asked. "I don't know. To be honest, I read a lot of books about heroes saving the world, and the heroes always seem like they know who they are, but I don't think it is that simple. I don't think a hero really intends to really be a hero. I feel like they all just want to help others, and through their actions earn the title as a hero from those they help." Ruben smiled. Scarlette stared at Ruben with a small grin.

"So, a hero is not a hero at all? A hero can be anyone who truly fights for what they believe in? Then what do you believe in Ruben?"

"That's a good question. If I had to think about it, I would say I believe this place is a prison. I am not behind bars, and my father doesn't force me to stay here, but I know I have no choice but to stay. I wish the world wasn't bound by the rules that are in place. I want to free this world, but at the same time... To this world, it is free. This seems to be the way things are because this is what is wanted. Can I really be a hero of a world that is not in need of one?" Ruben stared at the sky. He thought about the far reaches of the skies above and the possibilities of what could lie beyond the stars. His eyes wandered the skies until they followed an odd red hue coming from the farm.

"Scarlette, look at the sky!" shouted Ruben.

Scarlette paused, then looked away from Ruben to the sky above them.

"Something is wrong," Scarlette announced.
Ruben shot up as fast as lightning, and bolted toward the farm, fearing something terrible had gone wrong. He nearly knocked Scarlette to the ground as he raced by her. The forested area in which the fire pit was laid had been blocked on all sides, and the only way in was the small path cut into the trees. Rubens father cut the path and blocked it all off, so they could make a clearing for the fire pit at the cliffs. They used it as a getaway from the farm mostly to relax after a long day's work. A long path stretched from the forested area and all the way back to the farm. A walk that would normally take an hour. It was an organized arrangement of trees that was also created by Ruben's father, and it laid along the cliffs that were very dangerous, but worth the long hike.

Ruben ran as fast as he could, leaving Scarlette behind without a second thought. The dark sky turned a dim red as he ran closer and closer toward the farm. Flames became visible, and dread filled his heart. The flames grew larger and larger with every step. Ruben's breath was steaming in the cold, and his body was beginning to tire. He could not stop though. He used every single breath in his body to get to his father. The large wooden gate at the West entrance finally came into sight. Memories of him and his father building it last season filled his mind.

Scarlette came up to the west gate just behind Ruben, but he didn't even notice her following him. Her thoughts clouded her judgement. She threw her black cloak over her head and brushed her long pink hair off to the side over her shoulder. She reached into her side pouch and pulled out a small hourglass. She looked toward the farm, but Ruben was but a speck in the distance. She slowly walked toward the farm after Ruben.

He stood in the center of the farm, and he looked at the burning blaze that was shredding his life away little by little. His father nowhere in sight and the flames were spreading quickly from roof to roof. He didn't even blink as he scurried into the blaze of the closest building without concern for himself.

Rain slowly built up in the charred heavens above. Each drop like a tease to the dry field below, until it became a fierce storm that gave in to the field's greedy thirst. Ruben ran from building to building calling for his father. The rain fell harder, and harder as he searched. The red moon was dim with cloud cover, and the darkness soaked in a cheerless storm covering the whole land. Ruben dropped to his knees.

"Father!" screamed Ruben at the top of his lungs. His rage began to build, as his fists clenched in a firm grip. The farm slowly fell to pieces around him as he kneeled before the flames victory.

"Ruben!" a voice shrieked.

"Father?" He looked up in disbelief but saw no one. He couldn't be sure if he had heard anything, or if his mind was playing tricks on him, but didn't want to take the chance of it being nothing. He rose to his feet and called his father once again. The crackling of burning wood and crashing lumber falling to the ground made it difficult to hear anything. He looked with his eyes wide open and shouted over the flames, but his father didn't respond. The only place he had not yet checked was his father's bedroom inside the main cabin, though he felt it unlikely he would be there since he had come back for lumber. He quickly bolted over the fencing, and into the flames of his father's cabin with little hope left.

Scarlette came walking calmly out from the path and watched as Ruben ran inside the engulfed cabin. She smiled lightly and shut her eyes. The roof caved in over Ruben shortly after he went in, and he yelled out in pain. Scarlette's eyes opened wide, and her mouth dropped.

"Lumus!" Scarlette yelled out. She began to run forward, but as she did the ground began to shake. Scarlette looked back to the cabin, and she was amazed to see a blue light that began to shine through the collapsed cabin. Suddenly a yell from under the debris could be heard throughout the land once again. Scarlette took a step back and shielded her eyes from the light. Scarlette heard movement from the farm's north entrance.

"It seems the locals are coming." Scarlette turned back to the bushes, but she looked back to see Ruben collapse with his father in his arms just outside the cabin.

The day had come, signaled by the newly risen blue moon that dimly lit the sky, replacing the red moon of night. The air still smelt of smoke. Ruben woke up in a strange room. It was well kept and had a single window. He raced from his bed to look down upon a small village. He noticed a sign that read Aster Inn. He had never been to town before and had only heard stories of the Aster Inn from his father. He already got up and pulled the sheet off of quietly while staring at the door. Ruben was hoping that he could sneak out the window. He gazed outside just to find himself on the second floor with nothing below to break his fall. Realizing the door was the only option he grabbed his boots and reached for the handle.
It was silent outside, not a single sound filled the village. Still, he was uneasy and concerned. He had a million questions; what happened to the farm, and his father? Was it an accident? What happened to Scarlette? How was he still alive?
The door opened with a creak, and a large green-skinned demon with a black cloak looked back into Ruben's eyes. His heart skipped a beat, and he felt like he had to defend himself. He raised his fists to the demon.
"I am Alistro. You will come with me now human. Do not make me drag you." The demon laughed deeply as he turned, and walked back into the hall. The laugh did not comfort Ruben at all.
("Why would they keep me alive? What do they want with me?") He wondered as he collected the rest of his things.

"Come human!" Yelled Alistro over his shoulder. Ruben decided it would be best to follow Alistro until he could find an opportunity to escape. Alistro followed the long hallway to the stairs. The hallway alone seemed bigger than the farm he thought. The wood was a nice clean cedar, built in last years like the builder took pride in their work. Ruben found it odd that demons cared for craftsmanship at all. The stories he was told gave him the idea that they were all savage monsters that killed others for sport.

Ruben came to a landing above a stairway, which spiraled down to the floor below. Alistro was still walking the same speed, not once looking back to see if Ruben was following behind. Alistro stopped at the large double doors to the streets.

"Go," Alistro demanded. Ruben looked at him with confusion as he caught up with him.

"Go where?" Ruben replied.

Alistro picked Ruben up by his belt from behind and tossed him into the street. A cloud of dust rose from the ground causing him to cough.

"Get up boy!" Alistro demanded. Ruben got up quickly and immediately ran down the road away from Alistro. He looked back for a moment to see if he had been chasing him, but Alistro was gone.

"Boy? You test me?" Ruben turned around and stared Alistro in the eyes.

Alistro raised his fist. The punch forced Ruben off of his feet, and he flew a great distance back.

"Ah...Wow. Oh man, that hurt." Ruben coughed once again and wiped the blood from his lip.

"How did he get in front of me? What do you want?" Ruben cried out.

"Tell me what you know of Twilight. Tell me your purpose here. Tell me who sent you!" Alistro demanded. His eyes glaring at Ruben as he walked toward him.

"My purpose? What do you mean?" Ruben questioned. Alistro's cloak hid his face, his knees bent, and his fist clenched tight.

"Don't toy with me human! I'll rip you limb from limb until you tell me what I want to know! Don't waste my time!" Alistro's cloak blew back in the wind revealing his face. It was a terrifying face, tinged green and marked with a scar across his face.

"I don't know anything about this Twilight thing!" Ruben yelled out. He shifted left and right, looking for any way to escape. Smaller demons, almost little versions of Alistro came out from the shadow, and there were dozens of them.

"Meet my family, boy". Announced Alistro in that deep sinister voice. They surrounded Ruben, and clearly out-matched and out-numbered him. Ruben raised his fist to guard himself.

"Stupid human! You have no chance. Tell me what I want to know, so I can hurry up and kill you. Or you can be stubborn, in which case I'll toy with you until you squeal!" Alistro's voice became louder with every word as he walked closer and closer to him. The other demons formed a circle around them. The Inn was behind Alistro now, and Ruben was in the middle of the dirt road. He got to his feet with his head down.

"What happened last night was your fault, wasn't it?" His voice starting to get lower as his rage grew.

"You know what boy? You're not even half the man your so-called father was, so what makes you think you can beat me?" Alistro laughed hysterically, "If you must know, he was killed for sheltering a human child."

Ruben's brown hair fell to cover his eyes, a single tear rolled down his cheek.

"I will never forgive you, you monster!" Ruben shouted. He began to yell out in rage. His arms began throbbing, and his chest extended. His body started to emit a bright white light.

"Ruben, up here, catch! Scarlette yelled as she threw a silver crested sword down from the Inn rooftop.

Its beauty was unmatched, with gems in the hilt glowing even in the daylight. He didn't even look up, but raised his arm, catching the blade's sheath, then raised his other arm to pull out the sword.

"Alistro!" He yelled out as he ran toward the demon. He raised his head to reveal the anger in his eyes. As he charged forward the light emitting around his body flashed like an explosion, engulfing him completely. For a moment all that could be seen was a large white glow passing through Alistro. The light around Ruben had changed him. His pupils became a constant glow of white, and his hair shined like a star. The pure white glow changed him from the simple farm boy into a man. His ragged clothes materialized into a baggy white cloth; his old muddy boots now a silver gilded pair of boots laced with a silver lining down the centre, and gold trim around his ankle. In an instant Alistro had been defeated, his body sliced horizontally by Ruben's blade. The other demons that lined the street had scattered into the bushes.

"Scarlette? Scarlette where did you go?" He looked up at the rooftop over his shoulder, but she was already gone. He was alone once again. A white knight in the darkness of a world full of demons. Ruben looked at himself with marvel. His new clothes, and the change of his body. His lean figure had almost doubled in size, he felt taller too.

"What now...?" He said with hesitation.

"Well, maybe I can humour you with an old knight's story." A voice from the shadows said calmly.

"Who's there?" Ruben demanded.

"I am a friend, not a foe," announced the voice. A man in a dark green cloak came from the shadows just behind the inn. Ruben noticed the glint of golden armour hidden under the figure's cloak as the man walked forward. "My name is Orson," He announced. Orson turned his attention to Alistro on the ground.

("I have seen that demon before...Alistro. Incredible that Lumus could defeat him so easily after his first transformation. I struggled when I fought Alistro twenty years ago, and I was in my prime back then.") Orson shook his head with delight, then turned his attention to Ruben.

"I have been looking for you, my prince." Orson bowed.

"Prince? You must have the wrong guy." Ruben announced with confusion.

"No. I'm sure of it... You are the one that I'm here to find. I was the one that brought you here twenty years ago. I left you with the demon farmer Rozell. You must have a lot of questions I'd imagine. Let me explain what I can." Orson took a deep breath. "Firstly, the demon you call father is not your father, but I'm sure you knew that since you are human. He is simply one of the very few that I was able to put my trust in twenty years ago." Orson smiled.

"Not my father?" Ruben sat down on a rock nearby.

"He is my realm copy or familiar some would say." Orson threw back his hood, revealing an aged but familiar face.

"You! But how?" Ruben stood up in shock. Orson's face resembled that of Ruben's father's exactly, except that Orson was human, and did not share his father's light blue skin.

"I don't understand, how could this be?" Ruben shook his head, and the light around his body flashed intensely.

"You're not used to your power yet Lumus, you need to calm yourself." Ruben fell to his knees, and for a moment was still. When he was calmed down he looked up at Orson.

"Lumus? Why did you call me that? My name is Ruben." He stared at Orson.

"Ruben…? My familiar must have given you that name, but I did tell him your name. That is strange, but I suppose he had his reasons. Your real name is Lumus, the Prince of Light and Protector of Twilight."

"My name is Lumus? Twilight…?" Lumus held his head and closed his eyes.

"I know, my Prince, it must be overwhelming." Orson placed his hand on Lumus' Shoulder.

"My Prince, you will understand in time who you are, and this power you have."

Orson tried to smile, but he could tell it wouldn't help.

"So, you left me here with my father Rozell almost twenty years ago, and I was raised here in this world… It makes sense. I have always had the feeling like I didn't belong. I guess I always knew or hoped anyway." He replied.

"I'm sorry Lumus. I couldn't bring you with me. I didn't know what to do, and the only thing I could think of at the time was to leave you here with Rozell. I knew he would keep you safe, and I am sorry that he…" Orson looked at the ground.

"You don't have to Orson. I just wish I had this power to save him when he was in trouble. Some hero I am…" He smiled, but it quickly faded.

Orson wanted to ask but felt he shouldn't.

"We need to return to Twilight Lumus. I came here to bring you back. Lears has had twenty years to… Well, let's just say that Twilight is a different place now."

"Twilight, so it is real. Alistro mentioned it, but I had no memories of it until now."

"You remember Twilight Lumus? You were but a baby when we left. How could you remember Twilight at all?" Orson asked.

"This power. The moment I transformed. I have memories of many things. Things I have never actually experienced."

"I see. I don't quite understand, but maybe we can learn more about these memories later. For now, we need to leave this place. Alistro was just a grunt. I'm sure others will come looking for you.

"Wait, I need to find my friend. She was here a moment ago. She gave me this sword during my fight with Alistro. If we are to leave this world, I have to bring her with us." Lumus said as he looked around.

"She has gone ahead. I saw her head toward the Aster Mountains." A voice called out.

"Orson…" Lumus called as he rose to his feet, and stared into the dark path toward the Aster Mountains.

"Show yourself," Lumus yelled out as his glow illuminated the area revealing a green demon in the distance. Orson drew his blade and readied himself. The demon crouched down as if to prepare to dash at them. Suddenly the demon jumped with such speed that it looked as if he had disappeared before their eyes. Orson looked in all

directions, but couldn't spot the demon. Lumus turned around and looked at the Aster Inn rooftop.
"Ah, your reflexes are impressive. I sense something special about you." The demon said with his arms crossed.
"I am Brinx, Grenton Protector of Dystopia." Lumus and Orson looked at each other then back at Brinx.
"A protector of evil" Orson interrupted.
"No, the evil of this planet is not my concern. My concern is this planet itself. I live only for its safety and peaceful existence." Brinx uncrossed his arms as he corrected Orson.
"Demon trickery will not work on me," Orson said in a rage.
Lumus jumped just as Brinx did, with such speed that Orson couldn't believe his eyes. Lumus landed right beside Brinx on the Aster Inn rooftop.
"Ah, you're quick too? Impressive for a human." Brinx boasted. "I can only imagine what your familiar is like."
Lumus stared at Brinx without a blink. "My familiar?" replied Lumus.
Orson still stood below and began to walk closer to try to speak to Lumus.
"Lumus, you must know or have heard the tale before. There exists in this universe two worlds, or dimensions I suppose. Each in their own dimension of space, but everything here on Dystopia has a copy on Twilight. A person, place or thing must exist on both planets. From the beginning of time it has always been this way, but

only when I came to Dystopia with you twenty years ago did I start to believe this myself. If anything lives here, it must live in the other dimension, so the stories go. You're pure Lumus, you have been since you were born, but you were not born naturally. You were created using the blue core in the centre of Twilight. A wish was made in hopes that a perfect warrior could come here, and wipe out the demons so that we could have two peaceful worlds. Well, I shouldn't say we. Truthfully it was never our plan at all, but the plan of a child. The wish of a young girl created you, and all of Twilight's positive energy was used to make you. But when this happened, a rift in both worlds opened and sucked anyone under it through to the opposite world. Demons made their way to the core of Twilight, and I had no choice but to take you and try to escape. I took you outside, and we were both sucked into the sky. That's how you ended up in this dimension, but like I said, my prince, every person place or thing in one dimension must have a copy in the other dimension for the balance of our worlds. Our blue core turned red with negative energy since the positive was transferred to create you, and so the core of Twilight became unstable. After you and I came here another baby was born from the negative energy. I found that out when I had returned to Twilight twenty years ago. He was named Lears, and the surviving demons watched over him as he grew to be the one we all fear in Twilight now. He looks just like you, but pure evil

and hatred. Lumus, you are Twilight's last hope."
Lumus diverted his attention from Brinx to Orson.
"I understand, Orson. Ever since I changed into this form, I have been able to sense a strange power. I understand what that is now. It's him." Lumus crossed his arms and closed his eyes.
Orson stared in silence.
Brinx looked down at his hands.
("I have watched over this planet from evil all of this time, but this is far more important than this world alone. I must help in this cause. The true evil seems to be in Twilight? Then I must go.)
"Lumus, I will accompany you if you will accept?" Brinx asked. Orson had a look of disgust on his face, but Lumus smiled.
"You would leave Dystopia?" He asked.
"I have protected Dystopia for over one hundred years, and this new situation concerns this dimension too. I must see to this matter, and I am sure you understand my reason." Lumus opened his eyes to look at Brinx.
"Are you mad, demon? Why would we bring you to Twilight? Our mission is to get rid of you demons from our world. Why would we…"
"Orson." Lumus interrupted.
"My prince," Orson replied.
"Brinx, I can sense your spirit. You are not evil within. I will accept your offer." Lumus jumped down from the rooftop. Brinx followed after him.
"Prince Lumus, I don't understand," Orson said in confusion.

"Please Orson, just call me Lumus." He replied with a smile on his face.

"Orson, your familiar… he was killed trying to protect me." He hesitated to say if fear of his reaction. Orson turned his back to him suddenly. "I went to the farm where I had left you. I found nothing there but charred wood. I feared you had been killed, but I found the fire was fresh. I also followed the tracks from the demons to here. That is how I ended up finding you. Lumus, I should tell you when a familiar dies, the other gets his strength, and knowledge that the other had in his lifetime. The other learns every little memory over time. The only things you learn right away is the recent thoughts going through their mind before they die, which can be a terrible experience. I knew he was killed because I felt the transfer. I went to give him a proper burial." Lumus put his hand on his blade, cutting it slightly. A drop of blood spilled down his fingertips and fell to the dirt.

"You mentioned strength?" Lumus asked.

Orson took a minute to realize why Lumus had cut himself.

"Yes, his physical power is not transferred, but his spirit and his knowledge are. Anything he may have learned in his lifetime will eventually make its way to me." Orson explained.

"Hmm, that is quite interesting that you humans and demons share such a bond," Brinx added.

"What do you mean Brinx? If you exist then you would have a familiar too would you not?" Lumus protested.

"No, for us Grenton. We are grown from the great tree of Gaia," Brinx added.

"Orson is there not a tree like that in Twilight?" Lumus asked.

"Not that I know of, but I am sure we would know if little green men were running around in Twilight," Orson shot back.

Brinx laughed.

"If you are coming demon, then I will be watching you. We know nothing about you, and I simply don't trust you," Orson announced.

"I see. I am a Grenton. I am not human, nor demon. I exist to protect life, and I intend to follow you to Twilight to protect that very belief," Brinx explained.

"I suppose that…" Orson crossed his arms.

"Look, if my friend went up toward the mountain, then that is where I'm going." Lumus interrupted.

A flash at the peak of the Aster Mountains lit up the area.

"What? Someone has entered the portal to Twilight?" Orson called out.

("Scarlette? Did you go to Twilight? Why would she help me, then leave me behind?") Lumus thought to himself.

Lumus began to head toward the mountain to the north.

"I have been up to the mountain here before. The portal to Twilight is up at the peak, and that is exactly where we need to go." Orson said with confidence. Orson and Brinx followed behind Lumus as they began to walk.

"Brinx you said you were not a demon?" Lumus asked.

"That is correct Lumus. We Grenton are grown in a seed on the Gaia tree. Each of us is closely equal and born as I look now with some minor differences. The Gaia tree produces thirty orbs with full-grown Grenton's like myself, though they must fight to the death leaving only one. The Gaia tree then becomes that Grenton. I live forever without ageing, but if we do die in combat or natural calamities then my spirit returns to the Gaia tree, and then the growth cycle can start again with another shell for me to take over. For I am the tree, and this is just my vessel." Brinx spoke as he walked beside Orson, but Orson kept his hand on his sword under his cloak.

"Why wouldn't you all work together to protect the planet?" Lumus replied. Brinx laughed again. "When each of the orbs drop, a poisonous gas is released. The gas keeps anything or anyone from interrupting us from our battle. If there is no winner before the gas clears I eliminate the shells. If this happens, then another growth cycle will start, and I would have to select from a new batch. Brinx explained.

"Let me see if I understand, you all fight as if you have no other meaning for life, but those are just shells with no mind, am I right?" Orson asked.

"You are right Orson. I am the tree, and the poisonous gas is my defence against the Grenton that are defective. When there is one left I transfer myself into the Grenton that won, and I protect the

planet as that warrior. Not all Grenton are the same, they are all given a somewhat unique look." Brinx ranted. Lumus stopped walking.
"What is it Lumus?" Orson asked with concern.
"Brinx... what happens if you go into Twilight? If you die in another dimension then what will happen to you?" Lumus asked.
"I cannot fully answer that, my friend. I know that I have the ability to sprout a seed where I die if my host is damaged, but I must be buried. So if I must, I will sprout on Twilight." Brinx announced. Lumus' interest grew.
"What would happen to the Gaia tree in Dystopia if you die in Twilight?" Lumus asked with a concerned look.
"Like I said, I cannot fully answer your question. I don't know much of my kind since I have never encountered another of my kind." Brinx replied.
"I see... I'm sorry I brought it up." He said as he looked away.
"Not at all. We are all just looking for answers. Is that not what life is?" Brinx said with a smile. Orson tried to seem distant, but even he was taken by his words.
They continued up the path to the Aster Mountains. The wind picked up, and mist blew around like a constant cloud in front of them making it difficult to see. Orson led the way followed by Brinx and Lumus in the back.
"Orson, you know where you're going I hope?" Lumus figured he did but wanted to know more without seeming pushy.

"Yes, the Temple is near the mountain peak. I'm surprised your friend was able to get up here so quickly and to know of the portal… She must be something else." Orson shouted over the wind. "The Temple holds the only way for us to get home. I found it twenty years ago." Orson yelled again.

"You never explained where you were all this time? Why you left me here in the first place." He pointed out. Orson stopped, turning to face Lumus. He looked at him ready to say something, but turned back and continued to walk. Lumus and Brinx paused.

"When he is ready," Brinx said calmly.

Brinx then turned and followed behind Orson. ("Orson what happened all those years ago?") Lumus thought to himself.

The three arrived at a landing near the peak, and the wind seemed calmer.

"Orson, we should camp here and regain our strength." Orson stopped and turned around.

"Yes, a good rest would help us before we go to Twilight." Orson declared.

"I will keep watch from the trees," Brinx announced.

He jumped up into the branches without warning. Lumus gathered some twigs and slashed his sword off a rock to start the fire. Orson sat on a stone across from him. It was silent for a while before Lumus or Orson said a word.

Orson looked up and gave Lumus a full scan.

"Hmm? What is it, Orson?" Lumus asked. He paused.

"Nothing Lumus, it's just a shock to see you all grown up. You're not a child anymore, and your power is very impressive to look upon. Orson looked back into the fire.

"I have you, and my father Rozell to thank for that I suppose. I didn't know it, but you had helped me all my life. Why did you do all of that just for me?" Lumus asked.

"I did it for her. I did all of it for her. I was a soldier of Twilight. Protector of the Innocent. Sometimes demons were able to get into our dimension, but we don't know how, or how they managed to get to us even before the rifts open to let them in our world.

Twilight's Capital city of Capaz called for any young warriors brave enough to join and trained as knights. If we were to prove ourselves, then we would be able to take the knight trial. I became quite famous over time, and eventually, I became a first rank knight." Orson smiled and took a breath. Lumus thought that Orson was just like a real hero. One of the stories his father used to tell him about.

"The council of Twilight elected me to a special job once I became knight first class. I took it as an honor before I even knew what the mission was, but then a little girl came before me at Capaz palace, and I was announced her protector by the council. She was only nine years old. I had no idea who she was, and at first, I felt like I had trained to become such a great warrior and ended up a babysitter. I realized, however, that she was very gifted in the time that I spent with her." Orson paused for a moment to fix the fire before it went out.

"I see. You continued to carry it out even though you didn't agree with them?" Lumus asked.

"Of course, I'm a knight after all. It doesn't matter what they tell me to do. I talked with the child and asked her to tell me what she could. That's when I learned of familiars. Her familiar had died, and she had gained all of its knowledge, making her very wise. I was skeptical about familiars at first. I didn't really believe the whole idea of Dystopia, though it did explain where the demons came from all those years. She taught me everything about Dystopia as if she had been here before. I knew that my task was not a punishment after that moment. She and I became very close. She was like a daughter to me. We traveled to the Aster Mountains and arrived at the blue core where you were born. When we used the energy of the planet's core to create you, the rifts appeared in the sky, and it brought demons into the mountain straight to us. I was forced to take you to safety. I left the cave with you in my arms. My fellow soldiers fought off what demons they could but…The girl and I knew that you would be the only one to eventually fix the problem that we had created that day. When I took you and ran I heard her scream out my name. She was killed, and I wasn't there for her. I had failed to protect her, and

I told myself I would do everything I could to save you." Orson took another deep breath. He went quiet. Lumus just stared at him.

"I'm sorry Orson. I wish that this had not fallen upon you. Her death is my fault." Lumus put his head down.

"No Lumus, her death was not your fault it was mine, and it was the growing greed of our world. Twilight killed her. Not you. Her name will live on in me and the people of Capaz. I will never forget you, Scarlette." Lumus looked up quickly and looked at him with tears in his eyes.

"What did you say, Orson?" He stood up quickly.

"I said, Scarlette." Lumus turned to the fire and went silent. Orson stood.

"What is it Lumus? Tell me!" He demanded. Lumus faced the fire and turned his head to avoid looking at him.

"Scarlette is alive. That is to say if it is the same person," Lumus said softly.

Orson sat again. He was severely confused.

"Lumus, explain yourself," Orson demanded once again.

"Before all of this, a girl named Scarlette came to the farm many times. She only came when Rozell and I were separated. I didn't really realize that until now." He turned to Orson once again.

"Lumus did she have long pink hair and blue eyes?" Orson waited for him to reply.

"Yes, and a red ribbon around her neck that hung off to the side," Orson rolled both his sleeves up.

His left arm bare, but his right arm with a red ribbon tightly wrapped around his upper arm.
"She is alive," Orson said quietly.
"She must have survived. I don't know how, or how she got here and survived alone, but she's alive. Where is she Lumus? Please tell me." Lumus looked at his hands. His hair, and eyes still pure white from his transformation back at the Aster inn village. Lumus looked up at Orson with a smile.
"She helped me find myself when I was lost. She is the friend I was searching for after I fought Alistro. He explained. Orson looked back down at the fire.
"Then we will find her in Twilight. She must have her reasons for going alone. I should tell you of Twilight, and why we need to get you there. As you know, Lears has been causing problems in Twilight since you were born… Don't think it your fault at all. We of Twilight bare this burden, but we are hopeless to fight him. His power is far greater than any warrior or any army we have thrown at him. That is why I think you are the only one able to face him. He is your familiar after all. We need you to stop him. You are his equal in every way."
Orson continued to stare at the fire.
"I have only trained basic combat with Rozell. I don't know how useful I'll be against Lears, but I feel drawn to him like I must go to Twilight. For some reason, I feel like I know Lears, and I have to meet him again. When my power awakened… I felt like all of this knowledge came pouring into

my mind, but I can't just use it. It's like I am in an empty room, and I have to catch the pieces to understand them." Lumus began staring at the sky. Orson looked over with a smile.
"Twilight needs you more than you know Lumus. In time I'm sure you will learn who you are. Someone like you could bring hope back to the people. The world has fallen into dark times. Sure, life goes on and cities still stand, but Lears has been recruiting people from our world to do his dirty work. Demon attacks have been occurring more frequently, and the people are getting scared. Something is up in Twilight, and this is a perfect time for your return, but we shall talk more once we reach Twilight tomorrow. Get some sleep Lumus." He smiled as Lumus tried to get comfortable.
Lumus laid his head upon the dirt, slowly closing his eyes from all of the excitement.
Orson looked back to the fire once again.
("You must be exhausted Lumus. It's okay. You and Scarlette have survived, and my mission hasn't failed. It seems to have just begun.") He laid his head back on the ground with a faint smile that quickly faded as he fell asleep.

Chapter Two- Twilight

Morning came with the blue moon just over the horizon. The light was faint, but it was enough to wake Ruben from his sleep. He sat up quickly as he fled a nightmare. His eyes still had a faint glow to them. At first, he thought he was back at Rozell's farm, and thought he may have slept in again.
He noticed Orson laid where he last saw him sitting the night before. Brinx was standing on a hilltop staring down at the land below from a branch high in a tree. Brinx jumped down from his statue state from the trees above.
Orson woke up as Brinx landed with a thump. He stood up, gave himself a stretch, and rose to his feet with a yawn. Without a word, the three continued up the mountain path.
The road was fierce and steep. It was long and dreadfully cold, but they kept the same pace. They came to a dead-end with a rock-faced cave. The darkness inside made him feel uneasy. Orson seemed like he knew where he was going though. Lumus and Brinx didn't say a word.
"This is it, through this cave leads to the peak. It's not long, but it is incredibly dangerous." Orson said with a grin. Orson took his flint out of his pouch.
"Okay, now we need to......" Lumus walked forward into the cave, and let off a yell. His body

powered up making his body almost double in size, but most importantly emitting a very bright light. He looked at Lumus with a smile and put his flint away. He followed with Brinx into the cave after Lumus.

"This is called Twarn's cave, I think your light is a bad idea here, Lumus." Brinx became uneasy. Lumus turned his head while still walking forward.

"What is a Twarn?" Suddenly multiple red lights appeared on the cave wall ahead of them.

"The Demon favours light Lumus," Orson announced in a serious tone.

"Is that right?" Lumus replied, then he began to charge his body pushing out all of the light he could. The light around them became so bright that it lit the whole cave as if there were torches around the entire area. Orson drew his blade quickly. Brinx formed a layer of vines over his body making a helmet, a makeshift chest plate with leg guards. Lumus was still yelling as loud as he could. His body was growing in power, and the light shone off of him brightly.

The demon was a dark shade of green. It had long narrow ears, sharp claws, and a long tail with a blood red ribbon on it. Lumus noticed what looked to be a blade coming from the tip of his tail. He had begun emitting a faint glow and was ready to take on the demon. He turned to Brinx and Orson. "You two wait here, I would like to use this chance to test some of my abilities." Orson looked at him with worry.

"Are you sure about this Lumus? I have fought these things before, and I know how dangerous they can be." Orson said with a troubled look. Brinx reformed himself back to normal.

"It's your call Lumus." Brinx took a few steps back.

"I guess you're in the spotlight. Show us what you can do." Orson said without refusal.

The Twarn's eyes lit up a crimson red, and it made an eerie sound from afar. Lumus bent his knees and readied himself. With his right hand on the ground, and his left hand facing the Twarn.

"So, Twarn was it? I hear you have a liking for light, so let us see how you like this!" He yelled out as loud as he could. His muscles looked like they were growing, and his light began to flow from his body.

Brinx reformed his armour once again. It caught Orson's eye, and he took shelter behind a large stone. Lumus emitted even more power than before, then the light began to dim, and gather in his left hand. The Twarn was moving back and forth on the roof of the cave. Finally, it leaped head-on at him. He gave out a yell able to be heard for miles. Lumus drew his sword with lightning speed just as the Twarn made it to him. The cave went pitch black once again. There was a loud screech and a thud on the ground.

"Lumus are you okay?" Orson cried out.

"He is okay Orson. Just wait where you are." Brinx said calmly. His eyes flashed brightly for a split second.

"I can use my eyes to see what is happening," Brinx explained. He watched as Lumus rose back to his feet in the darkness. Even in the pitch black cave, Lumus was staring the Twarn right in the eyes. All Orson could see were the red lights of Twarn's body.

Lumus began to generate his power over his body once again. Brinx quickly switched back to his normal sight and covered his eyes for a moment. Lumus scurried for his blade which had landed beside him. As he grabbed the sword, he channeled some of his power into it. Twarn was injured and started crawling back and forth again on the cave roof. Lumus held his sword with both hands and stood firm while watching Twarn's movements to try to predict his next move. Twarn leaped at him once again, but he was ready this time. Twarn came flying at him with its razor-sharp claws. Suddenly Twarn froze in the air. Brinx had him trapped in the vines he was able to shoot from his body.

"Now Lumus! Strike him down while he is still!" Brinx yelled out. Lumus shot him a grin and began to run forward dragging his blade against the rocks on the ground. His speed grew faster and faster as he ran at Twarn. Sparks began shooting from his blade, then he leaped straight at Twarn and delivered the final blow. Twarn let out a monstrous cry and then fell to the ground with a hard thud once again. The cave still lit brightly, and Orson staring in disbelief now that he could see once again.

Lumus landed beside Brinx, Orson moved out from behind the stone as the Twarn turned into a white light. The light rose then shifted through the air toward the exit.

"Lumus, that was amazing," Brinx announced.

"Brinx... Good job," Orson hesitated to say.

"I just wanted to hurry things along," He shouted back.

Lumus walked over to Orson. Both staring as he walked off.

"Is that true Lumus? Could you have finished that on your own? I fought one of those before, and I almost died last time I came through here."

Lumus smiled and laughed a little.

"I guess Brinx is a tad bit impatient, and last time you were here maybe you could have used his help?" Lumus turned to follow Brinx.

("Maybe, but back then I probably would have tried to kill Brinx though...") He smiled and took his hand off his hilt.

The cave stretched far into the mountain. Brinx led Lumus and Orson with his impeccable sight since Lumus had tired himself out during his fight with the Twarn. Orson followed in the middle, and Lumus continued to follow behind.

"The peak is up ahead," Orson announced.

After a small turn, the cave exit had taken form. None of them really noticed until they caught sight of the blue moon still in the sky.

"I may need a moment to catch my breath," Lumus said as he tried to catch his breath. He sat on a rock just outside the cave.

"Lumus, the temple is just ahead. Shall we rest there?" Orson said softly.

"I suppose we shouldn't stop if we are close," Lumus replied.

Orson stood up once again.

"Are you sure, Lumus?" Brinx said, concerned.

"I can manage, let's continue," Lumus protested.

A small path leading up along the rocks followed through to the temple. Lumus went on ahead. Brinx stopped Orson as Lumus walked on.

"If you truly do not want me to join you in Twilight I will not go. I understand your worry about the situation." Brinx said sincerely. Orson looked at Brinx with a kind look.

"I have much trust in you after this short journey of ours. Although brief, you have been at our side the whole time. I would be honored for you to come back to Twilight, but I will be watching you never the less. I still don't trust you entirely." He said.

"I see, but if I was your enemy, would I have not killed you both while you slept?" Brinx walked away leaving Orson speechless. Orson took a moment to think.

"I suppose he could have. Even so... I don't trust him." He muttered to himself.

"Hey, what are you guys waiting for? Let's get a move on!" Lumus seemed very excited for his adventure to Twilight even though he was still pretty worn out. He had never seen anything past the farm gates.

The Pillars of the Dystopian shrine were mostly destroyed. Lumus' eyes were locked on the damage of the shrine, but Orson was thinking of something completely different. "The shrine wasn't this damaged last time I was here. Something must have done this recently." Suddenly, without a word, he drew his blade. "Scarlette…" Lumus said under his breath. "Keep your guard up," Orson said quietly. Brinx jumped off without a word into the trees soaring high into the sky. Lumus drew his sword and went back to back with Orson. The holy guardian statues of the great Dystopian shrine gone…destroyed. Orson was not one for gods and holy stories, but he believed it a shame to see such disrespect to such a place. Lumus shut his eyes and put his head down. A calm breeze passed brushing by his cheeks softly, and the silence drew out the small sounds farther off in the distance. He began to emit a light, covering his body. Orson moved from him.

"What is this?" Orson began to read a written stone text carved into the foot of one of the intact statues.

"The night is not the evil, the evil is the night" Orson paused. He continued to read.

"Those with a pure of heart may travel to the world of light. Those with an evil heart that dare try to pass to the light will meet uncertainty." He couldn't make sense of the passage.

("This wasn't here before, I remember reading a riddle last time.") Orson stood up noticing the light from Lumus and had readied himself with his sword once again. A short time passed, and he began to think that nothing was really there. Slowly, he moved toward Lumus looking side to side in case he was wrong. He was now face to face with Lumus, but Lumus looked up and opened his eyes quickly with a shout. Orson fell backward dropping his sword in surprise.

"What is it Lumus?" Orson's eyes followed where Lumus was looking. Two large, green eyes in the silhouette of the night stared back at him. The demon let out a monstrous roar, and squeezed through the roof of the shrine, ripping stone off the roof with ease.

The demon stared down with anger, then it readied itself to jump, but Lumus just stared with a calm face. Orson collected himself, picking his sword up, and arming himself once again. The distant demon jumped from the roof with a roar, soaring through the night sky. Suddenly just as the demon was in the air, Brinx came crashing upon its back slamming it from the sky, and into the ground with a loud smack against the rocks below. Brinx jumped off the back of the demon as it lay motionless on the ground.

"Those are called Night Wraiths. Usually dangerous, but this was a young one.

"If that was a young version, then I'd hate to meet its parents. Lumus let his light fade, then continued toward the shrine.

"Seems you have some tricks too, Brinx," Lumus added.

Brinx shot a grin back at him.

"The wild demons are no worry," Brinx added.

"A key opens the gate to the shrine." Orson interrupted. Lumus lit up for a moment and ripped the door open with one hand.

"We do not have time for keys," Lumus said with a serious face. Orson slowly pulled out an old looking key from his clothes.

"Last time I was here I spent hours searching for this key," Orson sighed.

"Sorry, Orson... I didn't realize you had a key." Lumus replied as he scratched his head with an embarrassed look on his face. Orson walked through the debris.

"It doesn't matter. We are in and that's all that matters." Brinx had walked past Lumus and Orson to the front of the portal inside.

He stood by the blue portal as Orson and Lumus walked up behind him. Lumus gazed into the blue sphere.

"This is the portal to Twilight?" Lumus reached out to touch it.

"Wait!" Orson yelled out.

"Lumus you must realize that when we enter this portal we will no longer be together." He said with panic in his voice.

"What?" Lumus replied.

"When you enter the portal you are randomly teleported to Twilight. The chances of us showing up together are very slim." He explained.

"What do you suggest?" Lumus asked. Brinx was still staring at the portal.

"Twilight is still not safe, and whatever there may be, you must stay alert at all times." Lumus took a step forward keeping his eyes on the sphere.
"We need to head to the Roon caves. There is a group of people there, and I'm sure we can at least learn something, and stock up before we head after Lears. The people have been gathering at this cave to try to live in secret. Lears doesn't know of this place, so it would be a good starting point for us." He suggested.
"Agreed" Brinx replied. He was still lost in the sphere even as he replied to Orson. "Brinx? Brinx are you okay?" Orson laid his hand upon his shoulder, with a quick shake of his head he came to.
"Sorry Orson, I must have been daydreaming. I heard what you said, but I couldn't help myself." Brinx replied while forcing himself to look away from the portal. Orson glanced at Brinx with an uneasy look.
"We cannot waste any more time. I will see you both in Roon caves. Just continue toward the West through a forest called Varlif, and Brinx... You may want to stay hidden. The people of Twilight won't see you as a friend." Orson explained. He paused one last time to look at Brinx, then to Lumus. He sighed, then walked into the blue sphere, and instantly disappeared.
"You're next Lumus," Brinx said calmly.
"Before we go... What do you really want to come to Twilight for?" Lumus replied.

"I suppose that is a fair question. I have been in this world since my first cycle. I have little memories of my people. I have not just protected the planet, but I have been searching for any other Grenton's, with no luck thus far." He explained.

"I see. So you wish to go to Twilight to see if there may be others of your kind. But you heard Orson. He has never seen any others of your kind before. Do you still wish to come?"

"I know there is little hope, but nothing is changing here. This world is full of monsters, and even though my genetics tell me to protect the planet... I can't seem to see this as the planet I am meant to protect."

"You know Orson distrusts you, and from his reaction, the people of Twilight may see you the same way."

"I know, but this is why I asked you if I could come. I can see it in your eyes. You want to learn who you really are. I sense that you and I are the same. I just want to know who I am, and I am willing to search new worlds if I am able. Orson may hate me for the color of my skin, but I will show them that I am no monster. I just want to find out who I am, and I am willing to risk my life for it." Brinx explained.

"I guess we are searching for the same thing in our own way. I won't stop you Brinx, and when we get to Twilight. I hope you find what you are looking for."

"And I hope you do too," Brinx said with a nod.

Lumus took a step forward and looked over his shoulder back at Brinx. Lumus smiled as he disappeared into the blue sphere.

The bright moon was overwhelming, and the gentle breeze ran through Lumus' hair. The once dark sky that he had known his whole life was finally gone as if the blue sphere was the passage to his own dream world. He laid flat on the ground staring up at the bright sky. Birds were flying peacefully, wild critters, and animals ran among the fields.

"This is paradise," He told himself.

The clear blue sky lit up his heart, and a smile struck his face as he lay like a child in the tall grass. He sat up, and his happy mood was taken away as swiftly as it came. A cloud of smoke in the distance too big to be from a campfire engulfed the distant sky. He immediately jumped to his feet, and he made his way toward the fire with thoughts of home and his father Rozell in his mind.

("This place... it is different. I cannot feel the planet. It's as if the planet is dead, no whispers no cries of pain, no sorrow to be heard.") Brinx thought to himself.

"You there! Demon!" Shouted an angry voice from afar.

"Demon?" Brinx blurted out. Four men armed with rusty blades made their way through the trees toward him.

"Fellow warriors, I do not mean you harm." he pleaded.

"Your trickery will not work on us monster!" The men replied.

"You will meet your end at my blade!" The man announced as he charged at him with the others following swiftly behind.

"You are making a mistake." He said calmly. Brinx crouched and jumped behind the men onto a tree branch.

"I will not fight you." He shouted.

The men turned in surprise.

"No demon will walk this planet while I still breathe, monster!" One of the men shouted.

The men charged once again at him, but he just leaped again to another tree. Two of the men took their bows from their backs and readied arrows. Brinx formed his defensive armor around his body.

("They leave me no choice.") Brinx stood up on the branch he had landed on. An arrow shot towards him from one of the men. Brinx caught the arrow and destroyed it with his hand. "I will say this once more, I will not..." Before Brinx could finish talking another arrow was shot. Brinx jumped again, but this time toward the men, slapping the arrow from his path and pouncing atop one of the men. One man ran in fear, while the other two charged once more with their blades. Brinx shot out vines from his palm, knocking one of the men unconscious. The other man continued with his blade aimed straight at him. Brinx and the last man stared at each other until the man thrust his sword forward.

"I am truly sorry for this," Brinx said sadly. He shot another vine from his free hand throwing the man far against a tree, knocking him unconscious as well.

("These people are brutal, and they seem no better than the demons of Dystopia…wild, and reckless…")

Lumus ran through the tall grass as fast as he could. The fire below roared just like his farm. His eyes teared as the memories flooded back.

"Help!" A woman shouted from the village. He was still running toward the fire but was searching for the source of the voice he had heard too. An enormous screech forced Lumus to cover his ears.

("Ah... What is that?") Lumus said to himself.

"Help! Please, somebody, help me", the woman called out again. Lumus drew his sword and looked around. He could hear the screams for help, but the ringing in his ears threw him off.

"Where are you?" Lumus shouted. He made his way closer to the smoke and found a small village in flames. No one was in sight, but the bodies of the helpless upon the ground. He dropped to his knees with a look of sadness in his eyes.

"I'm too late," he said under his breath. He stared at the burning homes of the village. He noticed a girl not even ten years old. She was missing an arm, and blood covered her dirty white dress as she lay on the ground.

"I… I was too late…!" Lumus cried out as his body began to light up. He began to emit a bright light, and it shot from his body passing through the flames. The flames blew away as the dirt lifted from the village.

"Anyone! Is there anyone there?" Lumus shouted once more. No one answered him though, and so he had closed his eyes with defeat. A single tear slid down from his face as he turned and walked away from the village.

The light from the blue moon was muffled by the thick treetops of Varlif forest. Orson walked alone happy that he appeared so close to the Roon caves, but he came to a large gate he didn't remember.

("I don't remember this gate here before.") Orson stood firm in front of the large gate to the West Mountains.

("A secret haven, but why would they have built this? It's only an invite telling the enemy that they are here...") He thought to himself. Noises in the bushes around him began to come closer.

"I'm not alone. Who's there? Show yourself!" Orson demanded. A pack of Krotin emerged from the bushes.

Pale green skin and light purple armour covered their bodies. They commonly carry small daggers or spears, and their speed makes them very dangerous in large numbers.

("Krotins? How could so many be here?") He thought as he drew his sword. A larger demon followed behind the Krotins, emerging from the bushes. It was an odd demon that resembled a cat in many ways, cleared the tree line toward him, but its species was unfamiliar to Orson. He was surrounded and outnumbered.

"Give up and I shall spare your life, knight." The demon stated

"Ah! The cat can speak." Orson announced with a laugh.

"You dare laugh at me human? Said the mysterious demon.

"I am Sir Orson Hefreny, Knight of Twilight, and protector of the people." Orson proudly announced.

"I didn't ask for your name, and it matters not, for now, you will be taken like all the others. Krotins, seize the human." Orson paused for a moment.

"Taken? Not likely. You be a good little kitty, and die!" Orson went charging into the crowd of Krotins swinging his sword recklessly, again and again.

"There's too many of them..." Orson began to get tired as he swung away.

"I am Antsos and you will remember my name human, for you will be begging me for mercy soon enough!" Antsos laughed.

("Antsos? I have heard that name before...He couldn't be?") Orson thought to himself as he fought off the Krotins. They began to overwhelm him, as they jumped on him and they eventually pulled him to the ground.

"I can't die.... here," Orson said as he fell to the ground, he was covered in sweat, and barely able to grasp his sword.

"Oh you will not die human, but you will wish that you had," Antsos said as he turned, and walked slowly into the darkness of the forest.

Brinx began his search, jumping at incredible speed through the trees with the wind blowing in his face. With no constant whispers of pain from the planet Dystopia, he could finally think clearly. He was unfamiliar with this new landscape, so he had no sense of direction. With no voice of the planet, he could not tell what direction was what. He made his way through Dark Wood Forest that leads him through thick woods, and overcrowded trees that did not let the moonlight in. The Forest was a great cover for him as he jumped through the trees undetected by anything or anyone who may consider him a threat like his previous encounter.

"I do hope Lumus and Orson are having better luck than I am." He muttered to himself.

Orson woke up slowly. He must have been knocked out when the Krotins attacked him. He looked around and noticed his sword and armour had been taken. Sounds of screaming and chains tightening were heard from afar. Cries of pain and agony filled Orson's head. He shut his eyes as blood started dripping down his face. His arms were bound, and his legs hung just above the ground. A tightrope fastened around his neck. He gave his head a shake to move the dripping blood from reaching his eyes. He slowly opened them to see a dark empty room with stone walls. Blood covered the floor around him, and partially the walls in front of him. Again cries of pain were heard coming from the halls.

("No window or any sign of light. Where am I?") Orson wondered. A door opened nearby, and he heard footsteps come closer to him. Orson's vision was still blurry, as blood continued to fall down his face to his eyes. A shadowy figure approached his holding cell.

"Who's there?" Orson cried out. Footsteps began to circle him.

"The question is, who are you?" The voice said. "Why would you be at the gates of Roon Caves? What did you hope to find there?" The voice said with a laugh. The footsteps continued to circle him slowly.

"I won't tell you anything you monster," Orson spit a mouthful of blood in protest to the demands.

"I see, so you won't tell me your name, or your reason for why you are here? So you are no use to me then?" The mysterious voice said calmly.

"I am a proud protector of Twilight and the defender of all these lands. You do not scare me. If I am taken down, another will rise up to take my place." Orson took a deep breath as if he had used all of the air in his lungs.

"Judging by your armour, and the glyph of Twilight on it you were someone of importance to the people?" The voice asked.

Orson coughed.

"I am Sir Orson Hefreny!" Orson said proudly.

The footsteps stopped.

"Hefreny?" The voice hesitated once he heard his name.

"You know my name then?" Orson said with a smile.

"I do actually, Sir Orson. You see your family has been quite the nuisance, but don't you worry. I will find your brother, as I have found you, and deal with him soon enough." The footsteps continued toward the exit. Orson tried to open one of his eyes for a look at whom he had talked to.

"Zelkem? He is alive?" Orson said with hesitation. The blurry image of the man turned his head to look over his shoulder.

"I am Lears by the way. Welcome to Twilight prison. Do make yourself at home, and enjoy your stay." Lears walked away with an evil laugh as the doors were shut tight, and locked behind him.

"My brother... Zelkem...?" Orson said as he started to cry.

The blue moon above was brighter than the one on Dystopia. Lumus smiled as he thought of the stories he read on the farm. They told of the hero in a world with darkness, but the hero would always look to the sky with a smile when things got to be too much. He continued across a bridge just past the Dark Wood Forest. There were no sounds of laughter; no kids playing in the fields. No people working the farms, and no one traveling the roads.

"The stories I read are nothing like what I thought. All I have seen is death and emptiness." Lumus said to himself as he began to walk across the bridge. His eyes caught a glimpse of a sign. It read

Nuran Region: Breedlands West, and Roon Mountains: Northwest.

The blue moon began to set, and Lumus looked at the sky in confusion. Lumus paused then looked down the Northwest road to the mountains.

"I'm used to the darkness, I might as well continue. Maybe Orson and Brinx are ahead of me."

Without warning, Brinx jumped from a tree near Lumus, landing just behind him with a crash. Lumus immediately drew his blade and had turned to point it at Brinx' throat.

"I'm glad this experience has kept you civil my friend," Brinx snickered.

Lumus shot a small grin as if to say he was happy to see him. Lumus put his sword away and continued to walk north. Brinx stood still for a moment, and turned his head, toward the sign pointing to Roon Mountains to the north. He smiled, and slowly caught up to Lumus.

The tall grass along the path blew gently in the night wind. Stars emerged in the sky. Brinx had his defensive armour on, and Lumus had his hand on his sheath. Both keeping an eye out for any movement. Brinx started to notice the tall grass moving more frequently than the wind blew. Without looking at Lumus he slowly drew a vine from his palm and stretched it to Lumus a little further ahead to get his attention. Lumus turned his head to see him looking in the grass. He noticed him nod to signal the movement in the distance. They kept their speed and said nothing to each other. Lumus spotted movement to his right just up ahead. Slowly they made their way to the end of the bridge, and Lumus stopped at the far side. Brinx stood in the middle, still looking at the tall grass. When they stopped, so did the movement. The steady stream of water under them was almost soothing, the night sky lit up with the bright red moon showering them with little visibility. Lumus drew his sword. Brinx formed his face guard, expecting a battle. The wind was still blowing gently, and the water was still.

The two warriors stood in wait, expecting to defend the bridge. Brinx ran back out to the road they had just come from and released a thorny vine from each of his palms. He shot them straight out into the tall grass on both sides of the road and began to spin, picking up speed rapidly. The tall grass tore easily making a huge circle around Brinx. Lumus concentrated on his energy, making a layer of light slowly brighten the area around him. He leaped into the sky, and the bright light around him pulsed from his body, and into his sword. As he fell back to the ground, the light retracted back momentarily, before being shot from his body again with such force that it ripped the grass around the north side of the bridge and into the sky. Brinx turned back to Lumus and walked across the bridge. They began to head north once again, knowing the threat was dealt with. As they walked away from the bridge a pack of Krotins slowly stumbled out of the grass, bursting into a white light that shot up into the sky as they died.

Antsos opened Orson's cell door, and three Krotins followed behind, carrying various tools stained with blood.

"So, Sir Orson, by orders of Lord Lears we come bearing gifts for you." The doors shut behind them, and Orson's eyes open wide with fear.

"Now Orson you will..." Antsos began.

"It's Sir Orson to you, demon." Orson interrupted.

"Is that so?" Antsos replied by backhanding him across his face. His head shot to the side. He paused, then spit blood from his mouth.

"My mistake. Sir Orson, you see Lord Lears believes you may be of some help to us," Antsos continued.

"I'll never help any of you," Orson announced proudly. Antsos hit him once more with another backhand to his face.

"You see my friend, you haven't any choice in the matter. My Krotin friends here have their toys with them to play with you. I'm certain that you will come around."

Antsos began to head for the door, but he turned to Orson and hit him once more.

"One for the road," Antsos said with a grin. He began to laugh as he left Orson's cell. Screams from Orson pulsed throughout the holding area, as Antsos walked down a dark hallway with a grin on his face.

"Lumus, I feel like we are nearing our destination," Brinx said worriedly.

Lumus looked further ahead and spotted a small mountain range shielded by forest.

"Let's head toward the forest over there. It should have a path to the caves that we can follow," Lumus replied.

"I hope Orson made it all right," Brinx said with an uncertain tone under his breath.

Rain began to fill the land swallowing it like a waterfall. Birds took refuge in the trees, and animals ran and hid. Brinx and Lumus approached Varlif Forest. The forest was wet, and the path was becoming muddy. Lumus took a short pause as he gazed back into the Breedlands. The thunderous lands lit up brightly with strike after strike to the flatlands below. Brinx didn't look back though, but he did pause to wait for Lumus. He looked back to the forest, with a sigh of relief for missing the downpour. Brinx let him pass, then followed behind covered in mud from his knees down to his feet. The moonlight from the night sky went into hiding from the rain as the cloud cover gave it the perfect hiding place.

Varlif Forest seemed endless, but Lumus pressed on in hopes of seeing Orson at every turn. Brinx kept his mind about the trees shifting his eyes from side to side for any hint of movement.

"I'll take a look from the treetops," Brinx said as he dove through the forest treetops. He jumped straight into the sky, bursting through the leaves of the trees. He was suspended in the sky long enough to see a large gate blocking the entrance to the Roon Caves further ahead. He landed back where he once stood with a crash. Lumus turned around.

"Maybe a little more warning when you jump off like that?" Lumus waved his hand in front of his face to clear the mud that had shot up at his face. Brinx pointed toward the mountain.

"Not far from here, just past these trees, there is a large gate built in front of the mountains. I believe that's our way in." Brinx declared.

Lumus was still wiping mud from his face.

"If you say so Brinx, let's get going then," Lumus said with a frown as he looked at his mud-covered clothes.

Brinx was lost in his thoughts as he walked alongside Lumus.

("I cannot feel the forest or the planet as I did on Dystopia. The forest doesn't tell me anything, and no cries for help, no plea for rescue...This feels odd to me.") Brinx thought to himself. He had a look of worry on his face.

("On Dystopia I was able to feel the planet's cries for help. The planet would guide me, but Twilight is different. With no Tree of Gaia, the voice is not speaking to me, and I am free to make my own choices.") He began to think what would happen if he had died on Twilight. With no voice of the planet, he thought his connection to Dystopia was broken, and if this were true he would not reincarnate if he had died. For the first time, Brinx worried that he would be vulnerable, and his courage began to falter with his thoughts.

Roon Caves was just ahead. Lumus walked on, staring ahead hoping to spot Orson. The giant gate that had been blocking the caves was open now. Without a word, Brinx leaped off into the forest cover, and Lumus quickly drew his sword. Lumus looked around but saw nothing. Brinx was nowhere in sight either as he had completely camouflaged with the green of the trees. Lumus saw a young man at the cave entrance walking out from the shadows. His hair was shaggy, reaching down to his shoulders. His brown hair matched his eyes. The boy wore baggy brown pants with a black belt around his waist, but no shirt. His arm guards looped around his middle finger and fastened around his forearm. Lumus focused on his sword. After a short moment, the sword became engulfed in the light coming from his body, then he pointed his sword at the man in the cave.

"That is one neat trick you have there. I guess you save a lot of money on candles." The man said with a smile.

"What are you doing in these caves?" Lumus yelled out. His sword still pointing at the young man. The young man sat on a rock facing Lumus. "I won't ask you again. What are you doing in the caves?"

The young man opened his mouth about to speak when someone emerged from the cave darkness. "Is that any way to treat Orson's younger brother Lumus?" Scarlette said softly with her head down. Her face rose, and her eyes met with Lumus'.

"Scarlette? Lumus dropped his sword to the mud, his mouth wide open, and his eyes expressing shock.

"Didn't expect to see me, Lumus?" Scarlette walked closer and put her bow on her back. Her long pink hair blew gently in the wind like a feather falling through the air.

Scarlette was wearing a chainmail skirt that went from her chest to her thigh. A belt worn around her waist, and long pink gauntlets going from her wrists to her elbows. Her black gloves on her hands stood out because they were covered in dirt, and her black cape with its pink lining laid flat under her bow.

"Scarlette, where did you go? Why did you leave me on Dystopia?" Lumus picked his sword up from the mud and cleaned it before putting it back in its sheath.

"You will learn all you need to know in time Lumus. By the way, this is Zelkem," Scarlette said with a smile. Suddenly Brinx came from the sky landing with a crash behind Zelkem and Scarlette. "This is Brinx," Lumus said with a laugh. Zelkem slowly turned around, staring into glowing green eyes. Zelkem fell backward in shock.

"I was just heading out, but please wait here until I return. I won't be long Lumus," Scarlette walked past him with a smile. He couldn't help but recognize her scent as she walked by. He immediately trusted her with memories of Dystopia flooding his mind.

Brinx and Zelkem went into the caves by a fire that they must have made while he was gone. They were talking just inside the Roon caves. Zelkem made hand gestures from a distance, but from where Lumus was standing he couldn't make out what he was trying to mimic to Brinx. He continued to lean against the cave wall at the entrance of the dim lit caves. He stared up at the sky to see the blue moon lighting up the sky. It was much brighter, he thought. It made Lumus think how this world had some similarities to Dystopia, like the moons. The blue in both worlds was still day, and the red was still night. He found it odd that opposite worlds would have that in common, but still, it passed through his mind quickly as he looked out from the cave and into the sky. The blue moon was setting in the distance over the horizon. Lumus decided to wait for Scarlette. It gave him a moment to really think about everything that had happened so far. Twilight, Dystopia, Scarlette, Orson, Brinx, and now his Orson's brother Zelkem. He wondered where Orson was, and what Scarlette had to do by herself, but he remained patient as he stood alone at Roon caves.

Chapter Three - A journey for Twilight

Scarlette walked slowly through the night with Lumus in her mind. With her bow in hand and her eyes trying to focus ahead through the morning mist, she made her way to a small pond. She sat upon a rock near the pond and laid her bow in the tall grass next to her. She looked up at the blue moon and shut her eyes; her body relaxed upon the smooth rock.

"Lumus...I don't want to disappoint you, and I will be by your side wherever you go. I cannot believe that you have become the man you are. You are a warrior now, but still pure as when we met on that fateful day. I feel like I know you better than anyone, but you still struggle to know who you are. I can understand that you were missing a part of you, but I hope now that you found it, you will be able to find the answers you were looking for." She spoke to herself as she stared at the stars in the sky with a smile on her face.

Images of the day Lumus came through the Twilight core crossed her mind like a slideshow of memories. The events leading to this day jumped through her mind continuously.

"I died... I died for you Lumus, and I'd gladly do it for you again. I will always be there to guide you. For you are the hope I always wished for us all. Maybe things didn't end up as I hoped, and I didn't think I would get so close to you, but I'm happy. I know you just arrived in Twilight, and I hate to make you wait, but I had to check something without anyone seeing..." She opened her small pouch hanging on her hip, and she pulled out a small hourglass.

"Too much time has gone by, but it couldn't be helped. Lumus would only have been ready when he was ready. I couldn't force him..."

She had a look of sadness in her eyes.

The wind blew gently through Scarlette's hair. She jumped down from the rock, and as she turned she noticed the mist had pushed from the shores onto the land. The forest path back to the caves was now covered with a thick mist. She noticed a shadowy figure stood in the pathway toward the caves. An eerie vibe of something she once felt before. Her heart jumped for a moment, and a chill went through her body.

"Lumus?" No one answered her.

"Zelkem? Brinx?"

She went to reach for her bow in the tall grass but kept her eyes on the mist-covered shadow. She hoped that the shadow was a friend, and not a foe, but wasn't about to take any chances. As soon as her hand had touched it, the shadow ran toward her with such speed as if its legs could skip across the mist. Scarlette readied her bow with haste and quickly reached for an arrow from her quiver. Before she was even able to place the arrow within her bow, the shadow was right before her eyes. She met eye to eye with the shadow. She realized what she was up against. The fiend was a shadow, and nothing more. A dark transparent being; its eyes opening to reveal a purple glare.

"I am Ged," announced the shadow.

Before she could respond, Ged jumped up with a swift kick, breaking her bow as his foot followed through, hitting Scarlette in the face. Scarlette flew from the impact, but before she landed, the shadow was already preparing another fierce kick from below her. The kick landed on her back, forcing her straight up into the air. He leaped into the air after her with his fist of shadows clenched tightly together, and he hit her with such force toward the ground that the rocks below crumbled from her fall. Ged stood above her body looking down at her. No face, and no emotion. All she saw before her eyes closed were the purple glaring eyes staring back at her.

"Scarlette!" Lumus called out. He came running out into the mist alone, looking for Scarlette in every direction around the pond. Lumus thought he could faintly hear an answer to his call.

"I think I just heard her," Lumus said aloud.

"Scarlette, where are you?" Zelkem yelled out.

"Your friend saves you today, girl. I will find you again and be sure to make you pay for what you have taken from me. Oh, and Scarlette…your knight friend Orson won't be making it to your little party." His form dissipated where he stood, becoming one with the shadows. Scarlette let out a moan of pain.

"Scarlette!" Lumus ran to her as she laid in the pile of rocks by the pond. Brinx and Zelkem came running into the mist, following the screams of pain.

"Scarlette!" Lumus called out again. He picked her up in his arms.

"Is she okay?" Zelkem asked in a panic.

"She is hurt pretty bad, but her wounds are just external. We need to get her back and let her get some rest. Let's head back to the caves for now," Lumus replied, trying not to seem worried.

He stood in the mist with Scarlette in his arms. The mist dragged along at his feet. He looked up to the sky before he walked back to the caves. The blue moon stood tall in the sky. Lumus thought it seemed to become a darker than usual, but he was still getting used to Twilight. He felt uneasy but decided to go back to the caves without any more delays. Brinx and Zelkem went on ahead through the tall grass. Brinx turned back to see a silhouette of Lumus holding Scarlette in the distance.

("There is hope for him yet, I see now what it is they all see in him. The compassion...") Brinx disappeared into the mist following behind Zelkem.

"Scarlette...It's me, Lumus. You're safe now." He said with a soft voice.

"Lumus...." She let out in a faint voice, "I'd do it all again for you, Lumus."

She fell unconscious in Lumus' arms.

Lumus stood still, looking into the distant woods across the pond. He noticed a glow almost like a set of eyes. After a second they disappeared just as quickly as they appeared. He didn't sense evil from it and quickly disregarded it. His mind ran in circles as he turned with Scarlette back to the caves. The forest path reminded him of the path to the fire pit back on Dystopia, but he quickly refocused when Scarlette started to mutter in her sleep. From time to time she made a sound, and her face winced from the pain, but still, she remained unconscious it seemed. Lumus moved faster each time he saw her in pain.

"Hey, Brinx?" Zelkem asked.

Brinx stood still, staring out of the cave into the dark, his smoky purple eyes shifting at every movement.

"Yes, Zelkem?" He replied, without turning towards Zelkem.

"I was just thinking. Where would we go from here? Do you think my brother will show up?" Brinx turned to Zelkem.

"It is a harsh world out there, but from what I have seen from his skills as a warrior, he should be here soon. As for where we go next, well, we cannot do anything until Scarlette is back on her feet. As for her condition, I have checked her body, and she seems to have no broken bones." Brinx said with a promising tone.

He turned back toward the forest to continue his watch. Zelkem paused for a moment to look at the fire.

"Yeah, some great warrior he is. That's all I ever hear from people when his name comes up. Ever since the day he abandoned me." Zelkem muttered to himself then sat by the fire a short distance into the cave.

"You speak of your brother as if you are angry with him." Brinx started.

He walked over beside Zelkem and sat down next to him.

"I may not be wise in the ways of family, but maybe we could discuss your dilemma?" Zelkem looked at him long and hard without a word. His face was blank, but Zelkem felt like he really was trying to help.

"My brother abandoned me after our parents died. The only thing he said before he left was that Twilight needed someone who would protect the people." He stared into the fire, his face now blank like Brinx' stare.

"You may think he has abandoned you, but maybe he left to give the world a chance? I have seen what your brother can do, and his skills are something not even I would willingly go against." Brinx got up and walked back to the cave entrance, but he turned back to Zelkem once more. He knew he had not seen Orson's skill in combat, but he felt it was what Zelkem needed to hear.

"Zelkem, have you ever thought that your brother was not the only one this world needed?" Brinx walked off toward the entrance but stayed within speaking distance.

Zelkem stared at the fire for a while thinking, but his eyes began to water.

("So what if Orson grew strong. He still left me. Some brother. He left me alone in a world where I knew no one. I was still a child with no home and no family. He couldn't even help his own brother.") Zelkem thought to himself. He wiped his tears quickly to avoid showing Brinx.
Brinx stood tall at the cave entrance with his arms crossed, and his head down.
"Look at the events that have unfolded Zelkem. If it wasn't for Orson this world wouldn't have had a chance. From what I know Orson has been watching over Lumus since he was a child, and without Lumus, this Lears character would have nothing in his way. Your brother single-handily gave this world a hope to believe in." He said while still looking out into the woods.
"Lumus…" Zelkem said under his breathe.
"He would watch Lumus like a brother to keep him safe, but not even me? His own brother?"
"You're missing the point Zelkem. Look at how you have grown up. Look at what you have become. A man made of no one's teachings, and a man with the spirit of his own free will. You are the product of your own doing. A man I see just as strong as his brother, and a will unbreakable by anyone."
"You speak as if you know me, but you don't."
"Your eyes tell me everything. I can see your sadness, and I can see your loneliness. Truth be told… I can see a warrior with more rage then most demons I have fought. Whether you think it or not, this world needs your brother more than

you do. If you try to face your brother with vengeance, you are only taking away from the very thing your brother left to fight for, and that is a world for you to grow up in without fear."

"You learned all of that from looking into my eyes?" Zelkem asked.

"You can learn a lot by reading people. I know you will not listen to me. You barely know me, and I can see that you also mean me harm, but since I arrived with Lumus you wish to hide that. I understand, and I won't stop you from doing what you believe is right." Brinx continued to watch the forest. Zelkem was speechless.

("Who is this guy?") He thought to himself.

Lumus came out of the trees with Scarlette in his arms. His eyes a bright white, and his hair giving off a glow even in the dark. He laid her down by the fire, and no one said a word. Zelkem sat staring into the fire once again. Brinx continued to stand by the cave entrance with a glare toward the trees.

"Thank you for checking Scarlette before you went on ahead Brinx," Lumus said with his focus on Scarlette.

"She is tough, Lumus. She will pull through. We just need to give her time." Brinx said softly.

"Zelkem are you okay? You seem a bit down." Lumus asked

"What's the plan Lumus?" Brinx interrupted. Lumus switched his attention over to Brinx.

"Orson said to meet here, so we stay put until he arrives." He said with a firm tone. Scarlette began

to cough lightly. She barely moved a muscle but turned enough to open her eyes to Lumus.
"Orson isn't coming…Ged told me…" Scarlette passed out once more.
"Ged? Who's Ged? Scarlette!" He said as he rushed to her side. He grabbed her arms, and gently shook her in hopes of getting more answers.
"Let her rest, she can't help us now. When she gets more rest maybe she will be able to answer your questions." Zelkem said softly.
"Lumus, I think I may know who she is talking about," Brinx announced. He turned into the cave, and slowly walked over to the fire, and stood behind Zelkem.
"If the Ged I'm thinking of is the same Ged she spoke of, then we may be in a bit of trouble." He added.
"Over one hundred years ago a noble warrior came to Dystopia. He was dressed in strange clothing and wielded a red sword, as deep as the red moon of night. I found him walking the woods after arriving through a blue portal. He began slaying demons everywhere he went. It seemed like his goal was to defeat any, or all demons he found. I followed him along his quest, and I found myself almost enjoying what it was he was doing. That was the first time I began to think that Dystopia was not the only place to live. I leaped down in his path one day, and he stared me down and raised his sword. I found myself in a battle rather than having a chance to find out more. When I tried to ask him about where he had come

from, I was ignored. I engaged him in battle, and I can't say he was an easy opponent. His skills were greater than my own. His speed was remarkable, and his swordplay unpredictable. I couldn't harm him because my duty was to protect the planet, and he wasn't there to harm the planet, so I couldn't fight back. I did my best to avoid, and even tried to reason with him, but I died that day. Ged went on to kill countless demons until I was reborn from the Tree of Gaia. When I found him again he was at the blue portal you know as 'The Passage to Twilight, or Dystopian temple' in the Aster Mountains. The blue portal allows pure souls to gain access back to Twilight, but for whatever reason, it may be Ged was denied his way back home. I watched from the trees as a swarm of reckless demons overwhelmed him, and killed him outside the temple." Brinx exhaled as he closed his eyes for a moment.

"So he was a warrior of Twilight that became evil?" Zelkem asked.

"Yes, and a fierce fighter. He must have taken out over a hundred demons before meeting his end." Brinx added.

"You are right Brinx, it is the same Ged." Scarlette rose from her resting spot. Her long pink hair flew down as she got up, and her face was without marks, and her spirit seemed back to normal.

"Scarlette? Are you okay?" Lumus shouted out.

"Please… I have a lot to say. Orson isn't coming, so I might as well tell all of you now." Scarlette interrupted.

"How do you know it was the same Ged?" Brinx said without emotion.

"I'll explain," Scarlette started, "It all began when I was nine years old, twenty years ago now. I went on an expedition to Aster Mountains with Orson as my guardian. They say that when your familiar dies, whether it be on Dystopia or Twilight, the other is given all memories and star energy." Scarlette said as she took a deep breath.

"Star energy?" Zelkem blurted out.

"Please Zelkem, I'll get to that. The star energy is what Twilight's brightest minds called the power of life. It is said in ancient writings that our entire galaxy was created from star energy. I didn't believe in this until I used it myself. I was selfish, and I decided that I would make a wish before anyone else stole my chance. I knew things they did not, because of my familiar that had died and passed on her knowledge to me. Even Orson didn't know of my true intentions. One hundred years prior to this, the temples were built, and every one hundred years a wish could be made using the core's star energy. I don't know exactly what our ancestors wished for, but the only logical thing would be the portal between Twilight and Dystopia. I have no evidence proving this, but it's my best guess. Ged was Twilight's strongest and purest warrior one hundred years ago. Our Ancestors sent him to do the same thing we tried ten years ago. Only Ged began to lose his sanity with every life he took.

When I tried my wish, the pure star energy that made our core blue was used to form Lumus. However, it was too much for the planet's core to take. That's why Dystopia and Twilight both used their cores to synchronize their energy. When this happened, rifts in the sky opened up, and that's how you, Lumus, ended up in Dystopia. The rifts opened the mirror realm of Twilight to Dystopia, and the core of Dystopia gave out its negative energy to balance the worlds once more. As a result, Twilight was left with no choice but to make another copy of our wish, that false wish is known as Lears."

The cave became silent, and the wind in the bushes outside grew louder, and louder until Lumus stood up.

"Lears is my fault; because of me all of those innocent people here on Twilight have had their world ruined," Lumus confessed.

"No Lumus, this is not your fault. You are the hope in this mess that I created. I didn't tell anyone that a wish could be made. I was a scared little girl, and I abused the power of the planet for my own selfish reasons." Scarlette protested.

Brinx walked back to the cave entrance. He backed up against the inner wall with his head facing outside.

"Continue, Scarlette. What happened next?" Zelkem asked.

"When the rifts in the skies of both worlds opened it sucked demons and humans alike from each world. Orson and I were in the innermost area with the core when this all happened. I think it was the core's energy that drew the demons to us. Orson took Lumus. He was still just a baby then, but I told Orson to protect Lumus at all costs. There was much panic and havoc but I still knew Lumus would one day be our ray of hope in the disaster that I had created. I stayed back with the other warriors of Twilight's Special Forces and fought off as many demons as we could" Scarlette paused.

"Then what happened?" Lumus said sadly as if he had already known.

"I died..." She hesitated.

"That's how I know about Ged, he was in the Realm of the Dead, and he taught me all about the realms. I learned a lot from him and he was very kind to me. He introduced me to a woman cloaked in a red and blue robe. She was very intelligent and seemed to have an answer to any question I could think of. She was called the West Zin, the goddess of the West galaxy." Scarlette took a deep breath.

"A goddess?" Lumus said faintly.

"When Ged had left her side, she turned to me and explained why she and Ged were always together. Ged was trying to earn back his life. She said if a life had been taken before its time then they will be given a chance in the Realm of the Dead to earn their life back. Ged had been there just under one hundred years." Scarlette took a deep breath. Lumus sat down with his head down.

"Scarlette... This is a lot to take in. I was blown away that another dimension existed, but a goddess?" Lumus looked to the ground and held his head in disbelief.

"I know, but I have to tell you. I need to explain it to you..." She demanded. Lumus looked up, and he locked eyes with her. He got that feeling of trust when he looked into her eyes. He smiled and nodded.

"West Zin explained that she needed ten years until she had the energy to complete the process to give me life again. Before I could ask why I would get my life back she told me that I was still to play an important role. When the ten years were up and she opened the multi-colored portal, and I was sent through it. I didn't age a day but when I had gone to the temple and made my way to Dystopia, Lumus was grown up. He was ten years old. And physically I was still nine." She explained.

Scarlette sat on a rock near the fire, a moss covered stone on one side but it didn't bother her. She stared into the fire that was nearly out now. Brinx was still facing outside, keeping watch it seemed. Lumus was speechless. He looked as if he had heard a ghost story.

"I know it's a lot to take in, but that's it. I've been living with that for ten years since I came back."

Zelkem had nothing to say. He got up and began to pace back and forth.

"Okay, so you died when you were nine, then you lived in a place for ten years but didn't age while Lumus grew up in Dystopia. You were given your life back and sent back here, at which point you were still nine years old. Then you traveled to Dystopia and met up with Lumus there, and ten years passed until you two made it back to Twilight? Did I sum that up alright?" Zelkem blurted out.

Scarlette was quiet. She looked at him, then back into the fire. A few seconds passed before she said anything.

"Yes, that's basically it." She finally answered.

"So now we know Orson isn't coming, what do we do then?" Brinx said still facing the darkness outside.

"We have two options, one: we leave now and search for Orson. Two: we stay here and search in the morning. Lumus said with a determined look.

"Brinx?" Lumus waited for an answer.

"Now."

"Scarlette?" Lumus tilted his head in her direction.

"Now" she replied. Lumus walked over to Zelkem and rested a hand on his right shoulder.

"Zelkem?" There was a short pause; Zelkem stared at the fire as if he didn't feel Lumus' hand. His eyes move to Lumus,

"Now." Zelkem agreed.

"Okay Zelkem, Scarlette. You two know Twilight better than the rest of us. Where should we start?"

"The Twilight Prison," Zelkem said with an uneasy look. It is northeast of here, but it is probably the most dangerous place on the planet.

"Orson could be there though." Scarlette blurted out.

"I don't really care. I didn't come here to join any of you. I was passing through. I just so happen to bump into miss pink hair here. I have no desire to go on a suicide mission to save a brother I could care less for." Zelkem stood up and walked past Brinx.
"If you leave now, you will never get the chance to prove that you are stronger. I saw it in your eyes." Brinx protested
"What do you know tree? You think I care about any of this? I hunt demons, and you are a demon. You are lucky I am giving you a pass." Zelkem barked back.
"You don't believe your own words do you?" Lumus added. Zelkem stopped.
"You may hate him, and I don't know the story between the two of you, but I know Orson risked his life for me. If you won't save your brother, then I will." Lumus walked past Zelkem with Scarlette behind him.
"Don't let your past be the cause of your future. Write your own fate." Brinx said as he followed Lumus and Scarlette.
("Bastards! They have no idea what they're talking about. Orson... why did you have to come back... Fine. I'll follow them for now, and I'll kick his ass when I find him!") Zelkem punched the wall of the cave before he followed after the others. After he walked away the wall cracked.
"Okay, I'll lead in front. Brinx, you take the back."
"Why does he take the back?" Zelkem asked offended.

"Can your eyes switch to night vision?" Brinx said with a laugh.

"No, but to assume they don't is insulting," Zelkem said with a smile on his face. Brinx seemed happy he decided to come after all.

The group ran into the night one by one. Lumus led the pack, followed by Scarlette, then Zelkem. Brinx jumped from tree to tree above the others, keeping his eyes open for anything moving in the dark. Zelkem turned his head as he ran to make sure Brinx was keeping up but was nowhere to be seen. Just as he was about to stop the group he saw Brinx leap from his left side to a large tree on his right, making no sound at all as he landed.

"Zelkem? What is this prison for?" Lumus was keeping up the pace as they ran east through the Roon Forest.

"Lears built it to imprison those he found useful or people he could turn to his cause. It's twenty-five stories tall, and the first floor is where they decide what floor the prisoners go to. The top is like a throne room personally built for Lears." He explained.

Scarlette was almost out of breath but still kept running. She couldn't let Lumus see her looking weak. She wanted Lumus to see her as help rather than being in the way.

"Lears has been seen at the tower only when new arrivals show up, but the so-called knights are too scared to make a move even if he isn't there," Zelkem added. Lumus was silent for a moment. Scarlette was pacing herself trying to catch her breath. Zelkem was behind by a bit, his attention on Brinx, amazed how he can leap and land without a sound. "People he can turn to his side? Lumus said quietly. You said Lears might be there if someone useful shows up. I'm certain that he'd find Orson useful if he knew he was with us. If that is so and Lears shows up, then we may have a chance to end this now." Lumus said with confidence. Brinx landed a short distance ahead of the group without a sound. "Lumus you speak as if you're ready to fight Lears now. I have to urge you to reconsider."

"Brinx…. I don't understand. We could end this now!"

"Or it could be a trap, Lumus" Zelkem said as he caught up with the group.

"I know your concern in the matter, but the fact is Orson could be there, and if there is the slightest chance that he might be then I must go," Lumus explained.

Scarlette had an unhappy look on her face, she disagreed in going, but she knew they couldn't leave Orson.

"If it was any of you in Orson's position I would be doing the very same," Scarlette added.

The group stood at the edge of the Roon Forest, and the open field through the mountains to the North was their next path.

"I can't leave my only family to die…even if he is an ass I'm going be the one to kick it. I don't care if Lears is there. I'll leave him to you, Lumus" Zelkem started to walk north on to the plains.

"I wouldn't leave Orson either, he's been loyal to me my whole life. It is time for me to show the same loyalty. I must protect Twilight with the same spirit Orson has given to me," Scarlette announced, as she followed behind Zelkem.
"I understand if you won't come Brinx, it may very well be a trap. For a friend, I'm willing to risk that. I know this isn't what you wanted to come here for, but this is why I'm here. Lears taking Orson was a mistake he never should have made. I will get him back; he is like a father to me in a strange way." Lumus turned away with a smile and began his race onto the plains behind Zelkem and Scarlette. Brinx gazed into the sky. His purple eyes looked up into the sky.
"I see. Scarlette has the drive to find her mentor and her friend. Zelkem wants to save his brother, but he would never just come out and say it, and Lumus would throw away everything for a world that doesn't know him, and a man he barely knows. Perhaps joining them will lead to answers I would not find on my own. I'm interested to see where their courage and respect for one another takes them." He crossed his arms and looked at his new friends as if he was proud. After a short pause, he took a step on to the plains after his companions.

Chapter Four- Twilight Prison

Time seemed to slow down for Lumus. He noticed the wind had stopped, and the clouds even seemed to follow the group. He had his eyes locked on the Twilight Prison, and he felt like he was drawn to it. Somehow, for some reason he felt... Happy.

"Guys, listen up! We just reached the border of Varlif Region. We're going to be entering Crystal Mountain Region now. Be on guard and keep your eyes open." Zelkem turned back around and began to continue the walk.

"Eyes seem to be on us already," Brinx said calmly. Lumus took a step back as he drew his sword. Scarlette pulled an arrow from her quiver, but she noticed her bow was not with her. Zelkem stood at the front of the group in confusion.

"Guys I know I said be careful but you may be a little..." Zelkem was cut off as a giant golden bird landed right beside him, bringing a gust of wind with him. Zelkem was thrown into the air and slammed hard into the thick ground.

"The Golden Twilight! Everyone! I lost my bow earlier. I won't be of any help," Scarlette said frantically as she stared at the massive golden bird flying nearby.

"Zelkem!" Lumus shouted as he tried to run to his side, but the Golden Twilight had his sights set on him.

"Brinx, I need you to get to Zelkem. I'll handle the bird. Scarlette take cover... Scarlette!" Lumus shouted at her, but she seemed mesmerized.

"Scarlette! Scarlette I need you to snap out of it!" He yelled.

"I have never seen something so devastating, but so beautiful at the same time. A bird with such grace that it's mere presence makes you feel like you have lost all of your worries. The Golden Twilight. A bird named after the grace of the planet..." A grin appeared on her face. "A rare sight for anyone to see in their lifetime." Scarlette thought to herself, completely unaware that Lumus shouting at her.

"Orson, you always wanted to see this bird, I wish you were here," She smiled.

Lumus ran with his sword against the ground, sparks flew as his speed rose. Brinx leaped over The Golden Twilight shooting green thorns from his hands.

"Ah, damn it!" Zelkem rolled to his side to dodge a blow from the giant beast's talons. He landed quite far from the group.
("I have to get up…no stupid bird is taking me out.")
He looked up as Brinx came crashing down beside him.
"Brinx, don't you do what I think you're…" Zelkem started.
Without a word, Brinx grabbed him and leaped off into the air once again.
"Damn it BRINX!" Zelkem shouted.
Lumus swung his sword violently at the Golden Twilight as Brinx landed with Zelkem beside Scarlette. "Huh? Zelkem?"
"Scarlette, you okay?" He asked.
"I would ask you the same Zelkem, you look horrible," Scarlette said.
"I bet you haven't had the pleasure of being tossed around in the air yet today," Zelkem replied sarcastically.
Brinx leaped off toward Lumus. Scarlette and Zelkem began to stare at each other in anger until they looked back at the Golden Twilight. Its brilliant light around its body flashed with a flap of its wings.
Lumus struggled to stand his ground against the fierce bird, with every attack the Golden Twilight threw one back, it was endless. The

bird landed swiftly. Lumus didn't budge and Brinx was too far to lend a hand. He stood alone with the large bird staring him down, and he stared back awaiting the Golden Twilight's next move. Suddenly it settled down, and continued to stare at Lumus without moving, and then began to approach slowly. He was ready to strike till he looked into its eyes. The great bird lowered its head to him and gently laid his head against his body.
"Lumus?" Brinx yelled out.
"It's okay Brinx, he's not violent anymore. I think it was just scared," Lumus assured him. As Brinx got closer to them, the Golden Twilight turned its back to Lumus almost like it was protecting him.
"Lumus?" Brinx said softly.
"It's okay girl, he's a friend." The Golden Twilight calmed down to Lumus' voice. It flapped its massive wings as its body began to glow. Just as it appeared, it soared off again into the sky with a shrill. The Golden Twilight flew through the clouds creating an opening in its wake. Everyone stared up into the open ring in the clouds where the Golden Twilight flew through.
"It's beautiful," Scarlette said softly.
"I've never seen anything like it. The Golden Twilight lives up to the legends that I've heard

over the years," Zelkem said as he sat down to catch his breath.

"I know you're tired Zelkem, but we must keep moving. Orson could be in danger." Lumus announced.

"Ah yes, the famous Orson." Zelkem got up slowly and began to walk toward the Twilight Prison once again.

Brinx followed behind, then Lumus. Scarlette paused, still staring at the sky where the Golden Twilight was last seen. Lumus turned back to her for a moment as she turned to rejoin the group, she gave him a little smile and began to catch up.

The wind began to build the closer they got to the heart of the Crystal Mountain Plains. It was mid-day and the blue moon shined brightly. The day was mild, and the wind kept the group from sweating. The Twilight Prison was within a few steps now, looking straight up it was still impossible to see the top. The cloud cover hid its true height.

"Lumus, we will need an escape plan, a place to meet in case we are to be separated," Brinx said as he stood motionless. His face locked on the tower as if analyzing everything about it. Scarlette stepped forward and drew an arrow from her quiver as she dropped to her knees.

"Pay attention Lumus. You too Brinx. You two don't know these lands as well as Zelkem and myself. These mountains behind me are the borders for Crystal Mountain Region to Dornet Region, that's assuming you go directly east. Northeast is the Aster Mountain Region. South across the great rivers is the Old Valley Region. I'm just telling you these for now so that you know your surroundings. You obviously know we came from the South West of Varlif region. Are you starting to understand a little more?" She asked with a smile.

"Yes, but I'm curious…how many regions are there?"

"There are twelve regions, Lumus. But some say thirteen with the water."

"Did you say the water?" Brinx said finally looking away from the tower.

"Well yes, I believe it to be the thirteenth region as well. There are still living creatures down there in the water. People consider the Breedlands a Region, but all people have there is one city."

"Scarlette," Brinx blurted out, "We are wasting our time here, get on with what you need to say."

Scarlette stared at Brinx for a moment, then realized they had no time to waste.

"Okay, the safest route we could take is toward Taurald; the city of this Region. It is to the South East. There is a small town there, and we simply need to acquire a boat and make for Capaz which is farther east by the river. Capaz is the capital city of the Torson Region.

"This is a pretty well-constructed plan Scarlette," Lumus said with an impressed tone.

"Well, Taurald is the closest for a quick getaway, if we get to Capaz I know people there that can help us. Capaz is my hometown after all. As for Librine, it's a long shot but I knew a boy from there named Dyne. I just hope he's still the boy I remember." Scarlette was fixated on the map she drew in the dirt. Lumus crouched down beside her.

"It would be best to meet in this city," Lumus added as he pointed to Scarlette's map.

"Capaz? That is perfect. Librine is too far, now that I think about it." Scarlette added.

"Quiet, there is movement at the tower gate," Brinx whispered.

Two guards came from the entrance leaving the gate open behind them. The guards lit six torches, three on each side of the gate leading down the path. The guards then returned inside, leaving the gate wide open.

"Lumus what do we do?" Scarlette spoke in a whisper.

"We go…we go now!" Lumus jumped over the rock they all hid behind and ran toward the gate, the others followed a few moments after him. He made it to the gate opening, but even with the torches, the inside was still dark. He didn't stop running though. As he entered the darkness, a loud shout of pain came from Lumus and he was thrown from the gates into the boulder they hid behind, shattering it to rubble as his body crashed through. The others stopped immediately. The night was setting in. The blue moon almost set, and very little light for a battle.

"Look! A knight! He was able to take Lumus down?" Scarlette cried out.

Lumus rose from the rubble and brushed off the dirt as if he took no injuries from the throw. The Lord walked into the light, his shoulder armour black like the night, and his helmet covered his face entirely. His armour was all a light black with gold linings. His sword was new but not impressive, it was a common long sword but nonetheless, should not be underestimated.

Lumus walked forward as he wiped the blood from his lip. He pulled his sword from his sheath, his head was down and his grip on his sword was tight. As he walked closer and closer to the dark knight, his grip on his sword got tighter and tighter. Scarlette, Zelkem, and Brinx stood still waiting for the dark figure to make a move. The looks on their faces were all the same, anger flittered over them as Lumus flew into the rocks. Just as they all readied to attack, Lumus began to power up, shining a light on his body and letting out a loud yell. His sword in hand, his eyes glowing a bright white as if it was shooting slowly from his eyes like beams of light in every direction. Zelkem stepped aside, as Lumus walked past. The Lord now with his sword pointed straight at him. Lumus stopped a few steps away. Both with their swords up and ready to fight. Suddenly a weird sound from the sky called out.

"Is it the Golden Twilight?" Scarlette said softly.

"No, something else," Brinx replied.

"Something bigger," Zelkem added.

The horrible screams got louder as the beast came closer to sight. Suddenly, a fire erupted from its mouth.

"It's a Dragon!" Zelkem shouted with fear in his eyes.

The dragon stopped in the sky, hovering high above them. Lumus was still staring at the

Lord, and the Lord stared back at him. It looked as if the dragon dropped something, and the small object got bigger and bigger as seconds passed. Suddenly it came clear to everyone that it was a person.

"Yhaaaaaaa!" The man came crashing down with a sword on his back. It was an odd red metal, like nothing the group had ever seen before.

As the large man landed, smoke rose from the ground making it impossible to see anything. Suddenly he emerged; his sword almost as long as his body. His hair was black with purple tips that reached for the sky, his armour black, and purple. His gauntlets resembled hands of a dragon but they had claws over the knuckles.

"You four, go about your business I will handle this Lord." The mysterious figure told Lumus. Without notice, he leaped at the Lord and clashed swords with him violently. Lumus' glow faded and his face went blank for a moment.

"Go! Inside! We need to find Orson; now is our chance." Lumus led the group inside through the darkness and they reached the inside of the tower. It was lit up with torches all along of the walls with beautiful murals covering the walls. Without saying anything,

Lumus began running up the stone stairs, a spiral of stone steps led to a floor of prison cells with bones in most of them. Guards were everywhere, but without stopping they took out any of the guards in their way. Lumus slashed any foes from the front. Brinx was covering the rear with his projectile thorns. Scarlette made her way behind Lumus. She felt useless without her bow. Zelkem finished off any that came from the corridors of other floors as they passed them.

The stone steps ended after an almost endless climb of stairs. A straight well-lit hallway led to more stone stairs. They ran by numerous prison cells but by the looks of those in the cells they were all dead. Lumus' anger grew more and more as he passed each blood-soaked cell. The tower seemed like an endless pool of blood.

"Lumus, wait!" Zelkem shouted, "There's someone alive in here."

Lumus turned slowly in disbelief.

"What?" he said finally.

"He is right, a girl it would seem," Brinx announced.

Lumus slashed at the cell door until it swung open.

"Who are you?" said a faint voice.

"I'm Lumus, this is Brinx, Zelkem and..."

"I'm Scarlette," She said as she kneeled beside the woman.

"She needs some clothes Lumus," Scarlette demanded

"What's your name? Are you okay to walk?" Zelkem said.

"My name is...my name is Zephry. My things are locked in that chest," she replied.

Lumus' hand began to glow as he grabbed the lock on the chest then suddenly he pulled the lock off with ease.

"Here, put these on, we must get going," Lumus turned back to the door.

"Why are you all here?" Zephry asked.

"We are here to find our friend Orson. We think he is here somewhere within this prison," Scarlette said as she handed Zephry her clothes.

"Orson, he's the big man from the cell across from me earlier. I think they took him upstairs yesterday and I haven't seen him come back. They did some terrible things to him. I screamed at them to stop but they wouldn't listen to me. Last I saw, a Lord came from upstairs but the thing is… I never saw him go up. Orson is a good man, he helped me survive by giving me some of his food."

She began to cry. Lumus' face went blank. Lumus wondered about the Lord they saw

earlier. "All of you go, get out of here and follow Scarlette's plan to Capaz. I'll go alone from here." Lumus began to head out of the room, but Scarlette grabbed his arm.
"Lumus you can't, Lears is up there. If you face him alone you might die." Lumus looked back at Scarlette with a grin on his face.
"I have to Scarlette. I have no choice. Now go!" Lumus ran through the hallway to the stone steps drawing his sword as he ran. ("This ends now Lears! I cannot and will not allow this to continue.")
 Lumus ran full speed up the endless spiral stairs hearing the others call out to him, he ignored them knowing what needed to be done. Soon their voices faded in the distance. He felt bad for leaving them behind, but he knew he had to face Lears alone.
Scarlette gathered the others and led them back down the tower. Zelkem led the rear and Zephry behind Scarlette. Brinx ripped the window bars out and leaped out. They made their way to the tower gates, where the strange man was still fighting the Lord, and both looked fatigued.
"Frostear?" Zephry called out.
"Zephry, I came to find you! Are you okay?" Just then the Lord had grabbed Frostear's arm and threw him into the tower wall. Zelkem

charged him, but only to take an elbow to the face, knocking him back off his feet. The Lord ran over, striking Scarlette with a devastating uppercut. While in the air, the Lord charged a kick, striking Scarlette across the rough terrain. Zephry jumped on his back, only to be grabbed and thrown to the ground alongside Scarlette.

"Hey buddy," Frostear said as he rose from the debris, "That was a huge mistake!" Frostear charged straight for the Lord with his large red sword above his head. The blade came crashing down, just missing the Lord. Using the large sword as leverage, Frostear threw his weight into his legs hitting the Lord directly in the face sending him flying in the air. His helmet flew off and his body flailed through the air, and he crashed hard into the ground.

("I have to be close, there can't be many more stairs than this.") Lumus made his way up the tower alone passing by all of the floors and only fighting the guards that stood directly in his path. Finally, he came to a large set of doors with brightly lit torches on each side. Two guards charged him, but Lumus took them out with ease. He yelled out loud as his body burst with a wall of light throwing the doors wide open.

"LEARS!" Lumus yelled out. A mysterious man in a black hood stood by the window. He turned slowly to finally look his rival in the eyes.

"Lumus, I felt you approaching," Lears said with an evil smile. Lumus ran at him with his sword glowing brightly. Suddenly Ged appeared, dropping to the ground kicking out Lumus' feet then delivering a kick to his chest that shot him back out the door.

"You shouldn't have come here Lumus, you fool. You brought everything to us. We have Orson, Twilight's purest knight. We now have your friends within our grasp, and I can now finish off that bitch, Scarlette. Oh, and Master Lears can finally kill you of course." Ged said with a laugh.

"Ged, go do what you need to do. I shall deal with Lumus."

"Yes, miLord," Ged replied quickly.

"How did the familiar of Ged get to Twilight?" Lumus questioned.

"Familiar? Did Scarlette not explain it to you? I am not from Dystopia. One hundred years ago I traveled to Dystopia to kill demons. I set out to prove my strength. It was there that I found and killed my familiar, but I fell against the other demons, even with my boost in power... I crawled back to the portal in hopes to return to Twilight, but I was denied passage. I remember begging like a lowly peasant. After losing my pride and my honor… I had given up on becoming powerful. I don't know why, but I was accepted back into the portal to Twilight. I returned just to die moments later. I then woke up in the realm of the dead, and I started my one hundred years of redemption to be reincarnated, but Scarlette took my place. At that moment I lost it… I couldn't accept that this child was granted passage over me, and I would have had to wait another one hundred years… I forced my way into the portal after her, but my flesh was ripped from my body. I was transformed into this creature… A monster that would never be accepted as a human ever again," Ged explained.

"That is enough Ged. You are dismissed," Lears yelled out.

Just as he appeared, he disappeared into the shadows. Lears took off his hood as Lumus got to his feet. The two looked at each other in silence for a moment. It was almost like they were glad to see each other.

"Lumus, I have heard of you, surprising really. A few demons from the beginning told me as I grew up that you were the first to emerge. Obviously, I didn't think anything of it, but as time passed… More people called out your name as I killed them, and as I burned their homes. Soon I found a young woman named Zephry and through her, I learned that Orson was the only one that may know the truth about you. So I searched for him all over. He seemed to be nowhere in Twilight. After that, I began to believe this alternate world of Dystopia just might exist. And if it did and he was there, then you might be there. That's when I began to feel a power like my own. I knew that you had returned. I was lucky to have found your friend Orson. He gave me a lot of the pieces to the puzzle you see. Now that I obviously know you exist, I also know how I truly came to be, and that there is another world for the taking. And you Lumus, you brought all of this to me. So I thank you," Lears laughed hysterically.

"I never wanted any of this, you are only here by a simple error in judgment. I'll make sure I fix that error for all of the people of Twilight," Lumus yelled, but he stared at Lears for a moment. He could tell he was hesitant too. Lumus stared at his own face, and it scared him. How could he possibly fight himself, or even kill himself? The thought of it made him cringe, but he stood up and kept eye contact with Lears. He fought the idea that it was himself he had to fight. He began to think of Lears as the monster that used his face to spread evil around the world, and that sickened him. They continued to stare at each other, but even Lears seemed frightened. Lumus knew this would be no easy fight, and he knew that he needed to win. For his friends, for Twilight, and for Scarlette. Lears snapped out of his dazed look and began to smile.

"Oh, how heroic Lumus, so you come to the lair of the villain and strike him down, then what? Do you skip in a field of flowers with the townspeople? Hahaha, not in this dream, for I have made it a nightmare, and it's my nightmare to manipulate," Lears said with a sinister laugh.

He picked up two unique swords off the stone table in front of him, one was a black-steeled blade with a uniquely designed hilt. The other sword was a red sword like the stranger's outside that Lumus met briefly.

"So that guy outside works for you too, the one with a sword like yours?" Lumus looked concerned that his friends may be falling into a trap.

"Hmm? A little off topic, I can't know every weapon my minions use, but if you're referring to this sword, it is red steel also known as dragon steel. It's quite useful. You see it is stronger than any other blade during the red moon. Although it does become just like any other sword during the blue moon it can be very useful in the red light though." Lears glanced at his sword as he spoke.

"Thanks, Lears… I just needed to know if my friends were okay. Now that you have confirmed that they will be okay, I can come at you with everything I have." He smiled.

He began to glow white, but Lears suddenly started to emit a black aura around him, and Lumus was a bit shocked to see how much he was like him.

"Well, Lumus are you ready to die?" Lears took a step forward as his face lit up with excitement, and he pointed his swords toward Lumus with a grin.

Scarlette scrambled to her feet outside. Zelkem was barely conscious, and Frostear was still in a stalemate with the Lord. Their swords clashed with each other over and over again. Sparks flew like a bunch of fireworks at a celebration. Neither would give up. Zelkem fell unconscious as he tried to stand up. Scarlette could barely lift her head up. Zephry stood up with all of her energy.

"Zephry?" Scarlette said faintly. A dim glow came from her hands, but her eyes were shut.

Zephry's lips were moving as if she was chanting something to herself. Suddenly, Zephry opened her eyes wide, but her pupils had faded behind the bright yellow light. As a small portal began to form in front of her, she was thrown off balance from Frostear crashing into the stones beside her. The glow dissipated and Zephry snapped out of it. She raced to his side. No one seemed to notice her glow but Scarlette.

("That yellow power, I have seen it before. Only a God has that kind of power, and I have seen it used only by the West Zin....") Scarlette thought to herself while she watched Zephry aide Frostear.

"Hang in there you dumb brute…" Zephry whispered.

"Zephry, I have been looking for you. I never thought to find you here," Frostear added.

"I was taken… Well, I really don't know how long it's been…"

"I felt like I owed you for all of the times you took me in when I needed a roof over my head." Frostear closed his eyes as he spoke. Zephry shook him, and gently slapped his face. He woke up enough to rise to his feet. He faced the Lord once again with a small grin.

"Hello my dear, have you missed me?" Ged grabbed Scarlette by the throat, catching her completely off guard. Slowly he lifted her into the air with just one hand causing her to gasp for air.

"I can't say I imagined this any other way girl, draining the life from you as you did to me in the Realm of the Dead. You stole everything from me when you entered that portal. I waited patiently for one hundred years! Then you come out of nowhere, and a nine-year-old gets precedence over me? I lost my mind when I saw you go in my place... I chased after you and this is what came of me. A shadow of my former self. You created this! I joined Lears to take over this world, but now that I have found you, I will not stop until I watch the last breath leave your body."

Scarlette gasped for air hoping to get enough to yell for help, but she couldn't. Her hands on Ged's wrists felt weak as she tried to pry them off, but she got weaker and weaker.

The Lord switched focus as he looked over to Ged... His eyes were glowing red until he noticed Scarlette. The Lord freaked out as he dropped his sword, and shook his head. When he looked up, his clear human eyes stared back.

"Scarlette!" Orson yelled as if he was too late to save her. He charged for Ged, knocking him to the ground and releasing his grip on

Scarlette. She fell to the ground unconscious. Orson walked slowly toward Ged with no sign of hesitation. The dust was covering Ged's vision as he got to his feet. He couldn't see in any direction. Orson threw him from the smoke while landing a devastating barrage of attacks on Ged. His rage made his strength grow far beyond Ged's. He was unable to guard a single attack. Orson dragged him across the ground like he was nothing, and without a moment of pause, Orson began to run, picking up speed as Ged was brutally dragged against the loose dirt and rocks along the ground. Scarlette began to regain consciousness and tried to sit up. She raised her arms enough to lift her head. She noticed Orson fighting a defenseless Ged.

"I can end this nightmare right now, Lears. I hope you're ready too. I won't hold anything back." Lumus told his foe.

"Finally Lumus, I can use my full power. I have never had anyone strong enough to even stand against me for even five minutes, but maybe you can." Lears shot back.

"Shut it Lears, I didn't come all this way to chat."

Lumus began to get angry, his body started to emit power.

"Lumus you fool, this is the end for you. I will take this world once and for all!" Lears flipped the stone table out of the way with ease. Lumus readied himself with his sword in front of his face ready to guard Lear's attack. Their swords clashed as they fought. One after another, their swords hit each other. Sparks flew as the battle below them roared. Lears flung a beam of dark energy from his sword, Lumus dodged it in surprise and as he landed. Lears shot another. Lumus was struck head-on, throwing him through the tower wall. He opened his eyes as he fell, now staring at Lears as he plummeted to his death. Suddenly he let out a loud yell as his body lit up like thunder. Just before Lumus crashed to the ground he stopped himself. His face almost completely covered by light, and he looked up to Lears once more, but this time lifting himself from his light barrier. For a split second Lumus touched the ground, but as soon as he did, he shot back up into the sky twice as fast as he fell. Lears backed away from the crumbling rocks of the once tower wall.

Orson and Ged continued to fight, not even fazed by Lumus falling and shooting off again. Orson's anger grew with every swing he took against Ged. A once peaceful man swearing to only protect others became rage itself. Zelkem woke up to watch his brother unleash a relentless barrage of attacks with no hesitation. His head waved in the air until he passed out once again. His face fell straight down into the rubble with a thud.

("What has Lears done to you, Orson…)" Scarlette thought as she slowly lifted herself from the rubble. Zelkem was face down on the rocks nearby, and Zephry was helping Frostear to his feet with his arm over her shoulder.

"He has lost control, Scarlette. We have to stop him before he hurts himself," Brinx said as he walked slowly toward her.

"Lumus and Lears are still fighting. They seem to have an endless source of power," Scarlette said as she stared up at the tower. Light and dark energy shot out from above as she watched in fear.

"Orson this isn't our fight, this is between me and the girl," Ged yelled out. Orson still headed for him without anything - or anyone - holding him back.

"Fine. I will give you everything I got. The girl will have to wait for her death."

Ged ran at Orson screaming. Orson's eyes locked on him as he came charging.

"You will not succeed Ged. I will not allow you to harm Scarlette, even if it costs me my life!" He yelled back as he readied himself. Orson and Ged ran at each other fiercely. As they hit, a blinding flash lit the area and the two went flying in opposite directions. Orson flew across the ground helplessly, but Ged flew out of sight. Brinx and Scarlette ran to Orson's side with haste.

"Keep back, he could still be enraged Scarlette," Brinx whispered.

"No, I cannot stand here while he is hurt. I can help him." She replied.

Zephry and Frostear joined Brinx's side. Zelkem started to wake up once again.

"Ah, fine run to Orson. I'm not hurt or anything," Zelkem said under his breath as he got up slowly. "Damn you, Orson, you become the enemy and yet you're still praised as the hero. I don't understand, I can't understand this. No matter how I try or what I do you are still the hero." He rose to his feet as he watched everyone help his brother.

Lumus and Lears continued to battle each other at the top of the prison. The world shook beneath them as they exchanged blows. The Twilight prison began to crumble slowly with each hit laid upon one another.

"I won't give in Lumus, you should know this by now. You've taken a beating, are you tired yet?" Lears said with a laugh.

"You know as well as I do that I've matched every hit you dished out. I won't give in Lears, not until I finish this and restored what I've done. You may share my face, but you represent everything I fight against."

"What you've done? You fool. They gave you your life, they gave you this power and they made you. Why do you feel compelled to fight me when you could easily take this world for your own?"

"Maybe because I'm not like you, and I care for others. The people of Twilight gave me life but because of my birth into this world, I have created nothing but death. I will fight any battle I need to, to make up for the pain I've caused. The people shouldn't have to suffer so that I can live!" Lumus yelled in a rage.

"It's a pity Lumus, a pity that I must kill my own brother. I gave you a chance to join me, but you had to be stubborn. Oh well, more for me! Hahaha!"

Lears jumped at Lumus with his swords facing towards his chest, and as he leaped into the air Lumus' hand began to glow.

("This is for the people, those that call this world their home.") Lumus let out a screeching yell as he pointed his hand toward Lears. The room lit up as the glow on Lumus' hand shot at lightning speed toward Lears. In mid-air, Lears caught the blast of energy in the chest, throwing him through the hole in the wall. He released a wicked cry as the energy engulfed his body, and it cast him into the night sky.

Chapter Five: Family Feud

"Lumus. Lumus can you hear me?" Brinx asked. He and Zephry were kneeling by Lumus' side. Lumus looked wrecked, his body drained and his clothes covered in dirt and debris.
"Hey Lumus, you must have passed out after the battle. We saw a huge beam of some kind shoot Lears off into the sky. You did it Lumus. You killed Lears," Zephry's face lit up with a big smile.
"Where are we?" Lumus said, concerned.
"Don't worry Lumus you're safe here," Scarlette said as she came through the door.
"We're okay here, for now. We are at the Inn in Taurald. We had to carry you out of the tower as it came down," she said with a sigh.
"I offered to take you out the window, but Scarlette wouldn't let me." Brinx crossed his arms as he turned to the window.
"Where is Orson? Is he okay? Ah. My body is battered, I can barely move. What happened?" asked Lumus.
Scarlette sat on the bed by Lumus. She put her hand on his.
"Don't worry we all made it out alive. We have Frostear, Orson and you to thank for that. You three fought to the end. I'm just sorry I couldn't have been more of a help." Scarlette looked away from him with a sad look in her eyes.
"Frostear? Who is this guy?" Lumus asked.

"I am a friend." He replied.

"He is a big dumb brute that came looking for me in the Twilight Prison, but you didn't need to risk your life for me!" Zephry complained.

"You know I had no choice," Frostear argued.

"I'm sorry, but we are all in the dark here. Who are you? Why did you help us?" Lumus asked again.

"My name is Frostear. I am a traveling hunter you could say. I hunt dragons mostly," He explained.

"So, you came looking for Zephry?" Brinx added.

"I did. I lost my home years ago, and since their dragons have become rarer over time, I have been having trouble earning money. I stopped at Zephry's hometown one night to find shelter, but she was kind enough to offer a stranger a room for the night. Over time, I continued to stay with her when I was in the area," He explained.

"You jumped off a dragon at the prison right?" Brinx added. Frostear smiled back.

"I suppose I can't hide that fact. I was able to tame the dragon, but it comes and goes when it pleases. I can call for it, but it doesn't always hear me." He walked to the window to gaze outside.

"I see. What will you do next?" Lumus said as he sat up in his bed.

"I came to find Zephry and I have. I will accompany her home then I will be on my way I suppose." He said quietly.

"Master Orson said he'd train me to be a Twilight soldier though. So I won't be in the way if I come along." Zephry sat opposite to Scarlette on the bed with a big smile.

"Zephry! What do you mean? What about your home? And the Zufore?" Frostear blurted out as he turned to face her.

"The Zufore have all been released by Lears or killed. My home is burned to the ground, and there is nothing to go home to. I will train to become a knight with Master Orson. I am tired of being in the way. I want to help!" Zephry screamed back in anger. Frostear stared at her for a moment, then turned to Lumus.

"Then I have no choice. I must follow Zephry. I told myself I would bring her home. Until she finds her home, I will have to come with her," Frostear announced.

Lumus smiled with a nod.

"We would be happy to have your strength Frostear and your courage Zephry. Speaking of… Orson, where is he?

"Orson and Zelkem left early this morning, Zelkem didn't say a word but Orson just said, 'We won't be long'," Scarlette replied.

"I believe they have some things that need to be resolved, but only those two can fight this battle," Brinx said as he turned back to Lumus.

The morning was cold. The birds chirped as the blue moon shone brightly through the trees. The river moved calmly by the Taurald falls. Zelkem stood at the shoreline looking down river toward the waterfall. Orson stood patiently a few steps away waiting for him to say something. Finally, he turned to Orson but remained silent; instead, he stared deep into Orson's eyes for a moment.

"I know you hate me Zelkem, and I know you don't understand what I did to…"

"No brother, I understand completely, I know why you abandoned me with no money, no food, and no place to call home. When I met Scarlette in Varlif region I was shocked to find out from her that you were still alive. I insisted on joining her, just to show you what your 'little brother' has become with no one to aid me. I have become a better man then you will ever be. You know when I thought you died I recruited a few guys brave enough to take on the demons. I and my band of brothers set out to save Twilight. After a few months, I was the only one left alive. All of my true brothers fell in battle against Lear's Lords. I continued to fight alone. I was after a demon named Antsos, and I learned that he was sighted near Varlif Forest, but when I got there he had already come and gone. That's when I found Scarlette. I'm glad I did though. Finding you alive has made my journey up to now worth it. So what do you think brother, do you think you can beat me?"

"Beat you?" Orson replied, "I'm not going to fight you Zelkem. Don't be stupid. I left because I was scared. I left because I knew I wasn't strong enough. When mom and dad died I wasn't just your brother anymore. I had to be both parents; two responsibilities that I myself couldn't handle. I left you in Geminite so that I could come back strong enough for both of us." Zelkem paced back and forth

"You never came back, brother. You never even came to see me when you became Twilights Golden Hero. Was I nothing to you then do I mean anything to you now?" Zelkem raised his voice. "I couldn't bear to see you after I left you like I did. As the years passed I sent out soldiers to Canby but when they reported that you were no longer there I sent more soldiers to all of the cities looking for you. I left my responsibilities as Knight First Class of Capaz just to find you. No matter how hard I looked, I couldn't find you. Shortly after that I returned to Capaz and was ordered to protect Lady Scarlette on a quest to the Aster Mountains, and the summoning of Lumus took place after that. I was sucked into a vortex in the sky with Lumus in my arms. I was gone for…"
"Twenty years," Zelkem interrupted.
"No, I was only there ten years. I found a way back to Twilight, but I left Lumus in Dystopia. I went back to Capaz to help who I found, but after a few days I left and traveled from city to city for ten years. I helped whom I could along the way. Anyone that may have seen you or had any information about you didn't help at all. So after ten years of searching while avoiding Lears, I went back to Dystopia through an ancient portal I found hidden in the mountains of Aster Mountain region. I told Lumus everything, and then he and I met Brinx just before returning to Twilight." Zelkem stopped his pacing to face Orson once more.

"It doesn't matter, none of this matters. I hate you, and I will always hate you. The only way you can prove any of this is to fight me. If you win only then will I believe that you left to get stronger to help me and not just yourself."

"Fine Zelkem, I will fight you," Orson announced.

"Don't hold back, I'm going all-out," Zelkem said as he took off his weighted arm guards.

Orson took off his heavy armour and gauntlets. For a moment the two brothers stared at each other without a sound. The river flowed behind Zelkem, the water whistled down the calm currents. The trees brushed lightly together behind Orson, and the path behind him that lead to town was covered with light dirt and rocks that now lay upon Orson's boots. Zelkem noticed that Orson had closed his eyes. Orson didn't move at all, and it didn't look like he was ready for a fight. Zelkem thought long and hard about whether to attack or not.

("I bet this is a test, big brother. You can't fool me, I'll strike first!") Zelkem lashed out toward Orson silently as he flew through the air. He charged his fist forward at Orson. The leaves on the trees stood still as Zelkem flew through the air. Just before Zelkem made contact, Orson's eyes opened and his hand rose to catch Zelkem's fist, stopping him dead in the air. Orson kicked Zelkem hard in the ribs knocking the air from his lungs. As gravity drove him to the ground Orson turned around, dragging his weight with him and throwing Zelkem with such force over his shoulder that he

had no chance to react. The air split as Zelkem
threw himself upright in the air, and as he came
down he landed on his feet with a gust of dirt
under his feet.

"Scarlette, do you hear that?" Brinx stood up as he
looked north.

"I hear something, like the sound of a thousand
feet". Brinx said softly.

"Krotins," Zephry called out, "It is time to go
now."

Zephry jumped up from the floor frantically then
bolted out of the door to the streets. Brinx and
Scarlette got up and headed outside. Lumus got
up slowly from his bed as Scarlette came back in,
"We need to leave now Lumus," Scarlette said as
she threw his arm over her shoulder to help him
outside.

"That's a lot of Krotins." Zephry's face turned pale
as she looked on to the site of hundreds of Krotins
advancing towards them.

"We need to leave now!" Scarlette dragged Lumus
along as she made haste toward the mountains
outside of Taurald.

"Frostear? Where is he?" Zephry said in a panic.

"You don't scare me rodents, I will show you no
mercy!" Frostear yelled threateningly.

He came running up the dirt path toward the
North entrance of Taurald his glowing red sword
in his right hand and a Krotin by the neck in the
other. Just before he reached the gate, he jumped
and turned to the hundreds of Krotins behind him,
and threw the one from his hand an arm's reach

away, He clenched his sword with both hands and turned it lengthwise after a short charge of energy. He hit the Krotin with the dull side of his sword to send it flying toward the mob.

"Frostear! Let's go" Zephry yelled out.

"Do you feel that?" Orson said worriedly.

"You're not getting out of this brother, I won't let this stop now!" Zelkem charged Orson.

"Krotins... Zelkem, the Krotins travel in large numbers. Lears uses them as small waves of expendable infantry. A small quake like this must mean..." Zelkem calmed down for a moment.

"Krotins? This area isn't known for any quakes. Lears must still be alive, and I think he has the Krotins attacking us. He knows we are still tired from the battle. We have no choice Orson we will finish this later, but for now we need to help the others," Zelkem replied.

Orson grabbed his armour as Zelkem began to head for the village.

"Scarlette, head for the Eastern path. That may be a way out," Lumus said as he tried to catch his breath.

"Everyone, this way! Let's get out of here now!" Scarlette held Lumus tight as she ran as fast as she could. Brinx, Zephry, and Frostear followed behind them as the Krotins reached the North Gates.

"We need to find Orson and Zelkem before we leave, Scarlette!" Lumus stood on his own.

"This may seem harsh but we cannot go back now, with their abilities I'm sure they will be fine."

Scarlette felt horrible as Frostear spoke. Frostear turned his back to the group and put his sword back into its sheath. Zephry followed Frostear as he began up the mountain path into the eastern mountains of Taurald. Brinx looked toward the village then back to Lumus,
"We should move on if you remember we made plans to make it to Capaz. If Zelkem and Orson follow the plan I'm certain they'd meet us there as well," Brinx assured as he turned to continue up the path. Scarlette threw Lumus' arm over her shoulder once more, and for a moment they gazed at Taurald as the Krotin violently destroyed everything they saw. After a short pause, Scarlette and Lumus followed behind the others.
"Zelkem, slow down, the others will be fine. I'm sure they left long before the Krotins arrived," Orson told his brother.
Zelkem turned his head to look over his shoulder. "And what if they didn't, brother? Another poor judgment call on your part. They could very well be in there," Zelkem replied. He hid behind some bushes waiting for a chance to look as Krotins passed by.
"You need to calm down. Lumus and the others can handle themselves and I know that they would follow Scarlette's plan to head for Capaz. We just need to head east to the Taurald Mountains." Orson hid behind a large tree, glancing over his shoulder in hopes that his theory was right and the others had already left.

"Fine. We play it your way, but you may want to come up with another plan brother. The Krotin seem to have reached the east path. Orson looked over to see the Krotin mobilizing at the eastern path in large numbers.

"Hmm, they seem to be acting a little different. Look, they are grouping. Normally they don't have the intelligence for tactics like that," Orson added.

"It would seem someone is telling them what to do, and that someone could be that guy at the gate. A man covered by a ragged cape blowing in the wind stood at the North Gate; his black hood covering his eyes and his sword as red as the night moon.

"I don't recognize this guy. Maybe a new Lord of Lears?" Zelkem began to worry.

"Lears has been building his army while I've been gone. I have no idea who this guy is either. I don't intend to start a fight with someone I don't know, we need to find out more about this guy." Orson sheathed his sword and made his way back to the river. Zelkem followed behind Orson. They made their way back to the river as the small quakes started up again.

"They're coming, hurry Zelkem," Orson ordered. Orson ran right to the edge of the river. As he did, he noticed the river was still. To his left, he noticed a blockade of boulders forming a dam.

"Zelkem we can make our way across the river. Look, it's still. Hurry." Orson jumped into the still water and began to swim across. Zelkem looked at

him for a moment to see trees falling and wildlife fleeing.
("Damn you Krotins, I shouldn't be running from beasts this weak.") Zelkem turned to Orson and jumped into the river. As he surfaced he noticed Krotins running along the dam by the waterfall. Slowly the beasts removed rock after rock. Orson turned to notice them too.
"Zelkem come on we need to hurry!"
The mysterious new Lord came walking slowly down the river path. The Krotins broke the dam-free, and as they did many of them flew over the falls yelling in fear of death. Orson and Zelkem began to be sucked down toward the falls.
"Orson!" Zelkem screamed out.
"Zelkem, hold on!" Orson yelled back. Their heads bobbed up and down under the water as they were forced down to the falls. As they flew over the violent falls with the Krotins and the boulders that began to give away, the man in the black cape reached the riverbanks. He looked up for a moment.
"He's not here, carry on after them. The rest of you follow me up the mountain path." He ordered to the Krotins.
Frostear stopped for a moment as the others passed him by. Zephry stopped as well and turned back to Frostear.
"What is it? Are you ok?" Zephry seemed worried.
"I feel something. Something I haven't felt in a while. I think my son is here..." Frostear looked at Zephry then back over his shoulder to Taurald.

"Your son? Well, that's good, right? Shouldn't we go help him if he is in Taurald?" Zephry seemed happy.

"No, he is more dangerous then you know, my son has gone down the wrong path. He has seen the power the darkness offers and has embraced it into his heart. If we want to live, we need to press on." Frostear turned from Zephry and hurried to the others.

"Can he really be stronger than you? Are you saying your son is so strong that he can beat you, or even Lumus?" Zephry asked, unconvinced. Frostear turned to Zephry.

"Zephry, there are many things you're forgetting - we are all still very fatigued from the battle at the Twilight prison. We would fall if we faced him now. I'm sure he knows that we are not at full strength, and he intends to kill us in our weakened condition." Zephry realized he was right.

"I see. Okay, Frostear. Maybe next time we meet him we can talk some sense into him and maybe he'll join us." Zephry walked past Frostear with a smile of hope on her face as if it was possible.

("She doesn't' seem to hear what I say, or maybe she is too optimistic to see the real danger in others.") Frostear thought.

"Come on you two, we can't slow down now. Let's get going; the Krotin could catch up." Lumus called back.

Scarlette seemed more concerned about Lumus getting hurt then the actual safety of the others. She held him tightly, almost hurting him more than helping him, but Lumus could tell from her eyes that she was scared and that she would do anything to protect him. Lumus began to think hard about his life, and the reasons that Twilight has fallen into such ruin.

The red moon began to set as the group made haste through the mountain path. They scurried through rough terrain and climbed over many obstacles as Krotins followed close behind. There was no sign of the hooded Lord. Lumus could feel Scarlette's grip on him weakening as they made it farther up the mountain. Brinx lead in front followed by Scarlette and Lumus. Zephry was right behind them but would check often to see if Frostear was still with them. He didn't seem to notice her odd interest in him. His mind was clouded by thoughts of his son in his head. Time seemed to slow down and the night was worse for visibility. With Brinx in front, they had only him to rely on as they traveled blindly. Brinx looked back frequently to make sure everyone kept pace. In his mind, he knew they were getting tired, and he knew that after the Twilight prison no one really had a decent rest, but he pushed on anyway, leading them through the pitch black mountains.

"Look," Brinx pointed to the peak, as the others used all of their strength to get over the last rocks to the top. The blue moon shot up over the distance once again the sky above turned pink. Noises of the Krotin faded as the blue moon became full. The group made it to the top of the mountain after a full night of traveling. The view was beautiful. Peridot Lake glimmered from the moon's light. Wildlife could be spotted around the shorelines. What Scarlette loved the most about it all was Leodot village, and it was just a short distance across the river to the lake. She remembered as a kid her father told her that Leodot was known for the Zufore, a flightless bird known for high intelligence and fast running speed, with feathers that were always different shades of blue. The darker the blue, the older they were.

Brinx shot a few vines from his palm and wrapped it securely around a heavy rock.

"I can scale down the mountain face with my vines. I can take two at a time. This would be the fastest way down," Brinx offered. He looked at Scarlette and Lumus first.

"Okay, let's go." Lumus agreed. He held on to Brinx' back and Scarlette wrapped her arms around them both.

"I will be back shortly," Brinx reassured the others as he started to descend.

To Scarlette's surprise, Brinx's vines had many uses as either a weapon against his foes, but also a very useful survival tool. Within a few moments, they had reached the ground. Brinx let them off and without a word began to pull the vine back through his palm pulling him slowly upwards, but before Brinx started to rise, Frostear landed a few feet away with a huge crash. A cloud of smoke rose from the ground, and as it cleared Zephry shouted out.

"Again, again!" like a small child.
"I would have to say my way is faster, Brinx," Frostear shot him a smile as Zephry climbed off of his back.
"Piscyst is just across the river," Scarlette said with a weak voice. Frostear approached Brinx.
"You wouldn't happen to be able to make a boat with your vines would you Brinx?" Frostear made Brinx smile this time.
"Maybe you can jump over it?" Brinx' smile faded as he walked toward the Shore of Peridot Lake.
"Scarlette, the current is too fast, we can't swim this," Lumus said as he regained balance on his own two feet.
"There's a bridge farther north. My hometown is up there, and it is about half day hike from here," Zephry started to glow thinking about home.
"No, I passed by there before I met you all at that tower. Piscyst is under Lears' control. I'm sure we'd run into trouble there."
"I agree," said Brinx, but back to square one then. How do we cross a fast-paced river?
"Zur Zur Zur…"
"What the heck is that noise?" Zephry looked at her to see a Zufore walking up the river from downstream.
"A wild Zufore, what luck?" Scarlette seemed relieved.
"Just one won't help us. We would need two more if we were to use them," Just as Brinx finished his sentence, a herd of Zufore crept over the hill downstream.

"Seems I was wrong, we are lucky."

"I can ask them to help us!" Zephry hurried over to the herd almost skipping in joy.

Zephry took a while with the herd of Zufore, but as she did the others rested along the mountain wall that they descended. Lumus closed his eyes; Scarlette looked over to spark a conversation but before she could Lumus had fallen asleep.

"So how far can those vines of yours reach?" Frostear asked.

"Hmm, a spark of interest in me all the sudden Frostear?" Brinx seemed insulted.

"Well, it's not every day you see a six-foot tall plant that can talk. This world is strange and I've seen more than you can imagine, but nothing like you." He replied.

"Yes well, my vines reach only three times my height. Maybe you can tell me about this sword you carry. I have never seen red steel. Where did you get it?" Frostear put his hand on his back to reassure his sword was still on his back.

"This? It isn't much of a secret. My homeland has a special rock called dragon steel. It's more of a plant that grows to a certain state, then during the red moon it changes into crystallized rock and continues to grow until day. During the night the steel becomes unbreakable, but during the day it's just like any other sword. The Twilight Army use to send recruits ready for promotion alone to my homeland as a first mission. They'd take some of the red steel and have it forged to their swords when they returned. It is how they were promoted to knights."

"Your people never tried to stop them from stealing your dragon steel?" Brinx seemed confused that a man his size would allow others to get away with stealing from him.

"You really are from another world, I don't know how you live, but on Twilight we all share the planet. Just because my clan lived near the red steel didn't make it ours to claim. We took what we needed, as did everyone else that came to Scorpial." Frostear explained.

"Fascinating, I have never known such humanity, let alone hear of an entire planet that does so." Brinx almost seemed shocked to hear his story.

"Frostear, Zephry seemed to know who you were when you showed up at Twilight prison. Have you two met before?" Scarlette mustered enough energy to ask.

"I use to pass through Piscyst often for supplies. I met Zephry on the streets trying to train a Zufore. After a few visits, we somehow became friends. I guess we started to become close the day I found her just outside of her hometown. She was being attacked by some low-level demon. I saved her, and ever since she waited for me to show up for supplies. After a while, I became used to it. As you know, recently she was at the Twilight prison. When I went for supplies I ran into a friend of hers that told me she had been taken. That is why I was in Twilight prison."

Brinx didn't respond, instead, he gave Frostear a simple nod of respect.

Zephry finally returned to the others but with a long rest needed by everyone, no one really noticed how long she was gone.

"Okay, I worked out a deal with the Zufore. They can help us cross the river in exchange for Mush-ati." Brinx didn't even bother to ask how she and the Zufore came to their terms.

"Mush-ati is very common. It is everywhere." Scarlette pointed out.

"Yes, but they want Frostear to give it to them. He needs to pick some and feed it to their leader." Frostear opened his eyes wide.

"What?" Frostear gasped.

"You need to feed him, so come on, hop to it," Zephry said with a smile.

"You have to be kidding me Zephry; do you know how ridiculous that sounds?" Frostear couldn't believe his ears.

"Hey, are you making fun of me?" Zephry raised her voice to Frostear.

"No... no way, I mean I'll do it yeah sure it's just... feeding a bird," Frostear almost seemed scared of Zephry.

("She seems so gentle, what the heck was that about, she just freaked out. What a woman.")

Frostear walked over to a Mush-ati plant and picked a few cloves, and looked over his shoulder to see Zephry with her hands on her hips and a stare that would scare anybody out of their shoes.

"I can't believe my eyes. I barely know Frostear but he's just not the type to be bossed around by, well.... Anybody," Scarlette had a very confused look on her face.

"I'm not sure I understand the people of Twilight at all...." Brinx had his eyes open wide. Everyone could tell he was shocked.

"I can't believe this stupid bird; it can get its own food why does it want me to do it?" Frostear mumbled to himself with a sad looking confused face.

"Alright, little buddy take the food and lets both get on with our lives. Come on, take it!" "You need to bow your head and put the food forward in your arms!" Zephry shouted over to him.

"Of course I do." Frostear began to bow; he put his arms out and displayed the food for the Zufore. The Zufore rushed forward with its head and gave Frostear a headbutt throwing him back to the ground.

"Zur! Zur!"

"Good work Frostear you did it! He accepted your offer." Zephry shouted over once again.

"Damn bird." Frostear sat on the ground holding his head with both hands, "If my dragon was here I'd have him eat you, you stupid bird."

"Lumus! Lumus get up!" Scarlette shook Lumus awake. Lumus slowly opened his eyes to see Zephry running over to Frostear sitting on the ground by the Zufore and Brinx with his arms crossed facing Lumus.

"I must have dozed off, what did I miss?" Lumus replied.
Brinx turned back to Frostear and Zephry.
"I don't think I will ever understand your human race." Brinx continued toward Zephry and Frostear. Lumus looked up at Scarlette, but before he could even ask she interrupted him.
"Don't ask Lumus; here let me help you up."
Lumus and Scarlette made their way to the herd of Zufore's.
The blue moon high above was as beautiful as it could be. No cloud cover, and no sign of the Krotins. The group had boarded the Zufore and crossed the harsh river, and now they headed for Capaz, stopping at Piscyst first. Brinx thought it would be dangerous to make a stop with the Krotin and a Lord so close. The best plan of action was to head straight for Capaz.
Scarlette was excited for a change; she grew up in Capaz after all, and it is where she first met Orson. He was given the job of Scarlette's protector because of his relationship with her father, and the two of them once fought together against a dragon that was wreaking terror on the northern cities of Twilight. Scarlette was young but for her age, she was thought to be the most intelligent person with her pinpoint accuracy in detailed reports of the core and how it functions. Orson was even shocked to listen to her speak; she was an impressive girl and had accomplished so much for Twilight. Now she returns to her hometown and palace of Capaz with all of her memories intact.

Chapter Six - Scarlette's Welcome

Orson woke up to find himself in a warm bed and freshly washed blankets. To his amazement, he had survived the waterfall and the rocks that followed after him. He immediately thought of Zelkem and shot out of bed. The bright light from day's moon shone beautifully as he hurried to get his armour back on. Suddenly the wooden door crept open.
"Excuse me sir - Oh I see you're awake, and already dressed too. Well, would you be kind enough to follow me then sir?" The man exited as fast as he entered, giving Orson no chance to say a word. He picked up his sword and fastened it across his chest. He grabbed the door handle, but he stopped for a moment and turned back to the window, he took this chance to take a view of where he was. He pushed open the windows and as they flew open the wind struck his face gently. Before he could get a good look, a few Golden Thorn Feathers flew by above him. He remembered them being his mother's favourite bird. It had feather's as bright as gold and little green spots shaped like vine thorns. He looked down to see he was not in any house, but a

palace. As he peered out the window he saw the Twilight Lake to the West, and the Aster Mountains to the North. Instantly he knew he had somehow made it to Capaz. He turned around to find the castle servant that entered earlier but to his surprise, Zelkem was in the doorway leaning on the doorframe.

"Zelkem, you're alive!" Like lightning, he raced over and hugged him tightly.

"Hey, hey now, c'mon. Yeah, we survived, no need for this." Zelkem didn't act happy to see his brother but in his heart, he was glad they both made it.

"We got lucky this time, a fisherman from right here in Capaz hooked us in his net. He brought us to Capaz and someone from the palace recognized you. If it wasn't for that fisherman, we'd probably be dead by now. Oh and I was told you were awake so I came to get you and bring you to the meeting room. It's across from the throne room. Let's get going," Zelkem spoke quickly, and he led the way to the meeting room.

"Ah I came back for you two," the servant mentioned, "Please, the council are eager to hear your report. Follow me this way please." Orson and Zelkem followed the servant down a flight of stairs and just past the throne room Orson didn't seem to take in the sights but

Zelkem's head was turning from all of the decorations and artwork.

"You know, I've never been in a palace before. It's a lot nicer than I thought. I'm kind of shocked that Lears hasn't demolished this place yet." Zelkem was still looking around frantically.

"Okay Sir Orson, the Councillor Gerald Manaki will see you now. We would like you to wait outside," The servant said to Zelkem with a demanding tone.

"What, I can't come in? Well, that's not fair." Zelkem turned his head down.

"I am terribly sorry sir but you are not of the Twilight Knights order, so you are not permitted an audience with the council at this time."

Zelkem started to get angry.

"Zelkem, wait for me in town. I'll look for you when I'm done here. Keep an eye out for the others. If they followed the plan, they should be here soon, if not already." Orson had his back to Zelkem as he spoke.

"Yeah fine, this is too much glamour for me anyway. Later." Zelkem responded.

He walked off with his arms crossed above his head. Orson turned to make sure he left. When he saw him head down the main entrance he turned back to the council door and entered.

"Orson it has been some time, I am glad to see you unharmed," started the counsellor Gerald, "You know the council has had its hard times during this whole ordeal, and we have limited resources at hand but to see you is a sight for sore eyes."

Orson was facing Gerald as the counsellor poured himself a glass of wine. He smiled and stared at Orson. He was a bald man, with decorative silver armour. His goatee was trimmed perfectly, and his mere presence felt intimidating. Orson knew to watch his manners since this man was known as the leader of the council of Twilight.

"So what has happened to the regiments? I need to know what happened to the Zodiac Knights, sir." Orson began.

"Yes of course, well you have been gone a long time, and with demons, at every doorstep in the land, we have not been able to offer help to everyone. The Zodiac Knights are working around Twilight to keep the demons at bay, but as time passes reports come in of more and more losses. I wouldn't worry though. As you know, the Zodiac Knights are twelve warriors that led Twilight to victory during the Dragon Wars. You are one of them after all."

"You said the knights are stationed at every town, I was just at Taurald and I saw no soldiers there." Orson seemed confused.

"Taurald is your Regiment am I right? Taurald, Leodot, Ariond, and Piscyst have all been moved, the Taurus regiment is with Gemini in Geminite, Ariond is with Cancer in Canby, and Pisces is with us here in Capaz. They are restocking supplies and heading out to Piscyst. I am currently waiting for reports of the whereabouts of the other five regiments. As you noticed, my Scorpial knights are within the city. All of our units are of only third or second class, very few first classes like yourself are left. That's why I needed you to know I'm leaving to Scorpial to aid in the fall back of a Lord."

"Sir where is the rest of the council? Are you the only one here?" Orson asked, worriedly.

Gerald looked at Orson for a moment.

"Yes, for now. The others should be arriving soon. Lady Concy as well. If you hadn't come back, this meeting would have been discussing a replacement for you. I know it has been a long time to wait to vote for a replacement, but reports came in from time to time with sightings of you. I see now that you were still around, but why not come back to the council?"

"I was searching for my brother. It's a long story, but to make it simple, I wanted to be sure he was safe," He explained.

"I understand, and I won't pry. I need you to greet Lady Concy and inform her what I have told you. I also need you to start the Council meeting in my place. After that, I need you to travel to Sagnet."

"Sir I have to decline, I will do the meeting for you but I have Lumus coming here now, and I'm traveling with him to stop Lears. I cannot leave him and Scarlette now."

Gerald dropped his glass of wine, shattering it on the ground.

"You're saying the boy survived with you? Lumus is alive, and to have Lady Scarlette back. I would very much like to talk with her."

"Yes sir, but we must gather here and find out our plans, we cannot leave yet, and I cannot go to Sagnet when there is much I need to do here," He explained.

Gerald walked over to the end of the long table and sat down at the end of the table on a fancy looking leather chair placing his hands under his chin.

"Orson, I need you to take action. But I see that there are more pressing matters for you. I will go to Scorpial's aid and you will be promoted to Knight Councillor Orson," Gerald smiled

"Sir?" Orson answered but felt a little disoriented.

"Look, we do not have time for formalities, but my word is law as Lead Councillor, so I will write a letter for Lady Concy to announce at our meeting. Now I must leave for my preparations. Do as I do Orson, and live by my words of advice, the days of tomorrow are the choices of today. Commit that to memory and you will not fail." Gerald's smile faded.

"Sir." Orson put his arm to his chest as he stood up straight and looked straight ahead of him.

"Orson, you are now Councillor; your new title gives you freedom of choice. You have authority to command knights of any nation along with the choice of whom you travel with. I will take your responsibilities of Taurald. I will send half of my knights to watch over Taurald. They will watch over things for the time being. You will have to appoint a successor to act as Councillor in your absences, but the council will need time to find a suitable candidate."

Orson nodded. Gerald took his leave and the door shut slowly behind him leaving him alone to think.

("Not just a Councillor? Knight Councillor? What does that even mean?") He walked over to the window to look down at the city of Capaz. After a moment, he smiled.

("Boy there really is a lot of people here, they don't even seem aware that Lears is out there, I wonder why they seem so peaceful?") Zelkem walked down the main road past all of the street vendors, many people shouted at him pitching sales of their stock. Kids played and ran through the tall grass in-between houses as he walked by. A small boy sat on a stump that seemed out of place for such a city. Zelkem approached him to spark a conversation, but as he did the boy jumped up looked both ways then shot off toward town.

("Well at least I can sit here till the others arrive, I just don't get it. There seems to be a lot of soldiers around here.") Zelkem looked over to one of the soldiers by the main gate. He stood there tall and still. Zelkem scrolled down to his emblem on his sheath. It was a diamond shape emblem like all of the other's, and there was a smaller diamond on the inside with a light blue orb in the centre but no other orbs, that's how he knew he was third class.

The colour of his crest under his neckline was emerald green. He knew he was from Piscyst regiment. The knight on the other side of the main gate had an orb on both sides of the small blue orb.
("Wow that guy's second rank, even the big guys do guard duty.") He looked a little closer and noticed his colour under his neckline was brown indicating that he was Capaz regiment. Zelkem crossed his arms behind his head and stretched out while letting out a yawn. He began to think of the others and where they could be. He thought about Taurald and all the people they left to die. ("I could have helped them, I could have stopped those weak Krotin. I regret just leaving them. Stupid… Orson's weakness is rubbing off on me.") Zelkem watched the main gate hoping the others would appear as he made himself comfortable.
("Knight Councilman, what does that mean, does he expect me to make the world better from a room… I can't be a councilman. I'm not a strategist, I am a warrior. Gerald was a warrior at one point too though. Maybe he sees that a warrior like me can change things like he did. He was the one that approved the core expedition, and he defeated over seven dragons in the Dragon Wars. Now he's going

to aid Scorpial. Maybe I should go to Sagnet, I could help the Sagnet regiment, but on the other hand, I cannot leave Scarlette or Lumus. Damn, I wish someone would tell me what to do.")

Trumpets played loudly as the Blue moon shined down on Capaz beautifully. Knights poured in with three Zufore's dressed in golden armour following behind them. Orson stopped abruptly, turned his head towards the music and walked to the closest window. ("Lady Concy has arrived with the Virphire regiment.") Orson turned away and headed to the meeting room.

"You there," Orson said, stopping a woman wearing a servant uniform, "I need you to give a message to Lady Concy. Tell her that Knight Councillor Orson will be waiting for her in the Council meeting room."

"Of course sir, I will tell her immediately." The woman took off with haste. Orson turned back to the meeting room once again.

("Hmm, what's this noise? A parade?") Zelkem jumped off his stump to notice a beautiful woman dressed like royalty. She sat to one side of the Zufore so her full dress could sit properly, her bright golden hair ran down to her shoulders and a tiara that blinded

Zelkem at first. He noticed a small diamond with a circular blue gem in the centre.

"Wow she really makes an entrance," Zelkem said, mesmerized.

"You there! Don't get any ideas you understand?" A man riding a Zufore passed by Zelkem; his lance was twice his body length and his chest plate was what looked like plain steel. He wore gauntlets that had green gems on the left arm but not the right.

"Look, pal, I don't need a lecture, so don't test me," Zelkem yelled back with confidence.

"Maybe a beating would suit you, boy," An older man dressed in dark green armour replied, as he rode up on another Zufore. He had a giant battle-axe on his back that looked like it would take five people just to swing.

"Did you just call me boy? Look, old man, I don't want to ruin your fancy parade but you're starting to piss me off," Zelkem snapped back.

The man got off his Zufore and reached for his axe. Zelkem noticed it was a double bladed axe after he took it off his back.

"Well, maybe I can teach you some manners!" The man swung downward at Zelkem so quickly that he couldn't respond. With a flash, the axe stopped. Zelkem looked up to see

Lumus holding the axe with just his index finger and his thumb clamped together.

"In these times fighting each other will not resolve anything. I was under the impression that people of Twilight were more understanding than to just attack people on the streets," Lumus said. The glowing layer of blue light faded from his body.

"You, what is this? Are you Lears?" The knight asked.

"My name is Lumus." Lumus let go of the axe as Scarlette walked up beside him. She removed her hood.

"Lady Scarlette. You're alive!" The man blurted out. The crowd backed away in amazement. Lady Concy rode up beside her knight.

"Joffree, that will be enough, report to the palace. You will be on guard duty until I say otherwise." Lady Concy made no sign of a joke in her tune. Joffree looked back at Zelkem with a smirk. Lumus stepped in front of him to stare him down. Joffree gave a short look at Lumus then turned for the palace.

"Lady Scarlette, I am happy to see you. It has been a long time since we last met. I'm sure you have much to say, but Councillor Gerald and I have to meet as well. I would like you to join us in the palace."

"I will accompany you my lady, but how did you know it was me?"

"Your hair. The only girl in the world with pink hair. Unique to only you. That is how everyone knows. Is that not why you wore your hood?" Lady Concy explained with a smile.

Brinx, Frostear, and Zephry came through the main gate on their Zufore's.

"Demon!" Joffree turned to ready his axe once again. Lumus stood in front of him.

"He is no demon, he is with us. These are our companions."

"Then you all shall join us at the palace." Lady Concy interrupted. She turned around toward the palace. Joffree jumped on his Zufore, confused by the demon's acceptance.

"I'm glad to see you guys, things were getting dull here," Zelkem said with a laugh. He had an odd smile on his face.

"If you want to continue with us Zelkem you can't stir trouble in our absence," Scarlette said sternly. They followed after lady Concy as the trumpets started up again.

"Lady Councillor Concy, a message for you ma'am," The servant quickly handed her a letter before jolting back to the palace.

"It's a message from Knight Councillor Orson? Right, Lady Scarlette and Lumus please follow me - the rest of you please wait in the throne room.

"Lumus I don't think I am welcome here, the people are staring at me with fear," Brinx said with concern.

"Just wait in the throne room, you're safe here Brinx. Scarlette, let's go." Lumus ordered, " and Frostear, keep Zelkem out of trouble please."

"You have my word, he won't be a problem." Frostear looked back at Zelkem; Zelkem sighed and threw his arms behind his head. Scarlette walked off with Lumus and Lady Concy.

"Scarlette, I am glad you're back. Really I am. Where have you been all these years? We really thought we lost you in the Aster Mountains that day." The three continued for the meeting room as Concy spoke.

"Some things are just best saved for the right time. Let's wait to see Orson before we begin catching up." Scarlette replied. Lumus stayed silent the entire walk to the meeting hall.

The doors to the meeting hall creaked open slowly; Orson sat in the head chair at the end of the long table where Gerald sat earlier. He faced the entrance with his hands under his chin just as Gerald did.

"Orson!" Scarlette yelled out, she ran over as he stood up with a smile. She hugged him long and hard before lady Concy interrupted. "Shall we sit down, we have much to speak about," Lady Concy said eagerly.
Lumus sat down as she finished, and Scarlette sat across from him. Orson sat beside her and finally Concy sat beside Lumus.
"So I suppose I will start. I have a few things I would like cleared up before you all begin. First would have to be, what happened in Aster Mountain twenty years ago?" Concy seemed excited to hear their story. Scarlette explained her story to Lady Concy. Lumus listened closely though he already heard her story and Orson's side of the story. Lumus noticed Lady Concy's amazement as Scarlette told her story.
"What about you in the mountains, Scarlette?" Concy interrupted.
"I died. Demons poured in from every cavern, and when I woke up I was in another realm called the realm of the dead. I know this seems strange Lady Concy, but please hear me out."
"Go on Scarlette." Lady Concy didn't seem phased by anything she said.
"Okay, well I had lived there with a man named Ged that had been there for almost one hundred years. He showed me around and

taught me a few things about the realm. Things here on Twilight began to get worse though, that's when the West Zin approached me. She is the creator of the west side of our galaxy. Normally after death, a person has to prove themselves over a period of one hundred years to earn their chance to become alive again, but because of my knowledge of the circumstances with Lumus, I was told to go back to help. So, I was let through a portal in Ged's place. Just as I left through the portal I saw Ged run toward me, but I had already made it through. I was teleported to Twilight, but West Zin opened another portal to Dystopia once I arrived. In Dystopia I stayed there for ten years to watch over Lumus. My body did not age in the Realm of the dead though, so I still appeared to be a nine-year-old girl. Lumus was ten then, I guess I felt like I was still nine and my life was just paused. After ten years Orson came back, I found the portal back to Twilight thanks to West Zin's information, and I went in after I saw that Orson was back with Lumus. I went in and made it to Ariond. I stayed with a family that told me about a cave people used to hide from Lears. I learned that Orson stayed with the same family that I did, and they told me that he was coming and going from Varlif forest a lot in his trips to Ariond. I figured Orson would bring Lumus there - at least I was hoping he would. When I went there I ran into his brother Zelkem, and he and I waited but only Lumus and Brinx showed up."

"You forgot to mention how Brinx came to the group." Concy interrupted again.

"Well I wasn't there for that actually," Scarlette replied, looking over to Orson.

"Brinx jumped us in the forest on the outskirts of Dystopia's Aster Mountains. Long story short, he asked to come, and Lumus allowed him. At first, I wasn't sure but he seems to have good intentions. Although, I still don't trust him entirely." Orson added.

"So, Lumus and Brinx came, and we waited a day before we left for Twilight Prison. We found Orson but he had been brainwashed by Lears. He fought Frostear, and after Ged showed up, Orson came back to his senses and helped fight Ged off. Lumus went after Lears but we are still unsure if he finished him. That's also where we met Zephry and Frostear. Zephry was locked away in the prison and Frostear helped to free her. Now they are our allies."

"Hmm, well if you didn't leave anything out I guess we are caught up then."

"Lady Concy, when did you become a council member?" Orson asked, interested in her story.

"The council was a collection of fourteen members before the incident at the core." Lumus felt guilty at Concy's comment.

"Now it is just thirteen members. We have one for each city and Gerald oversees each councillor. I read Gerald's letter by the way. Knight Councillor? I can see that he believes you will be more useful helping Lumus go after Lears than sitting in a room."

Orson stood up and walked to the window.

"I have a favour to ask," Orson explained.

"Certainly, what is it?"

He turned back to Concy.

"Zephry, the young woman that was rescued at the Twilight prison, I'd like to put her through the trails. I promised her she would be trained."

"Well as that may be, she would have to travel alone to Fargon region. Do you think that is wise in these times?" Orson walked to the door and turned,

"I'll be a moment," Orson said as he left the meeting hall in a hurry.

"What is he doing?" Concy complained.

A moment passed before he came back with Zephry.

"Now, Zephry, representatives of the council will permit you to become a knight of Twilight, but you must realize what it is you must do in order to do this. Normally a member would travel alone to Fargon region and retrieve a piece of dragon steel, but with Lears and his Lords and the way the world is, we don't think it is best for you to do this now," Orson spoke quickly.

"You're saying you don't think it's a good time, so you are still letting me decide if I want to or not?" Zephry responded.

"Well we can't turn down a soldier, it is their choice to go. If you do go and you get the steel, then we have no choice but to accept you." Concy didn't seem happy about letting her decide.

"I will leave tomorrow morning," Zephry replied, quickly leaving the meeting room.

"Wow she really wants to be a knight," Scarlette whispered, looking down at the table.

"I think she wants to get stronger. I think she knows that there will be more fights like the one we had at the prison. I'm sure she'll be ready next time something like that happens" Lumus added as he stood up. Scarlette got up after him.

"I see. Lumus I need to ask you to stay a moment."

"Lady Concy?" Lumus seemed confused.

"I'll wait for you with the others Lumus," Scarlette called back.

"Thank you, Lady Scarlette. I imagine you would have expected a bigger welcoming, but you have been gone twenty years," Lady Concy whispered to Scarlette before she left.

"I understand. The people of this city may not remember me, but I remember Capaz, and no matter how long I have been gone, I'm just happy to be home," She replied as she took off into the palace halls.

"Lumus, I know you must feel a little disoriented in all of this, and I know you still have a lot of questions too. So I'd like you to ask them."

Lumus looked over to Orson but he was looking out the window again, he looked back at Concy.

"I feel answers will show themselves when they need to, I don't need to know anything now." "Lumus?" Orson said softly.

"As a group, if you all intend to travel together, you all need to train a little. Zephry, Scarlette and you are still young, I would feel better if you stayed here a few days and trained. The palace has a knight training area in the basement, and if Zephry really does leave for her quest then you will be here for a few days anyway," Lady Concy added.

"Are you really going to let her go?" Lumus interrupted. Orson put his head down for a moment.

"It is not up to me," He replied.

"Fine, maybe I can learn how to use my abilities a little better in the meantime," Lumus agreed.

"I will set teams then," Lumus started, "I will train with Frostear since we are sword users, Concy can aid Scarlette with the bow, and Zelkem and Brinx can choose how they go about their training."

"I'll tell the others," Lumus left to the throne room. Concy sat down once again, and Orson sat across from her.

"Lady Concy you wouldn't mind helping Scarlette would you?" Lady Concy looked over to the window.

"I think I could use some training on my bow as well. It shall work out. I will have Joffree and Lysilus help too, it wouldn't hurt to train up for a few days. I would think Lysilus would be quite a match for your brother. Maybe we can arrange for them to work together."

"I wouldn't count on Zelkem," Orson looked back to the window.

"Are you insane Zephry, you intend to go to Scorpial alone?"

"I'm sorry Frostear, but I need to do this and no one can stop me. I need to become stronger. I need to prove to myself I can do this!" She yelled back. Frostear saw Lumus come through the door over Zephry's shoulder.

"Lumus, do you know anything about this? I don't know you very well, but I can see that you allowed this."

Lumus walked up to the group that had formed a circle around Zelkem sitting on the throne.

"Look, it is her choice to make, she can go if she chooses to." Lumus crossed his arms as Zephry sat down.

"Lady Concy and Orson told me that if we are going to continue to travel together we need to train together, so he is organizing with Lady Concy to train with us. Tomorrow we will begin with those that choose to. I am certain everyone has something to offer to someone else. Brinx you are very uniquely equipped. Frostear, you have exceptional skill. Zelkem your fighting skills have been proven with your survival here alone. Scarlette and I are still new to combat and we have things to work on, I am sure she agrees." Lumus shot Scarlette a look hoping she would.

"I haven't had much time to work on my accuracy, so count me in." Lumus looked back to Frostear.

"Orson was hoping you would teach him a thing or two as well," Lumus said with a grin.

"Yes, I'd be able to show him a few things I suppose."

"Zelkem what do you think? Lysilus and you could be a good match." Zelkem stared at the ground.

("Lysilus? That know-it-all in the cheap armour that freaked out in the street?)

"Yeah Lumus, I think I can show him a thing or two." Zelkem had a small smirk on his face.

Brinx walked over to the door without a word.

"Hey, Brinx? What do you think?" Lumus called out.

"I don't think training is needed for me. I'm one hundred and seven years old. I think I know everything I need to know."

"Only one hundred and seven?" Frostear blurted out. "Sorry to burst your bubble, but I'm five hundred and three years old and I'm helping, you think you have nothing to offer?"

Everyone's mouths dropped.

"You're... five hundred and three years old, Frostear?" Zephry said finally.

"Well, I am a Drayhelm after all. We live to about one thousand years old if we don't get killed." Zelkem's smirk disappeared.
"Wow man, are you serious?" Zelkem seemed shocked. Brinx turned around.
"I think I may have a few tricks that could help out. My vines can be cut and regenerate within a few seconds, maybe I can use that to test some of you?" Brinx gripped his wrist.
"Perfect, that could be a big help. Alright, guys, let's meet in the basement tomorrow after we see Zephry off." Lumus began to head for the door. Scarlette followed behind him. Zelkem slowly got off the throne.
"You know the throne is kind of comfy but it just isn't my style." Zelkem headed out behind Scarlette followed by Brinx.
"Frostear, are you really that old?" Zephry began to look sad.
"Yeah, why? What's with the look?" Zephry ran quickly toward the door.
"No it's nothing, never mind." She left Frostear in the throne room alone.
("Strange girl, does she? No that can't be it…could it?")
"Orson, did Gerald say where he was going, he didn't mention in his letter." Orson peered from the window.

"I believe he said he was going to aid Scorpial and that he had to leave right away."
Concy looked at him then over to the table.
("Scorpial, I don't remember the Scorpial regiment needing help.)
"I guess I missed that report about them needing help, he didn't say anything else?" Concy sounded puzzled.
"Not that I recall. He just sent me off and when I came back he was gone, I didn't even see him leave." A quiet knock was heard at the door, Orson turned around as Concy sat down.
"Yes, please enter?" Orson said bluntly.
"Hey sorry to interrupt Orson but I thought I'd tell you everyone is on board for tomorrow," Lumus announced. He froze for a moment and looked down as he let go of the door handle. A moment passed as if he had turned to stone.
"Lumus?" Orson cried out.
"Lears, he is alive. I can feel him." Lumus stood up straight, his fist clenched hard and he began to emit a dim light.
"He is back, I don't know how, but I know he is." Lumus grew in anger as his concentration focused on Lears.
"Lumus calm down, look we will deal with him when the time comes, and all we can do

now is focus on the now." Concy began to worry. She knew Lears was still out there but for Lumus to broadcast it in front of her, she worried like it was new information.

"Lumus I'll show you to your room. We can worry about Lears later." Orson walked over to Lumus and set his hand on his shoulder, and as he did the dim light faded and Lumus looked up at him with a smile.

"Yeah, yeah you're right. I beat him once I can do it again," Lumus declared. Orson smiled. The red moon was full, the town slept like a calm stream. Not a sound could be heard except the Capaz soldier that would occasionally walk by on their rounds. Zephry laid awake on her bed staring at the roof. She was worried that tomorrow would be her last day with her new friends. She almost felt that if she left she would never see them again. The window in her room was small but it allowed enough light into the room for her to find her way to the door. Zephry grabbed hold of the handle and gazed at it long and hard.

("I should go, but I want to see him before I leave. If I don't I may never get another chance. I want to tell him how I feel.")

Zephry's hand slipped off the small handle. ("What if he doesn't feel the same, what if he doesn't want to have anything to do with me?") She had grabbed the handle once more, her palm was sweaty and her eyes locked on her hand like she could turn the handle if she looked at it hard enough.

("I need to know. I need to find out before I leave.") Zephry turned the handle quickly and scurried down the long hall until she stopped at a wooden door identical to all the others. "This one I think, this is it..." Zephry grabbed the handle and slowly turned it. Slowly the door opened.

"Frostear? Are you awake?" Frostear sat on the floor in a beam of light shooting into the room through the small window. He didn't make a move, his arms out with his palms facing the roof and his legs crossed over.

"Frostear?" For a moment it was silent. Suddenly Frostear opened his eyes giving Zephry a bit of a scare.

"Hmm, Zephry what are you doing here so late?" Zephry began to blush. Well, I am leaving tomorrow and I thought I'd ask you something before I left."

Frostear rose to his feet. In comparison, he was exceptionally larger in size to her. Zephry took a few more steps closer as the door shut behind her. She walked into the light of the moon shining through the window, and as she did she tripped. Frostear caught her in his arms before she could fall to the floor. Zephry threw her hand softly behind his head. They looked deep into each other's eyes for a while. She pulled herself toward him for a kiss as she shut her eyes. Her lips landed on his slowly. His eyes remained open for a minute, then slowly closed.

Outside, high above in the sky, clouds began to push in front of the room, blocking the rays of light from shining down through the window.

Sounds of hard Zufore feet along the Torson region plains echoed loudly through the night. Gerald was racing fast along the flat terrain. No one was in sight, no animals, and no light. Gerald's cape flew in the wind as he picked up speed and his Zufore panted quietly.

("I wonder if Lumus' survival will change things, I am curious to see how things work out.") High above in the sky, the red moon seemed darker than normal as it shined down violently over Gerald racing hard along the plains.

("How come I didn't get my own room, I bet Orson did this on purpose. Look at him over there. What is he trying to do anyway."?)

"You know we have a few days ahead of us to train why don't you knock off the push-ups, I'd rather not smell you sweat as I try to

sleep." Orson paused for a second to look over at Zelkem. "I heard a rumour when I was younger that a few exercises before sleep would improve your endurance greatly, so every day for about twenty or so years I have done them." Zelkem rose to his feet.
"And I have to say I feel stronger when I wake up each morning," Zelkem added as he sat back down and rolled over to his side facing the wall.
"Yeah well, if you believe that then maybe you believe there are monsters in the lakes," Orson laughed.
"I don't believe everything I hear especially kids stories like those Orson, but you know, I did hear a story that I thought was worth looking into. Along time ago a soldier mentioned a tale of the great Zodiac waterfall. I think he said something about a secret entrance behind it. That would be quite the adventure to explore if it was true; wouldn't you think Zelkem?" Orson waited for a response but after a while, there was still no sound.
"Well, maybe some secrets aren't meant to be discovered. Good night brother."
Orson pulled his covers over himself as he went to sleep. Zelkem laid silently with his eyes open thinking hard to himself.

("Maybe one day we could go to that waterfall brother. Maybe we could be the first to see the hidden secrets it has to offer.") Zelkem smiled. The wind blew gently through the window as the brothers drifted off to sleep. The night sky sank as the city slept for a new day.

Lumus sat in a chair in his room down the hall from Orson and Zelkem. He had his head down and thought about Lears.

("Lears I can feel your power, I know you're out there. Next time we meet I will be ready to end things. I may have been caught off guard when I saw you, but it won't happen next time.) I shouldn't have held back on that attack to Lears at Twilight Prison. Damn it, because of that he sent those Krotins to Taurald village. Another thing I could have prevented. It will be different next time Lears I promise you that." Lumus called out.

"Coldblood, what is your report?" Lears faced out a window in a partially burnt house in Taurald. "Master Lears, Lumus and the others that follow him were here, they must have known somehow that we were coming. We chased them into the East Mountains toward Leodot. I sent Aire there, but they didn't show up." Lears turned to Coldblood.

"I see, send for Hedree and Antsos and tell Ged to report to me immediately. He has some explaining to do." Lears turned again to the red moon up in the sky.

"Master Lears, I hate to bother you once more, but Lord Ged has not returned. We have been unable to find him yet." Coldblood reported.

Lears didn't move this time. He continued to stare off into the sky. "Lord Coldblood, you had better find him. He has some information I'd like to hear so find him now, and give me no more excuses, do you understand?" Lears yelled back.

"I understand," Coldblood replied.

"One more thing, where is Levitz?" Coldblood paused for a moment.

"Lord Levitz is still following Lead Councillor Gerald. His last report said he was leaving Capaz toward the South."

"What is that old fool up to now? Who was he with?" Lears turned his head to his right shoulder interested to hear Coldblood's response.

"He was alone, Master Lears."

"That will be all Coldblood, return to Piscyst and tell the others I will meet them there." Coldblood bowed and left toward the North Gate of Taurald.

("Gerald you are quite sneaky, but I know what you're up to. I will reveal you soon enough.") Lears broke out into laughter.

Chapter Seven: Zephry's choice

All of Capaz slept with no sign of movement, except for Frostear and Zephry at the North Gates. They quietly made their way just outside of the city to be sure they were alone. A moment of silence crossed them like a light breeze. Zephry set down a small bag of supplies, then stretched as she turned to Frostear to say her goodbyes. He was already right in front of her as she turned around.
"Zephry, be safe out there okay? I know there will be a lot to frighten you on your journey but just remember why you want to finish your training, and you will succeed. If you run into trouble just get out of there as fast as you can. Don't take main roads, and stay hidden as best you can." Frostear said almost forgetting to breathe.
Zephry was blushing.
"You big softy, I'll be fine, and it's only a six-day trip. I'll go North to Geminite, and then to my hometown Piscyst. I can get a boat there to Fargon region. Three days there, and three days back, a piece of cake." Zephry smiled.
Frostear took a step forward and hugged Zephry tightly. Zephry was still blushing, but this time she smiled.
"I need to go before the others find out I'm leaving. I don't need to see five other sad faces... Although Brinx wouldn't really be able to show

that kind of emotion. He's too scary looking."
Zephry giggled as she let Frostear go.
"Be safe out there." Frostear blurted out. Zephry turned back to her bag. She threw it over her shoulder and started to walk away from Frostear. She turned while she walked, and waved back to him. He gave a quick wave as she faded into the morning fog. He waited a moment, then made his way back to the palace with his head down.
("How did this happen, how can I have these feelings so quickly for her, and a human? Maybe I am getting soft in my old age?") He thought to himself.
The fog thinned as he neared the palace, but it cleared to reveal Lady Concy sitting on the palace steps.
"You love her?" Concy said quietly.
"What are you doing here Concy?" Frostear asked.
"Well dear Frostear, after I was announced councillor of Piscyst I guess I needed to come see off one of my citizens." She said with a smile.
Frostear stopped at the stairs to the palace doors.
"You know what I mean, why are watching me?" He demanded
"I had to see the woman that replaced me, my dear. I had to see for myself." She replied.
"It's none of your business. You chose to leave me when you became part of the council. First of Fargon, but now of Piscyst?" He said with anger in his eyes.
"Don't get too mad Frostear, we don't want another Dragon War now do we?" Concy said

with a smile pushing past her, he made his way up the stairs.

"Oh Frostear, how is our son doing?" He paused for a moment then continued to walk into the palace.

"Coldblood, wherever you are, I hope you're nothing like your father." Concy looked out toward the plains where Zephry had started her journey. She sighed and turned back to go inside.

The morning came swiftly. Lumus rose early from his sleep and decided to make his way to the dungeon training area to wait for the others.

He waited patiently. The others began to show up just as he was about to go look for them. Scarlette came walking through the basement gates with Frostear, Zelkem, and Brinx.

"Has anyone seen Orson or Concy? Lumus sighed. "Fine, we will begin without them." Suddenly the basement door flew open once again.

"Orson and I are very sorry, you see the councillors have many obligations," Concy announced. Lysilus and Joffree followed in after Orson.

"Okay listen up, I'm not going to waste any time here. I will divide us into appropriate groups for our six days down here. So, let's begin." Lady Concy and Scarlette. Zelkem and Lysilus. Joffree, Orson, and Frostear. And finally, Brinx and I will make the final group. Don't forget we are not leaving this basement for six days, it is up to you whether you stay or leave now." Lumus felt confident everyone would stay. Sure enough, no

one spoke up. Concy and Scarlette took off to the south end of the basement to the shooting range. Frostear followed Orson and Joffree to the east section, which contained alternate terrains perfect for training in. Zelkem and Lysilus went to the west side. The west was flat, perfect for hand-to-hand combatants. Lumus lead Brinx to the north located directly below the palace gates. He took a moment to appreciate the architecture of the training facility.
"Lumus maybe now is not the time to daydream," Brinx called out. Lumus gave his head a shake. "Yes of course. We have six days, let's make the best of this." He announced. Brinx crossed his arms. Why pair us up together? Were you curious who was stronger? I can see you being stronger than the others, but I would be the odd one out I suppose." Brinx felt unsure of Lumus' choices.
"Well, I have seen what you can do, and I wanted to see if you can use your vines to maybe encase your body. Maybe something thick enough to withstand a swing of my sword." Brinx opened his eyes wide.
"I have never tried anything like that. It may be possible if I have enough time to focus." Brinx clenched his fists and bent his knees. He cringed as his body began to morph. All of the sudden multiple vines shot from him in every direction. Lumus had to dodge most of them that flew toward him. Brinx let out a monstrous roar as the vines came together. Tightly they wrapped his body, making him look at least five times his

normal size. Lumus was in a bit of shock. He could not believe his eyes.

"Well, it seemed to work. Although with this I feel a bit slow. It may be harder for me to move quickly. Take a swing Lumus, and let's see how I fair." Lumus took a step forward, and he drew his sword slowly.

"Alright, let the training begin." He announced as he dashed at Brinx. As he did Brinx let out another roar that caught the attention of all the others this time. Small debris came from the ceiling, Dust shot up from the floor and blew around the room. Lumus didn't notice though.

The battle started to heat up until Lady Concy entered the room.

"Brinx end this now. I have just got word that the councillors have arrived. Lumus, I'm sorry, but you will have to join me along with Orson. Everyone else can resume training." Brinx calmed down as Lumus lowered his sword.

"I have to be honest Brinx, I wasn't sure what to do there. I think you would have had me beat." Brinx began to shed parts of himself, returning to his normal size.

"Maybe Lumus, but you have something hidden inside you. It is that something that scares me, even with my strength I do not think I would have won. That form hinders my speed as well. I also think you should lose the sword. A strength like yours does not require such primitive tools." Brinx added.

"Twenty seconds of training, but I feel like I have learned something. Thanks, Brinx." Lumus said as he rested his sword against the wall. Lady Concy grabbed him and pulled him off.

"Come, we must hurry! I don't wish to keep the councillors waiting. Orson was waiting in the centre room with his arms crossed. He had a look on his face as if he was disappointed about leaving his training.

Lady Concy led the way back up to the main floor. Lumus followed closely with Orson behind him. "Now this is important, the councillors will be entering the city gates soon. Lumus, people are in a bit of hysteria about you. I am sure the councillors are very interested in seeing you as well. I have to ask you to wait in the conference room until I greet them. Orson will wait alongside me." Concy demanded.

"Maybe I should wash up first? I don't think it would be fitting for me to…" Lumus noticed that Orson and Lady Concy were sweating a lot as well.

"I wouldn't worry Lumus, I'm certain the councillors will have more pressing matters to address to us than our hygiene." Orson put his hand on Lumus' shoulder.

"Just give us a moment to greet the others. We will then meet you in the conference room." Orson instructed. Lumus turned around and began to head to the west of the palace.

"Orson, they are here." Lady Concy took a step forward as the large palace gates opened. The gigantic doors screeched open, and a beam of daylight shot in from the blue moon outside. The Councillors came in one after the other. Orson was happy to see so many old faces. He remembered fighting alongside most of them during the Dragon Wars. Lady Concy introduced each councillor as they entered.

"Introducing Councillor Mack Yozii of Ariond. Lady Councillor Anna Heloris of Geminite. Councillor Orgu Blank of Canby. Councillor Alexander Strife of Leodot. Councillor Owen Markus of Virphire. Lady Councillor Tilza of Librine. Councillor Tank Linjor of Scorpial. Councillor Cinnus Zarie of Sagnet. Councillor Brunius Dargon of Capaz and Councillor Geare Cogz of Aquoise. Please, fellow Councillors, follow me to the Conference room." Concy said with a bow.

She led the group toward the west wing. Orson stood at the rear with his head down.

"(Geare... I know him but from where?)" Orson seemed confused, but he saw the others leaving him behind so he quickly caught up.

"It has been some time, Lady Concy. How is Piscyst doing these days?" Brunius said with a smile.

"Piscyst is doing well councillor Brunius, and as you can see Orson and I have been taking care of Capaz in your absence." Concy bowed.

"I see, so that was Orson? I barely recognize him after so long. Does he know Taurald is without a councillor because of his leave?" Concy raised her head with hesitation.

"I'm not sure. He has been traveling with Lumus." Concy replied.

"Lysilus, gather everyone in the south room. I have some new plans." Joffree demanded.

"Sir? Yes, sir." Lysilus ran off to the other rooms quickly.

"Plans? Who says you're running the show?" Zelkem said in anger.

"Listen you little punk I don't have time for fools like you." Joffree barked back

"What did you say to me? You think I don't care? Why the hell would I be in a basement of some old palace training with all of you if I didn't?" Zelkem barked as he clenched his fists.

"Well you may have a fighting spirit Zelkem, but you are still no warrior. You should watch what you say." Zelkem stepped closer to Joffree just as the others entered the room.

"Listen you polished pawn! Wearing a badge and swinging a fancy sword at a few dragons doesn't make you a brave warrior either. You think because the dragons missed burning you up that you're something special? I bet everything you have was given to you. When's the last time you really earned something for yourself? And I don't mean a badge or some war trophy. Have you ever lived off the land? Have you ever saved someone without being ordered to? Have you ever helped someone because you felt it was the right thing to do, and not just an order? You're the fool, and you

are the one that should watch what he says."
Zelkem turned and began to walk toward the exit.
"Hold it! I'm not done with you yet." Zelkem
stopped and turned his head to look over his
shoulder.
"Oh? Some other crap you need to say before I
leave?" Zelkem said with a smirk. Joffree drew his
sword.
"If you think you're so great, how about you spar
with me? If you truly are a warrior I should be no
problem." Joffree declared. Zelkem looked over to
the others standing at the door.
"Zelkem don't do this, you have nothing to
prove," Scarlette yelled out.
"He has to Scarlette, look into his eyes. He is
looking after himself, just as he has his whole life.
This may be the moment he proves that he wants
to be here." Frostear explained.
"What does that mean? Has he said he didn't want
to be here?" Scarlette started to get confused.
"You don't understand; he doesn't have to say it.
Think back to everything that we know of him. He
fought Orson at Twilight Prison, and again in
Taurald. He never wanted to stay with us. Zelkem
just wanted to prove that he is stronger than his
brother. Now he is fighting with Joffree to defend
his position here with us." Frostear said with a
smile. Scarlette looked back to Zelkem.
"I see. So he is doing this for himself…" Scarlette
whispered under her breath. Frostear took a deep
breath.

"Well? What do you say, will you fight me?" Joffree laughed. Zelkem turned around.
"Hey Joffree, tell me again what they call you in your knight ranks?" Joffree griped his sword.
"I am Sir Joffree of the Piscyst Regiment! First ranked knight, you fool!" He announced with a maddening rage in his eyes.
Zelkem clenched his fist even tighter and widened his stance. Joffree ran at him wildly with his sword high above his head. Joffree brought his axe down hard on top of Zelkem's head. Just as Joffree's axe was about to hit him. He moved to the left quickly, and Joffree's axe crashed hard into the floor. Just then Zelkem grabbed Joffree's axe with his left hand using it as support as he forced his body up into the air. He landed a kick to Joffree's face, throwing him into the wall. His axe had stuck on the floor, and Zelkem stood beside it with a serious look in his eyes. Joffree got up quickly though.
"Impressive, but not good enough!" Joffree yelled out. Zelkem dashed toward Joffree. As they got closer to each other Joffree threw his left fist forward. As he did, Zelkem threw his right fist forward colliding with his. Joffree grabbed his wrist in pain as Zelkem spun and landed a kick to Joffree's face knocking him to the floor unconscious. He stood over Joffree with a grin.
"A true warrior cares for more than himself. Maybe you'd learn that if you pulled your head from your ass." Zelkem walked out of the training room and headed upstairs to the palace gates.

"Do you see Scarlette? Zelkem is one of us now." Frostear announced as if proud he was right after all.

"Are you sure Frostear? I think he is leaving." Brinx moved in front of the exit.

"Leave him alone. The boy doesn't need us now. If he is to join us, then he will when he wants to." Brinx crossed his arms as Frostear walked up beside him and Scarlette.

"I suppose the no leaving rule has been waved?" Frostear said with a laugh. Scarlette sighed.

Lumus stood watching the townspeople from the balcony window in Capaz Palace. Time seemed to go by slowly these days, he thought.

("Things sure have changed. I guess I have to learn to change with it. I went from a farmer to defeating Lears to training with the best fighters Twilight has to offer. He is still alive though. I can almost feel Lears as if he was here in the room with me, his very being calls to me, haunting me. What makes things worse is that Zephry is out there on her own, and the roads are not exactly safe. I don't really understand what I should do.")

Lumus looked down to the palace bridge.

"Zelkem? Where is he going?" He said aloud.

"Lumus, please have a seat." Lady Concy asked as she entered. The eleven councillors including Orson followed behind her. Lumus sat down at the end of the large table closest to the window. He tried to present himself as formal as he could pass off. As the Councillors sat down Orson closed the door behind him. Lady Concy sat opposite to Lumus.

"The first order of business. We must discuss regiment reports. Councillor Alexander, please begin." Concy announced. Alexander stood from his seat.

"As you all know by now Taurald has been destroyed, but many of the people inhabiting the town were able to escape just in time. There were many deaths within the decoy soldiers from Taurald that were killed during the attack. We are currently rebuilding but with so few soldiers we are taking every precaution. Also, a new enemy by the name of Coldblood led the attack yesterday. We believe this man is working with Lears." Alexander said sadly. Orson stood up.

"All of the people were decoys?" Orson interrupted

"The people that were in Taurald were in fact decoys, trained knights that laid in wait for Lears to attack them. In this case, the knights were outnumbered. You were there Orson, and you as well Lumus." Concy added. Lumus stood up.

"Yes, we were taken there late yesterday for recovery. That was the night before we fought Lears at Twilight Prison." Lumus sat down. Alexander looked at Lumus then over to Orson.

"I will be pulling my soldiers from Taurald within the next few days. I must protect Leodot from the same fate. I am sure you all understand?" Alexander added.

"We do. I will send some of my soldiers from Ariond." Mack announced. Brunius was still looking at Lumus.
"You two fought Lears and survived?" Brunius asked. Orson sat down.
"Actually Lumus fought him alone." Orson blurted out. Everyone looked over to Lumus.
"Yes, and I thought I had defeated him too, but I had failed. I can still feel him, and somehow I know he is still alive." Lumus said as he put his head down. Geare stood up.
"I have to know...., you say you can feel him. Do you feel his life force?" Geare asked. Lumus got up and looked out the window.
"I guess you could say that. It is more than that though, I can feel the energy he emits. I guess I have always been able to sense his star energy." He added.
"Could you explain what you are saying?" Tilza replied. Councillor Owen leaned forward, eager to hear his answer.
"His Star energy, you know… The power or life force that everyone has inside them. With every life experience with every life choice your star energy grows. When you die your star energy is placed into the galaxy contributing to the knowledge of the cosmos." Lumus replied thinking everyone knew what he was talking about. The entire table went silent.
"Lumus I don't think that is really something that happens. Who told you that?" Orson said tentatively.

"The Twilight Core speaks to me. Ever since I came to Twilight I can hear it, and with the core, I was able to defeat Lears. How do you think I learned how to use my powers so quickly? I thought you all knew this. The core told me about the dragons that are here on Twilight and the…" Councillor Tank stood up slamming his fist on the table, interrupting Lumus.

"What! Did I hear you say the dragons that ARE here? Are you telling me Twilight isn't rid of them yet?" Tank suggested. Lumus turned to the window again.

"Sir I don't know what your priorities are, but you have far worse problems than the remaining dragons. You should focus on Lears. He is the greatest danger to Twilight." Lumus muttered. Tank shut up quickly.

"I believe we are off topic. Please, everyone, settle down. We have an order to these meetings." Brunius demanded. They resumed their seats and took a moment to gather their composure.

"Let us finish the little things first. Each regiment is returning to their towns in three days, which will give us time to restock supplies. Orson, your townspeople are in Valley Cove as ordered. We have workers in Taurald rebuilding as we speak. That concludes the report, Lady Concy if you please." Brunius explained.

"Next we need to talk about Lears. We have taken fights to him many times, but have never been successful. We need ideas on this topic." Concy suggested. Orson stood up. "This may sound a bit crazy, but I say we use Lumus to fight Lears. To be honest, he is the only one that can. I have seen them fight, and I can't say I know anyone else that could stand up to Lears. Lumus, do you object?" Orson asked.

Lumus turned to the councillors and nodded his head in agreement. Lady Concy called for a vote and passed without any objections. Orson took Lumus outside the conference room and waited for Lady Concy.

"Lumus you are taking a lot on your shoulders with this, you know that right?" Orson said. Lumus put his hand on Orson's shoulder.

"Orson, do you remember a long time ago when you told me that you were frightened because you didn't know what you were up against. Well, I know what I am up against: Lears." He smiled.

"I said that to you when you were still a baby. How could you possibly know…?" Orson became silent as Concy entered the hallway.

"We don't have time to waste. Let's get back to the others." Concy demanded. Orson led the way back to the training area in the basement.

"Wait a moment, Orson before the meeting I looked out the window and saw Zelkem leaving the palace. Should we go after him?" Lumus announced.

"No, let's ask the others first. He would have a reason for leaving, and I'm sure they would know something." He replied.

"I will meet you down there. Orson, you and I must stay here. We have much to discuss with the other councillors. Remember you are councillor of Taurald. You have a responsibility to the council." Concy said with a tone. Orson stopped.

"Lumus go on without me. I will be there as soon as I can." Orson said through gritted teeth while looking at Concy.

He continued toward the training area alone as Orson returned to Lady Concy's side. "Don't be upset with me Orson, I don't want to be in here any more than you do right now. I know we can do more good out there than in this room." Orson left Lady Concy and entered the conference room.

("Maybe Orson can help Lumus, but I know I can do more good if I stay with the council. At least I can strategize against Lears in favour of Lumus... If he goes down, we all go down. It's just a matter of convincing the council") Concy thought to herself as she entered the conference room. The doors closed, and the sound of the doors locking caused Lumus to look back, but he quickly continued on his way.

Chapter Eight- Celebrating a Hero

The afternoon light from the blue moon shone down on Zephry as she made her way closer to Piscyst. She was tired, and sweat ran down her face. She finally took a moment to rest, but she smiled.
("Boy taking the shortcut northwest across Dornet was scary, but thankfully I didn't run into any problems. Hmm, if this is Leodot, I should move on to the mountains. I can rest in my hometown of Piscyst.") Her feet ached and Piscyst was another day's hike, but she pressed on anyway. She knew she only had five days left to get back to Capaz, but time wasn't the problem. The idea of running into trouble alone scared her. Up until now, she had her friends to help her when she needed them. To fight alone seemed impossible.
("The Dornet Mountains, this should be easy. I use to take these trails to Leodot with my father.") Zephry slipped around the East side of town along the mountains to avoid being seen by anyone. She reached the mountains at the end of her first day alone and pressed on.
 Lumus made his way through the halls of Capaz palace. His mind raced with overwhelming thoughts of Twilight's conflicts. He made his way toward the lower halls to the training area, hoping to find the others.

"Scarlette! Hey, how has training been going?" Lumus blurted out. Scarlette turned expecting Zelkem.

"Oh, Hi Lumus, well Joffree and Zelkem had a bit of a fight. Zelkem beat him down without breaking a sweat, then took off." She sighed.

"He will be back. The boy is not one to let things go." Brinx said as he stood up to greet Lumus with a nod.

"He was furious, but I know we will see him again soon. How did you fare with the council?" Frostear asked.

"Good I suppose, I was trying to explain my connection to the core, but Councillor Alexander seemed more interested in protocol," Lumus explained.

"You mentioned that on our way to Capaz. You were saying we all have a star inside us that grows stronger. It's a beautiful thought, but what did they say?" Scarlette asked. Lumus crossed his arms.

"Well not a lot of them talked, it was mostly Lady Concy, Alexander, Orson, and myself. Geare said a few things but he…" Lumus explained. Scarlette let out a gasp.

"Geare is a councillor now?" Scarlette said with surprise. Frostear and Scarlette frowned in unison.

"Yes, Orson seemed irritated with him too. Why, who is Geare?" Lumus asked.

"Geare was the first civilian knight. He received no training but was able to make it on to the council. He is abnormally powerful. A few of the knights were angry with him for making his way to the top without going through any of the trials. I heard that last bit about Geare. I thought I'd shed some light on the topic." Lysilus interrupted.

"That bastard killed most of my people. He took it upon himself to destroy us. The Dragon Wars started because of him. Dragons lived peacefully unnoticed, but Geare started to hunt us, thinking that he could make himself some money and a name for himself. He didn't know that the Drayhelms could willingly transform into Dragons, although I suppose not many humans knew that information either. Humans formed armies to fight us. We approached Geare, and explained that he was killing people, and not just beasts." Frostear explained with anger. Scarlette turned to him with sadness in her eyes.

"I remember my father talking to Councillor Gerald about Geare when I was still a child. He didn't show Drayhelms any remorse because he felt they were unnatural beings." Scarlette added.

"I shouldn't be part of this conversation. I'll join Joffree, but I'll ignore what you just said Frostear." He said with a bow, then he walked back to the other room.

"Geare went on to hunt us until he made his way into the council. We thought we were done with that little bastard, but then he turned his attention to the ruling nations and began to get people to fear us. After a while, Twilight formed armies that represented the Zodiacs. Then we were declared enemies of Twilight. Wave after wave we fought them. We tried not to kill the humans, but they killed us. Now you could count the Drayhelms that are left with one hand." Frostear stared at Scarlette. Scarlette put her head down with a disappointed look on her face.

"I'm sorry Frostear, I never knew that either. If we had known your people were the dragons we would never have attacked..." Scarlette replied. "Maybe, but after Geare killed so many of us, our people fell apart, and became more enraged. When a Drayhelm gets too angry they start to take on dragon attributes, such as scales, horns and our eyes change too. Once our anger hits its peak we prematurely transform. When this happens there is no changing back. The only other way to transform into a dragon is to wait until a certain age. Each body is different though, most can change at will around two hundred and fifty years old. Some may never transform." Frostear explained. Lumus turned his attention to Frostear. "Frostear how many Drayhelms are left?" Frostear looked up at Lumus. "Well, that's a hard question to answer. There could be more than what I know. There is Coldblood...my son. Lady Concy, my ex-wife. My father, you met at Twilight Prison. He was the dragon that I was flying on, and myself. There could be more. I know during the Dragon Wars a lot of Drayhelm fled. Others transformed due to their anger. People lost their loved ones and friends for just being what they were. It's possible they made it far enough to restart their lives but I cannot be certain." Frostear sat on the ground with his head down.

"Wait, that Lord from Taurald was your son?" Brinx said with hesitation.

"Yes," Frostear replied. Lumus kneeled down. "Lady Concy is a Drayhelm? Why does no one know this?" Lumus blurted out. Frostear locked eyes with Lumus.

"Would you tell people that you came from a race of dragons that strike fear in people's hearts, and was partially responsible for the Dragon Wars?" Frostear protested. Scarlette began to get upset. "How could the Dragon Wars be your fault anyway? Your people are the victims here." Frostear put his head back down.

"No, not all of the Drayhelm were good. When we get angry we change. The angrier we get the more evil our race can become. When we prematurely transform our rage is incomparable. We have had many leave our land in their dragon form, and hurt people of Twilight. There have even been cases of dragons killing people too." Frostear said with hesitation. Scarlette turned from the group to hide her tears.

"Scarlette? Are you okay?" Lumus asked in a whisper. Scarlette wiped her tears away before she turned back.

"I'm fine Lumus." She quickly replied.

"Everyone, we have made new plans," Orson announced as he entered the training room with Lady Concy. Frostear stood up and turned to the others.

"Not a word of this," Frostear muttered. Lady Concy took a step forward.

"Is there something wrong?" Concy asked. Brinx stood in front of Scarlette to hide her red face and tears.

"What new plans did the council decide on?" Lumus interrupted to change the subject. "Well Orson took the light in the conference room. He suggested that the councillors make way back to their towns to tell the people of Lumus. The councillors didn't believe that Lumus was really the one born from the planet. You see we have had others come and try to convince us they were Lumus. I suppose they had good intentions, but a false hope like that led the councillors to really lose hope and believe he was dead, or never existed in the first place. Once Lumus put on his light show they knew he was the real deal. With that they can go back and tell their soldiers, and the moral of our people will go up. That is what Twilight needs. Orson has also stepped down as Councillor of Taurald." Concy said as she looked to Orson. Scarlette looked upset.

"Why would you do that? Isn't being a councillor a great honour?" Scarlette yelled at Orson. Orson shook his head.

"I would say the real honour is to fulfill my promise to your father to keep you safe. I also made you a promise to protect Lumus. Those are two very important things I cannot walk away from." Orson replied. Lady Concy made her way toward the door.

"I must take my leave. Lysilus wake Joffree would you? I'm not going to ask how he ended up on the ground." Concy looked at Scarlette, breaking the tension in the room. Scarlette giggled.

Lady Concy made her way up to the main hall, and Lysilus walked by embarrassed with Joffree over his shoulder.

"Orson now that it's a bit quieter around here, who is going to watch over Taurald?" Orson crossed his arms with his head down as if lost in his thoughts. "I will step down as councillor, but Brunius will take temporary command of both Capaz, and of Taurald. Councillor Brunius returned with the other councillors two days ago. You may not have seen him." Brinx interrupted.

"He returned? What reason would he have to leave when the meeting was going to take place here anyway?" Brinx said with confusion. Orson shook his head once again.

"I believe he mentioned giving aid to Taurald. He went there to chase out the remaining Krotins. It is a coincidence that he came back at the same time as the others arrived." Orson replied. Lumus walked closer to Orson to inspect him. His hand reached out to Orson's shoulder.

"Don't worry I'm sure Twilight can handle things while you're with us. Remember we have some important things to do too. Let everyone play their part." Lumus smiled. Scarlette walked over to join Orson and Lumus.

"Yeah I'm sure they will manage, but I think we might need to discuss what to do next. Zephry is going to be gone a few more days until she gets back right? So in the meantime, we can plan what to do and rest until she returns." Orson seemed relieved with Scarlette's optimism.

The blue moon shone brightly. Zelkem was outside the palace gates leaning upon the solid red brick trying to clear his thoughts. As he closed his eyes he began to drift asleep, but only for a moment. Suddenly music blasted through the city. Zelkem fell to the ground, startled.

"What the hell, not a moment's peace...what are these people up to now?" Zelkem said angrily. People scampered about setting up shops and carrying out merchandise. Music floated through the air as people started to put up decorations.

"Hey, buddy what's going on?" Zelkem shouted. A strange man stopped at Zelkem's question. "Oh, have you not heard? Councillor Brunius is throwing a festival. Zelkem seemed confused. "A festival? At a time like this? Why the hell would he do that?" The strange man was frantic.

"Well two reasons; firstly, the councillors are departing, the other I assume is to show the people that Twilight doesn't care about the demon., Twilight will live on! The Knights will protect us so why should we worry? I must go I have much to do!" The strange man ran off with haste.

"That guy is clueless. They can't just celebrate when demons lurk around killing people. ...morons." Zelkem snarled. He crossed his arms and sat down where he stood on the side of the road. Music was still playing nearby. Zelkem tried to block out the noise as it irritated him more and more. Suddenly Lysilus and Joffree came walking out with Lady Concy riding a Zufore behind them. As they passed by the rest of the Councillors followed. Joffree spotted Zelkem from the corner of his eye, and Zelkem noticed him as well. As Joffree walked on, Zelkem shot him a devious smile.

"Hey, I can hear the music playing in the city from down here! They really pulled together in such a short amount of time." Scarlette lit up like the blue moon at its peak.

"Look let's enjoy the festival, we have three days, so let's break off for now, and try to have some fun." Orson seemed as if he was ordering the others to go, but without a word of protest, Scarlette dragged Lumus upstairs as Brinx followed slowly behind.

"Frostear, you have been silent this whole time. What's on your mind?" Orson asked. Frostear headed for the door.

"Don't worry about my problems, I can take care of myself." Frostear took off upstairs leaving Orson standing in the training room alone. Orson sighed. "Well, I guess that's what I get for being personal." Orson shrugged and headed up to the main floor behind the others.

Music roared as people danced in joy. Kids ran about from store to store as parents went frantically to each shop looking for deals. Lumus and Scarlette walked off alone, taking in the bright city in all its glory. Brinx walked off alone as he did people stared at him thinking the worst until Frostear walked up beside him.

"Can't have you walking off alone now, can we? These people are scared of you, I think its best you stick with me for a while." Frostear recommended. Brinx seemed to take comfort in Frostear's concern for his wellbeing.

"Maybe you should enter one of their events to try to fit in? I believe I saw a pie-eating contest near the palace." Frostear said. He laughed. Brinx stopped and turned his attention to a stage east of the palace entrance to find Orson standing alone. "What do you suppose he is up to Brinx?" Frostear asked. Without a word, Brinx made his way through the crowd to Orson. People noticed Brinx and started to step aside as he made his way through the main street to Orson. Orson just stood firm with his arms crossed, and a smirk on his face as he stared impatiently for Brinx to reach him. "What are they doing?" Frostear began to follow behind Brinx, but the crowds began to fill in again. Brinx made his way onto the stage Orson stood upon.

"Okay, Brinx let's give the people a show eh? Ladies and gentlemen welcome to the Festival of Capaz. Today I, Orson first class knight of Taurald have a special show for you today. I am going to show the people what we knights do for Twilight." Orson announced. The crowds swarmed the large stage, kids lined up close along the front of the stage as others jumped onto their parent's shoulders. Orson had planned a little brawl in hopes Brinx would agree to join him. Without a single word, Brinx was on board, and the two readied themselves to give a good show. Although Brinx looked like the bad guy he knew deep down he was doing this for the people to raise their spirits. Zelkem made his way to the back of the stage while watching Orson.

"Hey Brinx, don't be afraid to hold back. I'm sure he can take a punch or two." Zelkem yelled out. Orson turned his head to look over his shoulder. "Zelkem? Where have you…" Brinx interrupted Orson and took the chance to attack, and as he did Orson shuffled to the side narrowly dodging him. "Alright Brinx, try to put on a show," Orson said while getting his footing back. Brinx' face lit up with a grin.

"Just try to keep up." Brinx declared. Orson and Brinx lashed out at each other, every punch colliding off one another. Brinx jumped high into the air, launching vines from his palms. The speed of the vines firing toward the stage gave Brinx a weightless feeling until they crashed into the stage. Orson jumped back just dodging them. Orson climbed straight up the vines. Brinx started to retract them back into his palms, pulling him toward Orson. Brinx threw his head forward as Orson shot his fist at Brinx. The two hit with a flash, then both came crashing toward the stage. Just then Lumus and Scarlette joined the crowd to watch.

"Wahoo! Go for it Brinx!" Scarlette yelled out.

Orson got up from the stage slowly, Brinx could tell he did some damage to him in his last attack. "Come on, demon. Is that all you got?" Orson provoked Brinx for the crowd. The battle began to get intense, Brinx shot multiple vines from his arms at Orson launching him off the stage into a merchant's cart. As the debris cleared Orson stood up.
"(Wow he's actually going all out.)" Orson stood, proudly hiding his fatigue.
With all his energy he charged at Brinx one last time, knowing that this would be his last attempt to win the brawl. Brinx caught on that Orson was tired, and Brinx crossed his arms in front of his face willingly giving Orson an opening to his chest. With the last ounce of energy, Orson threw a punch straight at Brinx's chest, and as his guard fell. He threw another punch launching Brinx over the city walls into the trees.
"There you have it, ladies and gentlemen, the Twilight knights don't give up. I beat that demon down and I bet he won't be coming back anytime soon." Orson panted. The crowd roared with praise. Brinx sat upon a treetop looking down into the city. His wounds very minimal compared to Orson's. Brinx took a moment to watch the reaction to Orson's victory. After a moment he disappeared into the trees.
"Orson are you okay? You guys put on a pretty nice show, but where did Brinx run off to." Scarlette asked.

"I'm okay Scarlette, I assume he's keeping out of sight for now. It wouldn't make much sense if he came back. People think Brinx is a demon." Orson smiled. Lumus walked over and joined Scarlette's side.

"Actually they like Brinx. You can hear them, can't you? They want another show. They saw him walk in with us when we arrived. Maybe they think he's an ally or something." Scarlette pointed toward the crowds. Zelkem walked over laughing.

"You couldn't be more of a sellout. Is this what you Knights do? I can see now why Joffree was such a pushover. Orson hopped off the stage and walked off with a limp to the palace. Scarlette dragged Lumus away, leaving Zelkem and Frostear alone. Frostear noticed everyone walk away so he went off on his own. Zelkem turned to see him walk away. "Really? Am I even here? Zelkem went behind the stage and sat on the ground against the city walls.

Ged emerged from the shadow of Lears. Lears stood in an abandoned shack outside of Taurald. "Lord Lears, you called on me?" Lears stared at the wall with Ged behind him.

"I have decided to make Aster Mountains my new lair. Have some of my things brought over to make it more to my taste. I have also decided to make you second in command. I will give you orders for the Lords, and I expect you to complete them. With your abilities to jump through the shadows, I see this to be a very suitable job for you." Ged bowed.

"All is for My Lord." Just soon as he appeared he vanished. Lears turned and walked into the light shining through the window. "Just wait Lumus, the next time we meet you will see my true power." Lears exited the shack laughing hysterically.

Chapter Nine- Scarlette's Secret

Morning came quickly, Scarlette thought as she woke to the sound of the town bustling with life below. Merchants and travelers from yesterday's festival were all packing their remaining things to leave Capaz. Scarlette yawned loudly as she got up from her bed. She approached the window to see life in Capaz returning to normal and thought of the times she had looked out the very same window when she was a child. Thoughts of her mother and father waking her for her morning lessons came to mind. She went into deeper thought of them, and how she missed them as the days pass by. If the council didn't come to be then Scarlette would have been made the queen of Capaz. However, the loss of most royal families over generations through the many deaths in the Dragon Wars, Twilight produced the council so that anyone who distinguished their name through acts of loyalty to the people could be a councillor. Also, the council was a defense against the Dragons. Although the system works and the flow of control over each city is kept, Scarlette couldn't shake the feeling of being helpless.

The people still recognize her as the princess, but only as a title of no meaning. People that knew her family still believe that she is meant to rule all of Twilight, not only Capaz.

"What do I do mother... father? With limited time I can only do so much. Maybe going with Lumus is the only way I can do the most good? Princess or not, I still have a job to protect the people in your name. I will see you one day, and when I do I will tell you the story of how I helped purge Lears from this world. That is the only way I feel I can help." Scarlette spoke to herself looking up at the clouds.

She snapped out of her daydream to see people down below rushing to the city's main gates. She reached into her pouch and pulled out an hourglass. The sand was glowing, and Scarlette looked upset to see that half of the sand had already fallen through.

"What is this? What is going on?" Scarlette turned from the window and ran to the door. She ran out into the hallway and made it to the main hallway to the palace entrance where Lumus stood waiting for her. Before Lumus noticed her she hid the hourglass back in her pouch around her waist.

"Hey good morning! I was starting to get worried you wouldn't wake up on time to see Zephry return. The others have already gone to the gate. Let's go." Lumus smiled. Without a word, Scarlette followed behind Lumus in a rush of excitement.

The gargantuan doors opened to a bright light, almost blinding Scarlette, the Blue moon was bright as ever, and with all the clouds from the night before completely gone. Lumus lead the way down the main road past town square. People were still rushing out of their houses to invite the newest knight in years back to Capaz. Someone must have announced before she returned that she had undergone the pilgrimage since next to no one knew she had left other than Lumus and the others. Suddenly the answer came to mind; it must have been Orson since he was the one that set everything up for her in the first place.

People ran by shouting and cheered for their knights, while others walked by with improvised signs saying "Welcome back knight of Twilight". Just past the crowd of people ahead, Scarlette could see Councillor Brunius and Orson standing on a small stage. Scarlette could remember from when she was little that young knights that returned to Capaz were given their Twiblade just moments after returning. Behind the stage was the blacksmith working hard to finish the weapon on time. Lumus stopped just behind a few townspeople, and the ceremony had begun. Orson stepped up to the front of the stage to give a speech. Zephry made her way up the four small steps onto the stage, but she struggled to climb them since she was exhausted.

"People of Capaz! I stand before you to welcome home the newest member of the Knights of Twilight in about twenty years... Zephry Velurus. She has ventured to Fargon Region in the far Northwest area to obtain the Dragon Steel for her Twiblade to commemorate has passing into the rank of third class knight. I am proud to present to you Zephry, knight third class. Furthermore, we have a special guest to pass the Twiblade to our newest knight. I am sure you have all seen him around town, and have many questions about his arrival too. So here he is to present the Twiblade to Zephry, Prince Lumus." Orson announced with a grin.

The crowd went completely silent. Every head turned to Lumus in shock, although many have seen him around town no one really believed he truly was the Prince of Light. Lumus froze for a moment and looked around at everyone staring back at him. Scarlette gave a quick nudge to Lumus from behind, and he realized he should make his way to the stage.

"Hello everyone. I am Lumus. I am sure like Orson has said, that you all have many questions. To answer them I guess I would have to say the legend that I have heard since coming back to Twilight is true. A hero of Light was born from the depths of the planet. The hero was shut away to a world of darkness as his brother the prince of darkness took over his world, and threw the balance astray. Well to that I can only tell you I have found my world once again, and with all my strength I will bring balance and justice to Twilight once again. Lears shall be thrown into the darkness." Lumus yelled to the crowd, amidst the cheers.

Lumus turned to Orson, who stepped forward with the Twiblade he had received from the blacksmith during Lumus' speech and handed it to Lumus.

"Way to please the crowd Lumus," Orson whispered as he stepped back. Lumus turned back to Zephry and handed her the newly crafted Twiblade. "Congratulations Zephry Velurus, third class knight of Twilight," Lumus announced with a smile.

The crowd roared in excitement with questions answered, and hope brought back to their hearts. Zephry threw her arm high above her head holding the Twiblade in the air. Councillor Brunius and his personal guards exited the stage followed by Zephry, Orson, and Lumus.

The palace gates remained open until Scarlette, Zelkem, Brinx, and Frostear passed through. Councillor Brunius lead everyone to the throne room. Scarlette was surprised to see that the throne room had not changed at all since she had last been there as a child. The walls were marble stone with felt hanging down behind the throne, the symbol of Capricorn proudly displayed on it. Pillars followed from the main doors to the throne chairs. The group waited at the first pillars by the door as Lumus and Orson spoke to councillor Brunius alone.

"I have ordered the blacksmith to make you all new armour for your quest. Orson has told me you intend to leave after Zephry's return. I have had him make the armour similar to what your clothing is now. I have to say though, I was unsure of your green friend so he will not receive anything." Brunius smiled. Lumus laughed.

"Councillor, I don't think he would suit our clothing anyway," Lumus replied. Orson chuckled under his breathe.

"Very well then. Orson, I have to ask you though. With you leaving the council after just returning to us, do you have a successor in mind?" Orson looked over to Brunius.

"No sir, I have not made arrangements for a successor yet," Orson said while bowing. Brunius shrugged

"I see. Under rules of councillor responsibility, I have no choice but to make you remain Taurald Councillor until you do. I understand that Councillor Gerald has made himself available to take over until you find a replacement. I will make the arrangements with Gerald so that you may leave with Lumus. Under the circumstances, we have no choice." Brunius smiled. Orson bowed his head

"Thank you, Councillor Brunius." Brunius smiled once again and put his hand on Orson's shoulder.

"If a successor presents his or her self to me I will send word to the council at once," Orson replied.

"Very well then it will be done. Although this may take a while to find somebody suited for such a position." Orson knew that the councillors would keep Orson as councillor of Taurald regardless of how long he waited to find a successor.

A loud knock on the door echoed through the throne room, and the blacksmith entered pulling a wagon with a sheet over it.

"Councillor Brunius, I have completed your order." The blacksmith announced. Brunius immediately stood up, excited to see the outcome.
"Very well. Reveal them please." Brunius
The blacksmith pulled the sheet from the wagon, uncovering a variety of different armours.
"This is the blacksmith, Sir Paul Blackwood. He was once a knight of Capaz in the time of Scarlette's father. He designs all of the Knights' clothing and uniforms. A man of many talents" Brunius announced.
"Prince Lumus, this is yours." Paul smiled. The armour was silver with a black trim finish around the edges accompanied by a pair of stylish silver pants to match the chest plate.
"Sir Orson the chest plate you wanted is finished too." Paul handed Orson the armour with a bow. Orson received a dark grey chest plate with a gold trim. Also a large set of shoulder armour and arm guards to match. They were dark with gold trim on the edges. The pants were same as Lumus', but black in colour.
"Lady Scarlette I made you something unique." Paul handed Scarlette a half breastplate, the black trim followed around the top to the waist. She was also given a set of arm guards reaching from the elbow to her wrist, and a small cape with black on the outside and a light pink on the inside to match her hair.
"Sir Zelkem, I only made you pants in a dark brown. They are fitted and lightweight, but I did craft these weighted arm bands. Since you are a

fighter maybe they will be useful." Paul said with a grin. Zelkem grinned as he looked them over. "I hate to wear a shirt, so this works for me, why not show off the goods I always say." Zelkem boasted. Orson turned to Zelkem.
"When have you ever said that?" Zelkem sighed. "Lady Zephry I took the traditional third class armour and altered it to suit your look. It is a dark blue breast plate with matching pants and arm guards." Zephry stepped forward. "Thank you so much, I love dark blue it's my favourite colour!" Zephry said with excitement.
"Lastly, I have something for you sir Frostear." Paul struggled to carry off the large chest plate for Frostear. Frostear stepped forward to grab it for himself.
"A black and purple chest plate. I appreciate your craftsmanship, blacksmith." Frostear took off his armour and threw it into the wagon.
 "Perhaps you can melt it down for another use. These shoulder guards with the spikes are just my style." Frostear continued.
"Yes, and these are yours as well." The blacksmith handed two arm guards that were purple at the wrist with black centerpieces finished with a purple Fargon emblem.
"Oh, and don't forget your pants. I made all of the pants to match in style, although they vary in colour to suit your looks. Oh, and one last thing: Lady Concy requested this to be made for you, lady Scarlette. It is a new bow printed with your family crest. Lady Concy heard of how you lost

your bow near Varlif forest." The bow was silver from top to bottom with a silver quiver to match. Scarlette reached out and took the bow. Her hands shook as she gazed at its beauty.

"Sir Blackwood, It is an honor, and I never got a chance to thank you…" Scarlette smiled.

"Lady Scarlette. The honor is mine to serve a child of such grace. I'm happy I was able to serve such a family." Paul bowed to Scarlette.

"You may receive your payment from my guards at the door Sir Blackwood, and again. Thank you, sir." Brunius said as he sat down. Paul wished the group luck as he bowed his head. Quickly he turned and left.

"I will see you off from here. I have much work to do. Feel free to change in your rooms. You are welcome back anytime. Good luck to you all." Councillor Brunius stood up once more and made his way out of the throne room.

"Lumus we should get ready to go soon. We won't finish anything if we don't get moving." Orson said as he walked by Lumus, carrying his new armour with him.

"Orson, wait a moment! " Lumus called out at the last second. When everyone is ready we should meet at the main gates at the entrance of town." Lumus whispered.

Everyone walked off toward the throne room doors feeling slightly sad to have to leave the palace. Scarlette waited for everyone to leave. Lumus was last to go and he looked back to Scarlette, as she looked back to him and then turned around. Lumus knew she might need some time before leaving her hometown. He shut the door behind him and headed to his room.

"Mother, Father I have chosen this path on my own, and I intend to see it to the end. I hope I have your blessing from above." Scarlette closed her eyes for a moment while putting her head down. She paused for a moment thinking of her parents. After a moment she made her way to the door as a single tear rolled down her cheek. Then she opened the door to the main hall.

"Scarlette, are you okay?" Lumus stood in his new armour outside the throne room. Scarlette gasped. "I'm sorry to startle you, but I thought I would wait for you here once I changed. The others have already left for the North Gate." Lumus informed her. Scarlette looked over his shoulder to see the palace doors wide open.

"Lumus I need to tell you a secret that I have been keeping since before I met you in Dystopia." Scarlette worried. Lumus paused for a moment. "Is everything okay?" He asked.

"When I died in Aster Mountains I went to a place called the realm of the dead. It is where the souls of the west go when they die. As you know I met Ged there and I was granted life instead of him even though it was his time and not mine. The secret is… I didn't get my life back entirely. How can I explain this? I was given an energy that I can use to enhance my fighting. I became stronger, faster, and can endure more. The only problem is the more I exhaust my body the more my life force drains from me. There is no way of telling when I will disappear from this world back to the realm of the dead." Scarlette pulled the hourglass from her pouch.

"This was given to me by the West Zin. She said it contains the star energy that gives me life." She handed it to Lumus. Lumus notice the sand moving slowly to the bottom. He tried flipping it upside down. It didn't make a difference.

"Well, it was worth a try," Lumus said with a smile. Lumus felt his stomach drop.

"I have what the West Zin calls star life. She has given me the enhanced power to live, so there is no way to reverse it. I am sorry I held this from you." Scarlette declared. Lumus finally blinked.

"That's why you were up and about while I was in bed wounded at Taurald. Brinx had told me you took a beating, but you were barely scratched." Lumus realized. Scarlette walked toward the palace entrance.

"By the time we made it to Taurald I was back to normal. With that said I don't want to tell the others. I need to keep this a secret. Without warning, someday I will just disappear, and when that happens you must ensure that the others do not know the truth. The West Zin told me you were the only one who could know. She said that being near you would actually give me more time because of your pure star energy. The energy you radiate keeps me here longer." Scarlette blushed. Lumus turned Scarlette around to face him.

"So as long as you stay by my side you won't go back. Then I will never leave your side. Anywhere we go we go together." Lumus Declared. Scarlette let the tears that had gathered, roll down her cheeks.

"No, being with you will only slow the process, but not enough to keep me here. I just don't want this to affect anything." Lumus wrapped his arms around her as she broke down and cried.

"Nothing will take you from us. I will use everything in my being to stop it Scarlette." Lumus said as he wrapped his arms tighter around her. Scarlette knew he couldn't stop the process, but she didn't want to ruin the moment.

"It's time to go. The others are waiting. I'll change into my clothes, and meet you and the others." She said as she wiped her tears away. Lumus let go of her and walked outside the palace toward the North Gate.

"Are they going to take all day? We aren't going to get anything done just sitting around. Ah man, I haven't punched anything in a while, and I'm getting restless…" Zelkem started pacing back and forth.

"Calm down Zelkem, Scarlette is just having a hard time leaving her home behind again. If she needs time then the least we can do is give it to her." Orson began checking his armour, looking for any weakness it could have but finding none.

"Lumus is coming," Brinx said calmly.

"It's about time." Zelkem blurted out.

"Hey Scarlette isn't with him, is she not coming?" Zephry said sadly.

"She is probably staying behind," Frostear said.

"Hey Scarlette is on her way out, she's just getting changed." Lumus rushed past everyone to the gate and crossed his arms.

"Is something the matter?"

"No Orson, everything is fine. Just give her a moment. She is saying goodbye to Capaz." Lumus didn't turn around to respond.

"Hey come on it's not like she isn't going to see Capaz again," Zelkem exclaimed. Lumus shut his eyes.

"There she is, she's coming now." Zephry's spirit rose as Scarlette made her way to the group. She couldn't imagine going on this trip without her friends. The lonely quest to Fargon region had made her eager to catch up with her friends.

"Have you finished saying your goodbyes?" Frostear asked.

"Yes, I believe I did," Scarlette replied with a smile.

"Hey Frostear, farewells are for when you don't intend to see something again," Zephry replied with a grin. Frostear had a look of confusion about him.

"Are we all here, and ready? Let's get going then, we have a long way ahead of us. We need to head east past the bridge dividing Torson and Nuran regions, and after we make it past there we head south along the river to Librine. This won't easy, but it won't be impossible. Everyone keep your heads up, and keep your eyes open." Orson instructed the group, and the lead them out of the gate. Slowly the others followed. Zephry and Frostear lead the rear.

"Come on gramps keep up," Zelkem muttered as he passed Frostear.

"You're not going to start that again are you?" Frostear muttered.

"Start what?" Zephry asked.

"Nothing…" Frostear responded. Orson led the group with Zelkem and Brinx a few steps behind him, Lumus and Scarlette took the middle as Frostear and Zephry trailed a bit behind sneaking glances at each other from time to time. Frostear was silent. It didn't take much to make her blush he thought. She hasn't really said a thing to him since she returned. He had thought of her each day she was gone. What could be going through her mind he thought? Zephry was oblivious to Frostear's thinking. He was just playing the strong, and silent card. Finally, she broke and gathered enough confidence to ask.

"So Frostear, what are we to do?" Zephry asked while looking ahead.

"Like Orson said we head for Librine, and we will be there in a day or so," Zephry explained.

Frostear seemed confused why she would ask such an obvious question. Zephry shot him a look.

"No, I mean what of us? The night before my pilgrimage we…" Frostear cut her off before she went on.

"I don't think that is appropriate for casual conversation Zephry." Frostear protested. "Why not, they can't hear us from way up there. Come on, don't you want to talk about it?" Zephry tried to reason with Frostear.

"Where I come from, talking about feelings will block the real relationship. Simply put, I like you and you obviously can't leave me alone, so we will go from there. My people are not the mushy romantic types. So maybe you can respect that, and we can skip it." Frostear explained. She rolled her eyes.

"You really are blunt about this but I like that. I'll find a way to get to your heart." Zephry smiled.

"I will make a deal with you, Zephry. After our journey with Lumus, you and I will find a place to settle down, and live our lives together, is that acceptable?" Zephry's smile turned into a laugh.

"You sure do know how to sweep a woman off her feet. I guess if that is how I get you then that will have to do." Zephry giggled. Frostear smiled shyly.

"Orson, do you think this Coldblood goon will still be in Librine?" Orson turned to look back over his shoulder to Nuran River. After a pause, he looked over to give Zelkem his attention.

"I think if this 'Dyne' guy really did see Coldblood give the information to Antsos then he would wait for Antsos to return to report his mission." Orson continued to watch the area as he walked.

"You think so? Maybe he set off to meet somewhere else. I haven't met Dyne. Is that another council member, or is he a soldier?" Zelkem continued.

"Concy mentioned the name. It seems he came forward with the information. That's who we are heading to meet with. We have no other leads so this is our next logical choice to investigate." Orson explained. Zelkem threw his arms back behind his head resting his head in his hands, stretching as he walked.

"Or this could be a waste of time. Did you guys think that this could be a trap? Maybe Dyne works for Lears." Zelkem muttered to himself.

"Lumus do you think Frostear will really fight with his son?" Scarlette said in a sad tone. "Maybe. I don't really know their intentions. Frostear usually goes quiet when Coldblood's name comes up. Maybe they have some built up animosity to each other, who knows." Lumus checked to see the others behind him.

"I hope everything works out. At least it's a beautiful day." Scarlette smiled. Lumus smiled and started to drift off into his own thoughts.

"(I can feel something strange...almost like when I felt Lears nearby. I wish I knew what this was.)" Lumus thought to himself.

Wind rolled in off the small hills along the plains, the Nuran River just west of the group and picked up speed. The bright sky quickly vanished as the wind dragged in monstrous clouds high above.

"Looks like we may get a bit of rain. Does anyone see where we could take cover?" Orson asked, keeping a concerned eye on the clouds above.

"We shouldn't stop, a little rain won't hurt us," Lumus suggested. Orson turned to Lumus.

"When Lears began to take Twilight over, the wild animals became a lot more aggressive. It's not the rain that worries me." Orson replied.

"Rain Raiders," Zelkem interjected.

"Exactly. Those beast can swim through the rain as a bird flies through the air, it is quite a sight to see since they are one of the largest beasts in the Twilight Ocean. They can grow to stretch from Capaz to Librine." Orson added. Lumus gasped.

"Are you serious, how could something like that exist?" Lumus replied.

"They can predict rain. Specialists believe they live deep in the Twilight Ocean and must have some kind of sixth sense to feel when the rain will happen. Though they can't travel too far from the ocean. If it was to stop raining the beast would plummet to the ground helpless to move without water." Orson took a deep breath.

"I had no idea something like that was possible," Brinx said. Scarlette laughed.

"Really have you not seen your own reflection? People like you don't just fall from the sky. If you ask me anything is possible." Scarlette said sarcastically. The group went silent.

"I would like to battle something like that. I would like to see how I fair against the beast." Zephry punched Frostear's arm.

"Hey, don't be stupid. You could die." Frostear looked to the east toward Twilight Ocean.

"If we see one I'll try my luck." Zephry sped up to Scarlette's side.

"Sorry Lumus, girls only." She smiled.

"What just happened here?" Lumus said to Frostear as he slowed down.

"Come on don't get left behind…" Lumus caught up to Frostear keeping an eye on Zephry and Scarlette laughing, and giggling as they looked back at Lumus and Frostear.

"What did you say to her Frostear?" Lumus asked.

"I don't know, she hit me then stormed off. I am just as lost as you." Frostear replied.

Orson stopped at the river bend. He looked to see Librine in the distance.

Chapter Ten- Assault on Librine

"Okay... there is Librine. The rain let up, so we are okay to proceed. When we get there everyone split up into groups and look for clues. Try to be discreet, and above all be careful. Meet at the town inn when night hits the sky." Orson directed, and then walked off alone. Brinx and Zelkem followed behind heading to the south part of town. Zephry dragged Scarlette off toward the market in the east part of town.

"Alright, Lumus we are left with the housing district. The alleys can be somewhat confusing so try to keep your eyes open alright." Frostear headed off with Lumus trailing behind.

"Scarlette, this is the perfect time to get some shopping done! Look at all of the things they have for sale here!" Zephry ran from store to store looking at all of the different merchandise.

"Hey, Zephry we should be looking for clues around town not wasting time with this junk." Scarlette crossed her arms firmly disproving. Zephry turned her attention to her for a moment then back at the merchandise.

"Zephry aren't you listening?" Zephry turned to Scarlette.

"I am, look I found a clue." Zephry held her hand out with a pendant of the serpent on it.

"What is that? A serpent? What does that mean?" Zephry looked at the pendant.

"Well, Lumus said this guy had a serpent pendant right? Maybe this is where he bought his." Zephry suggested. The storekeeper snatched the pendant from Zephry.

"Young woman I hand make these pendants, so this is the only place that sells them. If you're not buying then please move along." Zephry turned back to the shopkeeper.

"Oh, I'm sorry. I didn't mean to take it." She apologized. Scarlette grabbed her hand.

"Come on, Zephry we are looking for clues of Lears' Lords being here, and now we know that Dyne is here." Zephry looked confused.

"Well, why didn't you tell me that? I just got back, remember..." Zephry replied. A man in a dark cloak bumped into Zephry as she was talking to Scarlette.

"Sorry miss, my apologies." The man said in a creepy voice.

"Oh um, yes well that's okay." Scarlette couldn't keep her eyes off the strange man.

("I feel something strange about him..."). Zephry, go find Lumus tell him to come to the market area now." Scarlette demanded. Zephry turned back to Scarlette.

"What is it? Is something wrong?" Scarlette took a step forward then turned to look back at Zephry over her shoulder.

"Yes, I think that was a Lord that bumped into you. Find Lumus quickly, I will follow him." Scarlette ran off to catch up to the strange man.

"I guess I'll go find Lumus, miss bossy…" Zephry muttered.

"Brinx don't you worry that some villager or angry demon hater will try to kill you? You always walk around town, but you never really seem worried." Brinx chuckled.

"I suppose they could try, but they would be no match for me, I would think. Not to mention the fact that I can be reborn" Brinx replied. Zelkem stopped.

"That's cool I guess." Zelkem sighed. Suddenly Zephry ran right past Zelkem and Brinx in a panic. "Something's wrong." Brinx jumped high into the air.

"Huh, Brinx? Zephry wait up!" Zelkem chased after Zephry as Brinx jumped off the way she came.

"Hmm, I hear Zelkem." Orson turned around to see them run past the intersection toward the west of town.

"Have they found something?" Orson turned to catch up with them.

"Lumus, this part of town seems like a dead end. Maybe the others have found something." Frostear said. Lumus looked at the sky.

"The Blue moon is setting. Let's head to the Inn." Lumus and Frostear turned to see Zephry racing toward them.

"Lumus! I found you finally…" Zephry was out of breath.

"Slow down, Zephry." Frostear seemed worried for her.

"Scarlette thinks she may have found a Lord in the market area, she sent me to find you, and she went on alone to follow him." Zephry bent down with her hands on her knees as she gasped for air.
"Lumus I'll stay with her. Go find Scarlette."
"Okay, come find us when you can Frostear. We might need your help." Lumus ran off through the street passing Zelkem and Orson as he ran.
"He is really fast! Ah, that means I have to run all the way back that way…damn." Zelkem sighed, then began to run back the way he came.
"Lumus?" Orson felt a strong gust of wind race by him, but Lumus was moving far too fast to hear Orson.
"Something is wrong." Orson ran after Lumus and Zelkem.
"Where did he go? How could I lose him?" Scarlette said as she wandered through the back alleys of the market area. The night crept over her as she tried to make her way through the dark alone.
"Are you looking for me? Ha-ha." A familiar voice called out. Scarlette recognized the voice.
"Ged. Come out and face me! Stop hiding in the shadows." Scarlette yelled out
"Ha-ha. You little bitch, you will show some respect when talking to me! Do you even know what you have done to me?" Ged cried out. Scarlette smiled.
"Actually you did that to yourself. You couldn't wait to get your life back, so you jumped into the portal that the West Zin opened for me." Scarlette

said with a smirk. Ged jumped from a nearby rooftop.

"You fool. You came and stole my life. If you didn't show up I would have been given passage to my new life. Reincarnation." Ged cried out once more. Scarlette readied her bow.

"You are selfish Ged, I had to come back to help Lumus. Without me…" Scarlette went silent.

"Without you what? You are useless in all of this. You play no role in his life. A waste just like you using the portal that was meant for me." Ged declared with anger. Scarlette gripped her bow tightly.

"There are some things you don't need to know. My role is my role, and the means of it are of no importance to you." Scarlette replied. Ged's eyes glared through the darkness. "Stupid woman, at least I got something out of your ignorance. Since my body became this physical shadow I am now able to jump from shadow to shadow. It is rather useful. Let me demonstrate my newest ability thanks to Lears." Ged yelled out.

Scarlette could barely see in front of her, she looked into Ged's eyes that were visible through the darkness, but she had no luck seeing them.

"(He must be on the roof. This path is flat so he couldn't be anywhere else.)" Scarlette thought to herself while looking toward the rooftops. Everything went silent, and Scarlette began to sweat.

"Stupid girl" Ged appeared behind Scarlette from the shadows, and before she could react Ged threw a devastating punch to her back, then hit her with a spinning kick, launching her down the street.

"You can't win. I will finally kill you, stupid girl." Ged celebrated. Scarlette managed to pull herself to her feet.

"Why Ged? Why even fight me? You were once a hero of Twilight. Can't you see it has fallen apart? I am trying to help Lumus fix our world. Why can't you see that?" Ged stopped. He looked at his hand wondering what he was doing.

"(I am Twilights hero, she is right that I once protected this world…)." Suddenly Ged cried and shook his head as if to free himself from his thoughts.

"No more games, Scarlette!" Ged cried out in a rage.

Ged leaped into the air, then charged down with both fists together. Just as Ged was about to land a harsh attack on Scarlette, Lumus charged in with a hard body check to Ged hurling him through the city walls into the fields outside the city. Lumus walked out from the alley street with a radiating light around him and made his way toward Ged.

"I will ask you once, Ged. Where is Lears?" Ged got up slowly and looked down at his bloody hands.

"Lears will find you when he feels the time is ready. You will fall before our power!" Lumus began to illuminate brighter.

"Wrong answer" Lumus let out a massive roar as his body was completely engulfed with light. The light was far too bright to look at Lumus directly. Lumus threw his arms in the air as the white light shot around him almost like lightning. Power from his body began to focus into his hands. The closer it got the louder Lumus yelled. Ged couldn't believe his eyes.

"(I can't dodge this, I'm too weak from his last attack.)" Ged scrambled to his feet in an attempt to defend himself; although Lumus noticed Ged's weakened condition he continued walking toward him. He clapped his hands together, and the energy from his hands hit Ged as if he had punched him. Lumus braced himself, spreading his feet, then finally he shot his palms toward Ged releasing a devastating attack of white energy directly at him. Lumus' palms launched the enormous blast across the field like a raging waterfall with lightning firing from every angle. Ged tried to block it by putting his forearms in front of himself, but the energy was far too overwhelming for him. The ground shot up as Ged took the attack. At first, he looked as if he could stop it, but soon enough he was engulfed in the attack, slowly lifting him off his feet. Ged's arms were thrown back as Ged lost control, and he flew up toward the sky as long as Lumus could hold out his energy. When the dust settled he stood still with his arms out and his head down. He began to breathe heavily for a moment, then he collapsed to the ground. Scarlette ran to his side as Orson and Zelkem reached the outer walls of the city. Orson kneeled down beside Lumus, and picked him up,

Lumus had fallen unconscious. Zelkem held Scarlette close, fearing the worst. Scarlette looked over at Lumus for a moment. She began to cry as she squeezed Zelkem tighter and tighter.

"Not for me…not for me Lumus!" Scarlette cried out as tears fell on Zelkem's chest.

"He will be okay if we let him rest. We need to head to the Inn. Scarlette, come with me. Zelkem, get the others, and meet us at the inn." Orson demanded. Scarlette pushed Zelkem aside and ran to Orson and Lumus.

"Right, Zephry and Frostear should be in the housing district, but where is Brinx? He jumped off in this direction before I ran into you, Orson." Scarlette asked. Brinx stood upon the city wall just beside the part that Lumus had hit Ged through.

"Zelkem I can reach the others faster than you. Go with them and I will find Zephry and Frostear." Brinx commanded. Brinx jumped off into the night as quickly as he appeared. "Zelkem give me a hand with Lumus. The Inn isn't too far from here. Scarlette he will be fine. He just needs to rest for a while." Orson asked. Zelkem threw Lumus' arm over his shoulder as Orson took the other.

"Zephry are you okay now?" Frostear laid his hand upon her back.

"Yes, I think I'll live. Should we go catch up to them? I'm worried about Scarlette." Zephry stood up, Frostear took a step toward the alley Lumus ran through.

"Zephry, it isn't safe here. Get out of here now!" Zephry became confused with Frostear. "What?

We are in a three-way intersection with the wall of the city to our backs. You will have to be more specific. Left to the city gates or right to the Market district? Hey, I just realized this city is a big circle." Zephry said obliviously. Frostear grew impatient.
"Head toward the market district, I'll catch up in a while," Frostear demanded.
"Fine. Jeez, you are so hard to figure out you know." Zephry stomped off in a rage.
"Finally that blabbermouth of a woman left. Is this the woman with whom you plan to replace mother? She is quite the catch, but don't expect me to call her mommy." Coldblood came lurking out of the shadows. His cape, worn and ragged, floated behind him in the alley, wielding a sword as red as the moon.
"Coldblood, it isn't too late come back with me please." Coldblood let out another laugh.
"Yes, you'd like that, wouldn't you. Father and son fighting side by side as heroes of Twilight. Really show the world how they were wrong about Drayhelms. You can't erase your past, father. We are killers. How you sunk so low as to follow someone who promotes everything I grew up to fight…, it makes me sick." Frostear stepped closer to Coldblood. "Let me see your face boy." Coldblood hesitated.
"I have been bad, father. Very bad." Coldblood took a step closer and revealed his face from under his dark hood.
"Your face…what have you done?" He recoiled in horror The wind began to go cold in the streets.

"(So he's turning, now I know why he has been driven into such a rage. The dragon inside must be trying to take over.") He thought with a disappointed look.

"I did what our race does best; I kill. Ever since the Scorpial region was domesticated we have been lost as a species. Scattered and hunted as monsters. We are the true race of Twilight." Coldblood laughed.

"You're wrong, son. Everything we were taught, everything I instilled in you was to live peacefully. Our leader just warped our minds into believing what we were doing was right during the war. He was wrong. Who are we to kill anyone?" Coldblood began to pace in circles around Frostear.

"So what are you saying? Our lives are lies?" Coldblood replied.

"No, but we have been misled. I left you to find answers. Do you know what I found? The world is full of people that want nothing but peace. People fight for even a chance, a hope. We were attacked as monsters, because of a human who felt like we were threatening that peace. I stand to help the humans understand that the Drayhelms are not their enemies. Now I fight to maintain that peace. Even against my own son if need be." Frostear threatened.

"Hahaha, yeah that does seem like quite the story. None of that matters to me. I don't share that love for the humans as you do, father. I will continue to fight them till my last breath. I have grown to love

the hunt, and I have found a new employer."
Frostear clenched his fist.

"Lears," Frostear responded.

"Yes, father that's right. I don't care who I kill, I enjoy doing it. I will prove to everyone that they were right to fear the Drayhelms." A single tear fell from Frostear's cheek.

"Father you will be the best hunt of all. That is why I have joined Lears. To kill you. You are the only one stronger than me. So I have made it my life to kill you. Well not to mention Lears set a bounty on your head to make it official. Your death will leave me the strongest of the Drayhelms." Frostear turned to get a better look at Coldblood's face.

"I will do whatever it takes to free you from this way of life. You have lost your way, and now I stand in front of a monster." Frostear added. Coldblood reached for his sword as Frostear did. "I'm sorry I failed you boy," Frostear added. Coldblood laughed.

"Enough talking! The hunt begins." Coldblood laughed.

Frostear and Coldblood circled each other with their swords held at the ready. Neither made an attempt for the first move as they circled the alley.

"You always taught me to never make the first move. It helps to read your opponent, but I have learned a few tricks of my own... try to read this!" Coldblood stuck his sword into the ground, and let out a monstrous roar. His arms shot out from his sides with his palms open wide. Slowly he pulled his arms forward and brought his palms together. Black energy began to form a ball. Coldblood's roar grew louder and louder. Frostear placed his sword in both hands to protect him from Coldblood's attack.

"Come now father, I would suggest avoiding this one." Coldblood began to laugh with such evil in his eyes. Frostear closed his eyes as the dark energy began to shoot around like lightning. He gripped his sword tightly and put one leg back to brace himself. Suddenly the light and noise were gone. Frostear still with his eyes closed pulled his sword down enough past his face to look upon Coldblood, but Brinx stood behind him with Coldblood at his feet.

"Brinx?" Frostear looked up with surprise.

"We have more pressing things to attend to. Lumus and the others have made their way to the inn so we should meet them there." Brinx informed. Frostear sheathed his sword on his back.

"This is important to me. You must leave…, I need to finish this." Without hesitation, Brinx kicked Coldblood aside, then took a step toward Frostear.

"On my way over here I have seen something that we cannot ignore. It seems Lears has somehow foreseen that we would come here. There is a massive army of demons on their way to the city as we speak." Brinx added. Frostear cringed. Brinx jumped off into the night leaving Frostear behind.

"(This isn't over, my son. We will finish this another time.") Frostear followed into the dark alley after Brinx, Coldblood was still unconscious on the ground.

"The inn is locked, aren't places like this usually open all the time?" Scarlette said in a panic. Orson stood beside Scarlette outside the Serpent inn with Lumus in his arms. She held her arms tightly to her body trying to keep warm. Zephry had an eye out behind them hoping for Frostear to catch up to them.

"Zelkem check around back, maybe its open back there," Orson commanded.

"So breaking and entering is part of the knight's code now?" Zelkem replied with a smirk. Orson glared at Zelkem.

"In a time of crisis the knights are authorized to use any means possible as long as the people are not brought into harm's way." Orson smiled back at Zelkem.

Zelkem turned to the alley behind the inn. He looked over back at Orson.

"So you guys make your own laws too? Just like the knights to think they're better than the people." Zelkem muttered.

Zelkem made his way into the alley, and as he did Brinx returned from the housing district, startling Zephry as he landed.

"Frostear is on his way, but we have something else to worry about now. As I went to look for Frostear I saw an army of demons making their way for the city. They will reach the gates in a matter of minutes. I saw maybe a hundred or so"

Brinx added. Zelkem came running out of the alley.

"The back is locked too," Zelkem said as he caught sighed. Lumus groaned as he woke. "We have to warn the people. Get everyone to gather in the alley where I fought Ged. The hole I made in the wall can be their escape. I will go to the gates and hold them off." Lumus demanded. Orson's jaw dropped.

"Are you kidding me Lumus? I don't care how strong you think you are they will kill you out there alone." Orson replied. Lumus looked up at the sky as the Red moon began to set and the blue moon began to rise.

"He won't be alone." A familiar voice called out. Frostear stood in the dark alley behind everyone with Dyne, and a strange creature. Zephry had already noticed him arrive before the others, speechless upon seeing see he was safe.

"Don't be frightened of my friend here, his name is Zynx. He doesn't talk, but he is quite the listener, oh and sorry for shutting down my Inn. Zynx and I went out to see what all of the commotion was about. Seems you guys have been busting the city up on your visit." Dyne announced.

Dyne stepped into the light in the street. He wore a light green tunic with a purple vest. His arm guards covered the ends of his sleeves. At his waist, he carried a small fencing blade with a steel handle. Zephry stared at Zynx.

"Whoa, you're one big kitty. What are you, like seven feet tall?" Zynx grunted at Zephry and then

stood beside Frostear. They were just as tall as each other. Zynx wore a dark green tunic that only covered his left lower half. He carried a large spear on his back with a chain holding it to his body. It looked like it was carved from a fully grown tree.
"Okay, go warn the people, and head to the west opening we made earlier, Frostear let's go," Lumus ordered as he turned to the North Gate. Lumus began to make his way to the gate as the others took off in all directions.
Zynx ran after Lumus and Frostear.
"Hey Zynx, don't be a fool. Be careful." Dyne muttered knowing Zynx wouldn't hear him anyway.
"Our priority is to keep the townspeople safe, we can't let this town fall as Taurald did. These are not knights like in Taurald, so we can't let anything through. I'll take the left and you take the right. If anything makes it past then you go back." As Lumus spoke he gazed at what looked like a swarm of demons flowing down Nuran Mountains.
"Lumus we have a visitor." Lumus turned to see Zynx with his large spear in his hands. He was silent as he walked up beside Lumus on his left side.
"Alright, I'll take the middle waves. Frostear and Zynx, do everything in your power to hold off the sides." Lumus demanded.
Lumus drew his sword from his sheath. Frostear pulled his from his back. Whatever happens, it is an honour to fight with...both of you." Lumus laid

both hands on his hilt as his white cape waved in the wind.

"Everyone head this way, and don't bring anything with you. There is no time for luggage. Scarlette is the market district empty yet?" Scarlette looked over her shoulder to count "Yes, Dyne, Zephry, and Zelkem moved on to the houses at the rear of the town," Scarlette replied. "We need to hurry. Scarlette I need you to go out with the people, and lead them to the back of town." Orson added. Scarlette paused to think. "We will be cornered if we go to the cape. Isn't there another way?" Scarlette replied. Orson took a moment to think.

"No, farther south is also a dead end, and we can't cross the river to Torson region…the current is too fast. At least at the cape, we can defend them as a last resort." Orson sighed. Scarlette paused again. "Okay, I'll take them," Scarlette said with a shrug. Orson turned to Scarlette once more.

"Scarlette I will have Zephry and Zelkem follow after you when they return," Orson added. Scarlette pushed her way through the panicked people.

"Zelkem that's everyone I think. Let's go meet with the others now." Zelkem turned to the small palace near the rear of the town.

"Zephry the Councillors left before us from Capaz right?" Zephry turned to the palace. "You don't think Lady Councillor Tilza is inside, do you Zelkem?" The dust from the people panicking out of the city left the streets cloudy, Zelkem could barely see the palace doors to see whether or not they were open. He figured if people from the palace left they wouldn't take the time to shut the doors behind them.

"Zephry everyone from this area has cleared out. Head back to the others while go on ahead to check out the palace." Zelkem said. Zephry coughed from the dust.

"Okay, Zelkem be careful, and hurry back to us okay?" Zephry shot Zelkem a smile. Zelkem turned back to Zephry with a smile, and a thumb's up.

"Don't worry, I can handle myself. I'll catch up soon." Zelkem ran off into the cloud of dust, Zephry turned and made her way in back to the east wall.

Demons flooded toward Librine gates wave after wave. Lumus looked to his right to see Frostear grinning. At first, it scared Lumus, but as he thought about it may be having someone with the love of battle was a good thing to have fighting alongside him. To his left Zynx pointed his spear toward the demons, his expression was abnormally calm for what they were about to face, although Lumus felt that wasn't a bad thing either.

"(Lears must be desperate to kill me. There must be hundreds of demons racing toward us. I have to stay calm like Zynx. If I panic the others will most likely panic too. I need to preserve my energy as well. Twilight prison and the fight against Ged wiped me out before. If I use too much energy I might collapse again, and then I would be adding to the problem. Maybe I can use all of my energy to blast through them all. I still don't know my limitations though. I might not have the power to finish them all.) Frostear it looks like you are anxious for this fight, but I have to try something. You and Zynx might have to finish this without me if it doesn't work, think you're up to it?" Lumus called out.

"I have a feeling you have made up your mind already. Fine, work your magic. I'll clean up your mess." Frostear replied. Lumus looked over to Frostear.

"Hahaha, thanks. Let's hope this works then." Lumus threw his hands in the air as Frostear took a few steps back.

"Hey Zynx, I suggest you step back a bit, you might not want to be too close to Lumus when he launches his attack," Frostear shouted, but Zynx didn't budge an inch. Lumus began to glow as his body tensed. The ground beneath him began to crumble, small rocks started to shake then lifted from the ground around Lumus. He distorted gravity around him to prevent any sort of blast, or kick back attack on himself as he charged. Slowly Lumus' body grew brighter and brighter. His hands shot out in front of him, and Lumus let out a monstrous roar.

"What is that?" Orson yelled out. Orson was knocked to the ground as the shaking intensified. Orson looked toward the city gates to see a bright light illuminating the sky above the North Gate.

"That's too much power he's going to kill himself. Lumus don't do it. Damn it, he's going all out." Orson made his way to his feet.
"Orson! What's happening? Is that light and shaking coming from Lumus?" Scarlette cried out. Orson's eyes didn't move from the sky.
"Yes, it is. I think he is going to try and take them all out with one shot." Orson replied. Zephry's jaw dropped.
"Can...can he do that?" Zephry added. Orson finally looked Zephry in the eyes.
"Lumus is the most extraordinary person I have ever met, I think if he wanted to he could destroy the planet with his power," Orson said with a serious look in his eyes. Zephry tried to shake her head as if she was in a dream.
"Scarlette?" Dyne called out. Scarlette stood completely still staring at the sky.
"Dyne, it's Lumus. He's about to attack." Scarlette whispered. Dyne turned to the city. Everyone stopped to look at the blue light Lumus emitted across the city. Even though they were scattered around the city, they could all see Lumus' light forming near the North Gate, and hear his voice for miles. The villagers all stared in amazement at the beauty of the light from Lumus.
"It...it's time. Frostear if this doesn't finish them off it is up to you and Zynx." Lumus said with a grin. Before Frostear could respond Lumus let out a final yell as he released a devastating blast of energy. The power from Lumus formed into a wall of light wider than Librine, and it stretched from

Librine to Nuran Mountains. The beam obliterated everything in its path and at the last second Lumus pushed his palms toward the sky, and the wave's path shifted from the mountains safely up into the sky. For a few moments, Twilight was silent. Lumus turned his head to look over his shoulder, and before he could say a word he collapsed to the ground. Frostear rushed to his side.

"(Lumus, you are abusing our power. You don't know what you are playing with. I wonder what would crush you more; the fact that you think you are winning, or the fact that each time you use that kind of power the planet loses some of its star energy. You are like a child with a new toy. Simply lost in what you think is yours to use. It is almost time that you and I will face each other in a real feat of power. Until that time go ahead and waste all the star energy you want.)" Lears' thought to himself as he stood outside a cave in Aster Mountains facing toward Librine in the south. In the distance, the blue light from Lumus' attack began to fade. Lears watched, and as Lumus' light faded, Lears smiled as he turned into the darkness of the Aster Mountain caves.

Chapter Eleven: Twilights Cry

Light showered the Nuran Mountains as the new day crept over the Mountains. Librine slowly repopulated as the villagers made their way back to their broken homes, often in tears and disbelief as they passed Dyne and Scarlette.
"Dyne, Lumus could be hurt. I can't bear to see him like that again." Dyne stood still watching as people slowly passed him by.
"I will find out what's going on. Head back to the city and regroup at my inn. I'll let the others know to meet there." Dyne said before racing off from Scarlette's side.
"(Lumus why do you keep pushing yourself to your limit? If you die you're just hurting more people than you would save. We still need you.)" Scarlette's eyes began to tear up.
"Zynx grab Lumus' feet we have to get him some help." Frostear was in a panic, Lumus wasn't breathing, and he was scared Lumus may have pushed himself too far this time. A few moments passed as Frostear and Zynx carried Lumus into town.
"Hahaha, (Lumus you did just as I had hoped and now you have sealed your fate.) I Prince Lears can now take this world fully. My grasp on this planet will crush the life from all those that stand in my way. I will rule as king when the dust settles." Lear's laughter scared even his minions. Ged, you

and Coldblood worked the distraction beautifully." Lears added. Ged, Coldblood, and Tigra all stood smiling behind Lears as he laughed a cold humorless laugh.

"My prince what will you have us do now?" Ged bowed as he spoke, waiting for Lears to respond before he stood up again.

"Gather all of the Lords. I am certain Lumus' followers are feeling the burn of their loss. We will strike at once. Scarlette will be yours, Ged. Coldblood your father awaits your return I imagine. Go now, and do not disappoint me. I will not accept failure.

Ged and Coldblood marched off with their orders in mind, both left grinning knowing their orders were the ones they both wanted the most.

"Tigra did you complete the mission I asked of you?"

"Yes My Lord, without failure as you commanded."

"Good, wait for your new orders I will have something for you soon, my friend." Tigra left after a short bow to Lears. Lears stood alone in the misty mountains staring at the core of Twilight.

"(This is where it all began. This core gave birth to us both, and in that time we were born we were linked as brothers. Lumus, I may be a copy of you, but I have evolved to be much stronger than even I could imagine. The link between us is broken now, so you are either dead or have found a way to hide your energy from me. Either way, I will still be the victor of the two princes. You so-called Prince of

Light and I the Prince of Darkness.)" Lears laughed aloud as his dark mind was occupied with even darker thoughts.

Zelkem ran swiftly toward Dynes inn, Zephry trailed behind him slowly. She was worn out as she struggled to keep pace with Zelkem. Suddenly, as Zelkem had predicted, Frostear and Zynx came from the North Gate holding Lumus in their arms. Dyne appeared from the east entrance that Lumus had blown open earlier in his fight with Ged. Zelkem quickly noticed Scarlette was nowhere to be found.

"Dyne?" Zelkem said faintly. For a moment he paused wondering what Zelkem wanted, then as Zelkem looked back to the east wall Dyne realized he was looking for Scarlette. "She is fine; she is helping people back into the city." He reassured. Everyone gathered at the inn with concerns for Lumus, town's people began to gather outside hoping that Lumus was okay. Even with the rain pouring down they stood quietly with hope for his safety. Frostear laid Lumus upon a bed in the room beside the entrance of the inn, everyone waited outside his room in the lobby while Orson and Frostear stood to watch in the room with Lumus.

"Zelkem, did Orson say anything to you about Lumus? Is he going to be okay?" Zephry whispered. Zelkem was leaning on the front desk looking out toward the front door with his head down.

"Zephry I know as much as you do, and from what I saw he didn't look good." Zelkem didn't look up as he answered her. She took no comfort from his answer.

"Dyne, did Scarlette tell you when she was coming back? I'm worried about Brinx too, he didn't return to the inn so he must be with her." Zephry whispered again. Dyne and Zynx were behind Zelkem also looking out toward the front door.

"Scarlette just told me to check on Lumus. I think she is too scared to find out if he is okay. It doesn't take a genius to realize she cares for him." Dyne replied. Orson stepped out of Lumus' room with a smile. Everyone looked up at simultaneously.

"How is he?" Zelkem said as he rushed over.

"Look we have a few problems. I think it's in our best interest to have everyone present. Zelkem I need you to find Scarlette, and Brinx too, he seems to be missing. Gather them, and we can start." Orson demanded. Dyne stepped forward.

"I'll go, I know the shortcuts in this town better then Zelkem plus I know where Scarlette is. I'll try to find Brinx before I return too." Dyne interrupted. Orson nodded.

"Agreed, Zephry could you calm the people outside. Let them know Lumus is alive and he will be on his feet in no time." Zephry shot up to her feet. Instantly, with a perky smile.

"You got it, I'll tell them right away." Zephry smiled. Zelkem was restless.

"Well, what can I do? I feel useless." Zelkem grumbled. Orson put his hand on Zelkem's shoulder.

"Well I was going to do this myself, but I still fear for Lumus. He should be fine, but I do not want to leave his side. I want you to find Lady Tilza. I don't think she is in danger, but I still need to know she is okay. Losing a Councillor would cause problems we don't have time for." Orson proposed. Zelkem was confused.

"Problems? You know I don't understand you knights, and what you do or how you work, but if she dies would another not be elected to replace her?" Orson tightened his fist.

"There are things you are unaware of. I need you to do this for me, and I need you to go now." Zelkem didn't say another word. He knew Orson was serious. He turned immediately and left the inn.

Scarlette stood alone east of town near Nuran Cape. She was left looking into the sky as a faint drizzle of rain came over her. She saw a rainbow appear in the sky and shut her eyes.

"(Lumus, I know you're okay, I don't know how, but I can feel your life force.") Scarlette thought to herself.

("Scarlette I am just fine. I knew I would be okay, I'm sorry that I worried you, and I'm sorry that I was so reckless. I have been wanting to test my limits since I arrived on Twilight, and I will recover quickly. Don't worry.")

("How can I hear you in my head?") Scarlette thought to herself, shocked.

("That's a good question; I don't have all of the answers though, so I don't know. Orson sent Dyne to find you and Brinx. I came back to town and met up with him. Tell Dyne that Brinx will be back with Zelkem shortly after you return.") Lumus added.

("Lumus how could you know this? Are you psychic all of the sudden?") Scarlette said in confusion.

("It seems that I am getting flashes of visions. Something I have never done before. But we need to hurry now. Lears has sent his Lords to Librine, and we need to gather now. It seems Ged was able to transport Coldblood back to their lair instantly. I felt their star energy briefly disappear, then return just as fast as they left. I feel like this is something my mind can do when I harness too much star energy, or maybe this telepathic communication is an ability I have yet to master. ") Lumus explained.

("I imagine they have some tricks we don't know about just like we seem to have some they don't know. I'm on my way to meet with Dyne now. I will see you soon.") Scarlette opened her eyes to see Dyne making his way to her, and quickly she ran to meet him.

"I don't have time to explain, but we need to get back to the inn Dyne. Please follow me as quickly as possible."

"Sometimes I wonder what goes on in Orson's head. He seems to go on a power trip the moment Lumus is out of the picture. Blah, I'm the golden knight. Blah blah blah respect me, blah blah blah. He just thinks he's so much better than everyone else." Zelkem reached the palace as he spoke aloud to himself. When he reached the gardens, a grim scent met him.

"This place looks messed up. The guards are dead..." Zelkem kneeled down to inspect the body.

"Lady Tilza is missing, along with her followers." Brinx jumped from a window overlooking the palace garden.

"Brinx why are you here?" Zelkem replied. Brinx began to make his way to the inn. He paused and turned to Zelkem.

"I heard screams during Lumus' light show and when I got here they were already gone. The fight was a distraction, or had a dual purpose." Zelkem stood up as Brinx turned to look.

"Do you think Lears was after lady Tilza?" As Brinx walked away he yelled back

"That's a good question, though its one I do not have the answer for." Zelkem raced to catch up to Brinx.

"Hi everyone my name is Zephry! Lumus sent me out here to tell you he is doing fine. There is nothing to worry about." Zephry spoke to the townspeople as she began to go red in the face. A man and his young son stepped forward.

"Ma'am my son and I have come to offer our thanks. If you all didn't come when you did then the demons could have destroyed our town." The small boy approached Zephry with flowers.
"Hello, miss I picked these flowers from our garden. My mother used to look after them and I know she would want you to have them. Zephry kneeled down to thank the boy; it took her a moment to pick up on the past tense the boy used to speak about his mother.
"I am sorry to hear of your loss. I will take very good care of these flowers in her name." Zephry replied. The street went silent as people started to head back to their homes. As the crowd thinned out Zephry noticed Scarlette and Dyne coming from the east wall.
"Scarlette! Hi!" Zephry shouted out. As she waved to them Brinx and Zelkem appeared from the south path from the palace.
"Oh hello, Brinx, Zelkem you were quick! I take it things are okay at the palace." Brinx walked past Zephry into the inn with Dyne.
"Are they okay?" Scarlette didn't respond as she slipped in behind the others, leaving Zelkem to be the bearer of bad news.
"Zephry maybe we should wait until we get inside." Zelkem held the door open for Zephry; she paused for a second then entered the inn, her face showing how puzzled she was.
"Orson!" Zelkem called out.
"Everyone is here." Orson opened the door from Lumus' room and looked to see everyone waiting

in the lobby. The air was thick with tension and unanswered questions.

"Lumus is awake, but he's still in bed. He asked for everyone to gather inside.

One by one everyone made their way into the small room and found a place to sit. Lumus struggled to sit up, but he smiled to let everyone know he was okay.

"Hey guys, I'm sorry to worry you with my actions. I have a few things to say, so just hear me out. Also what I have to say may not make sense, but I'll try to tell you what I know. First I guess I'll talk about what just happened, the fight with the demons storming Librine was not just an attempt to kill us. Before I powered up to attack I could…feel Lears. His thoughts and mine almost felt like we became one. Lears was planning on using the demons to distract us so they could go to the palace and assassinate Lady Tilza." Lumus declared.

"Orson and I were talking about that briefly. Why would they do that? What threat could she be to Lears?" Zelkem's fist clenched tightly as he spoke.

"Lumus, I feel I need to tell them. I was told in Capaz by the council that each council member knows a secret about the twelve guardians of Twilight." Orson said, his voice faint.

"Lears plans to awaken the guardians to harness their power for his own needs. Only he and I could face a beast of such strength, that's what Lears thinks anyway." Lumus added.

"Lumus is right about one thing for sure; Lears is trying to harness their power, and Lady Concy warned me of this before we left Capaz. She said the council will handle themselves while we dealt with Lears." Orson added.

"I think our plan of action is to reach Councillor Cinnus in Aquoise, then head to Sagnet for Geare. If Lears failed here, he may try to get the information out of other council members." Frostear said from a corner of the room. Orson's face turned red.

"And what of Lady Concy and Gerald?" Orson blurted out.

"From reading Lear's thoughts I know he doesn't know where either of them is, which means neither do we if they didn't arrive at Piscyst. Gerald left Capaz in a hurry. I don't know where he is either." Lumus added.

"He's in Scorpial. I remember him saying he had business there. We need to find him." Orson added.

"Even if he is, he will not be a target," Lumus replied.

"Frostear is right. Our priority is Cinnus and Geare since we do not know where Concy is." Lumus said. Frostear stepped forward.

"Actually I know where she could be. I think she is on West Islands, Southeast of Fargon region." Frostear interrupted.

"How could you know where she is Frostear?" Scarlette asked.

"She is Drayhelm and my ex-wife." Frostear walked to the window to gaze outside. Zephry walked behind him and put her hand on his shoulder.

"She is Coldblood's mother isn't she?" Zephry asked. Zephry shed a tear as she asked.

"I was going to tell you Zephry, It's just…complicated," Frostear added. Zelkem turned to Frostear.

"Ex-wife? Sorry, it's just hard to take in because you didn't say anything this whole time." Zelkem blurted out.

"I was the reason she left Fargon. Not many humans know that Fargon was the Drayhelm's homeland. Over one hundred years ago when the dragon war began I was a young dragon with a wild spirit. Concy and I met on the battlefield, not surprising since we were only an army of less than four hundred or so. As you probably know from your stories the Dragon War lasted about ninety years and in that time we fell in love and had Coldblood. Our leaders let her leave the army to care for a child, and as for me, I was on the front lines. Concy became more and more scared of humans making it to Fargon, so she decided to flee to Piscyst in hopes of giving Coldblood to the humans." Frostear explained. Zephry moved her hand from his shoulder.

"She tried to give Coldblood to the people in Piscyst?" Zephry became confused. "Before the war, Concy use to travel to Piscyst a lot. It was her escape from home. She told me it was a very peaceful place, and she loved it so much that she somehow became the Councillor of the town. If the people of Twilight knew she was Drayhelm…" Frostear smiled uncomfortably.

"I see now why you didn't say anything Frostear." Said Orson.

"If anyone found this out, someone other than me, then she would have been executed."

"I would like to think we have bigger problems these days instead of allowing something like this to cloud your judgement Orson." Frostear turned to look at Orson.

"Frostear, I'm sure I can speak for everyone in this room; we are all like family now. No one would betray his brother." Zelkem ground his teeth as Brinx put his hand on his shoulder. He looked back to see Brinx shaking his head, and realized now was not the time for his temper, and he nodded back to Brinx.

"Look I don't want to rush things, but Lears has sent his Lords to finish the job here in Librine, I think it's time we think of what we need to do next." Said Lumus.

"What a coward! Always sending something after us…Lears can't fight his own battles?" Zelkem muttered under his breath.

"I vote we leave now, warn the villagers and then head out. We can't face them now not with Lumus out of the fight." Orson announced.

"I agree with Orson, I believe we have a greater purpose than to stay and fight with the pawns. Also, they could be distractions to stop us from

helping the other council members." Orson added. Brinx walked over to Orson to show his support.
"Lumus, I think you should decide. What we think doesn't really matter. You are our leader." Said Scarlette as she sat at the end of the bed.
"Truth is, I am no leader. We are all equals in this with a common interest, defeating Lears. I feel we need to do everything we can to prevent Lears from finding the other council members. We should leave for Sagnet to find Cinnus. Then to Aquoise for Geare." Lumus slowly climbed out of bed.
"Let's go, we can't waste any more time," Lumus said with a smile.
Everyone gathered their things and left the inn. Orson, Zelkem, and Frostear went out into the city to spread the word they were leaving and that Lear's Lords were coming back. Scarlette and Zephry waited at the city gates with Brinx.
"Zynx has shown your friends to the city gates, Lumus. I must say my goodbyes here, as I have a business to run after all." Dyne smirked.
"You two aren't coming with us?" Dyne sat in a small uncomfortable chair behind the front desk and put his feet up on the desk.
"You know, even if I am the best fencer in all Twilight my skills wouldn't help you guys. Zynx and I would just get in the way." Suddenly the inn door slammed open, and Zynx came running past Lumus grabbing Dyne's arm and pulling him into the street.

"Alright, alright old friend we'll go, man, I was setting him up to beg us to come, now how will I hassle a payday out of going with them?" Dyne whispered. Zynx pointed to the city gates with a grunt.

"Fine, but when you run out of kitty treats, don't come howling to me," Dyne added. Zynx turned to Lumus, and pounded his fist to his chest with another grunt, and began to make his way toward the city gates after Dyne.

"Those two will strangely fit in with the rest of us." Lumus thought.

"Lumus!" Shouted Orson.

"Hey, we warned the villagers, every one of them said they would just continue on with their lives. I think they are going to stand up to the Lords. Either your actions gave them courage, or they are still blind from your big flash earlier." Frostear began to smile.

"It is their choice Orson, we did all we could. Maybe they are tired of running? Dyne and Zynx seem to be joining in our travels. I just had an eventful chat with them." Lumus laughed to himself. Orson took a look toward the city gates and saw Zynx was kicking Dyne's backside as if to speed him up, as Dyne made a lot of rude hand jesters to Zynx.

"Look we have limited time. The councillors could be in danger as we speak." Orson turned back to Lumus.

"You're right Orson, we should head out. Everyone is waiting for us at the gates." Lumus added. Orson began to make his way to the others as he noticed Lumus drop to his knees.

"Lumus what's wrong? Are you okay?" Lumus held his head in pain, bringing his head almost to the ground.

"I...feel the planet it's...crying. I can feel its pain. It's telling me to...stop." Lumus let out a scream.

"Lumus, stop what? What is it telling you to stop?" Lumus suddenly leapt to his feet and began levitating where he stood. His eyes opened wide, glowing brighter than usual. An unnatural voice began to emit from him.

"I am Omega. The planets voice, the soul of the planet. You and your friends have caused this planet to suffer. As the keeper, I will not allow this to continue." Orson took a few steps back; he looked back to the gate to see that the others have not noticed Lumus yet.

"If you're the keeper of this planet you would know that Lumus and everyone that is with us fight to save you." Lumus' body began to shine a light so bright it engulfing his body.

"The Natural species of my planet are the only ones permitted to fight for their home. This Lumus is an unnatural being. His actions are threats I will not ignore. In time a warrior of my making will make my point clear. All that follows the unnatural being will be targets, if you choose to fight this warrior, I will be forced to unleash the ancients of the world." Suddenly Lumus' body shot light in all directions, throwing Orson across the street. Lumus fell to the ground, unconscious.

"Lumus! Wake up!." Slowly Lumus rose to his feet with Orson's help.

"What happened to you? Are you okay?" Lumus grabbed on to Orson to help himself to his feet.

"The planet, it spoke to me… and it is very angry. Twilight thinks I'm unnatural, a threat to it somehow." Orson looked back at the others once more. They still seemed to be unaware of Lumus and Orson.

"Orson, let's keep this from the others, for now, we have too much on our hands to worry them about this. If the planet sends something, then I will face it if I have to, but Lears is our priority."

The light rain began to fade, as the clouds began to vanish. Orson and Lumus didn't say another word until they met with the others. Scarlette and Zephry had gotten new supplies while the others were warning the village. Brinx, Frostear, and Zelkem stood farther down the path leading toward the North, impatient to continue.

"Listen up everyone. I'm sure this is obvious, but it is always good to review plans before setting off. We need to head North through Nuran plains, then cross the main bridge into Torson Region near Capaz. We all agree that it would be best to avoid main cities for now. It seems we cause more problems when we visit anywhere. Taurald, Capaz, and Librine were all attacked while we were there." Orson announced. Lumus stepped in front of Orson.

"Also we won't be stopping until Sagnet. We have never traveled through the night. Orson tells me it can be a lot more dangerous so we need to keep an eye open. If we split up at any time we meet in Sagnet." Lumus started to walk away, but then he paused once more.

"One more thing: If I could see into Lears thoughts there is a chance he saw mine. If this is true we cannot afford to stop. Orson has told me this trip will take about three days, and we have planned to stop at the half way point, but that's it. If any of you don't think you can make this trip. It may be best for you to stay behind once we reach Capaz." Everyone looked at one another, after a short moment Scarlette stepped forward.

"Lumus, we all know what's on the line here. We all have something to offer in our own way. We all need to stay together because together we are a team…we are stronger. Truth is we all have been brought together for a reason. There is no coincidence, and no mistakes with us all being here." Lumus walked on ahead to look out toward Nuran Mountains. Orson came up to his left, and then Zelkem to his right.

"We all have the same mission then, to save Twilight from Lears." Lumus smiled, then turned around.

"Then we stick together. All of us have lost friends, family, and our homes because of Lears. To me, all of you are my family. Since the moment I met every one of you, there have been moments where we have all been there for me. So let me be there for you. If you will let me I would like to lead you on this adventure." Lumus spoke with real emotion Scarlette giggled.

"Lumus, I'm sure I speak for everyone when I say this, but you already are our leader. From Twilight prison to Nuran it was you who brought us all here together, without you, I don't know where any of us would be." Lumus took a minute to look over to the others and saw they were all looking at him.

"I see. I won't let any of you down." Lumus smiled once again.

The group made their way down Librine's main path, as the people cheered for them, and they threw rice into the streets. Lumus looked back one last time, and waved to them, simultaneously giving hope to the people as they have to give to him. Light glistened off the river just west of town. Scarlette admired its beauty as she walked by. Zelkem and Orson walked ahead with Lumus unaware that Scarlette was slowing down.

"Scarlette! Hey Scarlette. " Zephry shouted behind him. Lumus turned to see what was happening.

"Is everything okay? You look distracted Scarlette." Lumus said abruptly. Scarlette looked ahead to everyone staring at her face becoming increasingly calmed.

"No it's nothing, it's just everything seems so peaceful that's all." Lumus smiled. Frostear sighed as he, Zelkem and Frostear passed them by. Dyne walked by with Zynx, and as they passed by he looked over to Zynx.

"Hey, buddy you think these guys are going to be this dramatic about everything that happens?" Zynx grunted.

"Yeah, I thought so too," Dyne replied.

"Scarlette we should keep going, we can't stop now. We've barely even left Librine." Lumus laughed. Scarlette laughed too.

"You're right Lumus, I'm sorry. It's just… we haven't had many peaceful moments lately." Scarlette replied as her smile faded. Lumus turned to the group walking off.

"I know, Scarlette. But that's why we can't stop. I don't want just moments. I want it to be peaceful all the time. I don't remember a time when we weren't fighting, even when I lived in Dystopia. I fought all the time, sometimes it was life or death there. So I know what I need to do and I know with all your help I can do it. I don't want to fight anymore, but until this is all over I have no choice, and it is you, Scarlette… I fight because of you. Even though I was born from the planet, at that moment I heard your wish. These memories have been coming back to me over our time together. I heard that you wanted someone to protect you. A warrior pure and strong to defeat the monster from your nightmares. That was your wish, right?" Lumus said softly, Scarlette was speechless.

"I will fulfill your wish it's what drives me each day." Lumus turned back to Scarlette to smile and then continued to follow the others. Scarlette stared as Lumus walked away, speechless. She looked once more to the light glistening off the river, and then followed behind Lumus.

"Hey Orson, What are we going to Sagnet for anyway?" Zelkem asked, eager to hear his answer. Brinx shifted his gaze over to see Orson's response.

"Well... Sagnet is a respectable town, but its slums have some pretty bad neighborhoods. The plan is to get some information on anything we can about Lears whereabouts. I'm certain someone there would work for Lears, but we are mainly going to make sure that councillor Cinnus is okay." Orson replied.

"I may have an idea, Orson." Brinx interrupted.

"What do you have in mind?" Orson asked eagerly. Brinx sped up to Orson's side.

"Lears knows us all, this is obvious. Yet he does not know of Dyne and his beast companion." Dyne clenched his fists.

"What did you say, green man?" Dyne shouted. Orson spoke as if he didn't hear him.

"I see. So you think we could send them into the slums to gather information?" Brinx nodded.

"It's brilliant! If they are willing to do this then we have a plan." Orson looked for a response.

"So what do you think, Dyne?" Dyne laughed.

"So the plan is to send me and my buddy here into a pub and have a few drinks, and try to listen to a few drunks talk? I'd be a fool to object to such a mission, wouldn't you say buddy?" Zynx grunted. Dyne smiled at Zynx then looked back to Orson.

"Yeah, we're in." Dyne finished with a smile.

Lumus looked at the sky and noticed the day was slipping away. Scarlette trailed behind with Zephry. Brinx was now leading the group with Frostear at his side. Lumus began to speed up to the middle of the group, and as he approached Orson's side he began to power himself up, emitting a dim blue glow.

"I'm starting to understand how to use my powers. I think I can keep this up for a while, at least for most of the night. We can make good time as long as we can see." Lumus said with excitement.

"You're like a little night-light, it's beautiful." Zephry smiled with her eyes locked on Lumus. Up ahead Brinx stopped walking and began to look around. Frostear looked back at Brinx with a look of concern on his face, everyone stopped.

"Brinx what is it?" Orson said quietly. Brinx looked to his right, then to his left.

"We are not alone. Something is watching us." Zynx ran to the front of the group drawing his spear as he moved.

"I feel an evil presence too." Frostear drew his sword.

Lumus clenched his fist as he began to power himself up. He glowed brighter, revealing hundreds of Krotins all around them.

"Everyone listen up, Frostear and Zynx take the front, Zelkem, Orson to the rear. Zephry and Dyne take the sides. Scarlette with me in the middle." Everyone ran into formation. Scarlette drew her bow and readied an arrow. Lumus noticed Brinx jump off into the darkness, but Lumus ignored it. "Take them out! Watch your flank!" Orson drew his blade and swung his sword as Zelkem ran to his side.

Lumus clenched every muscle in his body as he drew in star energy. Scarlette shot arrow after arrow trying to stop the Krotins from getting close to Lumus. Scarlette almost danced around him, her movement's swift, and light. She was almost touching Lumus with every move. The horde of Krotins seemed endless. Dyne thrust his sword quickly as he dove out of the way of two Krotin rushing him. Brinx came crashing down on them as Dyne passed them by, he turned quickly to see him jump off again. Frostear's sword shone as bright as day. His sword gleamed a red glow in its wake, making it almost impossible to track where he was attacking.

"Lumus, what are you doing? If you do what I think you're going to do then we will all go down in the attack." Frostear shouted out. Lumus was curling his body as he began bending his knees, his glow started to brighten around his hands, but faded around his body.

"Scarlette... I can control it. Don't worry, I won't hurt you." Lumus seemed out of breath. Scarlette lost focus on the battle as she worried for Lumus. A pair of Krotin dashed at Scarlette without her noticing. As they drew closer, Zynx appeared from behind them slashing one from the side. The power of the attack ripped the Krotin clean in half.

The other Krotin kept going toward Scarlette, Zynx jumped forward with his massive paws and grabbed it by its head. Quickly he twisted his wrists until Scarlette heard a loud snapping sound. As she looked, Zynx threw the Krotins body to the ground.

"Zynx... Thank you." Scarlette said with a nod. Lumus let out a monstrous roar then threw his hands out away from his sides, he opened his hands and twisted his body. He took a deep breath and closed his eyes, and he spun around like a twister shooting beams of energy. Scarlette dove to the ground while the others just stood looking back at Lumus. After a moment Lumus came to a stop. Scarlette looked up at him, but to her surprise, he looked fine.

"Lumus...? How did you do that? You beat them all!" Orson said with disbelief. Brinx came crashing down behind Lumus.

"We made too much noise. If you are fine I suggest we move, and quickly." Lumus nodded.

"There is no point sticking around. Everyone collect yourselves, we need to get going." Orson demanded. Lumus' glow faded. The Red moon lit the way for the others to follow.

Several hours had passed, and the group made haste as the first glimmer of the day was rising behind them. Rain fell on them lightly as they scurried by the city walls of Capaz. Scarlette turned to lay eyes upon her home once again, thinking she may not return again for some time. Lumus led the group, and everyone kept pace until he stopped without a word. Everyone slowed down wondering what happened.

"Lumus, are there more Krotins?" Zephry asked with a hint of worry in her voice. Lumus hesitated before he turned around.

"It's nothing, I just thought I heard something. It's nothing. Frostear, Brinx, take the lead. We are getting close. The two ran off leaving the others behind, Orson walked over to Lumus slowly giving the others time to leave.

"It's not nothing is it?" Orson seemed sure Lumus was hiding something from the others. Lumus sighed.

"I heard the planet again. This was different though. It didn't speak this time. I just heard something…something else. I could almost see it from its vibration. Whatever it is, it's big." Lumus replied. Orson put his hand on Lumus' shoulder.

"Whatever is out there I know we can handle it together. The truth is we need to tell the others. If this thing was to attack us they should know to be prepared rather then caught off guard. We can't let this distract us now. We can tell everyone in Sagnet. For now, we need to save our energy for the rest of the trip. Let's get going." Orson walked ahead but soon stopped to look at Lumus once more to see him staring off at nothing. Orson continued behind the others.

Lumus turned to Twilight Lake, just west of the city of Capaz. He paused to search the area for movement, hoping to see a glimpse of what he had sensed earlier. After a moment Lumus followed behind Orson.

Everyone ran with all their strength, knowing they would have plenty of time to rest when they reached Sagnet. Lumus caught up to Orson, and as he did Zephry reached a little hill just a bit ahead. She slowly climbed up to take a look.

"Look there it is! There's Sagnet just beyond the river!" Frostear climbed up beside her as the others kept pace, heading South.

"Yes there it is, but we still have another day's trip around the bend and through Valley Cove Region. Sagnet is a big city, easy to see, but still deceivingly far from this point" Frostear smiled. "Don't feel too bad about it, if we can see it, then we can make it," Frostear added. Zephry groaned.

"You say that like it will be easy...Aren't you tired?" Zephry replied. Frostear jumped from the small hill. Then he turned his head back to Zephry. He laughed once more.

"I've lived through worse," Frostear replied. Zephry groaned once more.

"What does that even mean?" Zephry said in confusion. Frostear laughed, and then he made his way south to the others.

"Hey, don't leave me here! I know we're in a rush, but come on!" Zephry scurried behind trying to catch up. She leapt off the small hill but slipped on her way down. As she got up she noticed the red moon had not moved.

"Strange, I thought it would be early morning by this time, maybe we are making better time to

Sagnet then we thought." Zephry brushed herself off as she rose to her feet. She glanced once more at the sky then ahead at the group slowly making their way out of sight.

"Guys! Hey, wait for me!" Zephry called out. Zephry ran off to catch up with everyone. Her face was slightly dirty, and her clothes torn, but still, a smile found its way to her face. Lumus turned back to see Zephry in good spirits, then locked eyes with Scarlette who returned his smile.

Chapter Twelve- New Enemies

Bright above, the red moon still shone down, and it wasn't alone. The blue moon was making its way over the horizon. The night was meant to fade, and the day was to replace it. Things began to feel unbalanced among the darkness. Monsters were still roaming the plains on the hunt for food, while smaller animals stayed in the shadows in fear.

Lumus led his companions through Canby region, passing the bridge dividing Canby and Torson region. Even at night, the group pressed on, knowing that anything could happen, that even Lears and his Lords could appear at any turn. Lumus turned back to the group to make sure everyone was keeping up. Orson brought up the rear, but Lumus noticed he was trailing. Lumus turned to let the others walk ahead of him, but Orson walked slowly behind. Finally, he made it to Lumus. As he did Orson stopped and paused nervously.

"Lumus, I think we are being followed. For some time now I have felt like something was right behind me." Lumus looked over his shoulder.

"Are you sure? Maybe you are getting paranoid." Orson took a step forward, and his hand rose to his sword's hilt.

"No, something is there. Listen closely." A small Krotin hopped out of the tall grass beside the path.

"A Krotin!" Orson ran forward with his sword drawn. Lumus bolted in front of him, drawing his blade against Orson's.

"Lumus! Why are you stopping me?" Lumus looked back at the small Krotin.

"Look, it's injured and alone. I can't allow you to harm it." Orson took a step back. He looked at the Krotin and then back at Lumus.

"This is not the time to be kind, these creatures are our enemies." Lumus turned and kneeled down to the injured Krotin. Orson sheathed his sword.

"Hey little guy, are you all right?" The Krotin shifted on the ground in fear.

"I'm not going to hurt you, here." Lumus put out his hand.

"My name is Jasper." The creature said with a quiet, snakelike voice. Lumus stood up quickly in shock.

"Krotin's can speak? I had no idea." The group was out of sight, Orson realized, as he turned to see how far they may have gotten.

"Lumus, the others have gone out of sight. We need to catch up with them." Orson interrupted. Lumus was still staring at the Krotin.

"We need to get going. Well then. Jasper, are you able to walk?" Jasper looked at Orson then back at Lumus.

"I fear your companion wouldn't think that a good idea." Lumus looked back at Orson. "Yes well, when I look at you I see someone in need, not an enemy. You are welcome to join us if you like."

Jasper rose to his feet then fell to the ground once more.

"I fear I am too weak to accompany you," Jasper replied. Lumus smiled.

"I suppose I will have to carry you then." Jasper smiled back. Lumus bent down as Jasper climbed into his backpack.

"Ha-ha, well that works! I guess you fit, so try to get comfortable. Orson, can you grab his spear and shield please?" Lumus headed over the hill to the others. Orson shot a glance at Jasper and noticed his eyes were closed.

"(Maybe he isn't bad after all. Lumus, you really are living up to what we thought; you are even taking pity on the enemy. I'm surprised to see how pure you really are, such a rare thing since all of this began." Orson packed Jasper's things into his bag and followed behind Lumus.

"Look up ahead," Zelkem said faintly.

"It's Sagnet, we are so close." Zephry jumped in a fit of joy.

"Did anyone else notice we didn't take a break? That was a lot of walking." Zephry said laughing. Orson caught up with Lumus while the others stopped to gaze upon Sagnet.

"Lumus? Why is there a Krotin in your backpack?" Zelkem stared at Jasper as Frostear drew his sword. Jasper quickly retreated into Lumus' bag.

"This is Jasper. Orson and I found him a while back. Jasper, say hi to everyone." Jasper poked his head out and looked at everyone looking at him.

"I'm Jasper. Hello." Zephry took a step toward Jasper and put her hand out to greet him with a smile.

"Hi Jasper, I'm Zephry. It's nice to meet you." Jasper reached out to shake hands with Zephry and smiled back.

"It is nice to meet you too!" Zelkem crossed his arms with a puzzled look.

"I didn't know you little bastards could speak! I mean really we have killed countless Krotin's, and none of them said a word." Scarlette smacked Zelkem in the back of the head.

"Ah what the crap was that for?" Zelkem said while rubbing the back of his head. Scarlette walked oversee Jasper and then turned to Zelkem.

"Have some respect, Zelkem. You don't have to be so insensitive." Frostear still had his sword drawn.

"I can explain if you like. You see not all of us are as evil as people think. There are three types of Krotins; three species of my kind. The first is the evil ones you would see working for Lears. They don't have the ability to speak, and they are mostly monsters, brutal savages that live for violence. The second race is mostly gentle but territorial over their land. They live in the south of Twilight. Then there is my kind. We are what is known among my kind as the elders. We are a dying race ever since Lears came to be." Jasper explained. Scarlette bend down to hear him better.

"The elders of my kind lived in south Twilight in a large region called Dongaro. We lived in a cave north of the region's great city. One day many years ago a young woman brought many workers to our home, not knowing that we lived there. She had them build an orphanage above our home." Jasper explained. Lumus bend down beside Scarlette.

"Jasper, why are you a dying race? Does Lears have people in south Twilight too?" Lumus asked. Orson approached Jasper.

"Allow me to help, little one. Jasper's people were killed by a man named Don, he is a very wealthy man that used his wealth to build a huge city. He burned down the orphanage. I don't know why. All I know is that only five children survived. I knew them very well. I do however know that Lears was the one that ordered Dongaro to burn it down, again I don't know why." Orson explained. Lumus stood up.

"How do you know this Orson?" Scarlette asked. Orson turned away from the group and looked down.

"When I left you as a baby in Dystopia, I knew the location of the temples that serve as a doorway to and from Twilight and Dystopia and headed straight for them. I made my way back here to Twilight, and I searched." He explained.

"Brother what did you search for?" Zelkem asked.

"I was looking for you. I went back to our hometown Geminite and asked around. An old man told me of a small homeless boy who used to come to his home and steal his crops. He told me one day the boy stopped coming around. I left and searched for almost eleven years. I forgot about

Lumus because all I wanted was to find you. Lears hadn't made an appearance at that point." Orson said as he wiped his tears. A single tear fell down Zelkem's cheek.

"That's how I know about the orphanage. I traveled to South Twilight, thinking you may have gone there. I found a woman that told me her sister built the orphanage, I had little hope at that point, but I went there hoping you may have made it home. I stayed there for almost a year. I left one day, chasing a rumour of a boy stealing food from people's homes. When it led to nothing I returned to find the orphanage had burnt down, and…" Orson's eyes began to tear again. Scarlette rose to hug him from behind.

"And my wife was dead, she didn't make it out of the fire, someone must have trapped them in the orphanage." Everyone gasped. Zephry finally stepped forward after a long pause.

"Your wife?" Zephry gasped. Scarlette hugged Orson even tighter.

"After I found her body I realized that I had lost everything. My family, my knights, I even lost Scarlette to those demons in Aster Mountains. I was beaten. I lost myself that day. I spent a few months tracking demons and killing them. It was the only thing that made sense to me. One day I left south Twilight and entered the temple to Dystopia, and that's when you found me, Lumus." Orson explained. Zelkem turned away, wiping tears from his face. Zephry had started to cry as she listened to Orson's story. Jasper sank to the ground where he stood.

"Don took the five children you spoke of. He used them, and last I heard they were trained as his personal bodyguards." Orson turned, knocking Scarlette off his back. "What did you say!? I left them in a cabin we built together. I don't believe you." Orson yelled. Jasper closed his eyes.

"When the fire started we raced out to try to free the children and the woman with them," Jasper explained.

"My Rose!" Orson shouted out.

"Yes, Rose. She was a kind woman. When we emerged to the surface, Don's guardsmen slaughtered my people. My elders and my friends…everything that meant anything to me. I set out to learn the summoning magic from my elder's old tales in order to get revenge. That is why I am here. Unfortunately, I have learned that summoning magic has been long lost." Jasper said, defeated. Orson began to calm down.

"Look at the moons, they're eclipsing" Lumus interrupted. Frostear sheathed his sword. "This is not right. Being a Drayhelm, trust me when I say this has never happened. At least not in my lifetime." Frostear announced. Jasper stood up.

"I heard the purple one say the sky shall turn purple like a poison, and…" Lumus looked down to Jasper.

"And what Jasper?" Brinx asked.

"The light shall fade." Jasper finished.

"The purple one?" Lumus muttered to himself.

"I don't see the big deal, the moons will eventually pass each other and will return to normal. It's probably just something that happens once every few hundred years or something." Dyne interrupted. He looked up smugly to the sky, as Zynx stood beside him without making a sound, staring at the sky.

"Maybe it is nothing. We still have to find Cinnus and Geare. We need to get to Sagnet quickly." Lumus demanded, and walked over to Brinx, facing Sagnet. He turned to the others, and then without a word continued toward his goal. As the others followed suit, Zelkem lingered and looked over at Orson before following the others.

"Orson, are you okay." Scarlette stood behind Orson, attempting to smile.

"I have come to peace with Rose's death long ago. I just haven't been able to talk about it with anyone. I tried to be strong for everyone." Orson said with a faint smile.

"Orson you don't always have to act so strong. Sometimes your true strength will only show when you let everything out. Too much on your mind, means you won't have full focus on the matter at hand." Scarlette said before following the others. Orson stood alone with his head down.

("Scarlette, when did you become so insightful.") Orson thought.

"So this is Sagnet? Dyne, are you ready?" Lumus stepped aside for him to pass.

"Drinks on you Zynx! See you guys later at the inn." Dyne and Zynx walked off toward the slums.

"I'll head to the counsellor hall. If Cinnus is here, chances are he's held up in there." Orson said. Zelkem followed behind him without a word. Orson noticed him follow but remained silent.

"We should head to the inn and wait for them to get back. Where is Brinx?" Lumus added. Frostear sighed.

"He's a quick guy. Just before we entered the city he jumped off somewhere." Frostear continued toward the inn.

"I guess that's kind of his thing," Zephry said as she smiled and followed Frostear.

"Lumus the money I got earlier from Lady Concy should cover the inn, but I'm afraid we are running low on funds." Lumus sighed when suddenly a bag of gold coins landed in front of Scarlette and Lumus. Scarlette picked it up then looked around in confusion.

"Sorry I can't come out, I'm sure the villagers wouldn't like to see a Krotin walking around," Jasper said from Lumus' bag. Scarlette smiled.

"This is yours Jasper? Thank you, but how did you get this?"

"Us Krotins aren't thieves, we used to mine our own gold in our caves, and when we needed food we would take it and leave a few coins behind," Jasper added. Scarlette looked at Lumus, still smiling.

"That's so sweet." Lumus locked eyes with her, wondering why she was smiling at him. She walked past him toward the inn.

"Are we off to the inn Lumus? There isn't a whole lot of space in here." Jasper said. Lumus hesitated, he was watching Scarlette walk away.

"Yeah let's get some rest, Jasper. Maybe you can tell us more about you. " Lumus finally replied.

"Master Lears, Lumus, and his followers have arrived in Sagnet. I believe they are searching for the councillor Cinnus." Coldblood said as he bowed. Lears gazed out toward the moonlit sky, the wind brushed by lightly as he laid his hands on the window ledge overlooking the scenery below.

"Yes, I can feel Lumus' power in that direction. He no longer concerns me, at least not for now. I can sense something else out there. Whatever it is it has a great power almost equal to Lumus and myself." Lears turned to Coldblood.

"Have everyone in that area retreat immediately. We shall leave this mess to Lumus. I can use this opportunity to focus on my other plans for Twilight's future." Lears demanded. Coldblood nodded, and turned to leave, just before he reached the door he turned once more to Lears.

"Master, what of the councillors our Lords are tracking?" Lears turned to Coldblood on a rampage. His energy radiating off him like a lightning storm.

"Must I repeat myself Coldblood? They no longer matter! We have bigger things happening now. Have My Lords' return at once. Lumus and his followers have no idea what pursues them. I believe we have just taken Twilight as our own without lifting a finger." Lears laughed. His laughter and rage combining into something terrible to behold.

"It will be done, master." Coldblood bowed. "Before you go Coldblood, I want you to send word. The councillors are not a priority any longer. Also, send word to Aire. I want him to track Gerald. Best for us to keep tabs on our investments." Lears closed his eyes tightly as Coldblood left the room. His body covered with a dark aura as he smiled.

"Zynx you would think this place would be a little more energetic? There are three people here, five if you count us? Hmm, maybe they all left town when your ugly mug showed up." Dyne let out a laugh. Zynx grunted lightly.

"Hey, waitress? Care to get us a couple of drinks? Jeez, you would think the business would be welcome... take your time love." Dyne shook his head. This place has to be the worst..." Suddenly Zynx shot to his feet. His teeth bared as he faced the doors, quickly grabbing his spear.

"Whoa boy, down. Down boy." Dyne looked over at the door to notice some purple smoke coming in through the bottom of the door.

"What in the world is that? Zynx you ready to fight buddy, buddy?" The waitress dropped the drinks she was carrying and quickly turned and ran to the back. The other three strangers followed behind her.

The smoke crept in faster and faster, the wooden door began to slowly expand and split in the middle, then suddenly flew through the bar into the bottles along the back. A strange silhouette entered the doorway.

"Would you two be friends of the one they call Lumus?" Dyne drew his blade.

"Who is asking?" The strange figure stepped into the light of the bar, revealing a man with purple hair and dark purple eyes to match. He wore a cloak and light clothes that matched his hair.

"I am Kontaminate." Dyne's jaw dropped, as Zynx raised his spear up a little higher.

"Is this some kind of joke? We didn't even get our drinks yet. What's the big idea?" Dyne dropped his guard. Kontaminate had an odd grin on his face.

"You don't seem to want to help me. Very well, I shall dispose of you insignificant little pests." Kontaminate raised his hand and a dark cloud of purple energy formed in his hand. Zynx raced at him with his spear. The energy around his body exploded, sending Zynx flying into the back of the pub and into the streets. Dyne raised his sword to Kontaminate once again.

"Hey, you bastard! I'll kill you for that!" Dyne leaped forward as Kontaminate swung his handful of energy from the air down to the floor. Just as Dyne was close enough he raised his hand to his face shooting the energy at full blast. Dyne flew straight through the pub's roof landing in the streets just pass Zynx.

"Lumus, now I can feel you. It seems your energy is revealed when you sense danger." Kontaminate laughed.

Lumus jumped to his feet, causing Jasper to fall the ground.

"Lumus? What's wrong?" Scarlette rose from her bed. Frostear entered the room from the sounds of Jasper hitting the floor.

"What happened?" He asked. Lumus closed his eyes.

"Something is here. Something powerful. It is coming from the slums. How did I not sense this sooner?" Lumus shook his head, opening his eyes as he raced out of the room with Frostear close behind him. Scarlette turned to Jasper and said.

"Stay here, this could be dangerous." She ran off leaving Jasper alone. Lumus stopped in the street. He closed his eyes once more and quickly facing toward the slums once again.

"This way!" Lumus shot off down the main street, and Frostear hastily turned to Scarlette. "Zephry left to the councillor's mansion to check on Orson and Zelkem. Go back tell them what is happening now!" Frostear yelled. He turned his attention back to Lumus.

"I don't even know what's happening..." Scarlette whispered she ran toward the mansion.

"That's right Lumus come to me. It shall all be over soon." Kontaminate stood peering into the main street waiting for Lumus. Dyne and Zynx lay unconscious nearby. Neither of them was moving. Lumus came to the top of the hill, and he glared down seeing the pub in ruins, then to his comrades lying face down in the street. Lumus turned back to the pub to notice a figure walk out toward him from the shadows.

"What is this? Lears? No this... is someone else." Lumus said in confusion. Lumus walked slowly down the dirt path from the top of the hill to meet face to face with this strange figure who looked just like him.

"So you finally showed. I have come to end your existence. You are an unnatural being. A poison that must be remedied. Lumus stared Kontaminate in the eyes

"A poison, you say? All I see from you is destruction and pain. Look what you have done here and yet I'm the poison? What does that make you?" Lumus replied. Kontaminate shot Lumus a grin.

"A simple answer, I am Kontaminate. I am here to poison this world. Infect it to cleanse it. I will enter the bodies of all living entities to kill everything you have altered. That is my purpose."

Kontaminate smiled as he stared at Lumus. Lumus clenched his fists.

"Who sent you? Why do you look like me? Were you born like Lears and I were from the planet's core too?" Kontaminate laughed.

"No, I was built with purpose, with a plan. You are an accident, a miscalculation in human actions. The one responsible for everything you see sent me to correct this world. Because of you, the people have come to harm and they have been thrown into a world that never should have come to be. For the crime of existing you have been targeted for disposal. I will use any means necessary to eliminate you. Even use the lives of others against you." Kontaminate glared at Lumus. Lumus stepped forward.

"I understand but I have too much to live for now. I will fix all of the wrongs my existence has brought. Then and only then will I willingly be taken to the other side." Lumus replied. Kontaminate hesitated for a moment.

"There are two? There is another like you in this world? I must investigate this being. My master only knew of one. Two brings more questions that I alone cannot answer. You have not yet seen the last of me. When I return you and I will fight, and I promise you my masters' desire to make the world as it should be will come to be." Kontaminate then suddenly lit up with a bright purple light and with a flash, he flew off into the sky.

"He can fly?" Lumus stared off into the sky until Kontaminate became a distant speck. He finally gave his head a shake and looked back over at Dyne and Zynx. Frostear was already with them. Brinx had appeared from the shadows, the hood of his cloak shadowing his face, but his eyes still glowed from within its depths.

"Lumus!" Scarlette called out. She came running down to the ruined pub with Orson Zelkem and Zephry behind them.

"What happened?" Orson seemed out of breath.

"It's difficult to say. Looks like Lears is not the only copy of me after all. I wonder if he was the one that spoke to me before." Lumus said with little certainty.

"Let's head back to the inn. We shouldn't stay out in the open, and Zynx and Dyne are in very rough shape." Frostear pointed out. Scarlette and Zephry made their way up the street. Zelkem and Frostear picked Dyne and Zynx up and carried them up the street. Zelkem hung back with Brinx and Orson. Lumus stood still without a word.

"I know everything is all unclear right now, but we don't have much choice. Let's go back to the inn and regroup." Zelkem said with a hint of worry in his voice. He waited for Orson and Lumus to move before he started toward the Inn. The Inn door was shattered into splinters, the windows broken with glass everywhere. The torches on the walls were all burnt out. The darkness within the inn made Zephry uneasy. Lumus and the others all gathered outside.

"Lumus, who do you think would do this? None of the other buildings are damaged except this one. Was someone looking for us?" Zelkem said. Scarlette felt a cold chill in the air.

"Orson comes with me, everyone else waits here." Lumus demanded as he powered up to emit a soft light around himself. He made his way into the inn with Orson behind him.

"Jasper was still inside, wasn't he? I told him to stay here. If he is hurt it would be my fault." Scarlette's eyes began to tear. Zelkem walked over to put his hand on her shoulder while he still carried Dyne on his back.

"I'm sure you did what you thought was best. None of us would have guessed the inn was going to be attacked." Zelkem looked over at the inn once more. Zephry stepped forward and cleared his throat.

"When we ran by the inn earlier it looked fine. We couldn't have been gone from here for more than ten minutes, right?" Zelkem moved his hand from Scarlette's shoulder.

"I would have heard the glass shatter; I don't know how this could have happened," Zephry said with worry. Brinx removed his hood.

"Look they are coming out!" Zephry called out. Lumus came walking toward them from the inn. The light was gone from his body, and his face looking down as he carried Jasper in his arms. He was bloody and beaten. There was no life left within his body, and Lumus knew it. He walked past everyone to the main street. Behind him was the pub far down the road they had just come from; in front was the way to the town's cemetery. Orson followed Lumus up the trail, as everyone followed behind.

"He was a good soul. He only meant to protect his people. For that Jasper, you have my respect. Although our journey together was brief, I still call you my friend. " Lumus said as he kneeled down, and laid Jaspers body into a hole Zelkem had been digging.

"I will be sure your people will be revenged for this Jasper. I promise you." Orson stepped back. "I promise the one responsible will die for this." Orson turned his face down as he spoke. Scarlette cleared the tears from her face with her sleeve.

"We should plan our next move," Brinx said with his cloak back on. Zynx woke up under a tree just inside the city gates where Frostear and Zelkem had set him and Dyne down. Zynx reaches down and gave Dyne a slap on the face.

"Ah, the heck was that for?" Dyne managed to open an eye enough to see he was okay.

"Look, buddy, I'm not as tough as you, I can't just pounce back up like you. No pun intended." Dyne laughed himself back to sleep.

Lumus stood over Jaspers grave with Zelkem, Orson, and Brinx to his right. Scarlette, Zephry, Frostear were on his left. They all looked at Lumus.

"Orson, Cinnus was okay right?" Orson stepped forward.

"Yes, and I asked about his Tilza. She had fled to Capaz. With Kontaminate around we need to be a lot more careful. We need to assume Geare is okay. I have asked Cinnus to send word of what is going on. The Knights will be able to take things from here. It is obvious Lears is somehow involved. Brinx shook his head.

"I know. Kontaminate flew off toward the North." Brinx added.

"Across the Twilight Lake." Zelkem interrupted.

"Correct. What is on the other side of that lake?" Brinx asked. The group went silent. "There is my hometown!" Zephry blurted out.

"The Aster Mountains are also over there. They overlook Capaz." Scarlette said faintly. "Then it can't be helped, we head back to Capaz. It will be another three days back." Lumus added. Zephry sighed.

"Maybe we can save some time if we swam across the lake." Zephry blurted out again. Orson laughed.

"That isn't a bad idea," Orson added. Zephry sighed again.

"I was kidding, we can't swim that far..." Zephry replied. Orson turned toward the lake. "No Zephry. We can take a boat. This is a fishing town is it not? All we need to do is find a captain to take us. When we were down in the slums I saw plenty of boats. There has to be someone to take us." Orson explained. Lumus walked over to the street and peered toward the lake.

"That would save us about two days. Orson, go see Cinnus and tell him we are taking a boat. Zelkem you, and Scarlette find us a captain. Everyone else stocks up on supplies we need to move now." Lumus ordered. Orson bolted off toward Cinnus's Palace. Zelkem and Scarlette headed toward the destroyed pub. Lumus looked up at the sky to see the eclipse moons high in the sky.

"(Lears, and now Kontaminate, this is getting complicated. Jasper rest well. You have lost so much, but I won't forget you. Thank you my friend.") Lumus thought to himself, then made his way toward the docks.

Orson came walking down the docks with Cinnus at his side. Cinnus seemed relieved to see Lumus in his city. Scarlette, Zephry, Frostear, and Zynx carried crates onto a large vessel. The ship's mass rose twenty feet into the air, the deck was big enough to fit a hundred people Zelkem thought.

"Hey Dyne, Brinx. How about helping out huh?" Zelkem called out.

"And take all of your glory? No sir, this is one battle you can be the hero of." Dyne laughed. Brinx turned his attention to Lumus, and Cinnus over by the destroyed pub. They were too far away to hear though.

"Lumus you don't have to worry about the damage. I understand that we are basically at war with Lears, and there is bound to be some damage." Lumus smiled.

"Thank you, Councillor Cinnus. We have found a captain that has agreed to take us across Twilight Lake." Cinnus smiled.

"At a cost I see. That would be Captain Nex. He is a good man, provides this city with a lot of tourism, because of that massive boat of his. If the stories are true it is the largest one on the planet. So he's making you earn your ride by putting your friends to work?" Cinnus laughed. Lumus smiled again.

"Yes, he refuses to let me help though. All he said was, save your strength lad, but I must thank you again, Councillor. We need to be going though." Lumus said with a bow. Cinnus stepped toward Lumus and put his hand on his shoulder.

"You be careful, Lears has been in the shadows all these years. We may fear him, but truthfully all people see are his minions doing all the work. I don't think anyone knows what he can really do." Lumus sighed.

"Yes, well I can't say for sure. I guess I will see for myself when I confront him." Lumus tried to reassure Cinnus. Cinnus smiled.

"Don't worry Lumus. Time will show you the way. Just wait while fate finds you a path. Lumus smiled but didn't say a word.

Orson made his way to the boat. Lumus turned to follow. He turned his head back to Cinnus.

"Thanks again Councillor. I hope to see you again soon." Lumus said as he waved farewell.

Lears stood in the deepest part of Twilight at the planet's core. He stared into the light of the core with his arms crossed.

"Soon Lumus. Soon." Lears laughed with a sinister smile on his face deep in Aster Mountains.

Chapter Thirteen- Kontaminate

The wind gently brushed against Scarlette's face as she stood at the bow of the ship. Zelkem leaned on the railing overlooking the lake. He occasionally glanced over at Scarlette. He noticed once in a while she would close her eyes, and throw her head back. He smirked.
"What is she trying to do?" He whispered to himself. Brinx snuck up behind him with his eyes on Scarlette.
"I would assume that she is currently living in the moment, it would seem she realizes the dangers ahead and is taking in what she can in case we meet our end upon facing Lears." Brinx interrupted. After his short rant, he gave Zelkem a moment to respond, but he didn't say a word. Brinx snuck away just as fast as he appeared.
"Lumus!" Orson shouted out.
"Come over here, the captain would like a word." He added. Lumus was sitting against the ships center mass. His head was down, and he was almost relaxed, His head rose, and he turned to Orson. Gave him a quick nod, and began to stretch as he got up. Lumus took a quick look back at Sagnet but was still in view.
"Lumus please, we need a word with you," Orson said calmly, he didn't want to let the others know there may be something wrong.

"What's the matter, Orson?" Lumus walked over and entered the captain's cabin with his attention to the window facing Dornet region. Orson sat down in an old chair. He looked over to Lumus and then looked over to the seat across from him. Captain Nex was sitting at a grand table made of old mahogany. His feet were up, and his arms crossed with his eyes closed. Captain Nex wore a black vest with brown baggy pants. He also had a brown undershirt with a black belt stretched from left his shoulder to his right side.

"Lumus, I have been given new information from a mate of mine residing over in Canby. My contact and I exchange information here and there to keep up to date on sea-related events. At any rate, he has mentioned a large unidentified creature making its way up the south waterways. From the note, I can say this is no friendly creature, and it must be dealt with immediately. So here is my question for you, you and your mates are all adventurers, and have skill in battles, so I offer you this..." Captain Nex sat up, he walked over to the window behind his desk.

"Do you see that cave there by the waterfall?" Captain Nex continued. Lumus stood, slowly made his way beside the captain, and peered toward the waterfall.

"I see a small opening, yes" Lumus replied. Captain Nex nodded.

"In the cavern leads a single path to an underground waterway. That is the resting ground rumoured to be the beasts' lair. I propose you, and your mates go inside, and slay the beast." Captain Nex sat down once more. Orson stood with his arms crossed, and his head down.

"I know we are going to find Lears, and we need to end his plot, whatever it may be, but I have been talking to the captain, and we both agree that this is a priority. If we let this beast continue roaming the seas it will potentially harm the lakeside towns, and anyone out at sea such as us if we are to need Captain Nex's services once more. So we need to know if you agree since you are our leader." Orson explained. Lumus turned to Orson. "Yes. We shall deal with the beast. Our goal is to stop the harm to the people of Twilight anyway we can. Lears can wait, with luck he will still be where we think he is, but we can't let the people live in fear of anything, not just Lears. Captain, Do you know how far the cavern goes until it reaches the creature's lair?" Lumus asked while looking out the window.

"Unfortunately no, but I can position my ship behind the falls to stop it from escaping while you, and your mates make your way down." Captain Nex replied. Orson nodded. "Yes, also Lumus we should leave a few of us on the ship in case the beast tries to attack it while we are gone," Orson added.

"We need to leave half of us on the boat as a distraction, and as a defence, so the rest can enter the lair. Orson, you keep Scarlette Zynx and Zephry on the ship, I will take Brinx, Zelkem, Frostear, and Dyne with me." Lumus ordered.

Orson nodded then headed for the door. He turned his head back to Lumus.

"I will tell the others the plan, also I will have the ship turned to our new course." Orson left the captains room and shut the door behind him.

"Lumus I must say I thought you would have said no to all of this. Orson told me why you all need to cross the lake in the first place. I thank you, sir, when this is all over the sea will be a safer place." Captain Nex sat in his chair. Lumus took a look out the window for a moment.

"It will be a better place for everyone. It is because of me that everyone lives in this nightmare. It is only right I am the one to set things right again." Lumus explained.

The boat began to turn; Lumus and Captain Nex made their way to the deck. Brinx, Frostear, Zelkem, and Dyne stood by the cabin waiting for Lumus. No one said a word as Lumus walked by. Orson had the crew ready the cannons from the one side to all face the waterfall for their defence. Captain Nex raised his arm, with a swift movement of his hand his crew shuffled to various locations around the boat. The boat turned just missing the water crashing down into the lake, Lumus ran up to the railing and took a quick look below. There was a small landing he could see that looked safe enough to jump down to. He turned to Brinx, and the others with a quick nod then turned and jumped overboard. As he landed he rolled and scanned the area once more. Brinx leaped just past him with a soft landing. Zelkem jumped over and landing with a minor thud. Dyne walked over to the side of the boat.

"Yeah, I'm not jumping down there. You guys must work out a lot cause that would hurt like crazy." Dyne slowly climbed over the railing. The crisscrossed rope along the side waved along with the boat. Dyne looked down and sighed.

"You guys are nuts, and what's at the end of this crazy ride? A big creature we know next to nothing about…wonderful." Dyne yelled out. Dyne made it about half way down the ropes when a small wave shifted the boat up against the rock line. Dyne reached but missed then fell crashing down onto the rocks below. Zelkem approached his side.

"I hope you're better with that rapier then you are with heights…" Zelkem reached his hand to aid Dyne.

"Real funny there little man, how about we leave the one liner's to me yeah?" Dyne disregarded Zelkem's hand and made his way to his feet. He brushed himself off and turned to see Lumus and Brinx waiting at the cave opening. Zelkem and Dyne looked at each other, then Frostear came crashing down beside them. "I guess it's time to get serious," Zelkem said with a laugh as he waved his hand to brush away the dust.

"Look we don't know what to expect, everyone keep your eyes open, Brinx you lead the way with your night vision sight, and I'll take the rear. Try to be as quiet as possible so we don't stir up any unnecessary trouble." Lumus said as he allowed

the others to pass him. Brinx entered the cave following Dyne and Zelkem, then finally Lumus.
"I will stand guard at the entrance. Don't worry. If the beast somehow makes it up here he will have me to deal with." Frostear said. He smiled as the others continued into the cave.
"Okay they're in, everyone get ready there is no way to tell how long this will take." Orson alerted the others. Orson looked up at the falls. Scarlette readied her bow. Frostear closed his eyes while he drew his sword. Zynx unclipped his spear from his back harness. Orson looked back to see everyone was ready in their own way, once more he looked back to the cavern entrance.
"(Lumus, be careful down there, this isn't our fight as much as you may think. Defeating this beast is really only slowing us down.)" Orson thought to himself.
Brinx leads the way down the narrow cave, he paused once in a while to listen for anything up ahead. The others didn't question his methods, they just simply followed as he proceeded. Brinx noticed further up, there was a small opening letting down a small amount of water from the falls above.
"Lumus, it seems the cave structure is not as strong as we thought. It would be best if we made haste to the beast's lair." Brinx said as he kneeled to see where the water was heading from its fall.
"There seems to be no water on the ground here, the water must be falling further down. Lumus moved up from the back to investigate for himself.

"Yeah, I agree. Never know what may happen, or when the rocks may give out." Lumus turned his attention to the light up ahead.

"Look over there; I can see some light shining in down this path." Lumus pointed out.

Zelkem sighed.

"Let's hope this beast likes company," Zelkem replied as Dyne laughed.

"Yes, I suppose that would be nice for a change. Although we wouldn't be down here in the first place if it was known as a friendly monster now would we." Dyne laughed once more.

Lumus made his way toward the light with Brinx, and Dyne close behind. Zelkem kneeled down to look at the water falling down the cracks. He put his hand on the ground to detour the water.

"What is that?" Zelkem stood up to notice the others had gone without him. Zelkem looked to the right. It was pitch black, but Zelkem could tell that the area was wider than the others had thought.

"Hey, guys I found…" Zelkem stopped talking as he entered a large room. Lumus Brinx and Dyne all stood just a foot from the path, they entered the beast's lair, and it stood staring back at them.

"Spread out, don't give it a chance to attack," Brinx called out.

The beast was pure blue with gold around its four legs, its neck stretched high, and its tail ended with a large golden spike. It almost resembled a dragon but had too many other features that seemed unique to this monster.

Lumus began to glow with a yell. Brinx leaped over the beast. Zelkem and Dyne both dashed to opposite sides to get to the beasts back.

Dyne and Zelkem stopped before making it to the back of the cave. Brinx landed on the beast's back. Brinx landed on the creatures back causing it to fall to the Zynx charged with his spear, but a fierce strike from the creature's tail flung him across the cave. Lumus launched himself at the creature toward its face. He threw a devastating kick that stunned the creature. Lumus landed just in front of the cave entrance.

"Everyone move!" Lumus called out. Dyne and Zelkem ran behind Lumus. Zynx laid on the ground still winded from the creatures attack. Dyne quickly realized and ran to his side. Dyne used every ounce of strength to lift Zynx over his shoulder. Lumus yelled out will a flash of light. He put one hand up, and his palm facing the creature. Lumus shot a large sphere of light at the creature, but to his amazement, the creature's tail countered Lumus' attack back at Lumus. Lumus was hit with his own attack. He had no time to dodge at all. His own attack flung him back into the cave walls behind the entrance. Dyne looked at Zelkem, and Zelkem looked at Dyne.

"Lumus and Zynx are out Dyne. Make sure you watch over Zynx. I'll hold this thing off!" Zelkem assured Dyne.

"Don't get yourself killed man!" Dyne called out. Zelkem ran at the creature with his fist clenched. The creature let out a roar and noticed Zelkem running toward it. It swiped its tail at Zelkem, but he jumped to avoid it. Zelkem stopped then began to chant words under his breath.

"Rambosho!" Zelkem yelled out.

Suddenly Zelkem's fists began to glow faintly. He took two steps toward the beast then disappeared. Dyne was watching with confusion.

"Where did he...?" Dyne whispered to himself.

After a pause, Zelkem reappeared striking the creature with a hard punch to its head but then disappeared once again. With a second of delay, Zelkem appeared again with lightning speed striking again. Each time he disappeared, he reappeared faster and faster. Eventually, to Dyne, it seemed like Zelkem was in a dozen places at once. Each time striking with powerful blows to the creature. Zelkem finally appeared above the creature with his fists facing down as he dove into the creatures head. The creature fell hard to the cave ground. A small shake woke Lumus from the cave floor.

"Zelkem!? Lumus looked over, then he ran to Dyne's side.

"He did it Lumus, I don't know how, but he did it," Dyne said with relief. Zelkem walked over with the light around his fists slowly fading.

"Zelkem... That power? You have learned how to utilize star energy?" Lumus asked.

"I suppose, though I didn't know that was what it was called. I call it Rambosho. I learned it from... well, that's another story." Zelkem smiled.

Suddenly a huge crash shook everyone to the ground. It continued for some time. Lumus rose to his feet.

"Orson, the boat." Lumus ran out the cave door. Orson turned to the others.

"Come on, the roof could collapse. We need to move outside." Lumus shouted.

"You want to live to see the next day don't you mates, move your asses to shore!" Captain Nex and most of his crew stood on the rocky shore watching their massive boat sink to the bottom of the lake.

"Salute men that is your life sinking there." Captain Nex said as he squeezed clenched his fists. Lumus now stood behind Captain Nex out of breath from running up the waterfall path.

"Captain, what happen here?" Captain Nex turned to look Lumus in the eyes.

"The boat drifted into the falls." Captain Nex replied. Lumus looked out to the lake. "Captain we ah, we defeated the beast." Captain Nex turned his attention to the sky. "Then what is that?" Captain Nex pointed. He pointed up to the sky. A small shade was seen in the purple moon. Almost looks like a dot. In a flash, the dot disappeared from sight. Lumus readied himself.

"Captain, get the rest of your men into the cave," Lumus demanded. Captain Nex starred at Lumus for a moment.

"You heard him, boys, get your asses in the cave. ....Seven eight and nine. That's everyone Lumus." Captain Nex called back. Lumus' power started to shake the land. His entire body began to glow brighter and brighter. His eyes overflowed with energy.

"Lumus, what is it?" Zephry asked. Lumus could hear the fear in Zephry's voice. "Kontaminate is back. Everyone follow Captain Nex through the caves." Lumus bent his knees and tightened his fists.

"Lumus are you sure? We can help you here." Scarlette tried to yell over the gust of wind blowing off of Lumus. Orson grabbed her arm and pulled her into the caves. Lumus looked back to see everyone has made it safely into the cave.

"I warned you Lumus, I told you that you had limited time. I had to see this Lears for myself. Now that I have I know that you both must die. Abominations will not be allowed to live. Now die!" Kontaminate shouted.

Kontaminate began to glow bright purple. His back stretched out, and thorn-like spikes pierced out of his back, and elbows. He landed on the rocky shore facing Lumus. Lumus had his back to the path entrance. Lumus charged Kontaminate and threw a heavy attack at Kontaminate, but he had missed. Lumus jumped over Kontaminate and elbowed him in the back sending him flying across the ground. Kontaminate got up quickly, and he raised his arms and closed his eyes. Lumus crossed his arms in front of his chest and braced himself. A light from Kontaminate's hands formed a ball. Lumus starred at Kontaminate waiting for the attack. He separated the ball of energy into both hands and he rushed forward at Lumus, just before he reached Lumus he through the energy from his left hand throwing his body into a right spiral Lumus slapped the energy away, firing it through the massive falls. Kontaminate was still spinning in the air, suddenly the other energy shot out at a tremendous speed hitting Lumus square in the chest. The impact blew Lumus off his feet and slammed him into the rock wall. Debris fell, covering Lumus entirely.

"Surprisingly easy to defeat you Lumus. I have to say if Lears is as weak as you, then I am wasting my time here." Kontaminate turned his back and made his way to the cave entrance.

"It's not over!" Lumus yelled. Lumus flew like the speed of light out of the debris. He grabbed Kontaminate by the head while he flew by, just before Lumus hit the wall he stopped while spinning his body. He released Kontaminate in one swift movement sending him straight out the falls, and into the sky.

"(Ah, I can't move. How can he throw with such power? I can't even slow myself down. What…what is that?)" Kontaminate could see a small light coming from behind the falls suddenly it got bigger, then he knew. It was Lumus flying through the falls directly at Kontaminate, but Kontaminate couldn't move to defend himself.

"I choose my destiny!" Lumus yelled as he flew from behind the falls, and landed a devastating punch, at lightning speed, to Kontaminate's face sending him flying far into the sky past the clouds.

Lumus looked back up to notice Kontaminate wasn't even in sight.

"I must have hit him harder than I thought." Lumus sighed.

"Falling from this far is going to kill me, come on think…think." Lumus tried to mimic Kontaminate's attack but aiming it at the water below.

"Alright here goes nothing!" Lumus faced his hands toward the water below, he closed his eyes, and slowly a white light grew bigger and bigger from his hands.

"Now!" Lumus opened his eyes and shot the energy with everything he had. The force of the blast was enough to stop him, and even raise him into the air a bit. The water shot up in every direction around Lumus. After a short pause the force gave out, and gravity took over. Lumus fell lightly into the water just missing the stern of the boat that got caught on the rocks just below the surface. As he made his way up the rocky shore, and into the cave entrance Lumus looked down to notice a huge hole in the ground. Lumus peered down into the hole for a moment. After a quick look around he continued down the path.

"Lumus! We heard a bunch of loud crashes. Next time I'm coming with you." Scarlette hugged Lumus tightly.

"I'm fine, you don't need to worry Scarlette. Zelkem earlier you noticed a crack in the ground. During my fight with Kontaminate, I think it opened. The cavern below is very massive, and it got me thinking, with enough people we can turn this place into an underground city." Lumus explained. Orson sat down.

"Lumus you could be on to something there, what if we dug tunnels to each of the major cities. We could then tell the councillors of the tunnels, and if Lears or anything for that matter attacks, the people can escape to this place." Orson added. Zephry smiled.

"Oh, we get to name the city! We should call it Neutral City!" Everyone turned to Zephry. Lumus sat down beside Orson.

"Actually Zephry that is a perfect name. We need to think hard about this, I gave a quick look down there, and there is no actual sunlight so we would need to plant outside. I was hoping to make the city self-sustaining." Scarlette suggested. Lumus put his head down. "Lumus I'm not an expert, but this chamber is big right, big enough to plant a lot of crops? Also, it is right beside a waterfall so planting and watering would be easy in this chamber right?" Captain Nex added. Lumus looked up and surveyed the chamber.

"Yes, Captain Nex you are a genius," Lumus said then smiled. Captain Nex smiled too.

"I know you have much to do with Lears out there, and all those monsters stirring up the planet, so you leave the digging to me and my mates." Captain Nex said with a proud tone. Scarlette walked over and gently took Captain Nex's hand.

"Thank you, Captain Nex." Scarlette smiled.

"You don't have to call me captain anymore. I don't have a boat anymore so just call me Nex." Nex replied.

"Alright, so we will rest here tonight, then head back to Capaz in the morning," Lumus announced. Nex walked over and put his hand on his shoulder.

"While you guys rest we will start to dig you a tunnel to reach Capaz. Remember, send anyone you can to help. Not too many people just anyone that can be useful to the starting of the build." Nex added. Lumus nodded then walked off to find a place to rest. He looked to his side, and everyone was already sitting on the rocks. Zynx stood staring out toward the waterfall. Lumus walked over to join him.

"Hey, Zynx, why don't you get some rest with the others? We have a long walk back to Capaz tomorrow." Zynx didn't move, he stood still staring out the waterfall. Lumus looked out, but couldn't see past the heavy falls.

"I'll leave you on guard duty then." Lumus smiled, then stopped for a moment with his eyes open wide.

"(Kontaminate, he is still alive. I can feel his energy from here.) Zynx can you feel Kontaminate too?" Lumus asked. Zynx finally turned to Lumus, then pointed toward Zangus region in the far north.

"Yeah I'm guessing he would have landed by now, but I can sense his energy from here. He isn't gone yet, it seems he is going to be a problem after all."

Lumus added. Nex walked over to join Lumus and Zynx. Zynx crossed his arms as he turned back to the falls.

"Lumus I couldn't help to overhear your conversation. If that chap is still kicking do you think it wise for my men and me to stick around here?" Lumus shifted to Nex, he paused for a moment and sighed.

"Truthfully I don't know. I think he is really only after me. I think once we leave he will know, and his reason for coming here will fade. Kontaminate is a threat yes, but only to me. You and your men can continue without worry. We should just focus on what we both need to do. I have a feeling Kontaminate isn't one to back down, he will follow us, and I will have to face him once more." Nex laughed.

"Yes, but now he knows you are no pushover I'd assume. I don't know what you did, but when those lights through the falls faded, and we heard that loud bang in the air your friend here turned and has been standing calm in that very spot ever since. I think he can feel his energy as you can." Nex said with a concerned look in his eyes. Zynx turned his head to Lumus. He nodded and turned back.

"I will count on you for that ability in the future Zynx," Lumus said.

Lumus walked over to Scarlette and Zephry, the two had fallen asleep. Lumus smiled and looked over to see Zelkem, Frostear, and Orson had fallen asleep as well. Brinx was kneeling by the cave path looking out. Lumus assumed he was keeping an eye out while the others slept. Dyne wasn't in sight Lumus noticed. Lumus looked around to double check, but he still wasn't found.

"Brinx, have you seen Dyne?" Lumus whispered. Brinx didn't even turn to face Lumus. "Yes, he followed down to the lower chamber with Nex's men," Brinx replied.

"(He must be helping with the dig. I guess I'll leave him to do as he wants.)" Lumus thought. Lumus headed close to the falls on a small rock and laid down beside it. He moved around for a moment to get comfortable. He ended up lying on his back with his arms crossed across his chest. Scarlette snuck over, and laid beside him, she cuddled close and threw her arm over his chest.

"Scarlette?" Lumus looked down to see her eyes were already closed. He smiled for a moment and slowly closed his eyes.

"Lord Lears, I seek an audience with you," Ged announced. Lears stood over a large table looking at some maps.

"Yes enter, what is it Ged?" Ged entered from the shadows. Coldblood, Aire, Levitz, Hedree, Jol, and Tigra followed after him.

"My Lord we have gathered as you asked. The others have their reports." Lears looked up to see everyone has made a semi-circle around him. Lears crossed his arms behind his back.

"I see. Then I will start with Tigra. What news do you have Tigra?" Tigra took a step forward, he dressed in a dark cloak with a hood. He carried no weapon, but his claws hidden in long fur.

"My Lord I have been in Varlif region in the town of Ariond. The people there have only heard rumours of Lumus and his followers. No sightings of Kontaminate yet in Ariond." Tigra said as he bowed to Lears. Lears moved on to Jol. A small girl with a dark green cloak, and a light green mask covering her face, except for her eyes.

"I don't know you, Ged. Why do you bring this child, and call her a Lord? Is this a joke?" Lears began to lose his temper. Ged stepped forward.

"My Lord she is an orphan from Seaside Orphanage in south Twilight. This child is highly trained with daggers. She is quick and agile, even at her young age she is unmatchable in stealth." Ged stepped back.

"Hmm, step forward child." Lears smiled. Jol stepped forward.

"My Lord I have seen Lumus, and his friends pass through Valley cove region heading North." Lears sighed.

"Is that all?" Jol felt nervous in front of Lears.

"Well child, you have proven more useful than the rest of these fools." Jol stepped back. Hedree moved forward.

"My Lord I was…" Lear raised his hand to Hedree.

"Ged …" Ged stepped forward once more. To make this easier explain where these new people came from would you?" Ged bowed.

"This is Hedree I personally recruited him from Geminite, the Ebony and Ivory region in the southern part of North Twilight. He was a cage fighter, the champion actually. His hand to hand combat is very impressive." Lears looked back to Hedree. Very well continue.

"Next is Levitz, I found him by Piscyst robbing, and murdering a traveling merchant, and his followers," Ged announced. Levitz wore arm guards from his wrist to his elbow. He wore a black shirt with a green vest over top, and a double-ended dagger was latched to the back of his belt, his pants were tight till his knees, and began to get baggy from there to his balky boots.

"Last we have Aire. A hand to hand specialist. I found him wondering the Northern border of Zangus and Dornet regions. I have posted him in Aquoise" Aire wore a pink shirt with a black vest over it. His pants and boots matched as well. He wore a wristband on his left arm and a bracer on his right hand that stretched from his hand to his elbow.

"I don't feel like wasting my time listening to failed reports, step forward if you actually have something to report," Lears demanded. A few seconds went by then Ged, Aire and Coldblood stepped forward.

"Aire was it? What do you have to report?" Lears walked back to face Aire.

"I have seen a man fall from the sky in a purple light. I heard a loud crash, he must have landed in Zangus region just after I met with Ged. The man passed by me while I hid in the trees by Dornet boarder. I saw him head south toward Torson region." Aire stepped back. Lears turned and uncrossed his arms from his back.

"My Lord, what Aire says is true. I have collected information, and it seems his name is Kontaminate. The people of Leodot talked about him stopping there, and telling them he was looking for Lumus, and you." Ged added. Lears turned to Ged.

"Looking for me? This fool must be insane to be looking for me." Lears laughed.

"My Lord as a Drayhelm I can tell you I sense this being isn't human. I can't say what he is, but I am certain he is not human. Nor does he emit the energy of a demon. I can't say what he is." Coldblood interrupted. Lears turned to the large table.

"I see, Ged you shall keep me posted on this. On to more important topics. Some of you are new here, so know that I do not accept failure. Remember that. Second. Ged and Jol stay where you are the rest of you will follow orders I have already given to Tigra. Now leave my sight." Lears demanded. Everyone left the room in a hurry. Lears went back to his maps at his table.

"My Lord I believe it wise to add more demons to patrol the area," Ged suggested. Lears looked up at Ged.

"You do not need to tell me how to go about my business, if I need something of you, you will know. Jol, child I have a new task just for you. I want you to go to go to south Twilight and deliver a message. Tell Dongaro, I have not forgotten." Lears smiled. Jol quickly nodded to Lears, then fled out of the dark chambers.

"Ged you have brought me many new Lords, we have finished recruiting for now. I want you to focus on keeping these fools in check. I promote you to Overlord Ged, Your title means that you are now in charge of the other Lords. You will use your shadows to travel as you have, but now I want you to keep tabs on them. Watch them, and make sure they don't betray me. We want the people to fear us. I don't want these new Lords killing the people I am to rule. I decide who dies, make them remember that." Ged took a moment to soak everything in.

"Yes, Master. I will tell them immediately." Ged said as he bowed to Lears. Lears turned back to his maps.

"From now on Ged, You are the only one to enter my chambers. I don't need to deal with the peons anymore, I know who they are now. Keep them in line. Now go." Ged backed away slowly as he bowed. He vanished into the shadows in the blink of an eye.

"Kontaminate, so that is the other energy I felt. It seems that another player has entered the game." Lears clenched his fist and began to draw in dark energy around his entire body. Suddenly demons emerged from portals all around the room. Over fifty demons appeared within seconds. They were a sleek black with a shine to them in the light.

They were shaped like large dogs with razor sharp claws, and a massive head like a wolf without the fur.

"Have six of you outside my door, the rest of you spread out throughout the tunnels." With a devastating shriek, the demons ran out of Lears chambers like a pack of rabid dogs. Lears looked back to his maps of Twilight.

"Where are you hiding Lumus?" Lears continued looking over his maps.

Chapter Fourteen- The Infection

The ground was cold from the night Lumus though as he woke up. The only sound was the colliding of waves on waves as the waterfall continuously came crashing down. Lumus was first to wake, as he opened his eyes he noticed Brinx was exactly as he was when Lumus drifted to sleep. Scarlette was still wrapped around Lumus. He wondered why she curled up to him before he fell asleep. Lumus tried to slowly sit up without waking Scarlette, but as he tried to rise to his feet, she woke up. Scarlette stretched with a yawn and greeted Lumus with a smile. Lumus smiled, then looked over to see Zelkem, and Orson waking up too. Over by the falls, Zynx curled up into a ball sometime after Lumus drifted off, and Dyne laid beside him with his head on Zynx, using him as a pillow. Nex and his men were nowhere in sight. Zephry was already awake. She had been cupping water from the falls in her hands, and walking it over to the flowers. Lumus rose to his feet, along with Scarlette.
"Zephry have you seen Frostear?" Lumus asked.
"Yes, he is speaking with Nex in the cave below."
Lumus found it odd that she didn't look back at him, she seemed to have her attention on the flowers. Lumus turned to see Orson walking toward him.

"Lumus we should see if Nex and his men have made any progress. Let's let the others follow when they are ready." Orson quickly turned to the cave path. Lumus had seen Scarlette walk over to Zephry while Orson spoke to him. Lumus followed behind Orson toward the small cave. "Lumus, it's unrealistic that they made it that far. We should think about making shelter since we may be here a while." Orson said as he led Lumus down a dark path.

"That all depends how far they are, although I did notice trees in the underground chamber last night. We could haul some of those up, and see if we can start some buildings." Orson laughed. "Look at this, those crazy pirates built a stairway to the lower level already. Lumus went ahead while Orson began checking how sturdy the stairs were.

"Orson, you should look at this." Lumus' eyes widened as he entered the lower chamber. The cavern was well lit with rows of torches all lit along the walls. The cavern went about the length of the lake itself. Lumus looked over at the Northern wall to see almost thirty unmarked graves. To the left were two of Nex's men building a house by the looks of it. Another five men were working on a larger building. Orson walked down the steps behind Lumus with amazement.

"Impossible, all of this overnight. They chopped down most of the trees, built a cemetery, and even started building houses." Orson was surprised. Lumus turned to the right to see two torches, one on each side of what seemed like a cave leading deeper down into another cavern.

"Ah you are awake, are you? So I have a bit to tell you then. Meet me in the headquarters when you're ready." Nex yawned before he turned away. Lumus and Orson looked at each other, Orson then looked over at Nex.

"Nex, the headquarters? You mean that large building your men are working on?" Lumus asked quickly. Nex turned around for a moment.

"Yes." Nex turned around just as he did Lumus noticed a smile on his face.

"He is proud that we are amazed by all of this." Orson laughed.

"Well I suppose I would be proud too, this is a lot to finish in a matter of hours," Lumus added. Lumus and Orson made their way through the dim cave to the large building. Nex had called over his two men to join them. Scarlette and the others were in wow at the progress. As everyone entered the half-constructed building, Nex sat in the only chair in the room and crossed his arms.

"Well then, as you can see we have been very busy. We have not taken a break since you all went off to sleep. I have a few things to go over with you." Nex took out a map from a small bag and placed it on the table.

"Now gather around. Dyne be a good lad, and grab that torch would you? Now then, as you all have seen we have taken down the innermost trees, and have dug up the stumps. We used some of the wood to bury our mates and form the fence around their graves. Over to the left here we are beginning the construction of housing. The building we are in now will be headquarters. This building will have nine rooms, one for each of you. We can assign homes to people as we start to recruit. First, we will need farmers and harvesters, do any of you know anyone like that?" Nex sighed. Zephry raised her hand.

"Actually I would like to volunteer for that job. At least to get things started." Zephry volunteered. Scarlette looked over in confusion.

"Umm, Zephry? Shouldn't you come with us?" Scarlette sounded worried.

"I won't be away long. I use to live on a farm with my family back in Piscyst. It only makes sense that I stay, and I could help get things rolling. Dyne laughed.

"You are right on that one darling. I will also stay." Zelkem shook his head.

"I figured the lazy guy would want to sit back with his feet up. Ha-ha." Dyne sighed. "Actually I am the one that drew up the blueprints for the houses we are building. Back when I was in Virphire I worked on a construction crew to rebuild homes lost in the Dragon Wars." Dyne replied. Nex nodded.

"He was up last night helping with the blueprints while you were sleeping. Actually, we have Frostear to thank as well. He was able to help move the big trees. We tried to help him, but he said little men can't lift big things." Nex added.

Dyne laughed. Lumus crossed his arms with a smirk.

"Nex I am very grateful how serious you are taking this, and how much you have accomplished..." Nex smirked.

"But you want to know about the digging. I thought that would be a priority, so my men and I worked on that first. To our surprise, we had a small tunnel heading east out toward Capaz, as we went further in it got wider and wider. All we really had to do was dig up at the end of the tunnel. The tunnel just about lined up with where we had to dig. Truthfully there are two holes we dug. The first led to the bakery in Capaz and did we ever scare the young lady over there. She pelted me good too." Scarlette giggled

"That's excellent news! So we can head over to Capaz anytime now, right?" Nex sighed. "Well yes, but you are still in for quite the walk, and some of the torches have gone out down there. You will have to bring some torches with you, but other than that you're good to go. Oh, I need to give you this too. It is a list of basic supplies we will need to get things going. If you can get a couple of you to do that I'd be grateful." Zelkem shook his head.

"Something tells me I'm getting supplies." Lumus took a quick look at the list.

"Okay, I don't want to waste time. Zephry you will stay here, and work on the crops..." Zephry snatched the list and added some things to the list.

"I can't plant anything without seeds!" Brinx walked up behind Zephry.

"I will assist her since I basically am a plant. I have a few things I can offer to the job." Brinx added. Lumus smiled.

"Okay, Orson and I can go look for the councillor Bruins. I have a few things I would like to ask him. Scarlette and Zelkem can get the supplies. We can walk down together, and meet back here whenever we finish our tasks. Zynx if you don't mind I would like to get you to move some trees with Frostear." Zynx snared and then walked off toward Frostear.

"Don't worry Lumus that means he would be happy to help." Dyne laughed. Okay, are you all ready to head out now?" Orson turned to Lumus. "Yes, the sooner the better. Scarlette and Zelkem nodded. Great, let's start walking.

"Don't forget the seeds! Hurry back!" Zephry yelled as they faded into the darkness of the cave. Orson walked up beside Lumus and Scarlette leaving Zelkem a few steps behind.

Orson stretched while cracking his neck. He slowed his pace and returned to Zelkem's side. Zelkem walked silently. Scarlette began to wonder about her hometown. It has only been just about a week, and she is grateful that she gets to once again revisit her home. Lumus was quiet too, Scarlette noticed him looking forward without his eyes even shifting from the path ahead. He must have a lot of things on his mind she thought. She turned her head to see Orson and Zelkem chatting away, again she looked back at Lumus but this time she smiled.

"Lumus, what are you thinking about?" Scarlette squinted as she smiled. Lumus finally broke his concentration to look over.

"Frostear's son," Lumus replied.

"You mean Coldblood?" Lumus turned back to look down the path.

"Yes. Ever since Sagnet, I feel like I felt another power like Frostear's. I just feel like Coldblood was watching us, but it could just be my imagination. Kontaminate on the other hand, I have no idea what knowledge he may possess. I have begun to think, where did he come from, and how did he get to Twilight? Does he really exist just to kill Lears and I?" Lumus looked back at Scarlette. Scarlette sighed with a small grin.

"You are thinking too much, think about it, he is all alone, and you have all of us. Even if your strength is equal, you have an edge. Every one of us would fight on your side." Scarlette turned to see a crack of light up ahead. Orson sped up past Lumus and Scarlette to look up toward the light.

"This is it. We can use this ladder to reach the palace. Orson climbed up as he reached the top he poked his head up to have a quick look around.

"Lumus this is the first-floor guest chambers. If we go through here we can head left out the door to the main hall." Orson said as he looked around. Orson climbed into the room and looked out the window. Scarlette and Lumus made their way into the room. Scarlette looked over at the bed.

"That is odd, the bed is a mess? Usually, this place is pristine." Lumus opened the door to the palace a small crack and peaked out.

"I don't see anyone, nor do I hear a thing." Scarlette and Lumus turned to Orson.

"The city is too quiet. There is nobody in the streets. Something is wrong." Orson drew his sword. Zelkem crept up the ladder.

"Hey thanks for leaving me in the dark, you guys have the only torches you know." Zelkem looked around the room.

"Lumus take Scarlette for the supplies, Zelkem and I will find Brunius," Orson suggested.

Scarlette opened the window and headed into the streets. Lumus hoped over the window seal behind her.

"Lumus, Zelkem and I may be a while. If you can keep an eye out while you wander through town, people may still be around. Maybe we can find out what's going on." Zelkem walked over to the door and opened it wider. He looked around then walked into the hall.

"Wow, this place seems completely empty. Where is everyone? How does a whole town just disappear?" Orson turned to Zelkem.

"Keep your voice down until we know what is going on." Orson turned back to see Lumus and Scarlette walking off into town. Orson notice there was no damage to the buildings, or any things lying on the ground.

"(If there was a struggle people would have dropped things in their panic, I suppose that is a good thing.) Zelkem we need to head..." Orson turned to the doorway, but Zelkem wasn't there. Quickly Orson ran to the door with his sword drawn. He looked out to the right then as he turned to the left Zelkem was standing directly in front of him.

"Whoa, hey no need for the muscle. Put that thing away before you hurt yourself." Zelkem yelled out. Orson sighed." You fool don't just disappear like that." Zelkem laughed.

"I'm barely a foot from the door. Anyway, shouldn't we be looking for Brunius?" Zelkem turned and began to walk off down the left hallway. Orson put his sword back in his sheath. "Zelkem, Brunius enjoyed the library. It is possible he is there, it's this way." Orson pointed down the right hallway. Zelkem turned around.

"Well lead the way then, I don't know this place like you do," Zelkem replied. Orson began to make his way down the hallway with Zelkem following behind him. Orson had his hand placed on his sword before each turn, Zelkem noticed each time he did but laughed to himself each time he saw it.

"Lumus where do you think everyone has gone? Do you think everyone is collecting somewhere in fear of Lears? Or even Kontaminate?" Lumus walked just beside Scarlette although they each faced opposite ways looking for anyone left in town.

"I'm not sure. If they did all leave to go somewhere safe I guess we wouldn't have much use for all the tunnels down below. On the other hand, Lears wouldn't collect everyone from the town. He wants to rule, and I have a feeling that he doesn't kill unless he needs to." Scarlette looked at Lumus then back to the left.

"A feeling? You can sense his thoughts can't you?" Orson added. Lumus stopped.

"Not exactly, Ever since I saw him for the first time in Twilight prison it's almost like I can see what he is thinking in his head, but it is too fussy to see clearly. Sometimes I see images, and other times I can just hear him." Lumus replied. Scarlette turned to Lumus.

"If that is so, then he would be able to see and hear your thoughts?" Lumus looked up at the eclipsed moon directly above them.

"I don't know. I suppose it is possible." Scarlette kicked some dirt on the ground.

"Can you see Kontaminate's thoughts?" Orson hesitated to ask Lumus shrugged.

"No, Kontaminate is different. Lears and I have a link because of the way we were born, Kontaminate on the other hand, I'm not entirely sure where he came from. He may look like Lears and myself, but he isn't the same." Scarlette looked up at the moon.

"Did you know the Blue moon's nickname is Cobalt, and the nickname for the Red moon is Scarlet. I was named after the Red moon, at least that's what I was told. I believe that Cobalt means Silver and white, it was nicknamed Cobalt because when the blue moon rises over the horizon it looks silver with a white glow. Pretty neat huh?" Scarlette looked over to see Lumus staring at her. "I didn't know that I just realized I don't know a lot of things. I feel like I have been sheltered all my life. All I really know is what I learned on Dystopia, survival skills, basic combat, and farming. Everything else I learned from you when you came to the farm." Scarlette laughed.

"Yeah, I guess you are still new to Twilight. You will learn so much more Lumus. It isn't all bad like we both seem to be used to. In all fairness, I don't know all that much either. I died when I was eleven years old. All I really learned in that time was how to run this city like my father." Lumus smiled. "I guess we are more alike than we thought," Lumus added.

"Zelkem hand me that book there." Zelkem paused.

"What book there is like a thousand books?" Orson shook his head.

"How have you survived this long? Give me that one with the read spine." Zelkem shook his head mimicking Orson.

"Really…they all have red spines… Shouldn't we focus on finding your councillor buddy?" Orson pushed Zelkem aside.

"This one, those are a dark orange you fool, and Brunius isn't here. At least I can grab a book that may have some insight into myths, or legends." Zelkem smirked.

"I'm not going to say a word, too easy. Oh, and what do you plan on reading about these monsters for?" Zelkem walked over to a desk with a map of Twilight on it. He sat down in the chair facing the map.

"I haven't seen a map of the world in some time. Why are these so rare, you think someone would make one map then just create copies for travelers? Actually, when we find where everyone went, I'm going to make copies, and sell some maps, its genius." Zelkem laughed. Orson took a deep breath, then continued to look for his book.

"I don't care I'm taking this map. Hey, you have hookups here right? Tell them I'll get them a copy would you?" Orson leaned on the bookshelf.

"Tell who Zelkem? Everyone is missing. Orson yelled. He took another deep breath then continued to look for his book once more.

"No need to yell…I'm still taking the map." Zelkem looked closer at the map. He noticed Twilight prison was on the map, there were also three small x's marked on the map. "Orson I know you are busy looking for your red book, but I don't think this map belongs to Capaz" Orson stood up and turned to Zelkem.

"What do you mean?" Orson walked over to the table.

"Someone has drawn the Twilight prison on here, and what are these marks? I think Lears was here, or at least one of his Lords. That means Lears may have had something to do with the people that are missing. We should hurry back to the others.

"Scarlette the door is locked. Is there a back door?" Lumus turned his head to the left of the general

store. Scarlette ran past at the door with her shoulder knocking the door off its hinges.
"There it's open. Grab a bag to carry the supplies." Scarlette walked into the general store ahead of Lumus. Lumus had a shocked look on his face.
"Should we really have done that?" Scarlette smirked at Lumus.
"Yeah, I guess this isn't the time for rules." Lumus hurried to the back and began to fill a bag with seeds and medicine. Scarlette stopped at the side door and peered into a room. "Lumus I hear something in here." Lumus dropped his bag and rushed over.
"Let me have a look." Lumus walked slowly toward the room. His hand pushed the door open as he walked in the room.
"Hello, is there anybody in here?" Lumus saw shelves and bags labelled with various merchandise for the store.
"Hello?" Suddenly a woman poked her head up from behind a few barrels.
"I recognized your voice lady Scarlette." The lady said with a scared voice.
"Penelope?" Scarlette rushed over and hugged her tightly.
"My lady I am glad you are safe," Penelope said with a smile. Lumus turned to Scarlette. "You know this woman Scarlette?" Scarlette giggled.
"Of course I do, Penelope used to deliver goods to the palace for me." Lumus turned his attention to Penelope.

"I hate to break up the reunion, but Penelope do you know what happened to everyone here in town? Where did everyone go?" Penelope wiped her tears from her eyes.

"I was taking an order over to the palace like I usually do, it was mid-day yesterday. As I walked out of the palace I noticed the moons had eclipse, and the sky was an odd purple. I guess it had been like that for a while. I was just too busy to notice I suppose. I was just about to arrive here at my shop when a bright purple light crashed through the town gate. When the dust cleared I saw a man with a purple light surrounding him. At first, people began to cheer, we thought it was you. When the man's head rose his face had such an evil look upon it that even now I get chills just thinking about it. He claimed to be a god. Then he began stabbing people in the streets." Scarlette gasped.

"He stabbed people!?" Penelope crossed her arms to hold herself.

"They didn't die though, they…" Lumus checked the window.

"They began to change. At first the people he stabbed cried out in pain, then their hair changed purple, and then…" Scarlette rested her hand on Penelope's shoulder.

"What happened Penelope?" Penelope looked up at Scarlette then to Lumus.

"They grew what looked like spikes, almost like horns around their body. I heard the man say, spread the infection, my children. That's when I fled into my storeroom." Lumus notice a tear race down Scarlette's cheek.

"A purple man, it could only be Kontaminate. He must be amassing an army since he lost to me at Lake Twilight." Lumus said as he clenched his fists. Scarlette sat on the ground.

"Lumus, what if he has moved to another town, what if he is doing this to everyone?" Scarlette replied. Lumus turned back to the window.

"We need to get all we can carry, and head back to the tunnels." Penelope moved a few sacks of grains off a hatch.

"A man came through the floor just before this all happened. He told me you would be coming. I had a carpenter build a hatch that locks from inside the tunnel. We can use this to go down there. Though I should ask, where does it go?" Penelope said as she cleared the hatch. Scarlette brushed away her tears with her hand.

"The tunnel leads to a large cavern under Lake Twilight, we have many friends there. We have Captain Nex, and a few of his men helping us build a town there." Scarlette said with a smile. Penelope smiled with what little hope she had left.

"Then, of course, I would like to join you there, maybe I can offer some help to you?" Penelope looked at Lumus, still with a smile. Lumus opened the hatch.

"Of course you can, but we must hurry back. If Kontaminate is going to each town and infecting people, then we have to come up with a plan to stop him. Scarlette you and Penelope head back with everything you can carry. I will find Orson and Zelkem." Lumus said. Scarlette nodded. Lumus headed to the door and turned back to see them heading down.

"I found it! Orson, I think this is the one we need. It says Opal thirteen, Myths of Demons that's the one right?" Orson hurried over to Zelkem and grabbed the book from him.

"Yes, this is it. Okay, lets head back to the tunnels." Zelkem stood up and looked over to the doorway leading into the palace halls.

"Orson, the torch in the hall went out." Orson looked over at the door.

"What is that light? Purple lights?" Orson reached for his sword, and after a pause, he looked over at Zelkem. Zelkem took a torch from the wall nearby. When he turned back the lights were gone.

"Where did the lights go Orson?" Orson had his sword facing the door with his eyes focused.

"I don't know they just disappeared. When I say rush we rush toward the door. On three. One. Two." Lumus came crashing into the library glowing bright, he rolled on the ground toward Orson and Zelkem, and he stood up quickly lighting the room. In front of them was a woman with purple eyes and two large spikes, one on each arm. The woman lifted her arms facing the spikes up at the three of them.

"Lumus, what the Dystopia is that?" Zelkem said with a panic.

"Kontaminate has infected the town. All of the people have become his puppets." Lumus replied. Orson panicked.

"Scarlette, where is Scarlette?" Lumus shifted his head toward Orson.

"She left into the tunnels with a woman named Penelope. They are safe." Orson paused.

"Penelope? I know her. She owns the general store." Orson replied.

"Yeah that's all awesome but can we focus on this crazed Kontaminate wannabe?" Zelkem interrupted. Lumus began to focus his energy.

"Stand back." Lumus raised his hands in front of his chest. After a small pause he let out a yell, and a gust of energy flung the woman into the stone wall by the door.

"Let's go now!" Lumus yelled out. He raced toward the door. Orson and Zelkem didn't hesitate. They made their way back to the hall and ran down the hallway that had the tunnel to Neutral City. As they ran past the last corner a man jumped out and grabbed Zelkem.

"Ah, Orson!" Zelkem cried out.

"Zelkem!" Orson raced back, but before he could make it to Zelkem the man stabbed Zelkem in the back. Zelkem's face went faint. He dropped to the ground grabbing at his body as if he was on fire. When Orson looked back up to the man with tears his face went into shock.

"Councillor Brunius? You bastard!" Orson raised his sword to Brunius and dashed at him. Lumus jumped on his back and pulled him back.

"Orson he is infected, he doesn't know what he is doing," Lumus shouted.

"But Zelkem…" Orson said faintly. Lumus pulled Orson back, and threw him behind, then raised his left hand with a flash, throwing Brunius through the air. Orson ran to Zelkem.

"Brother I got you. You're going to be okay." Orson cried out. Zelkem rolled back and forth on the ground screaming in pain.

"Orson move back from him." Orson stood up. As he backed away Zelkem began to change. First, his hair slowly turned purple then two spikes shot out of his arms. Zelkem was on his hands and knees with his head down.

"I think he has fully changed Orson." Orson was still staring at Zelkem.

"Changed into what Lumus?" Lumus looked over to Orson then back to Zelkem. Zelkem raised his head and opened his eyes slowly. They had become completely purple, his pupils were gone too. He smiled back at Orson and Lumus as he rose to his feet. Lumus rushed at Zelkem with his fist clenched. He jumped in the air as he punched forward. Zelkem tried to punch but missed, Lumus hit him directly in the face knocking him out cold.

"Orson we need to go." Orson's face was overwhelmed with tears.

"Not without my brother. I will not leave him like this." Orson cried out. Lumus grabbed Orson by his armour.

"We don't have a choice, I don't want to leave him any more than you, but we can't take him through the tunnels. We can't risk the safety of everyone. Zelkem would do the same thing, and you know it." Lumus stared into Orson's eyes.

"I know what you're feeling right now, but until we know how to reverse this we have to leave him. Let's go!" Orson kneeled. He put his head down for a minute, then stood up once again.

"I will be back for you brother." Orson turned and rushed off. Lumus followed behind him. He turned back to Zelkem after a moment. A tear slowly ran down his face, after a short pause he raced off down the palace hallway behind Orson.

Chapter Fifteen- Lumus Vs Kontaminate

The tunnel to Neutral City seemed darker than before Lumus thought. He felt like he was running as fast as he could, but even so, he could not catch up to Orson. Lumus began to slow down. Finally, he came to a stop and began to gasp for air.

"(I must have tired myself out with those attacks. If those little attacks can wear me out then I really need to watch it. Maybe I should practise with my power more. Come to think of it, the last training I did was almost two weeks ago now. I didn't really get to train too much either.)" Lumus thought to himself.

"Lumus?" Scarlette said faintly. Lumus looked down the tunnel.

"Scarlette is that you?" Lumus replied. Scarlette came walking up the tunnel with Frostear.

"Lumus are you okay? Where is Zelkem" Scarlette asked. Lumus stood up straight.

"I take it you saw Orson run by? He ran ahead of me earlier" Lumus said with concern Frostear shook his head.

"He ran up to the waterfall cave. All we heard was Zephry cursing like crazy, and yelling about him trampling her flowers." Lumus leaned up against the tunnel wall.

"After I left you Scarlette, I went back to find Orson and Zelkem, when we were heading out Zelkem was grabbed by Councillor Brunius. He stuck him with one of his spikes, and Zelkem transformed into one of them. We had no choice but to leave him behind." Lumus explained. Scarlette fell to the ground.

"Penelope told us about the infection, she told us about the people. Nex and his men are digging to the farthest towns first. We all decided the farther the reach the more we can save. If Penelope is right and this happened yesterday, depending on what way Kontaminate went, we could have a day if he goes to Aquoise, or if he went south, well there are a few ways he could have gone, but we have about four days to reach anything past Sagnet toward the West." Frosted interrupted. Lumus nodded.

"That seems like the most logical decision." Scarlette stood up in tears.

"Everyone is worried Lumus. These aren't just monsters. This is our family and friends. We have to do something more than digging." Scarlette cried out. Lumus shook his head. "What else can we do? If we go by foot, then we would just be guessing. At least with Frostear's plan, we can really save people." Lumus replied. Scarlette tried to wipe some tears away.

"We can't just give up that easily. Will it take them some time to dig those tunnels? Couldn't we at least go to Aquoise, or to Librine, they are the closest towns. We can at least check to make sure they are safe." Scarlette retorted. Frostear nodded.

"She is right. We can break into two parties, and check them both in half the time." Frostear added. Lumus closed his eyes.

"I can feel Lears. I think he is on the move. He is leaving Aster Mountains." Lumus said faintly. Scarlette shrugged.

"Who cares about Lears!? It's Kontaminate that's a huge threat right now." Scarlette interrupted. Lumus opened his eyes to see Scarlette staring back at him.

"I know Scarlette, I'm just curious about their plans. I wonder if they might help." Lumus suggested. Frostear laughed, then turned to head back.

"I'll meet you guys back at the cavern." Scarlette didn't stop staring at Lumus.

"Lumus you know we can make a difference if we go to those towns. We have to stop Kontaminate, and he could be out there." Scarlette had a look of worry in her expression. Lumus crossed his arms.

"Yeah I know, but we can't fight the people, he is using them to fight. If we go out there we will be fighting the very same people we are trying to protect." Lumus replied. Scarlette turned toward the cavern.

"I know that. I know it is dangerous, but if it means that we can take out Kontaminate then we have to try. If we go out there, we don't have to just walk in the front door you know. I'm saying we can just go see from afar. If it's too late we turn and head back to plan other strategies. Until we figure out how to cure the infection we should avoid any unnecessary fighting with the people." Scarlette tried to convince Lumus. Lumus walked over beside Scarlette.

"You're right. Let's go ask the others who will come with us then. If we just do surveillance, and nothing more. If we find Kontaminate, then I will deal with him." Lumus smiled. Scarlette smiled too. "Thank you Lumus," Scarlette said as she hugged Lumus.

"(That bastard, using our own people against us. Ah…Zelkem. You are a pain in the ass, but you are family, as much of a headache as you are, I still love you, and I can't let this monster get away with what he has done)" Orson thought to himself as he paced in the chamber behind the waterfall. "Orson I've found you." Scarlette stood at the cave door with a sad smirk on her face. "Lady Scarlette." Orson stood as he wiped his face dry. "Is there something the matter?" Scarlette walked over to the waterfall and reached her hand out to catch water.

"Orson, Lumus told us what happened to Zelkem. I promise you Kontaminate will pay. Lumus has taken Dyne, Frostear, and Zephry to Librine. You, Zynx, Brinx and I will travel to Aquoise. We are going to find Kontaminate. If he has been to either of the two towns we will help any way we can." Orson joined Scarlette's side.

"I understand. I am ready to leave at once my lady." Scarlette turned back to the entrance of the tunnel.

"We leave immediately. Kontaminate has maybe a day on us. There is no time to waste. We can help Zelkem, and we will stop Kontaminate at any cost." Scarlette turned away and faded into the darkness of the cave.

Lumus closed the hatch to the tunnels behind him, Penelope's shop was quiet. Dyne leaned on the wall by the door. Frostear and Zephry were already outside scouting the streets. Lumus walked over to Dyne and gave him a nod. They made their way out into the street to join the others. A purple light from the eclipse lit the streets. Frostear and Zephry noticed Lumus and Dyne exit the shop. Frostear nodded at Lumus to signal that the streets were empty.

"We need to head South East across the bridge east of here. No stops, no detours, if Kontaminate is there I don't want him to escape. If any of you don't want to go speak now, there will be no turning back. Penelope mentioned the eclipse last time Kontaminate showed up, He must be close." Lumus looked around at the others, no one made a sound. "Then I'll set the pace, keep up I won't be stopping for anything." Lumus began running toward the south gate with Frostear behind him.

"Lumus seems a lot more serious than usual. I know a lot is happening, but he seems to have changed." Zephry said with a chill.

"You remember what Lumus said before, we are like family now. I'm certain Lumus is thinking of Zelkem. What happened is terrible, and I am with Lumus with anything he decides. He has proven time and time again that he really is the hero Twilight needs." Dyne said with a smirk. Dyne turned to catch up with Lumus.

"I understand all of that, he just doesn't have the same look on his face. He reminded me of...Lears." Dyne stopped without turning around, he paused for a moment then continued to run. Zephry lost sight of Lumus and Frostear; Dyne had almost reached the gate. Zephry looked up at the sky holding her hand in front of her eyes to block some of the light.

"I wish Twilight would go back to the way it was." After a moment Zephry began to make her way toward the gate.

"Everyone wait a moment." Lumus stopped suddenly just after the gate.

"I know that the others are going to Aquoise, the thing that keeps going through my head is if Kontaminate is there, will they be able to face him alone? I have decided to go to Librine alone." Lumus announced. Frostear smiled.

"I know Zynx is lost without me so I'll do as you ask." Dyne turned toward Aquoise, as he did Frostear shot Lumus a nod, then turned to follow.

"Hey, where are you both going?" Zephry finally caught up, she was out of breath, and dripping sweat already.

"I need you to go with them Zephry. I know Orson isn't in a clear mind, and he may do something reckless without all of you with him." Zephry looked over to the others walking toward Twilight forest.

"You don't think I'm going to just let you go off alone. I haven't been with you as long as the others, but I know you can sense Kontaminate. That seems to be something that everyone is overlooking here." Lumus turned his head.

"They are all fully aware that I can feel his star energy. That is why they left Zephry." Lumus replied. Zephry sighed.

"So, you are really going to face him alone. Why send everyone to Aquoise?" Zephry seemed eager to hear his response. Lumus turned back to Zephry with a smile.

"I just want everyone to be at a safe distance for the battle. I don't think Kontaminate will just let me win." Lumus replied with a soft laugh. Zephry laughed too.

"Okay, I won't stop you. Good luck Lumus." Zephry smiled for a moment before she turned to follow the others.

Lumus turned to Librine. He clenched his fists as he powered up. The air around him blew in a spiral, his head was down, and he had closed his eyes. After a short pause, Lumus raised his head and dashed toward Librine.

Scarlette, Zynx, Orson, and Brinx reached Capaz. Everyone made their way to the main street near the palace. Scarlette made her way up the ladder in Penelope's shop.

"I wonder if Lumus and the others are okay." Scarlette walked out of the storage room. She noticed everyone was waiting outside. She opened the door and walked outside to see Frostear, Dyne, and Zephry.

"Hey, where is Lumus? Why are you all here?" Scarlette began to panic. Frostear stepped forward. "He means to fight Kontaminate alone. He won't take us along because he knew we would just be in the way." Frostear replied. Scarlette began to cry. "Why? Why would he go alone?" Zephry ran over and hugged Scarlette.

"I think Lumus knows Kontaminate is here for just Lumus, this is something he has to do alone." Zephry backed away from Scarlette. She looked around to notice everyone was looking at her. "We may not have Lumus with us, but we still have a mission to complete. Until Lumus returns we need to focus on that mission." Zephry protested. Brinx became interested. "What mission is that Zephry?" Brinx asked. Zephry looked around.

"We need to go to Aquoise to find Zelkem, and help him return to normal." Frostear cheered. Orson finally had a happy look on his face. "Zephry how do we know Zelkem will be in Aquoise?" Orson asked.

"Like we have been doing since the beginning, best guess. Kontaminate said in Sagnet that Lumus and Lears are abominations right? So if he is going after Lears why not send his infected to distract Lears while he fights Lumus?" Zephry declared. Scarlette whipped her tears away. Frostear was in shock. Finally, Brinx walked over to Zephry and rested his hand on Zephry's shoulder.

"That is a brilliant plan. Listen up everyone we have wasted enough time here. Let's get moving to Aquoise. Brinx jumped off into the sky, Dyne Zynx and Orson made haste toward the North Gate. Scarlette turned to Zephry before they left.

"Thank you Zephry." After a quick hug, Scarlette followed the others. Zephry smiled as she watched everyone leaving.

"Hey wait! Why am I always the one left behind?" Zephry yelled out.

Lumus' speed was ferocious, not even the fastest Zufore could keep up with him. Lumus noticed the eclipse getting brighter as he got closer to Librine. When Lumus glanced ahead he noticed Librine's city gates.

"Librine, I made it." Lumus began to slow down as his light faded.

"I can feel him, he is close."

"Ha-ha, you think you could sneak up on me Lumus? I am the ultimate weapon. I am a force used for centuries to clear planets of abnormal species. I am the last thing you will see." Kontaminate called out. Lumus laughed.

"I can feel your star energy. I have to say I'm embarrassed for you. You are strong sure, but I am not far off from you. As for Twilight, I won't let you hurt anyone else. This is it Kontaminate I hope you're ready for the end." Kontaminate smirked back at Lumus. "Every time my creator wakes me to cleanse a planet I find it interesting to see what it is, and what it was. I can see these humans are the species that belong. There will be no harm to them unless you decide to neglect your makeshift fate. If you don't my infected children will continue to go from town to town infecting the planet." Lumus gripped his sword tight as he drew it from its sheath.

"Enough, let's end this already!" Kontaminate held his hand out, a purple light made the shape of a sword.

"I see, so this is what your species calls a weapon on this planet. Very well." Lumus shrugged.

"I hope you know how to use it because I have become quite good with mine," Lumus said with a grin. Kontaminate laughed.

"I do enjoy your species. I have not been a human for some time now." Lumus looked at him in confusion.

"What do you mean you haven't been a human for a while?" Kontaminate began to swing his sword around as he looked toward Lumus.

"Simple answer for a simple person. You see I sleep in the cosmos up in the space that your kind has yet to fully learn about. I have been to planets where they have become so knowledgeable that they were able to build ships to enter space. I have been to planets where there were no humans at all. My job is to kill anything my master has not created. You and Lears are two things created by the planet, therefore I was sent here to kill you both." Lumus clenched his fist.

"Your creator? Do you mean like a god?" Kontaminate laughed.

"Your kind knows nothing of the gods of our world. There is Omega Zin, ruler of this galaxy. Under him are the North Zin, the East Zin, the South Zin, and your god the West Zin. Your planet falls on the west side of the galaxy. Then there are the Zodiacs of the twelve. These are the gods of legend. Not even my master has seen them. Anyway, I have given you enough information. At least now you will have something to think about in the realm of the dead." Kontaminate laughed.

"Kontaminate dashed straight at Lumus, his sword just missed Lumus as he jumped over him. Lumus swung at Kontaminate, as he did Kontaminate turned to deflect Lumus' strike with his energy sword. Kontaminate raised his hand to Lumus' chest, a bright light flashed in Lumus' face. Lumus was thrown across the field.

("Ah, what was that he didn't even move. He just pushed me with his hand.") Lumus struggled to get up. Kontaminate walked slowly over to Lumus as he tried to get to his feet.

"Seems I know your powers more than you do. Interesting, I will tell you this Lumus. Your true power is not this blade nor is it the star energy within you. Your power is drawn directly from Twilights Core. With a vast amount of power at your fingertips, you could easily become a threat to the universe. Now you see why you are abnormal and must be destroyed?" Lumus finally made his way to his feet.

"So what do you draw your power from?" Lumus asked.

"I draw my power from Omega Zin. So you can only imagine how much power I really possess." Lumus laughed. He fell to his knees as he continued to laugh.

"You think the god of our galaxy will grant you all of his power? Not even I am that naïve. Remember you are a copy of Lears and me. We can feel your Star energy. Oh and another thing, I don't ask the core for its power!" Lumus began to glow brightly. He threw his sword through the light at Kontaminate, but he just deflected it. Suddenly Lumus flew out of the light with his fist aimed at Kontaminate. He let out a bombardment of punches, then grabbed Kontaminate by his head. Lumus jumped with Kontaminate unable to fight back. He slammed Kontaminate into the ground with a loud crash.

"Do yourself a favour Kontaminate, stay down." As Lumus stared into the dust a small needle flew out of the debris and hit Lumus in his neck. He quickly pulled it out, then fell to the ground once more.

"Ha-ha, you fell for it. Thought you had me beat did you? I cannot be beaten." Kontaminate began to laugh. He raised his arms to the air.

"Now I just have one of you left. I already have my army of infected ready to attack Lears. All they need is a general." Kontaminate turned back to Lumus with a smile.

Lumus grabbed his neck in pain, he immediately began to sweat as his body began to change. Lumus was on his knees screeching in pain. His body began to form spikes from his shoulders, then another pair burst through his elbows. Lumus began to swing his arms violently. He ripped his shirt off and scratched at his chest.

"The venom is taking over your mind. Soon Lumus, you will become fully infected." Kontaminate crossed his arms and turned toward Aquoise. Lumus fell to the ground with a twitch. Kontaminate turned his head to see Lumus over his shoulder.

"Transformation complete Lumus. As your master, I command you to stand up." Kontaminate said in a serious tone.

Lumus twitched for a moment his eyes dazed. Kontaminate picked him up by his hair with one hand.

"I gave you an order Lumus," Kontaminate said.

("I can hear him, but I can't move my body. I can't believe I have been infected. Is it all over? No. I can't let it end this way. I won't let it end like this. I will use every ounce of energy to free myself. I just need to find the way to the power of the core from my mind. I need to hurry. Kontaminate seems to be getting angry. I just need to close my eyes and I can focus.")

Lumus hung from Kontaminate's hand motionless. His mind was nearly under Kontaminate's full control. Kontaminate looked into Lumus' eyes closely.

"Are you fighting the venom Lumus? Good for you, I see you have more will then the humans.

You can try all you want, in the end, the venom always wins." Lumus slowly closed his eyes.

"Ha-ha, I can wait all day Lumus." Kontaminate tossed him across the field toward Librine.

("Good at least I don't have to look at him. Now I can focus. Twilight show me to the core. Show me the way. Guide my mind back to my body. I can't allow Kontaminate to harm Twilight.") Lumus thought to himself.

"Lumus can you hear me?" A voice called out to Lumus.

("A woman's voice, who are you?") Lumus heard a voice in his head.

"I am the West Zin. I am the creator of Twilight, and of Dystopia. You need to listen to me. The only way to defeat Kontaminate is to draw power from both Twilight and Dystopia. It is the only way to defeat him. If you draw too much at once from Twilight you will cause the planet to become unstable, and Twilight may summon the Zodiacs."

("That's right, last time the planet used too much positive energy, Lears was born. West Zin what are the Zodiacs?") Lumus replied.

"I created them as a defence for the planet. Twilight was the purest planet until the Dragon Wars. I created the Zodiacs to destroy anyone who disrupted the core's balance. You and Lears have recently been agitating the planet. You cannot keep this up. When you were born, I was able to shift the balance, but Lears was born. We were lucky in a way. The Zodiacs were held in confinement." West Zin replied.

("I understand, but if I draw from Dystopia's core would the negative energy affect me?") Lumus said faintly. There was a pause for a moment.
"I don't know, I didn't create you or Lears. I don't even know what the limit of your power truly is, but I can tell you that the planet will not be able to give you enough power without Dystopia's help." West Zin said. Lumus went silent. His body still laid on the plains just outside of Librine. Kontaminate waited with his arms crossed, and a smile on his face facing Aquoise.
("West Zin, I know what I must do.") Lumus created an image of himself in his head. He stood in a white space. There was nothing in sight. Lumus was floating he noticed. He looked down then up. Still, there was nothing.
("It seems I did it, now to test this out.") Lumus used his imagination to move an image of himself within his mind. A road appeared under Lumus. He slowly floated to the road then looked ahead. A town appeared further up the road, then an old man morphed from the town gate. Lumus began to walk to the old man.
"You have entered the realm of realms. As you requested I am here to guide you." Lumus looked up to the town gates.
"I need to get inside the gates," Lumus said.
"I warn you, young master. Inside is the world of shambles." Lumus turned to the old man.
"The world of shambles? What do you mean?" The old man turned away from Lumus. He went silent.

"Old man, what is behind the gate?" The gate turned into a keyhole where the gate once was. A voice radiated from the white space as if it was coming from everywhere at once. "You are the key Lumus." The voice faded after repeating a few times.

"I am the key?" Lumus turned to the keyhole, the large gate had turned into a large keyhole big enough for Lumus to walk through. Lumus looked into the keyhole to see the purple light shining out. "He is taking his time with his transformation. Hurry up Lumus!" Kontaminate gave Lumus a swift kick to the gut. Still, his body lay lifeless on the plains. Kontaminate turned back to Aquoise. "Ah, the whole place is shaking." Lumus turned to see the road he was on began to crumble.

"I am losing focus, something must have happened to my body. Okay, now or never." Lumus ran toward the purple light to appear back on the farm in Dystopia. The shack was on fire, and Lumus noticed a boy run into the flames. "That is me? I tried to save Orson's other self. I couldn't help him. Huh? Who is that? Scarlette? What is that in her hand?" Suddenly the old man appeared beside Lumus. "That is the hourglass she received from West Zin in the realm of the dead." Lumus jumped back.

"Why am I here, why would the door bring me to this place?" The old man walked over to a tree, and walked behind it, as he walked behind the tree he changed into Lears, then walked back over to Lumus.

"This is all in your mind Lumus, you see what you're mind wants to show you. This is your memory of the first person you couldn't save. Strange isn't it? Scarlette was there so quickly yet she just stood there. Why would she not help you?" Lumus unclenched his fist and turned to Scarlette. She watched the farm burn, then turned into the woods.

"How can I see this? I wasn't outside to see this." Lears turned to Lumus.

"Your eyes are only the gateway to your soul; they can see what is physical. Your mind, however, can sense energy. That is the real eyes of your being. If you can feel the power of something around you it is just like seeing it with your eyes." Lumus shook his head. "What does any of this matter?" Lears laughed.

"All of this matters, you are trying to regain your mind right? How can you have what you don't understand?" Lears walked over to the shack. "Remember Lumus what you see is not always what you can see." After a pause, Lears smiled then walked into the shack. The flames engulfed him, but he didn't make a sound. Suddenly the shack blew up with a flash. Lumus closed his eyes, and he quickly covered his face. He noticed nothing had hit him, nor did he feel the heat from the flames. Lumus opened his eyes. He looked around to see himself in Capaz Palace. Lumus looked out the window, it was dark, and the streets were silent. He turned to the bed beside him to see himself sleeping.

"This is Capaz, I slept here many nights. What is special about this night?" Lumus turned to the window, then turned back to himself sleeping, but when he looked back it was Scarlette. She got up and stood beside Lumus.

"I guess I shouldn't be surprised about this realm anymore." Scarlette pointed out the window down to the palace steps.

"Do you see?" Lumus turned to look out the window he blinked as he turned his head. When his eyes opened again he was now standing outside with Scarlette beside him at the bottom of the steps.

"What does this matter? What does any of this matter? Scarlette faced Frostear and Concy as Concy spoke.

"I suppose I would live based on my will to help others. If I knew I was going to die, I would help anyone I could before my time was up." Scarlette turned to Lumus.

"Would you?" Lumus stood speechless for a moment. Scarlette turned back to Frostear and Concy and Pointed to them. Lumus turned to look. Frostear and Concy argued then they both walked off.

"We are a few feet away, but I can't hear them." Scarlette points once more. A man in a hood stood outside the palace.

"Who is that?" Scarlette walked over beside the hooded man.

"Come Lumus," Scarlette said as she pointed up. Lumus walked over to join her, he turned to see

Brinx on the palace roof, glaring back at them. He turned to the hooded man.

"Brinx was watching over us as we slept." The man reached for his hood and pulled it back. Lumus gasped as he took a step back.

"Lears was here? How did he get past the guards?" He asked. Scarlette laughed.

"You know that Lears could take a few guards down it was Brinx that stopped him that night from killing you. The question is, why did he tell no one that he was there in the first place?" Lumus looked up to Brinx.

"I know Brinx, I know he has his reasons." Lumus turned to Scarlette, but she was gone. Lumus looked all around, but no one was there.

"Brinx wouldn't betray us, he has fought by our side this whole time," Lumus said to himself.

"Very well, if you believe then it is as you will." Lumus ran up the steps then turned to yell back.

"So whatever I think I can make a reality? Then I want all of my friends to appear before me!" With a flash Scarlette, Orson, Zelkem, Dyne, Zynx, Frostear, Brinx, and Zephry all appeared at the bottom of the steps.

"What do you will of us?" They all said at once. Lend me your strength; show me the way to beat Kontaminate. Lumus looked up at the sky the core of Twilight was high above glowing brightly, when he looked back down he was no longer in Capaz. He was back in his body on the field outside of Librine. His body had changed into one of the infected. Although he kept some of his normal features, his elbows and shoulders had spikes coming from them. Around some parts of his face and torso was purple from the venom, but he kept his mind after all.

Lumus stood up, and he closed his eyes. He clenched his fists and began to illuminate.

"Oh, Lumus so you are ready for your first orders. I want you to head to…" Lumus raised his hand, and just as Kontaminate did, Lumus hit him with a flash in the back sending Kontaminate through the land, and rocks like it was nothing.

"Lumus opened his eyes. They were glowing a bright blue. The skin around the spikes began to heal. The spikes fell as if they weren't attached, and his skin turned back to normal. Kontaminate got back up in a hurry to see Lumus was back to normal.

"Impossible, nothing has ever been able to fight the venom! I will kill you, you abomination. Kontaminate ran at Lumus as fast as he could. Lumus dashed toward Kontaminate. At the last second Lumus noticed his sword he threw at Kontaminate, just as Kontaminate reached Lumus, he bent down grabbed his sword off the ground and slashed through Kontaminate. Lumus slid along the rocks then turned to Kontaminate. Kontaminate began to cough up blood.

"I guess you have won Lumus. My master told me to tell you this if I was to lose. He said a hero born from the planet shall be the only one able to defeat the monster born of the planet, but only if he was to find himself. Kontaminate dissolved into energy, then blew away in the wind.

"This…This was all a test? Omega Zin never wanted to destroy the planet.

"No, he didn't Lumus. The Omega Zin only wanted to test your mind and spirit. I speak to you now from my world, and I have a favour to ask of you." Lumus looked up to the sky, night had fully set in while he was in his mind. The moons had returned to normal as they went their separate ways in the sky.

"What could I do for a god?" He asked.

"Lumus, I need you to defeat Lears and rebuild Twilight to normal. I know this will be no easy task, but I beg of you. Please restore Twilight for me." Lumus closed his eyes.

"I will, I won't stop until Lears is defeated." Lumus turned back to Capaz with a smile on his face.

Chapter Sixteen- Twilight rebuilds

The day had finally come over the hills on Nuran region. Lumus limped toward Capaz. He looked back over his shoulder, paranoid that Kontaminate would be behind him. Lumus made his way to the bridge in front of the East side of Capaz. The town's people had returned, and they had begun to clean the streets. Lumus looked over at the palace to see Orson. As Lumus passed the corner house to the palace entrance he noticed Zelkem leaning against the palace walls. A smile struck his face as he fell to one knee. Orson saw Lumus collapse and ran to his side.

"Lumus I knew you would win! So you ended up sending Kontaminate packing after all. We kind of figured that you did since the infection wore off. I have to say it was close too." Lumus looked up and smiled.

"I'm glad that everyone is okay. How is Zelkem?" Orson turned to look over his shoulder.

"Well he is a pain in the ass, but he's family. He will live. The others have gone to rest. I have to wait for the Councillors to return, so I stayed awake with Zelkem." Lumus stood up, as Zelkem glanced in their direction and began to make his way over to them.

"The councillors are coming back to Capaz? It seems like we were all just here." Lumus said. Orson laughed.

"I suppose you are right. Although this is not just a meeting about their assigned cities, this will also be to congratulate your victory over Kontaminate. It seems we have also been getting false information from some of our cities. I suppose we have nothing to worry about, but this tells us Lears has more of a grasp on our military then we thought. It will be hard to trust anyone after this." Orson sighed.

Lumus looked up to the palace where Brinx once stood from his visions. The roof looked just as it did, but he couldn't think of a time when he looked up there. Lumus closed his eyes and tried to think why he had memories of something he had never witnessed. Could he have glanced up at the roof and had forgotten he thought?

"Lumus is something the matter?" Orson turned to see Lumus with his eyes closed, and his head tilted back.

"No, it's nothing. I am just relieved that things have settled down. After a rest we can continue after Lears, I just hope we still have time to reach him, before he moves again." Orson shrugged.

"It would be best if we focus on rebuilding first. We have much to do still. Also, I have sent some soldiers to aid our friends down below with the tunnels." Lumus turned to Orson quickly.

"Orson if there is a leak in the military do you think it is wise to have sent them?" Orson laughed and replied "I knew you would say that. I thought about that too. I asked Brinx to watch them, he is down there now. They don't know that he is watching them though." Lumus replied as Zelkem joined them.

"Welcome back, Zelkem!" Lumus said as he walked away toward the palace doors.

"Thanks! You too" he replied.

"Zelkem, I've been meaning to talk to you properly since you, well, transformed back. I just want you to know, I mean, well…"

"Orson, are you gonna get all mushy and sentimental on me!?" Zelkem laughed.

"Aw, hell, you know what I mean. I don't know what I would have done if we hadn't got you back". Orson awkwardly grabbed his brother in a quick hug, and then stomped off

"If you tell anyone about this, I'll deny the whole thing," he said over his shoulder.

Orson followed Lumus to the palace doors and made his way down the main hall to the throne room. Lumus stopped at the doors as Orson proceeded inside. The throne room was decorated for the celebration. Lumus looked around to see long ribbons from wall to wall. Flowers lined the walkway to the throne as Orson walked down he checked each one for perfection.

"Is this all for us Orson?" Lumus finally followed behind Orson.

"Yes, this is going to be a big celebration I hear," Orson replied. Lumus stopped once more.

"You mean you didn't plan this?" The doors shut with a loud thud behind Lumus. He quickly turned around to see Councillor Gerald standing behind him.

"I thought our heroes should be treated as such wouldn't you agree Orson?" Orson continued to the seats at the end of the room.

"Lumus as you can see Councillor Gerald is responsible for the preparations." Orson sat down on the steps just before the throne chairs. Lumus turned to Gerald.

"Councillor I didn't know you had arrived in Capaz. Have you been here long?" Orson asked. Gerald walked past Lumus toward Orson. He turned to Lumus.

"I arrived just as you engaged Kontaminate. It seems I was too late to lend a hand. I brought some soldiers and had heard you were in the area from my scouts. By the time I arrived you had finished off Kontaminate. I secured the city and sent word for all of the councillors to meet here. If I am not mistaken they should all arrive soon. Until then, I plan to fix the city to its former glory and help the people as much as possible. Orson requested a couple soldiers for, what was that for again Orson?" Gerald turned to Orson." Orson stood up.

"I needed them for some repairs. Thank you again for their aid." Orson replied. Gerald laughed. "I see, well regardless, if it is to help the city that is why I am here." Lumus approached Gerald. I thank you for the assistance. I would like to take my leave to walk through the city. Excuse me." Lumus said with a forced smile. He turned to the doors, and let himself out.

("He is hiding something. I need to see what is happening underground.") Lumus made his way to Penelope's shop. As he made his way around the corner he noticed a lot of Gerald's guards roaming the area.

("I need to slip inside unnoticed, maybe through the back door.")

Lumus went the long way around the shop toward the city wall and grabbed a cloak off a clothing line. He wrapped himself in it to conceal his face, then headed down the alley behind the shop. Lumus waited in the shadows as some of Gerald's men marched by. Quickly he leaped into the street, and opened the window to climb in, then shut the window behind him. He waited for a moment then covered the window.

"There I don't think I was seen. I really hope I am just being paranoid." Lumus opened the hatch to Neutral City and climbed down the ladder.

"Orson, is everything okay with Lumus? He seemed a little distracted." Gerald asked. Orson moved over to the window.

"I assume he has a lot on his mind. If you had a twin regardless of how he entered this world would you find it easy to kill him?" Orson replied. Gerald laughed.

"Kontaminate was a monster in a skin that resembled Lumus, nothing more." Gerald protested. Orson turned to Gerald.

"Never the less, the situation would be easy to no man. If Lumus seemed distracted, then I say leave him with his thoughts for now. This is something he needs to deal with on his own. You have to remember Gerald. Lumus is still new to this world. Everything that happens to him, happens to him for the first time. Even his power is relative." Orson made his way to the door.

"Are you leaving Orson? I have much more to talk with you about." Gerald called out. Orson reached for the door.

"It will have to wait, the councillors have arrived." Orson made his way through the doors leaving Gerald alone.

"Master do you have new orders for us?" Gerald turned to the shadows behind the throne. "Have the soldiers watch Lumus and Orson closely Tearus. They are up to something and I want to know what it is. Orson took two of your men correct?" Tearus stepped forward.

"Yes My Lord, they are currently with him. They did not know the location in which Orson was taking them. I will have them give you a full report as soon as they return." Tearus turned back into the shadows and disappeared with the others as if they were never there.

"These fools think I won't find out what they are up to, I own this world. Lumus and Lears will soon see why the Drayhelm is to be feared." Gerald walked down the throne steps and slammed the doors behind him. After a moment Lady Concy came from behind the banners by the north windows.

"So that is your plan, Gerald. Well, you are not the only dragon with an agenda. You can show yourself Tearus, I can still smell you." Concy said with a grin on her face.

"Ah, lady Concy. I am surprised me nor master Gerald was able to catch your scent. Maybe being around humans have worked out for you, but I cannot let you leave here alive" Tearus said with a laugh.

"You underestimate me Tearus. I have not come alone." Concy turned her back to Tearus. He used the opportunity to dash at her, but Frostear leaped out and thrust his sword through Tearus' chest. "You would betray your kind too!?" Tearus fell to his knees. Frostear pulled his sword from Tearus, then turned to the doors to the main hall.

"Lumus isn't to know of this." Frostear barked.

"I shall keep the council out of this as well. I wouldn't want the council to think the Drayhelms are coming for them. This was an act of a small group." Concy added, but Frostear just walked away.

Lumus made his way through the tunnels in a haste to catch up with Orson. His cloak blocked his light from revealing himself. As he made his way down the tunnel he continuously checked behind him to be sure no one was following him.

("Finally I found you, Orson. I just need to sneak in front without them noticing." Lumus concealed his face and crouched as he tried to sway by Orson and Gerald's men. The guards looked at each other than down at Lumus. For a second Lumus stopped as he waited for them to look away hoping they hadn't caught him. After a pause, they looked at each other again, then continued with Orson. Lumus quickly passed them, then began to move quickly to make some space between them.

"This should be far enough. This may set us back, but it is better to be cautious rather than sorry." Lumus let out some of his light, it reflected off the walls blinding Orson and Gerald's men. Lumus threw a punch at the roof in front of him to cave in the tunnel. He quickly ran behind the others before they regained their sight, and hid in the shadows once again.

Orson took a few steps back, his arm covering his face.

"What happened? Is everyone okay?" Orson tried to open his eyes, but his torch had gone out. One of Gerald's men stepped forward with his torch to light the path ahead.

"There was a cave in Councillor. I don't think we can proceed." Orson crossed his arms. "This is solid stone, there must have been something to have set off the cave in," Orson said with confusion.

"Orson, what's happening down here?" Orson turned to see Lumus walking up behind him. He looked at the rocks in front of him, then back at Lumus.

"Lumus why are you down here?" Orson asked, but he had a smile as if he already knew. "I heard you guys came down here so I thought I could lend a hand. What did you come down here for anyway?" Orson turned to Gerald's men. You two are dismissed. We cannot proceed so there is no need for your services." The soldier handed Orson the torch, then the two soldiers looked at each other. After a pause, they passed Orson and Lumus to head out of the tunnel.

"Lumus this was your doing I take it?" Lumus walked over beside Orson with a dim light around him.

"I had to stop Gerald's men from finding out about Neutral City," Lumus replied. Orson looked at Lumus still with his smile.

"I was trying to get some more help for the rocks in the North tunnel. How could that hurt?" Orson replied.

"I was with Gerald earlier. I don't trust him, Orson. I can sense something about him. My gut tells me not to trust him that's all. I wanted to be safe rather than sorry." Lumus said as he looked back down the tunnel toward Capaz. Orson looked back at the rocks.

"Now we can't get back to Neutral City. How do you suppose we get back?" Lumus pushed Orson aside and put his hands out in front of himself. His hands let off a bright flash as Lumus quickly pushed his arms out to his sides. The rocks blow into the cave walls like it was nothing.

"There now we can get back. The stone roof is solid, but near the bottom, it is just dirt and clay." Orson laughed.

"So what do we do now?" Lumus grabbed his cloak from the ground and threw it over himself.

"I will follow Gerald's men. Head to Neutral City, and gather everyone back in town. I need to know what Gerald is up to." Lumus replied. Orson turned as Lumus walked back to Capaz.

"Lumus be careful." Lumus turned and gave Orson a smirk as he faded into the darkness of the tunnel.

Lumus began to run down the tunnel to catch up to Gerald's soldiers, he didn't want to lose them before he found where they were heading. He came up to the ladder to the shop above.

"They should be passing by the palace by now." Lumus climbed the ladder to see Gerald and his two soldiers standing with him in the shop. He quietly jumped out of the tunnel into the storage room, then hugged the wall beside the door.

"Lord Gerald the cave collapsed inside the tunnel, Councillor Orson told us nothing about what he wanted us for either." Gerald was pacing.

"So you fools learned nothing about Lumus and Orson while being with Orson for over three hours?" Gerald said with anger. The soldiers looked at each other.

"My Lord, Orson didn't speak to us at all after we entered the tunnel." Gerald stopped. "Return to the others. I will deal with you two later." Gerald ordered.

Lumus heard the two soldiers leave, but then the pacing began again.

"Hmm." Gerald paced from one side of the shop to the other. After several minutes he stopped, then Lumus heard the door to the street open once more.

"Why is he so curious what we are up to? What does he care what we do?" Lumus pondered for a moment.

"(Gerald must have left, I need to follow him.)" Lumus moved to the door to see someone covered by a black cloak in front of him.

"Hello Lumus, I was expecting Orson, but this may work out better than I thought." The voice said, but Lumus couldn't see the man's face. Just a devious grin. Lumus stepped back and raised his guard.

"Who are you?" Lumus called out.

"You don't recognize my voice? I thought you could sense me where ever I was?" The man laughed. Lumus gasped.

"Lears!?" The man reached for his hood and pulled it back.

"Lears! What are you doing here?" Lears raised his head revealing his sinister grin.

"I was in the neighbourhood, and thought I would drop in," Lears replied. Lumus notice Gerald through the window. His arm rose and pointed to the shop. His men looked like they were gathered around the entire general store.

"You were expecting Orson? Why would you be looking for him?" Lumus replied. Lears crossed his arms.

"If you must know I was told he was here. I was planning on killing him, but maybe you would like to play instead?" Lears laughed again. Lumus took another step back.

"You really want to fight? Fine, but not here. If you want to do this, then we leave the city. Just you and me." Lumus said while keeping an eye on the men outside the window. "What makes you think I'll play along? If I wanted to fight you, I'd do it here, but I'm not here to fight you. Not yet anyway. I came to investigate Kontaminate, but Gerald convinced me to come here." Lears turned his attention to the window

"You are working with Gerald?" Lumus replied quickly. Lears quickly looked back to Lumus. "Not exactly, though he may think we are partners. Actually, I came here to stage a fight with Orson to bring attention to Gerald. I'm sure you noticed his men surrounding the building. Well, my little plan was to fight Orson in the street bringing you, and your friends out in the open. Gerald would then transform, and attack you by surprise." Lears peered out the window.

"Transform?" Lumus said under his breath.

"You didn't know Lumus? Gerald is a Drayhelm. One of the oldest actually. Oh, maybe I shouldn't have said that." Lears smiled.

"What do you benefit off all this?"

"Nothing but questions today huh Lumus? I simply want to expose Gerald. He seems to think he runs this planet with his power of lead council, but when they all see he is a Drayhelm they will most likely kill him. He seems to think he can give me orders as if I will obey just because he has been leaking information about you, and your little gang." Lears took a small step back from the view

of the window. Lumus lit up as his anger grew.
"You can leave Lears I will expose Gerald, and you and I can settle this later," Lumus said. Lears laughed once again.

"You think you can tell me what to do too? Don't be foolish Lumus. I have had plenty of time to train my power. You, on the other hand, are as useful as a lamb. How about a little show for the people of Capaz? They can see their hero in action."

Lears began to emit a black energy around him. His cloak swayed in the air like a flag in the wind. Lumus watched as Lears let out a yell releasing his energy into his hands. As Lears clenched his fist Lumus rushed at him. Lears dodge swiftly, and grabbed Lumus by the neck, then let out a barrage of punches to Lumus at random. One after the other Lumus was defenceless to guard or break free. His grip on his throat was strong, and his punches hit with no pause. After a few more hits Lumus passed out.

"Not yet Lumus, the people are yet to see how little hope they really have." Lears stepped to the side throwing Lumus through the shop window. People in the street panicked and ran from the area. Lears walked out and smiled at Gerald's men as he walked around to Lumus. Gerald's men rushed Lears, but Lears had somehow improved his speed. He was able to dodge every attack and slap them aside as if they were nothing. Lears Laughed.

"Do you see? You have no hope. Your saviour is too weak to stand against me!" Lears turned to look at the palace. Gerald was at the foot of the steps. Lears seemed to have vanished into thin air. Gerald blinked, and he was gone. The rest of the council joined Gerald on the palace steps. The people looked at Lumus lying lifeless on the ground. Suddenly a scream came from Gerald. Lears had appeared in front of the council and grabbed Gerald by the throat

"Come now Gerald, show the good people what a monster you really are," Lears yelled. Gerald let out another scream as Lears forced him to his knees. He held the back of his neck with such force Gerald was left with no choice. He began to transform into a Dragon.

Lears leaped into the air, higher than any normal person could jump. Gerald's clothes began to rip apart as he body changed. His flesh peeled revealing scales. Horns instantly grew from his head, and a massive tail sprouted from his lower back. A roar came from Gerald so loud, it could be heard across the land. Lears stood on top of the palace with a sinister grin. The council rushed away in fear of being trampled.

"My work is done dear people of Twilight. I have unleashed a true Drayhelm upon you. Now he has transformed out of anger. As the legends go, Drayhelms that change of anger cannot return to their previous state. So now choose, kill the leader of the council you trust so very much or die by the beast your people fought so hard to eliminate."

Lears still smiled as he watched the people panic below. Lumus was still lying unconscious, and Orson had not yet arrived with everyone. Frostear watched from a window inside the palace.

"The fear has just been reborn. This event will change Twilight forever. Will the people never escape our curse?" Frostear spoke to himself while watching Gerald.

People ran from their homes, and into the streets. Gerald had fully transformed and had started to destroy nearby homes, and shops. His size grew larger than the palace, and his wings spread half the distance of the city, smoke blew from his nose as his claws shredded building after building. Gerald's eyes caught glimpse of Lumus lying on the ground outside Penelope's shop. His crimson red eyes glared for a moment as if he remembered Lumus. He spread his wings wide and blew a breath of fire from his mouth with a monstrous roar. As he looked back down Lumus was gone. Gerald's rage grew as he searched for Lumus. Gerald walked a few steps searching for Lumus. Suddenly an arrow struck Gerald in the chest. Gerald looked over to Scarlette standing alone, with another arrow loaded into her bow. She launched another arrow without delay, but as it flew toward him he threw his massive claws down to the ground and lowered his head. Scarlette ran toward the outskirts of the city, then quickly turned a corner to take cover, for a quick second she looked at Gerald just to see flames rushing at her. She quickly turned her head back around the corner, then raced off down the alleys. Orson made his way toward the palace. Frostear jumped from the palace window and joined Orson. They ran behind Gerald each with their swords drawn. They quietly made their way back to the palace. Orson turned before entering and made a signal by raising his sword above his head to Zelkem. Zelkem stood with Zephry on Gerald's right side. They hid behind some rubble just out of sight. Zelkem turned to Zephry and nodded, then they separated around each side of the remains of the building. Zelkem ran, and jumped onto Gerald's leg, then latched onto his wing to climb up Gerald. Zephry went around to his left side unnoticed. As Zelkem had his attention Zephry ran over to the inn and climbed onto the roof. Zelkem lost his grip and began to fall. As he fell Gerald swiped his tail sending Zelkem flying straight down the eastern street. Before Gerald could pursue Zelkem, Zephry leaped from the roof off the inn with her sword facing down. She stuck her sword in his leg making Gerald screech in pain. Zephry swung back then forward using her weight to leap up, but Gerald spun around causing her to miss him entirely. She hit the ground with a roll and turned back to Gerald quickly.

"Frostear this way, the roof hatch is at the end of the hall." Orson led Frostear down the west hall to the back of the palace with their swords still drawn.

"Here you go first, and I'll follow." Frostear nodded then made his way up the ladder. Orson quickly followed.

Brinx jumped down from the sky landing beside Zephry just in time to carry her off as Gerald slammed his tail down. Zelkem turned onto his stomach and tried to push himself up. He turned to look at Gerald, but his eyes were unable to focus. He began to shake his head, then his strength faded, and arms gave out as he fell unconscious.

Zynx sprinted across the main road just in front of Gerald with his spear ready to throw. He leaped into the air and launched his arm back. As he was just about to throw his spear Gerald flapped his wings hard and shot a strong gust at Zynx. The sheer force instantly threw him through the air back the way he came. He fell on the main road rolling violently. Scarlette ran out as Zynx flew by, and caught Gerald's attention with her bow loaded. Quickly she shot an arrow aimed at his face, then without a pause, she disappeared into the alleys once again. The arrow hit Gerald on his nose. He let out a screech and staggered back toward the palace. Orson yelled over to Frostear they both took a few steps back then charged off the edge hurling their swords at Gerald. Orson landed first, his sword pierced Gerald's back. Frostear pierced just above Gerald's wing. The two hung on as Gerald came tumbling down to the ground. When the dirt settled, Orson, Frostear, and Brinx stood in front of Gerald. Zephry ran to help Zelkem, and Dyne helped Zynx to his feet.

"I'm sorry I'm late, buddy," Dyne said with a faint smile, but Zynx pointed to Lumus.

Orson turned to the others and looked around frantically.

"What happened to Lumus?" Dyne came walking over to the others with Lumus' arm over his shoulder.

"Don't worry he is still breathing." Dyne yelled out. Orson turned back to Gerald.

"This was tough, I'm just glad everyone is okay." Dyne walked up beside Frostear. Scarlette walked a little closer to Gerald.

"I never though Gerald of all people was a Drayhelm. I had my suspicions, but I didn't even think this. I have never actually seen a transformed Drayhelm so close before." Scarlette said while brushing the dirt off herself. Zephry looked behind her to notice the town's people had returned. They stayed quite a way back and gazed from afar.

"Dyne please bring Lumus back to Neutral City, I will stay here with Orson, and try to plan what to do about Gerald and for the Capaz. Brinx can you do an outer city sweep? Make sure Lears has really left." Orson announced with a serious tone.

Scarlette looked over to Orson. As everyone began to walk away Gerald's eyes opened wide. Scarlette screamed, causing her to fall to her knees. His wings flapped hard, causing everyone to cover their eyes to shield the dirt. Orson looked up to see him heading toward Aster Mountains.

Scarlette rose to her feet and turned to Orson. "What do we do? Should we pursue him?" Scarlette shouted. Orson's eyes didn't leave Gerald.

"No, we are in no condition to give chase. Bring Lumus down below. Everyone else will help out in the city." Orson demanded.

"Orson, Zelkem is in and out. I think he needs to rest too." Zephry whispered. Dyne looked at Zynx barely standing behind Scarlette.

"I'm no doctor, but it looks like we all need to rest," Dyne said faintly. Orson walked slowly toward the Palace.

"Very well, you all go get some rest. I shall organize the cleanup, and join you shortly. Frostear threw Lumus' other arm over his shoulder to help Dyne. They made their way toward Penelope's store. Zephry followed with Brinx and Zelkem. Scarlette waited until they all had left.

"Orson this is bad, we don't know what Gerald will do, he is no more predictable than a wild beast." Orson stood atop the palace steps.

"I know. He could come back at any time, but some of the people have lost their homes. This is all because of us. Every time we are attacked people get hurt in the crossfire. I'm going to do the only thing I know I can do. I'm going to help the people see the light in these dark times." Scarlette looked over her shoulder to the town's people returning to their destroyed homes. People from all over the city began clearing the rubble from the streets.

"I will stay here with you Orson. I will send word to gather the council in the main hall." Orson smiled.

"It will take some time, but things will return to normal. Are you heading to the palace then?" Scarlette nodded to Orson.

"I didn't see where the city guards went. I'm guessing they retreated with the people." Orson turned to notice the town knights working on clearing the streets.

Scarlette worked up enough energy to smile.

"Thank you, Orson." Scarlette turned and made way for the palace.

Orson turned back to the people. He noticed the stage from the last celebration was still in one piece. He made his way through the street and hopped up. The people noticed Orson, and slowly one by one everyone turned expecting a speech.

"Hello everyone, I know we have been through a lot. I know this isn't the first time that our town has been attacked. I honestly don't know what to tell you any more." Orson paused for a minute and looked around from face to face. He could see the confusion in their eyes.

"The truth is Lears can try to bring us down all he wants, we, the people of Capaz will always rise from the ashes and rebuild. He can never defeat us because we cannot be defeated!" The people roared with applause, and cheers as Orson jumped off the stage. Scarlette had watched the speech from the palace doors. Her face lit up with a smile as she closed the doors behind her.

Frostear led everyone down the tunnel with Lumus now on his back. Everyone followed behind except Dyne who was walking a slow pace behind. Zephry looked over her shoulder to see if Dyne was still in sight. He looked as if he was dragging his feet, but it was hard to tell in the dim light.

"Dyne are you okay Zephry blurted out."

Everyone stopped and turned to Dyne. "

I just don't know what we are doing anymore. At first, we were just trying to fight Lears, and end all of this madness, but as each day passes we seem to be falling farther and farther from our goal. I mean really, Lears was a problem, but then we have purple god-like beings, Drayhelms, and not to mention each time we try to battle these bastards, we end up destroying a town in the progress." Dyne said as he slammed his fist into the cave wall.

Dyne sat down and held his head. Frostear walked over to Dyne and grabbed him by the back of his tunic. He raised him into the air to look him in the face.

"Things may seem rough, but don't think for a second that we have lost. You need to remember Lumus beat Kontaminate. Lears will be dealt with in time, and as for Gerald I will deal with him when the time comes." Frostear dropped Dyne and walked past everyone with Lumus still hanging off his back. Dyne made his way to his feet and watched Frostear fade into the darkness of the tunnel.

"Maybe he is right, but we need to be better organized if we intend to win." Zephry ran over to Dyne and stomped hard on his foot.

"Ah! What was that for?" Zephry got real close to Dyne with a deep stare.

"You idiot, did you not just witness what we did together? We just fought off an Elder Drayhelm. Do you think that was unorganized?" Zephry frowned with a wide-eyed stare. Dyne kept stepping back, but Zephry matched every step forward as he moved away.

"Yeah, I guess I didn't think about it," Dyne replied. Brinx turned to Dyne.

"We have accomplished so much together so far. The more time we spend together the more we grow. Teamwork like that can't be false. It's our combined will to change the world for the better that drives us to work together as we did. If one of us loses hope we will all fall apart. As much as you may feel these doubts, we need you. Don't lose hope, or we will all fail." Brinx turned back and made his way toward Neutral City. Zephry walked alongside with him. Zynx stood beside Dyne. He looked at him for a moment as Dyne looked back up at him. After a pause Zynx gave Dyne a kick in his leg, then turned and followed the others.

"Ah! I get it. You of all people, come on man." Dyne rubbed his leg for a while before he looked up. His torch became dim as the flames began to shrink. Everyone had gone ahead and left him alone. He looked back down to see Zynx's kick had put a rip in his pants.

"Damn, these are my favourite pants. Ah, forget it, complaining only gets me yelled at." Dyne shrugged then made his way to the others.

Orson entered the main hall of the Capaz palace. He smiled at Scarlette then approached her.

"The city has cleared most of the debris out the North Gate. We have begun rebuilding in the town plaza. It is amazing to see everyone work together even after all that has happened to them." Scarlette stood from the throne.

"Orson, the councillors will need to choose a new councillor. They will ask my input along with yours. I wanted to know what you thought." Orson walked to the window. "Brunius has returned from the infirmary. He has recovered from his infection from Kontaminate." Scarlette took a long look at Orson.

"Scarlette you would be who I would want as the new lead councillor. No one else would be worthy to give order to Twilight then you, my lady." Orson still looked out the window down to the streets. Scarlette looked down to her satchel strapped to her waist. She took a minute to realize she had not checked her hourglass for some time now. Orson turned back to Scarlette.

"I understand though Scarlette. You want to follow this through with Lumus, as do I. I would elect Lady Concy." Scarlette smiled.

"I agree, my vote will also be for Lady Concy." Orson turned from Scarlette and made his way to the door. He turned as he opened it.

"I must go meet the council in the meeting room. My lady, you would have been a great leader for Twilight." Scarlette smiled as Orson made his way out of the throne room. Scarlette made her way to the window and glanced down the North Gate. Scarlette noticed Orson exiting the palace. He stopped for a moment, then made his way to The North Gate to greet the council members. Scarlette turned and sat once again in the throne chair.

A few moments after Scarlette sat down the Councillors from every city had walked in. She thought in her head that they had made their way through the palace very quickly.

"Lady Scarlette is it true?" Geare blurted out. Scarlette stood quickly.

"Calm yourself, Geare. We will have our answers soon." Lady Concy said politely. Orson was last to enter, he shut the doors behind him. Councillor Owen and Mack started to circle in front of Scarlette, the others formed the circle as they noticed.

Scarlette waved to Orson, he made his way beside her to face the others.

"I am sure you have all saw. Lead councillor Gerald was, in fact, a Drayhelm. Geare you may have been absent during the attack, but yes. Gerald was, in fact, a Drayhelm." Orson announced. Lady Concy had a look of worry on her face as Orson continued.

"Lears appeared too and antagonized him until he lost control. Gerald transformed just outside the palace. Luckily no one was harmed, but we were unable to defeat him." Orson added. Orgu laughed.

"I would have crushed him," Orgu said proudly. Lady Tilza smacked the back of his head.

"Pipe down you old fool! Continue Orson." Orson smiled at Tilza.

"Gerald fled to the North. We are not certain exactly where. However, that will be dealt with. As you all know we now need to elect a new lead councillor, so we will put it to a vote. Orson raised his hand.

"My vote is Lady Concy." Mack raised his hand.

"Scarlette" Orgu raised his hand.

"Scarlette" Everyone left raised their hands, and simultaneously said Scarlette. Scarlette stepped forward.

"Thank you, all of you, but Orson and I have talked this over already. Although my father was once the leader of Capaz I have no right to be voted to take the lead of you all." Scarlette protested. Lady Concy stepped forward.

"Lady Scarlette, You are, and always have been the one to take your father's place. He would have been lead councillor if not for untimely death. You must take his place." Concy added. Scarlette sat down.

"I appreciate your words, but I have to decline, and I vote for Orson." Orson looked at Scarlette with surprise.

"My lady, I cannot, I must be with you and Lumus to see this quest through," Orson argued. Scarlette sighed.

"If I remember correctly Gerald traveled as he wished. I don't see why you cannot do the same." Scarlette added. Brunius entered the throne room and made his way toward the others.

"I heard what you all have said, I have been trying to decide whether I was ready to return after what happened to me." Brunius raised his hand "Orson". Brunius said with his hand raised.

Everyone paused, then raised their hands after a moment. They all shouted Orson.

Scarlette sat up and pushed Orson into the Throne. "Congratulations lead councillor Orson," Scarlette said with a smile.

"If this is so, then I have a few conditions." Orson said. Lady Concy stepped back.

"You are lead councillor. What you say is law, My Lord." Concy replied. Orson smiled. "The first new law, all members of the council must agree on a decision for it to pass. Furthermore, the funds for all of the cities will be distributed equally where they need to be. I also request that we use some funds to rebuild Capaz. What say you?" Orson demanded. Everyone cheered.

"I would also like to enlist Lumus as a Citizen in Capaz, and use some funds to build him a home here in town," Orson added. Everyone cheered again. Orson stood up.

"I would like to ask just one more thing. I would like the council to make Zelkem a third rank knight. I ask he skips the trails due to the path we shall take toward finding Lears. Everyone cheered, but councillor Geare.

"Councillors Cinnus, Anna, and Tank turned to Geare.

"I don't agree to that. The trail is a rite of passage to become a knight. We cannot just allow anyone to become one." Geare protested. Orson nodded. If that is how you feel councillor Geare then it will not be." Geare looked at the other councillors looking back at him.

"Very well Orson, your brother shall become a knight third class, but when this is all over he must take the trails as everyone else has, even if he earns his way to first class," Geare added. Orson smiled.

"Thank you councillor Geare, Zelkem will become my apprentice as well as lady Zephry," Orson replied. Tank crossed his arms.

"We haven't had to take an apprentice since the Dragon Wars. You haven't trained a knight before Orson. Do you think you can handle two?" Orson turned his attention to Tank.

"From what I have seen in combat with them I believe those two will surpass even you," Orson said with a laugh. Tank shrugged.

"Ha-ha that I would like to see." Tank replied. The councillors made their way to their rooms, Orson stayed behind with Brunius and Scarlette. Brunius took his seat on the throne as Orson walked over to the window.

"I have to apologize. When I got over my infection, it took me some time to see straight. I needed some time until I could return to the palace." Brunius hung his head as he sat. Orson sighed.

"Brunius we understand, notice how the rest of the council didn't question you? I know they trust you and have seen what you have done over the years for the council and Twilight. You don't need to be sorry for anything." Scarlette smiled.

"Thank you, Orson. Lady Scarlette I will be the leader of Capaz that your father wanted you to be until you are ready to take my place." Brunius smiled. Scarlette turned to the window.

"I know you will Brunius." Brunius left the throne room with his head held high. "Scarlette are you okay?" Orson tried to see her face.

"I am fine Orson you should head down to the plaza, they may need your help." Orson stopped moving toward Scarlette.

"I see, if you need me, then you know where I'll be." Orson made his way to the door. He turned before leaving to see a shine of light from outside glisten off Scarlette's cheek as a tear fell to the ground. He had a sad look on his face as he closed the door behind him.

Chapter Seventeen- A Glimpse of Darkness

Lears sat proudly in his chair at the top of a large staircase overlooking all of his Lords below. The stone around them freshly carved into their new fortress. The corridors were brightened by the many torches along the walls. Columns lined the cavern from the door leading to the Aster Mountain trails all the way to Lears on his new throne. Five shadow demons stood behind Lears, digging as he sat.

"I have called you all here to witness my next act of hatred toward the pathetic people of this planet. We have terrorized and killed people burned their cities, and even built a prison to house those that defy us. Now we will take it to the next level. Now I will show them my true power. I will unleash a moon-sized attack on Twilight." Ged looked worried.

"Lord Lears, won't an attack that size... Won't it kill everyone, and us along with it?" Ged blurted out. Lears laughed.

"Ged, you worry over nothing. The attack will seem life-threatening, but in truth, it is my way of luring Lumus and his friends out of hiding." Lears laughed once again. Coldblood sighed.

"So we are trying to finish them off once and for all?" Ged asked. Lears stood from his throne.

"Exactly, and when they are out of the way we will commence in taking out the rest of Twilight and rebuild it as I see fit." Lears sat back down. Antsos glanced outside as he heard a roar.

"Master, I believe the Drayhelm is back. Coldblood turned his attention to the cave opening.

"His name is Zuul. Gerald was a name he gave himself to fool the council. Lord Lears, now that Zuul's rage has transformed him there is no telling what or who he will attack." Antsos announced. Lears stood up once more, but this time he made his way down the stairs past his followers to the cave door. He noticed Zuul circle back to the mountains.

"This Dragon is nothing to me." Lears raised his hands and formed a ball of dark energy. Slowly it grew bigger. Lears closed his eyes and began to glow with a faint dark light around his body. Zuul noticed the energy from the air. With a roar, he dove down directly at Lears.

Lears' eyes flew open as he cried "Let's see how the great Zuul handles this!" The ball of energy grew larger than Zuul as he was hit head-on. He was pushed farther into the sky as the energy rose. The dark energy came to a stop, then stayed high in the air. Zuul was pushed with such force out of sight. Lears yelled out once more and dropped his hands.

"My Lord, are you okay?" Antsos asked with concern, Coldblood stared up into the sky. "My Lord, I believe you sent it off into space," Ged added. Lears turned back to the cavern entrance.

"We won't be bothered by him for a while." Lears laughed as he passed Ged. Coldblood stared up at the sky.

"I should mention that us Drayhelms can hold our breath for almost a week while in our dragon form. You may have just made him angrier. He will be back, My Lord." Coldblood explained. Lears stopped for a moment, then continued toward his throne.

"Zuul is not important; what we must do now is march for Twilight Lake. Lumus will be coming to see the main event, I'm sure." Lears sat on his throne with a sinister grin on his face. Ged approached Lears and kneeled in front of him.

"My Lord, what are we to do when we find them?" After a pause, Ged looked up at Lears. His eyes were closed, but he still smiled.

"We will kill them all. Leave no one alive." Lears demanded. The Lords roared. Ged rose to his feet with a grin.

"As you wish, My Lord." Ged backed away slowly, then turned for the cavern entrance. Coldblood and Hedree followed behind him. Jol and Antsos waited for them to pass then followed as well. Levitz and Aire were about to follow, but Lears stood up once again.

"You two wait a moment. I have a special job for you." Aire glanced at Levitz, who stood silently waiting for orders. "I want you two to remain hidden. When the battle starts I want you to abduct the girl with pink hair." Aire crossed his arms.

"What use is the girl to us?" Aire asked. Lears stared at Aire. He raised his hand to Aire, then shot a quick blast of energy towards him, causing him to fall to his knees.

"Aire, the next time you speak, remember that I do not care for your opinion. The girl may know some things that I want to hear for myself. You don't need to know more than that. Don't fail me; I will not tolerate failure. Lears loomed over Aire as he spoke, as Levitz remained silent. Aire glance back at Levitz once more, who remained unmoved. He nodded at Lears, then turned to the door. Aire turned to look over his shoulder then staggered to his feet, following Levitz without a word.

Ged led the Lords across the fields from the southern mountain line toward Lake Twilight. He didn't turn back to see if the others were following him. Instead, he watched the sky, thinking that he is knowingly walking under the path of Lears' attack. The energy flowed like lightning in a transparent ball with dark light spewing out like little volcanoes.

"Everyone stop. Zuul is above us." Ged yelled out. Coldblood looked straight up. For a moment he scanned the sky.

"He is silent, but he knows we are here; that is certain," Coldblood added. Ged glanced over to Coldblood.

"Are you sure he knows we are here?" Coldblood was still staring at the sky.

"He is circling the area, waiting for a chance to strike," Coldblood replied. Ged took a moment to think. He looked across to the fields.

"If we were to have entered the plains he would have attacked us. While we are under cover of the cliffs he can't get a good enough chance to strike. We must find a way past without Zuul attacking." Coldblood moved past Antsos and Jol.

"Our best bet is to follow the cliffs back and…"

"And what?" Ged interrupted.

"If we go back how do you think Lears will greet you? Only gone a few minutes, and already we have failed the mission. No, we find a way to press on, and we do it without returning to Lears." Ged looked up at the sky. After glancing between the field and the sky once more he turned to the cliffs.

"We take the cliffs all the way to Lake Twilight" Ged demanded. Antsos laughed.

"Lord Ged, there is no path along these cliffs. We would be climbing the whole way." Antsos added. Ged turned to Antsos.

"I know, but unless you have a better idea we follow the cliffs." Coldblood put his hand up to stop them.

"Wait, Zuul is leaving. I think he has gone." Antsos finally looked up. After a pause, he turned to Ged.

"Zuul has flown above the dark energy. I can no longer see him." Coldblood said as he continued to stare at the sky. Ged jumped off the small cliff onto the grass below. "He means to push the attack on us?" Coldblood turned to see Jol already fleeing back toward their headquarters.

" Jol has the right idea. If Zuul brings that attack down on us, then we are done for!" Coldblood didn't wait for a response from Ged. He quickly turned and followed behind Jol.

"Ged, it would be wise to flee." Antsos agreed.

"We are supposed to be the Dark Lords of Lears, and you all act like cowards. I will not flee; I shall complete the mission." Ged shouted.

He dashed as fast as he could across the plains. Antsos turned toward the headquarters. He glanced toward Ged, then the sky.

("Fool, you are going to get yourself killed.") Antsos thought to himself. Ged made his way to Lake Twilight, he peered down into the lake from the cliffs. As he looked from side to side for a place to wait, he noticed Aire and Levitz climbing the cliffs to the West. "I guess they are taking the high ground... smart. I shall stay low then." He thought as he ran over to a couple of rocks with a small gap in between them. He climbed over into the gap and hid in the shadows. He looked up to the sky once more, but couldn't sense dragons like Coldblood, nor did he have the cat-like sight like Antsos.

"I suppose if Zuul does push the dark energy down I can just enter the shadow realm, but my power is currently weak from transporting the other Lords here. I can't enter the shadow realm for some time. Maybe this wasn't as well planned as I had thought." Ged said to himself.

"Lumus... Lumus! You should come see this." Scarlette stood by the window in disbelief. Lumus turned from Orson and Frostear.

"What is it? Is something the matter?" He replied with concern. She didn't say a word or even turn to face him. She just stared out the window. He walked over to join her at her side.

"What is it?" Lumus turned to the window beside her. His eyes widened.

"How did I not sense this energy? Orson ran over to the other window with Frostear. "This must be Lears, right? What could he possibly gain from something like this?" Orson asked. Frostear looked up into the sky.

"It's Zuul. He is trying to push the energy from above." Frostear added. Lumus opened the window. "I don't understand. Is Zuul attacking us?" Scarlette asked in confusion.

"This is star energy from Lears. I think he is fighting Zuul. It looks like they are just past Lake Twilight. Zuul has now shown us where Lears is hiding. Orson, have everyone meet us at the city gates; It's time that we end this." Lumus demanded. Scarlette turned to him, surprised.

"Are you crazy? Look, we can't go out there. If we all head over there now Zuul could drop that massive ball of energy on us too." Scarlette shouted. Frostear made his way to the door and quietly said "Then we go aerial. I'll call my father. He can fly us up to Zuul." Lumus turned and made his way toward the door.

"Lumus are you two really going to go? Don't be crazy! This, for once, is not our fight so please don't go looking for trouble." Scarlette cried out. Orson walked over to Scarlette's side.

"I agree with Scarlette. We don't need to fight. It would be wise to let our enemies battle each other, then we can move in on them once they are weakened. It may be a low tactic but when your enemy fights dirty, you must fight dirty." Orson added.

"I don't care that they are fighting, and I don't care who wins between them. That massive ball of energy could kill hundreds or even thousands of innocent people. Frostear, please call your father." Lumus demanded. Scarlette looked out the window once again. Orson crossed his arms facing Lumus.

"I understand. Scarlette and I will continue overseeing the construction. Do what you feel is right Lumus." Orson replied. Frostear left the room. Lumus watched him walk outside, then he turned back to Scarlette.

"I won't do anything foolish, I promise. I will stop the attack, then I will return here." He looked Scarlette in the eyes. She didn't say a word. She just turned back to look out the window.

Lumus left, shutting the door slowly, and made his way down the main hall to the Palace lobby. He noticed Frostear by the main gate. He walked down the road toward Frostear. He turned to see Scarlette watching him. He smiled, and after a pause, he turned back and made his way toward the main gate.

"Frostear, are you ready?" He asked.

"I think it would be best if we got a good distance from the city before I call my father to us. People may not react well toward a dragon near the city." Frostear added. Lumus smiled to agree.

"You're right. We can make our way to the forest line by Lake Twilight. That should be enough cover from the city."

Coldblood and Antsos returned to Aster Mountains. He stopped just outside the passage to their new lair.

"Go ahead Antsos," Coldblood said faintly.

"Are you not coming?" Antsos replied.

"I can feel Zuul's rage, we must warn Lord Lears. Antsos entered the lair with Coldblood just behind him. Coldblood looked up to see Jol had already arrived.

"Lord Lears, Zuul has come back. He seems to be pushing the energy toward us." Antsos announced as he bowed.

"What did you say Antsos? Lears said in a rage. Coldblood, you said Zuul wouldn't return."

Coldblood shrank back from Lears. "My Lord, Zuul is much stronger than normal dragons. With age we Drayhelms grow in strength." Coldblood added.

Lears stood beside his throne with a look of worry on his face.

"My Lord, what will you have us do?" Lears turned to Antsos.

"I will have to deal with Zuul myself. I was hoping to avoid fighting him." Antsos laughed.
"My Lord, you can destroy Zuul with ease. Why do you think so little of yourself?" Lears turned fast hitting Antsos with the back of his fist. Antsos flew across the room slamming into the wall.
"Don't be a fool. I know I can destroy Zuul, but if I was to use my energy on him; it would take time to recover. With Lumus so close to finding us I need to stay at full power."
Antsos coughed up blood as he tried to stand. Jol took a step back with fear in her eyes. Coldblood headed for the door slowly.
"Are you going somewhere, Coldblood?" Lears said maliciously.
"My Lord, Zuul has started to push the energy. It's slow...but it is building up speed." Coldblood said as he looked up into the sky. Lears calmed down as he turned, and he sat back on his throne.
"I can also sense my father, he is flying not too far from here," Coldblood added.
"Your father is a Drayhelm? Does that mean we are dealing with another dragon?" Antsos blurted out from the ground. Coldblood laughed.
"No Lord Antsos, my father does not yet have the ability to transform. He is riding upon another dragon. That dragon is my grandfather. Lord Lears, I believe he is coming to stop Zuul." Lears had is eyes closed when Coldblood looked up at him.
"Lumus is with him. I can feel his power coming closer. We will fall back for now. Coldblood, block

the entrance. Jol and Antsos, light the inner tunnel torches." Lears stopped as the others ran to complete their orders.

"Antsos, where is Scar?" Antsos stopped facing the dark tunnel behind Lears.

"My Lord I have already brought Scar to the lower tunnel. I have made him comfortable, I assure you." Lears waved his hand as if to release Antsos. ("For now, Lumus, I will let you live. I have bigger plans for you to come. Zuul has done most of the work for me, but at least I was able to give you a small parting gift. I still have Ged, Hedree, Aire, and Levitz to keep you company.") Lears burst out into laughter as he turned to head down the dark tunnel behind the others.

"Frostear, look down there. It's Zuul!" Lumus held on tightly to Frostear. The wind was stronger than Lumus thought it would be. He could see Frostear calm without covering his eyes from the wind. ("How does he keep his eyes open at this speed? I can barely keep mine open at all.") Lumus thought to himself. Frostear pulled up and to the right on the dragon's neck. Suddenly with a roar, the dragon flew up to the right side of Zuul. He was too busy attacking the energy to notice.

"Lumus now is your chance. Go!" Lumus managed to stand up. He faced toward the energy while holding onto Frostear for balance.

"I'll see you in a bit, Frostear. Thanks for the ride." Lumus leaped into the air with his arms out wide. He fell just above the orb of energy. Just before he hit it he pulled his arms into his sides and dove straight into the energy. Zuul noticed Frostear as he made his way behind him. He turned, and hit his feet against the energy to push off toward Frostear. As Zuul pushed off of the energy, Lumus reached out and grabbed Zuul by a claw on his left foot. Zuul screeched as he looked back. Lumus pulled him into the energy with him as Frostear watched.

("How could Lumus have enough strength to pull Zuul in? The energy alone must be draining his power just from being in there.") Frostear thought as he circled around the orb, hoping to find a way to help, but he didn't see anything he could do. As he flew just above the orb, Zuul burst through and latched onto Frostear's father. Zuul's razor-sharp teeth sunk deep, but Zuul's eyes opened wide as he was pulled back into the orb. Slowly Frostear was pulled in with his father. At the very last second, Frostear jumped off into the open sky. A single tear rolled from his eye and drifted into the air above him as he freefell back to Twilight. A bright flash of light forced him to cover his eyes as he fell. When he was able to see again; the orb of energy was gone, his father, Zuul, and Lumus were nowhere in sight. As he searched for them he looked down to notice he wasn't falling. Frostear turned his head to see Lumus holding onto him. "Lumus! How?" Lumus just smiled as the two of them slowly fell through the sky back to Twilight. They set down on the ground gently. Frostear noticed three claw marked across Lumus' chest. Blood ran down his stomach under his shirt and began to soak through the fabric. He looked up to the sky. Nothing was there, no traces of Zuul or his father. He looked back at Lumus, and noticed the blood. Lumus was still standing, but his eyes were closed with his mouth open as if he was sleeping standing up. Frostear ran over to him as he fell forward, unconscious. Frostear caught him just before he slammed into the ground.

"I got you Lumus. It will be alright. I will get you patched up." Frostear stood with him in his arms He turned and looked off toward Capaz.

"It may be a longer walk than I thought," Frostear said to himself

"I don't think you will be heading back to Capaz just yet." A familiar voice said from the shadows. Frostear turned to look over his shoulder.

"Aire and Levitz. What are you two doing here?" Frostear asked with a faint smile. Levitz made his way around Frostear as Aire crossed his arms and stared at Frostear.

"Well, Levitz and I saw an opportunity to kill Lumus once and for all. We decided to abandon our mission to do so." Aire announced. Frostear watched Levitz.

"Levitz wanted to take you on. He doesn't talk much, so allow me to formally introduce Levitz, the assassin of the Dragon Wars." Aire smiled.

"You don't need to introduce him," Frostear said as he threw Lumus over his shoulder. "Ah, I see you know him?" Frostear laughed.

"No, I meant I don't need to know his life story since I'm about to kill him." Levitz continued to stare at Frostear without a move. Aire began to laugh.

"You don't think you have a chance, do you? Levitz has killed more of your kind than you can count. He has single handily put your race near extinction." Aire added.

Frostear took a deep breath. After a moment of silence, he dashed over to Aire, in a flash punching him in the gut with such force that he coughed up blood on Frostear's face. "I'll deal with you in a minute" Frostear whispered into Aire's ear. He pulled his fist back and straightened Lumus on his back. Aire fell to his knees as Frostear turned to Levitz. Levitz's eyes opened wide in disbelief.

"I bet you are curious about my speed. You see the Drayhelms that you have killed in the past were probably younglings. Only elder Drayhelms have the ability to move as I do. I may not be able to use this ability often, but it will be enough to take you two down." Frostear smiled with a glare. Levitz pulled a dagger from the sheath on his leg and another from the sheath on his arm. He planted his right leg forward with his right arm up.

"Still you think you can fight me. Even while I carry Lumus I can…" Levitz blinked for a second, and Frostear was gone. He searched the area and even the sky, but he was nowhere to be seen. He realized he would have to be behind him. Slowly Levitz turned, but Frostear was already clenching his fist before Levitz was able to fully turn; Frostear punched Levitz with such force in the center of his back that he was paralyzed, unable to move. Frostear walked around him.

"You won't be killing any more Drayhelms. Though only a few of us remain." Levitz fell to his knees. His body went limp, but he was able to hold his head up.

"That was for my father, I'm sure he would have wanted to kill you himself, but I'm glad I get that pleasure." Frostear grabbed Levitz by his throat and lifted him into the air. He stared into his eyes as he squeezed tight. Levitz turned solid black like a shadow and then vanished. Frostear wiped the blood from his face, but as he did the blood turned black and faded. It reminded him that Aire was still behind him. He had made his way to his feet.

"I thought Lumus and his followers were soft," Aire announced. Frostear smiled.

"Who told you that? Maybe Lumus and a few others would have let you live, but I think the only way to deal with a problem is to eliminate it for good." Frostear replied with a smirk. Aire held his chest with one arm. His other arm hung at his side. Frostear's attack had left him with no energy. Aire had trouble breathing but still managed to stand.

"I am surprised my son could tolerate working with Levitz in the first place, knowing that he killed so many of our kind," Frostear said in disgust. Aire laughed.

"Who do you think helped Levitz find all of the Drayhelms?" Frostear turned toward Capaz. Aire turned into a shadow and disappeared just as Levitz had done.

"Ged, you can tell Lears that we are coming for him. Your shadow clones are an insult. Next time try to fight me one-on-one and see what happens." Frostear shouted as he walked away with Lumus still on his shoulder.

Ged watched from the shadows on the hillside. After Frostear had made his way out of sight Ged showed his face with an evil grin.

"I am impressed, Frostear. You were able to see through my shadows. It's too bad he doesn't know what Aire and Levitz are really up to." He smiled as he turned into the shadows and faded away.

Chapter Eighteen- Orson's Promise

The light from the blue moon poured into Orson's room as the day started without him. Outside his room was quiet. No one walked about, no voices whispered in the halls. Orson's legs stretched to the end of the bed, then fell over to the side of the bed, causing him to wake up. He reached for his sword that lay beside him. His eyes shifted around the room until he realized where he was. He put his sword on the bed and began to slowly put his armour on. He gazed out the window to see that people had been working through the night. All of the debris was moved away and people had begun fixing the damaged walls and shattered windows in most of the homes and shops. He looked over to the right and noticed a handful of people starting the foundation on a new home.
("They have started to build Lumus' house. The people really do care for him.") He turned and picked up his sword, strapped it to his waist and sighed. He turned to the door, then in a hurry turned back to the window. He saw Frostear straight down the main road carrying Lumus over his shoulder.
"Lumus!" His eyes opened wide.
He ran to the door and down the hall to the palace doors. Scarlette was waiting outside, staring at the steps. At first, she didn't hear him, having left the door open behind her. He looked down to

Scarlette. She turned to him to see the worry in his eyes. Without a word, he ran off into the street. She stood up with her hands covering her face in panic. She didn't follow Orson as he took off down toward the main gate.

"Frostear is he okay!" He yelled out.

"I wouldn't worry, I patched him up on the road." Frostear walked past him without stopping. "Are you sure? There is a lot of blood on both of you." Frostear didn't stop walking. He tried to keep up beside them.

"Lumus got clawed by Zuul," Frostear announced. Orson stopped walking, utterly shocked by the idea.

"What happened, Frostear?" Scarlette shouted out. He stopped at the steps in front of her and rested Lumus on the bottom step. He looked up to see Scarlette crying.

"We went to stop the dark energy falling from the sky. Lumus jumped into the orb of energy, then he dragged Zuul into it with him. My father was dragged into the energy by Zuul, and I fell from his back. Lumus will have to explain the rest of that, but I wouldn't worry. Lumus may have been clawed, but it's already healing. I think he just used too much power." Frostear turned to head for Neutral City. Scarlette dropped to her knees beside Lumus. She held his hand as she cried.

"You may want to think about how many people Zuul would have killed if he wasn't stopped. Maybe you will realize what we are all fighting for when you hear it from Lumus." Frostear paused for a moment, then continued walking away. Orson crossed his arms and watched him walk away.

("I hate to admit it but he is right.") Orson thought to himself. He turned to Scarlette.

"Look Scarlette, you need to think about this; all this time we have been searching for Lears, and his Lords. What did you think would happen when we finally met face to face? Shake hands and just say 'sorry for the trouble'?" Orson asked. He walked over to Lumus, picked him up and carried him up the palace stairs in both arms.

("Maybe Frostear rubbed off on me, I was a little harsh on her too.") He thought and turned back to Scarlette to apologize, but when he turned around he was shocked to see Ged standing in her spot and holding her over his shoulder.

"Don't be sad, golden warrior. She has had this coming for a long time now. I will treat her with the attention she deserves. Oh, and tell that Drayhelm that he is next." Ged said with a laugh. He opened a portal within a shadow on the ground and jumped into it. He quickly dropped Lumus and jumped to the bottom of the stairs and slid into the portal after Ged and Scarlette. Lumus rolled down the steps, still unconscious. As he hit the ground the shadow portal disappeared.

("Ah, where am I? It's cold and this ringing in my ears won't stop.") Orson thought to himself as he wiped his eyes.

He stood up and opened his eyes to see a solid white ground that seemed endless in every direction. He looked to the sky, but it was pitch black. He wasn't on Twilight anymore he thought to himself.

"Welcome to my world, Sir Orson," Ged announced. Orson turned around to see Ged and Scarlette. She was unconscious near his feet. Orson looked at Scarlette closely.

"Don't worry Orson; she is still breathing." Ged kicked her across the flat white surface.

"Hey, you bastard leave her alone!" Orson yelled out. Ged smiled. Then he threw his arms up into the air. He clenched his fists and dropped his arms toward her. Multiple transparent shadows came racing down from the sky encasing her in a small cage of bars with a solid black roof on top.

"Don't want her waking up and interfering now do we? You see, this is my world. I call it the Realm of Shadows. In this world, I can manipulate the shadows above to create whatever I see fit. For example, this small prison for Lady Scarlette. Oh and this!" Ged raised his arms once more and clenched his fist like before. This time he dropped his arms beside himself. A large shadow came crashing down on himself. Orson took a step back and covered his face against the gust of wind from the shadow landing on Ged.

"What kind of trick is this?" He blurted out. Ged began to laugh. As the shadow faded it revealed a bald man with a goatee. His armour almost matching Orson's in style, but dark red rather than gold. Even his sword sheathed around his waist was very similar. Ged smiled. Then drew his sword and pointed it at Orson.

"In this world I am everything. In this world I am anything…in this world I am God." Ged shouted with a devious smile. Orson drew his sword.

"This is it Ged, we are ending this now." Orson smiled.

"You can try, but remember I was the golden hero over one hundred years ago. You can't match me with a sword, Sir Orson." Orson unbuckled his sheath, letting it fall to the ground.

"Things change, Ged. I am the new and improved version of you." Orson's smile faded.

Ged and Orson ran at each other at full speed. Their swords clashed with sparks. Ged pushed Orson away, throwing him off balance. He slashed again, but Orson let himself fall. He turned his sword and thrust it at Orson as he rolled out of the way and jumped to his feet. He smiled as he thrust his sword forward at Orson once more, but he quickly dodged just to be punched by Ged. Orson regained his balance and rubbed his face as they circled each other.

"Ah, not bad. Using the thrust as a distraction for that punch." Orson spit off to the side. Ged's smile faded.

"I am no fool, Orson. You are holding back." He raised his sword. Orson could tell he was after a real fight.

"Try this, Ged" He tightened his grip on his sword and yelled out before he dashed at him.

("He knows how to channel his star energy into an attack?") Ged thought to himself as Orson jumped into the air with his sword above his head. He locked eyes with Orson for only a second, then Orson disappeared. A moment went by and Orson reappeared in front of him, unleashing a devastating slash to his chest. He flew through the air, then slammed into the ground. He rolled for a while unable to move.

"It is over Ged. Like I told you before; I am the new and improved knight." Ged rose to his feet slowly.

"Don't mistake carelessness as weakness. You may have surprised me with that attack but I too have been able to channel my strength into an attack. I am impressed though. Very few people can do this. Remember, star energy is the very life that we are, that we breathe. As we age, we build more and more star energy. You can use as much energy as you can without dying, but it will take time to rebuild that energy." Ged explained. Orson sighed.

("Why does it seem like he is trying to teach me. This is a fight to the death, right?") Orson thought to himself.

"Well? Are you ready to go again?" Ged asked with a grin.

"I used a lot of energy on that attack, is that what you're telling me? That may be true Ged but look at you. You are barely able to stand." Orson added. Ged gripped his sword.

"That may be true as well, but here is another fact for you. Your physical energy and your star energy are separate. Though you may have lowered my physical stamina, I can still perform an attack worthy of winning the fight." Ged raised his sword above his head, then let go. His sword slowly flew up into the air.

"I can't see the swords, they are moving too fast. How was he able to do that?" Orson held his sword in front of his face.

"Your mistake is thinking you could defeat me," Ged announced from within the wind tunnel with his glowing eyes fading into the heavy winds. Orson stood strong, trying to keep his balance against the strong winds.

Ged smiled and pointed his hands toward Orson. The wind picked up as the sword hurricane jumped into the air and sprang toward him. His sword blocking his face, he watched Ged, and not the attack. As the swords made their way to Orson, he readied his footing to try to avoid them. Just as they were in front of him, he noticed Ged couldn't see him over the wind. He leaped to the left, then dashed past the attack at Ged. He made his way past the hurricane, then caught Ged off guard. Ged had no choice but to release his hands. Orson quickly slashed him across his chest, but his crimson armour took most of the attack. He jumped back as the hurricane of swords faded. His sword was thrown by the dissipating wind, and it landed behind Orson.

"Well planned, Sir Orson. You were able to see the weakness of the attack so quickly, and now my sword is out of reach... I did not foresee you would maneuver in such a way." He boasted with a smiled. Orson held his sword pointed at him just out of striking distance.

"It's over Ged; you are unarmed and low on energy. I have won." Orson announced. Ged reached to his back and grabbed the strap holding his armour over his shoulders.

"I am not finished yet, Sir Orson. You have only managed to slay my armour." He laughed. His armour fell to his feet revealing a light chainmail underneath.

"The fight has just begun!" He yelled out. Orson smiled.

"So it has, Sir Ged." Orson reached to his back still holding his sword at Ged. He unclipped the straps, letting his armour fall to the ground too.

Ged raised his hands to the sky as he grinned with his eyes closed. Two large shadows came crashing down to his hands. After a moment they made shapes then color appeared revealing a sword in one hand, and a shield in another.

"Let us keep this a traditional fight. A knight's fight." Orson bent down to his armour, and picked up his chest plate. He took the center of the armour out which turned out to be a shield built into the armour.

"Okay Ged, let us begin." Orson smiled with his sword and shield ready.

Ged ran at him with his shield out in front, and with his sword behind him. Orson ran with his sword out front and his shield at his side. He swung, clashing with Ged's shield as Ged swung his sword around. Orson pulled his shield up to block then brought his sword back, his elbow bent. Ged dropped his shield to block Orson's lower attack. He stepped back as Orson did the same. They circled each other while staring into each other's eyes. Orson took a step forward, but Ged mimicked the opposite. Orson raised his sword as Ged did the same.

"It seems we are equal with the sword, Orson. I have to say I am interested to see how this plays out." Ged smiled. Orson didn't say a word. He was looking over his shoulder at Scarlette. After a moment he looked back at Ged. Orson dashed at him, their swords clashed again and again. Sparks flew from each hit as they matched attack after attack. Sweat dripped off the pair, but as they moved so fast it almost appeared to fall in slow motion. Finally, the battle stopped. Again they stepped back and circled each other. They panted with exhaustion. Sweat dripped down both their faces as they silently planned their next moves. Ged jumped into the air and pointed his sword at Orson. He moved, and rolled to avoid his attack, Orson now on one knee turned to see Ged's fist coming for his face. The roll had left Orson disoriented and the fist struck his face. Orson slide across the ground. The punch seemed to have more strength behind it, then he had thought. He slowly made his way to his feet. Ged was just standing in dead silence. His breathing returned to normal.

("How, he didn't have enough time to recover, not even close.") Orson threw his shield away and gripped his sword with both hands.

"This is it, Sir Ged. I have had enough." Orson stood strong. Ged's face was calm, but inside he knew he was thrashed. His body was tired, and his star energy had been drained from his last attack. Orson ran at Ged with his sword raised high in the air as he built up speed. Ged raised his shield and stood his ground. Orson swung hard downward at him hitting his shield with such force that the attack forced Ged to his knees. The tip of Orson's sword pierced the edge of Ged's shield just above his head. Slowly his strength gave, and the shield lowered until it was pushed onto his lap. He surprisingly released one hand from his shield and reached out to Orson. As Ged sprang up, Orson's sword pierced through Ged's chest. Orson pulled his sword from Ged and took a step back.

"You may have won Orson, but as they say you have only won the battle, not the war." Ged smiled.

"Ged what have you done?" Orson asked. He laid spread out on the ground, blood started to form a puddle beside his body.

"It is simple; I have lost. I may not have been able to kill Scarlette myself, but I will return one day." Orson turned to look at Scarlette. The shadow cage slowly faded. Orson looked back at Ged. His clothing and flesh turned into a liquid and started to turn black. The liquid turned back into shadows then returned to the sky. He had returned to his shadow form.

"Remember this: A knight's honor is only measured by the loyalty with which he devotes himself to his cause. In the end, nothing else matters. Whether you're with someone or you always die alone. It is the curse every knight is burdened with."

The shadow from Ged's body rose into the air to reveal only a skeleton. Orson stood up, in awe, and turned to Scarlette. After a bright flash, Orson was relieved to find himself back in Capaz just outside the palace. He noticed Zelkem and Zephry helping Lumus to his feet. Scarlette was regaining consciousness just behind him. He quickly rushed to Scarlette to make sure she was okay. Scarlette smiled as she stood up.

"Ged is finally gone. That is one less thing to worry about." Scarlette said with a sigh of relief.

"I believe we haven't seen the last of Ged. He is a shadow, and wherever you go there is always a shadow behind you." Orson said with a cheerless smile. He turned toward the palace and went inside. Scarlette walked towards Lumus with a faint smile on her face.

"Are you okay Lumus?" She asked. Lumus had a smirk on his face.

"It will take more than Orson dropping me down some stairs to keep me down," Lumus said with a laugh. Scarlette sighed then burst out in laughter.

Zelkem put his arms up with his hands behind his head.

"Well he is concussed, might want to have that looked at Lumus." Zelkem walked off toward Penelope's shop with Zephry.

Lumus shook his head. After a moment he turned to Penelope's shop and watched Zelkem and Zephry enter with the door shutting behind them. Scarlette took a minute to look at Lumus then at Penelope's shop, then back at Lumus. She thought Lumus was daydreaming, but the moment the door shut he turned to the palace.

"Scarlette will you wait for me in Neutral City?" Lumus didn't wait for a response, he made his way up the palace steps. Scarlette took a breath as she watched Lumus walk away from her.

("What is he up to? Going to the palace would only mean he wants something from Orson or the council.") Scarlette headed toward Penelope's shop. She made her way to the door, and she turned once more to see Orson walking down the palace steps with a man dressed like a messenger.

"We have only just returned from a fight with Ged, who is that man? That badge? He must be a messenger. Scarlette wondered for a moment.

"Sir Orson, again I must say it is an honor to have met you. My kids will never believe me, and thank you for meeting with me, especially in your condition." Orson smiled, almost embarrassed.

"I am happy to be of service, thank you again for delivering this parcel all the way from Librine. You must have great courage to have traveled alone." Orson added. The messenger paused while looking at his next parcel.

"Not at all. I have guards that travel with me and my caravan." He looked over his shoulder toward the city gates, he couldn't quite see them but assumed they were there.

"In any case, I must go. Good day, Sir Orson."

"And to you." He replied.

Orson opened the parcel to find a pendant. For a moment he paused. Suddenly a tear rolled down his cheek. He dropped the packaging but clenched the pendant with both hands. After a moment with his eyes closed, he made his way back to the palace. Scarlette watched from the window of Penelope's shop almost in tears, watching him. He entered the palace, and made his way to his room where Lumus had been waiting for him.

"Orson, is everything okay?" Lumus asked.

"I just got something by messenger, it seems I have to leave for a while," Orson announced. He moved to the dresser and grabbed some things. He began wrapping some of them and tied it to his chest.

"Leave? What is the matter?" Lumus asked. Orson didn't stop, he opened a drawer beside Lumus and took out a small coin purse.

"Someone I used to know died some time ago. A pendant I gave her was given back to me before I left. After that, I met some young kids that I spent some time with, and I trained them and helped them get by before I left South Twilight. I gave the pendant to a small girl as a memento and told her if she ever needed me to send the pendant, and I would return. So I must go." Orson finished gathering everything then turned to the door. Lumus stood in the way.

"You know I can't let you leave without offering to come with you." Lumus smiled.

"I'm sorry Lumus, I have no choice but to do this alone. I will be back in a week. Until then, stay here and take some time to learn more about Twilight. Everyone deserves a break, and maybe some downtime will help everyone get their morale back. You can also use this time to focus on Neutral City. We are going to need it if Lears plans on attacking any more cities." Orson announced as he looked around to see if he forgot anything.

"I suppose we could use this time to build and expand," Lumus added. Orson looked back at Lumus.

"Make sure you coordinate with the council to set up the tunnels. Even if Lears attacks we will have those tunnels as a backup. I will return as fast as I can Lumus. Be safe!" Orson gave Lumus a nod. Orson left the room and raced down the hall. He made his way to the side entrance to the Zufore stable. He hopped on a Zufore and made his way to the main street through the city gates.

("It will take a few days to get to South Twilight, but if I don't stop I can get there faster. The pendant could only mean she is in trouble. Hold on Zana, I am coming. I have been foolish to have left those kids. I knew I should have brought them back with me. At the time it wouldn't have worked. Looking for Zelkem, and having Lumus in Dystopia. I haven't made the best of choices, and I won't allow this to be one of those mistakes. For Rose...I can't fail. Those kids were calm and courageous even in the face of so much danger. Zana, Doxas, Noah, and Saxsus. Good kids, just getting by in such a dark time. I took care of them, taught them to hunt, fish, cook, and even fight. Even built a small cabin with them. They always reminded me of Rose, and maybe that is why I cared for them so much.") Orson had been lost in such deep thought that he hadn't noticed he had already passed the Canby region. He continued to travel west toward Geminite until he came to the outer mountains that divide Canby and Geminite. ("These mountains won't be any good for the Zufore.) It looks like we must part ways, my friend." He said as he got off his Zufore.

He took the saddle off the Zufore and he watched as it ran off to the East. He turned back to the mountain after the Zufore ran off. He looked around to find a suitable path, knowing that Geminite was a town normally accessed by boat. "I couldn't imagine Lears making his way to Geminite. It seems this would have been a better location to make a defensive stand." Orson gave his head a shake then made his way toward the rocky terrain.

Orson knew it would take the whole night to cross into Geminite, but he knew he couldn't stop. In the back of his mind, he could see images of Zana's smile looking up at him like a father. He couldn't let her down. Somehow he mustered enough strength to continue.

Night slipped by as he climbed through the jagged mountains. Each step was hard to find since the terrain was so unpredictable, and the sky was still covered in red. He carried on though. Finally, he noticed over the peak of the mountains; it was Geminite, The biggest trade town of Twilight. He saw a small cave off the slope of the mountain overlooking the city.

"Must be a mine of some kind. I can use the path to get to the city quicker than I thought. The boat is still docked too. I won't have to wait if I can get there on time." He thought to himself. He stood up on the rocky terrain. As he did he noticed a soldier come running through the shadows toward him.

"You there! Who are you?" The soldier called out. Orson lost his footing and fell down the rocky side of the cliff on to the path.

"That armor! I recognize the sigil on your chest plate. You are Sir Orson. The golden knight of Twilight!" The soldier sheathed his sword.

"I need you to hold that boat. It is of great importance that I am aboard when it sets out." Orson demanded. The soldier put his arm up to his chest and put his hand over his heart to salute him and then ran down the path toward the docks. Orson struggled to his feet. The fall from the cliff along with the climb tired him out, but continued on, slowly making his way down the path under the red sky. The streets stretched out then zig-zagged down a steep series of streets leading down the mountain to the heart of the city. He made his way down to the bottom and saw the ship had not departed.

("The soldier made it on time to stop the ship. Good.") He thought. He made his way through the market district leading to the dock. Normally the vendors would be yelling out to sell to anyone walking by. He found it strange they were silent until one vendor dropped to their knees. Orson continued to walk, and as he did each vendor along the way dropped to their knees to bow their heads to him. A smile struck his face as he passed by. When he arrived at the docks he looked back to see them still kneeling with their heads down.

"Sir Orson. We have halted the boats for your arrival." A young soldier announced. Orson turned to the soldier.

"Thank you. Will the boat be leaving soon then?" The soldier looked up at him with a salute.

"Sir Orson the boat is ready to leave at your command." Orson looked over at the boat. The crewmen all held on to ropes looking down at him. After a pause, the men aboard the ship kneeled to give their respect to Orson.

"You know they admire you. Just like Zana did. We all did." A familiar voice announced. Orson quickly turned to see a young man in a red cloak, and a black hood. He waited for the man to continue. The hooded man walked over to his side.

"I sent the necklace." The man said in a whisper. Orson turned to the man grabbing him and throwing his weight into the man. He slammed him into a dock support beam. The man's hood slid down to reveal a familiar face.

"Doxas!?" Orson said in surprise. He loosened his grip, then backed away with a glare.

"It has been a long time, Orson. Look at you now. The respect of the people, and fancy armor of the higher classes. You have really made a name for yourself since I last laid eyes on you." Doxas laughed.

"Why are you here, Doxas?" Orson stood up straight.

"Zana is dead. She died two weeks ago." Doxas announced. Orson fell to his knees. He looked up to the people on the boat. They turned away as he watched them. He looked at Doxas, his face twisted with anguish.

"How did she die?" He said with a tear in his eye.

"After you left, the Don took us in. South Twilight has been fighting over land, and while in need of work we went back to all we knew. At first, we refused, but Noah and Saxsus felt we should side with him because he owns all of South Twilight. Zana didn't want to split up the four of us. I ended up following her. I found it the only way to protect my sister." Doxas smirked.

"I suppose I failed her. I should have been there for her or told her that I didn't agree with the way we were living life, but you know Zana. She always did what she thought was right. Trained as assassins, and still, she thought it was the right thing to do. She was brainwashed by the Don, and she thought that by taking out the marks assigned to us that somehow we were killing bad men. Men that were murderers and thieves. Zana just wanted it to be true." Doxas explained.

"So she died fighting for a false master? I have heard of this Don. I have brought it up many times to the council here in North Twilight. The vote always turned out the same, seven opposed, and five agreed. The council didn't want to dwell into business they had no part of. The vote was to defend our shores if they were to attack, but I never thought it would come to this. Doxas, I will go to South Twilight, and I will deal with the Don myself." Orson turned for the boat, but Doxas stood in his way.

"No, I promised myself that I would avenge her death. You haven't been in South Twilight in over twenty years. This is no longer your problem. Like you said, North Twilight has no business in the South. I sent you the necklace so you could pay your respects to Zana and Saxsus." Doxas turned to the boat.

"Saxsus died as well!?" Orson cried out. Doxas turned to look over his shoulder.

"Zana killed him. He betrayed us, and he left her no choice. They both died that day. Noah left us for dead, and even now he sits at the side of the Don. I will deal with this. Don't follow me, Orson." Doxas said as he raised his hood. He walked on to the boat, after a word with a man on board. The men pulled in the bridge and raised the anchor.

("Zana... Saxsus. I should have been there for them. I should have kept them safe. I'm sorry, Rose. I wasn't able to help at all. If anything, I made things worse. I'm so sorry.") Orson thought to himself as the boat drifted into the sea.

He stood up and made his way to the city gates of East Geminite. He found a soldier to give him an escort through the mountains in the North. As he made his way out to the mountains he turned back to Geminite.

("I hope you can forgive me, Rose.") Orson tried to smile, but he just couldn't bring himself to do it. He turned back, and he followed the soldier toward the mountains with a tear rolling down his cheek.

Chapter Nineteen- Zodiac Awakening

Lumus stood outside Capaz palace with his head down and his arms crossed in front of him. People of the city were still working on completing his house, but that wasn't why he was waiting. Scarlette had told him that Orson was going to South Twilight, and Lumus didn't want to make a move without him. Brinx hid in the trees looking out toward the Southwest.

Zelkem sat on a rock at the entrance in the north end of town. He waited patiently for Orson to return. Most of the time he kept his head down, but once in a while, he would look up to the entrance, hoping to see him. Zelkem gave a quick stretch then laid back on the rock for a nap. People of the city walked by staring at him as they crossed, but Zelkem didn't care. Slowly his eyes closed with a smile on his face.

Frostear returned to the village with a few animals over his shoulder. He had his head down, and his eyes focused on the ground, but as he passed Zelkem he reached his right arm out and grabbed his foot. Frostear didn't let go though. He continued to walk dragging Zelkem off the stone.

"Ah what are you doing? Frostear?" Zelkem cried out. Frostear laughed.

"Hunting," Frostear added. Zelkem squirmed on the ground trying to shake free. People started to notice, but when they saw Zelkem scrambling on the ground, unable to shake free of Frostear, they began to laugh.

Scarlette stood by the window in her room upstairs in the palace. She shook her head when she saw Frostear and Zelkem. Scarlette turned from the window. She reached into her side pocket and pulled out a small hourglass. She frowned with an intense stare.

"The sands are almost depleted. I need more time. Please hurry, Orson. We don't have time to wait for you." Scarlette said to herself.

She jumped when she heard the knock at her door.

"Scarlette are you there?" A soft voice enquired.

"Yes. Just a moment." Scarlette grabbed her hourglass and quickly put it back in her side pocket. After a pause, she walked to the door, but it opened before she could reach for the handle.

"Hey Scarlette, sorry to just barge in, but Lumus is calling everyone to meet in Neutral City. I still have to find Brinx and Dyne. Luckily I found Frostear dragging Zelkem in the street, and Zynx is already down below waiting with Lumus." Zephry smiled.

"No problem Zephry, I will head down now." Zephry turned to the hall then stopped for a second as she tilted her head and turned back to her.

"Oh yeah! Sorry, have you seen Brunius anywhere?" Scarlette shook her head.

"No, I have been in my room for some time now. Why do you need Brunius?" Zephry smiled though she was disappointed.

"Well, Lumus wanted him to meet with us in Neutral City too. I think Brunius and Lumus have been coming up with a new plan of action. Maybe we will finally set out again!" Zephry turned back to the hall. Scarlette waited until she turned the corner at the end of the hall until she shut the door. She sat on her bed and reached into her pocket once more. She looked at her hourglass with sadness in her eyes.

("I have no choice. I need to tell the others before…The West Zin told me not to, but Lumus needs to know what is about to happen. ") She stood up then took in a deep breath. She gave her head a shake then left her room for Neutral City. Zephry made her way down the palace steps in the main lobby. Brunius was waiting for her by the main doors with his arms crossed, and a small grin to greet her.

"Hello, Zephry. I never got a chance to congratulate you on becoming a third class knight." Zephry began to blush a bit.

"Thank you, councillor Brunius. I am honored to become a knight of Capaz." Brunius shook his head.

"No, not of Capaz, but I'll have to explain that later. In any case, I heard you were looking for me?" Zephry had a look of confusion and worry in her eyes.

"Yes. I was asked by Lumus to gather all of our friends in Neutral City." A moment passed with an awkward silence.

"Yes, well it seems Lumus has come to find the answer he was looking for?" Brunius smiled with his hand on his chin, as if he was deep in thought. Scarlette walked down the stairs to join Zephry's side.

"What kind of answer is that?" Zephry blurted out. Brunius laughed.

"Well if he hasn't told you maybe I shouldn't be the one to tell you. You both know Lumus, and if he hasn't told you something yet, then I imagine it's only because he wants to tell you himself." Brunius continued to laugh as he exited the main doors.

"He is right, Scarlette. Lumus must have a lot on his mind. Maybe he is just waiting for Orson to return until anything is said. Seems strange though. Am I not a knight of Capaz? I wonder if Brunius means I will be a knight of my hometown instead." Zephry took a minute to ponder the thought.

"Don't stress about it too much, Zephry. Either way, you are a knight, so it doesn't matter the place… You will always be one of us." Scarlette smiled, and she grabbed Zephry's hand as she gently dragged Zephry with her outside.

Neutral City was full of people from all over North Twilight. Lumus stood on a platform built for holding weapons, though the platform was currently bare. Scarlette and Zephry made their way through the crowds of people with a surprised look in their eyes.

How did so many people get down here? I didn't see too many people enter the city outside." Zephry spoke with a loud voice to try to speak over the many people talking. Scarlette stopped in front of the platform. She looked Lumus in the eyes. He smiled, then looked to his left. Without a word, Scarlette led Zephry to the left of the stage. She was surprised to see the councillors from every city hidden behind a curtain. Even Brunius had arrived already.

"Zephry can you find the others? I should talk to the council." Zephry looked at the crowd, then back at her.

"Yeah, I'll ask Lumus if he has seen them." Zephry smiled. She walked through the crowd, but she struggled to get through. Lumus stepped to the center of the platform to address the people.

"Hello, people of Twilight. As you may already know, I am Lumus. I know many of you have questions. I will try to answer everything I can, but please let me start by telling you my story." Lumus smiled with his hands raised.

Scarlette entered the hidden area with the council. Brunius greeted her as she entered.

"Scarlette I'm glad you are here. We were discussing how we might name you the new Lead Council of North Twilight." Brunius said with a smile. Scarlette paused.

"That was sudden. I mean… It would be an honor…" Scarlette looked at her pocket where she kept the hourglass.

"In these troubled times, I would like to take that role. It's just that Lumus needs me now, and in the coming days, we may need to take the fight to Lears. At this time I cannot take the role of lead councillor. I truly am sorry." She announced. Brunius and Lady Concy whispered to each other for a moment.

"We understand, Lady Scarlette. When the dust settles perhaps you would reconsider. Scarlette bowed politely then she turned to the platform to see Lumus still talking to everyone.

"Lears has caused everyone so much pain, and I do understand that he is responsible for so much of your anger. I have made it my mission to take the fight to Lears with your golden hero, Sir Orson, at my side. Together, we will take Twilight back from the darkness. Together, we will fight today to live tomorrow. I have summoned the council of Twilight here as well, and they will go over the rest of our plans with you. I must leave, and take the fight to Lears. FOR TWILIGHT!" Lumus shouted, then bowed to the audience. He went off the stage toward the council.

"Lumus. Are you sure you don't want us to..." Concy began to talk, but as soon as Lumus looked at her, she stopped.

"Thank you Lady Concy, but my mind is made up. As we have already talked about this, you must understand my reasons." Lumus interrupted.

"Then best of luck to you, Prince of Twilight," Concy replied.

The Council members followed Lady Concy out onto the platform. Brunius reached out to Lumus to shake his hand.

"Good luck, Lumus. We are here if you need anything." He added. Scarlette watched Brunius follow the other councillors, then she turned back to see Lumus making his way toward the tunnels to Capaz. She moved through the crowd quickly to catch up before she lost sight of him.

"Lumus!" Scarlette caught his attention. He turned to wait for her.

"Please keep your voice down. I don't want people to know I'm leaving. I thought Zephry told you?" He added. Scarlette seemed confused.

"What do you mean? She was supposed to tell me what?" She whispered. He took Scarlette's hand and pulled her with him through the crowd toward the tunnels.

"She was to tell you that after my speech I was going to meet you all outside the North Capaz gates. Don't worry I will explain everything outside." He whispered back.

They made it to the tunnel. Once inside Lumus began to slowly run. He began to pick up speed as he noticed Scarlette was able to keep up. They came to the ladder to Penelope's shop. Once outside, Scarlette noticed the streets were bare.

"Scarlette hurry!" Lumus announced. He ran off toward the North Gates.

("Why is he in such a hurry? What is going on?") Scarlette thought. She finally caught up to him.

Everyone was waiting and greeted them with smiles.

"Orson you're back!" Scarlette ran up and hugged him.

"I'm sorry I worried you Scarlette. There was something I just needed to do on my own." He explained. Scarlette laughed awkwardly.

"I know, you don't have to explain anything. You're back and that is that." She smiled.

"I'm sorry too Scarlette. I forgot to tell you about us meeting Lumus out here. I went down to Neutral City. After I left you I had realized everyone was outside, so I went to find them." Zephry confessed.

"It is no problem Zephry. I had to speak to the council anyway." Scarlette added.

("Now that I think about it I never did talk to them about the hourglass. Maybe it's for the best. They might take that information a little too hard. It would be best to keep the other world to myself.") Scarlette thought to herself.

"Scarlette? Hey Scarlette?" Zelkem shouted out. Zelkem had placed his hands on her shoulders to shake her free from her daydream.

"Ah, I'm sorry Zelkem. I must have got lost in thought there." She laughed. Zelkem moved a few steps back, and he turned his attention to Lumus.

"Everyone I have been keeping you all in the dark about what the council and I have been discussing. The council has named us the Knights of Twilight. We are bound to no city and are given access to anything we need to aid us. I have given things a lot of thought recently, and I have determined that we need to take the fight to the enemy. As you know I was born from the planet's core, and with that, I was born with unique abilities. I have had this feeling like something was coming for a while now, and it turns out I was right." Lumus explained.

Orson crossed his arms and turned to the side to face Capaz.

"Shortly after arriving in Twilight, I began to feel an enormous power coming from the oceans. After some time I felt another, then another. I now believe twelve enormous powers from all around the planet will reach the surface in a matter of days." Lumus continued.

Everyone gasped. Brinx shook his head. He turned to the north, but no one seemed to really notice him.

"I have come up with a plan that you all will disagree with, but I had no other choice. I have talked to the council and explained my reasons." Lumus added. Dyne stepped forward as he spoke.

"Out with it Lumus, you are just beating around the bush. Just tell us what you have planned." Dyne demanded. Lumus closed his eyes.

"He is already here," Lumus said as he turned to look toward the north.

"Lears and his Lords came over the hill just north of them. Everyone but Lumus readied themselves for battle.

"Please. Everyone stand down. I asked him to come." Lumus shouted over everyone.

"Lumus are you insane? Lears is our enemy! Why would you call him here?" Scarlette yelled back. Lears stepped forward with a grin on his face.
"Lumus was right to call us here. Though it angers me not to kill you all now. We must work together, otherwise, we will have no planet to fight over." Lumus walked over to Lears and reached out his hand. They shook hands, then walked out to see both groups.
"Lears and I have been able to sense these powers for some time now. I have conversed with the council and with Lears in secret to plan the safest way to approach this situation. Twelve powers are coming from the ocean all around North Twilight, and the council knows their armies will be no match for them. Everyone here has some kind of influence over star energy which makes us the only chance to defend the planet. Though we are still learning the concept of star energy, we know that the more we train the stronger we become with it.
Aire pushed Coldblood from his path as he walked forward.
"These are the beasts of legend? The Zodiac of Twelve?" Aire blurted out. Lumus and Lears looked at each other.
"Aire what are you going on about?" Lears shouted." Zephry moved to the center of both groups, and she faced Lumus and Lears.
"The Zodiac of Twelve. The legend is very well known to every one of Twilight." Zephry smiled. Dyne joined Zephry's side.

"Zodiacs of creation born with the planet from the beginning of time. Twelve beasts defended the planet from meteors long before man. Craters filled with the tears of the twelve creating oceans for man to be born and watch over life as the twelve rebuilt their strength." Dyne took Zephry's hand after he finished his speech.

"So it wasn't a legend after all. It looks like they are coming back from their sleep. I am also new to this legend, but might I ask why they wake now at all times?" Brinx asked from the back of the group.

"They are waking up because of us, because of Lears and I. Lumus ran his hand through his hair. Regardless of why they are coming, we need to take action now. The council has agreed to keep all knights within their cities to protect them if we fail. Lears and I have decided to make teams of both groups to strike each beast simultaneously." Lumus added. Orson shook his head with a sigh.

"Lumus are you sure that is wise? Why wouldn't we pair up with ourselves?" Orson blurted out as he looked over at Lears with disgust.

"Lears and I have thought this through. Each team chosen was devised by their abilities and willingness to work together. We understand that we are enemies, but this threatens the very world we have been fighting for as Lears said already. I feel that the teams we chose will be strong enough to face these creatures." Lumus explained.

Scarlette walked over to Lears and raised her hand to shake his. Lears looked at Lumus then back at her. He tentatively shook her hand

"Thank you, Scarlette. Together we will face these monsters, and maybe after we can learn to live together in peace." Lumus walked over to Lears' group.

"Thank you. All of you. All of you coming here means you are willing to work with us." Lumus smiled then turned to walk back to the middle with Lears. Scarlette returned to her friends too.

"The groups will be as follows: Orson and Aire. You will be traveling to Ariond. Zynx and Antsos will be traveling to Taurald. Zelkem and Jol will be going to Geminite. Dyne and Levitz will be traveling to Canby. Brinx and Hedree will be traveling to Leodot. Frostear and Ged will be traveling to Virphire. Zephry and Coldblood will be traveling to Librine. Lears will go to Aquoise, and I will be going to Piscyst at Lake Twilight." Lumus announced.

"What about me, Lumus?" Scarlette asked with an odd look.

"I was hoping you would come with me," Lumus replied. Scarlette shook her head.

"No. I will go to the beast that is said to come for Capaz." Orson stepped forward.

"Scarlette doesn't be mad, but you won't be able to take on such a power by yourself," Orson begged. Scarlette laughed.

"Why? because I am a woman?" Orson stopped dead in his tracks.

"No, my lady, that isn't what I meant. I just don't think it wise for you to go alone." He explained. She smiled.

"I am a long-range fighter. I will keep my distance as I fight, so I will be fine. Enough said. Lumus, go on." She demanded, Lumus walked over to Scarlette, and he rested his hand on her shoulder. "Scarlette, the beast for Capaz is also at Lake Twilight," Lumus whispered. Her anger subsided. "Oh, I see. Then fine. We can go together Lumus." She smiled uncomfortably. Lumus smiled as he returned to the center of the groups.

"We are short people for the other three locations, so groups that are able to must head to the closest free location to assist as fast as they can," Lears added.

"You forgot about us, Lumus." Everyone turned toward Lady Concy, who waved to the group. Doxas appeared from behind her too.

"Doxas!" Orson yelled out in surprise.

"Concy?" Frostear seemed confused about her arrival.

"Mother?" Coldblood pushed Hedree and Levitz out of his way to see her.

"I see we are not too late for the meeting. I found a young man looking for Orson. I thought I would bring him to you. I also wanted a reason to join the fight." Concy added.

"What about the council?" Orson asked politely.

"They know it is my decision to go. Lumus who is that behind you?" Lumus and Lears turned simultaneously.

"Kontaminate!?" Lumus yelled out as he stepped back in a panic. Lears didn't move. He looked over to Kontaminate to give him a quick scan from top to bottom.

"So this is the one sent by the gods to kill me? Were they trying to be funny by making you look like Lumus and I?" Kontaminate's face had a blank expression.

"Omega has changed his mind." He announced. Lears leaned closer to Kontaminate as he spoke.

"Omega? Interesting. I should have words with this Omega." Lears said in a mocking tone. Kontaminate locked eyes with him.

"I am merely here to assist in this problem. Not negotiate with parasites like you." Kontaminate added. Lears opened his eyes wide with amazement.

"Do you know who you are talking to!?" Lears began to coat his body with a transparent black energy.

"LEARS! Let's hear him out before you lose your cool." Lumus cried out.

Zelkem tried to push Orson out of his way, but he stopped and held him back.

"Zelkem I know how you feel, but you need to cool it," Orson whispered as he struggled to hold him back.

"The West Zin created these twelve creatures when this planet was formed to protect against any threat that may harm the planet, and they were awoken when Lumus and Lears met and fought some time ago. The planet reacted to the surge of power and caused them to rise once again. I was sent to assist in the disposal of these creatures as Omega has ordered me. West Zin no longer has the strength to handle this alone." Kontaminate added. Scarlette looked down at her pocket containing her hourglass. Lumus smiled as he tried to judge what Kontaminate had said.

"Good, we can use all the help we can get," Zephry said.

"Fine, you can go to Sagnet just west of Lake Twilight. I won't stop you… this time." Lears walked over to his group. Lumus gave his head a shake.

"Well, that leaves Scorpial for Lady Concy and…Doxas was it?" Lumus suggested. Doxas bowed his head to him.

"Yes, sir," Doxas said politely. Orson laughed as he let go of Zelkem.

"I had a question, Mr. Kontaminate?" Zephry squeezed past Orson and Zelkem as they let go of each other. Kontaminate looked over at her.

"I just wanted to know why this Omega guy would want to help us. Don't get me wrong, but last time we saw you, didn't you try to kill us? I also had one more question. Is anyone else freaking out that gods exist, or is that just me? Scarlette smiled and turned not to show her reaction as she giggled.

"Agreed. I am a bit taken aback by the fact that the gods do exist. I haven't given it much thought myself, but if they are willing to help out, then I'm on board." Kontaminate stepped forward just past Lumus.

"You misunderstand. Omega is helping the West Zin, and only because we cannot afford to lose Twilight. The core of this planet is a vital part of our galaxy just as any other planet." Kontaminate explained.

"So the gods don't care for the people, they just care for the planet? Some gods…" Zelkem added.

Frostear continued over to Lears and his group. "Ged how about we get this charade over with?" Frostear didn't wait for an answer. He just continued walking past like he didn't care whether Ged followed or not. Ged didn't say a word. He walked away with Frostear toward the south.

"Gods or no gods, we need to go. These beasts are coming regardless, and they won't wait for us. When everyone is ready to head out, then leave when you are able. Scarlette are you ready to go?" Lumus said. Scarlette hugged Orson before she joined him.

"Be safe, everyone!" Scarlette said, full of concern for her friends.

("This may be the last time I see them, but I will always watch over them when I'm gone. Be safe, everyone.") Scarlette paused to remember the moment.

Lears and Kontaminate both left without a word. Lears didn't even talk to his group before he took off. Lady Concy and Doxas started to head south. Dyne watched them leave, thinking it was weird for them to head south until he realized going north meant going around the Aster Mountains. Dyne looked over to Levitz.

"Are you ready then?" Dyne asked.

"I suppose the sooner, the better," Levitz replied. Dyne and Levitz started toward the South for Canby.

"So, golden boy. Are you ready to get on with this?" Aire said with a smug laugh. Orson waited to answer. The short pause infuriated Aire. Other groups were partnering up and heading out, but Orson just stood still. Aire finally walked in front of Orson to see his face, but his eyes were closed.

"Okay Aire, before we head out I want to ask you a question," Orson said. Aire smiled.

"This should be good. Well go on, golden boy, what did you want to know?" He asked. Orson opened his eyes to look Aire eye to eye.

"What do you plan to gain from this?" Orson asked.

"What... What do you mean?" Aire seemed puzzled.

"I mean, you fight for Lears and he clearly uses you. Let's say Lears wins and he kills Lumus. What do you think would happen to Twilight? Why would you not fight to help Twilight stray from darkness?" Orson explained. Aire was taken back for a moment. He looked down and clenched his fists.

"You may not have seen what happen the day Lumus was born, but even as a small child I still remember that day. The large black hole in the sky. My uncle was taking me on a fishing trip to Lake Twilight. We must have been just outside of Capaz, just a bit south of Aster Mountains. That's when the demons came from the sky. At first, they were rushing to the caves. I remember seeing so many of them trying to enter the caves at the same time. The ones left outside started to look around, and that's when they saw us. My uncle took me by the arm, and we made our way to the bridge toward Capaz, but the demons caught up to us and dragged my uncle away. I was left crying on the bridge. That is when Antsos appeared. He just looked at the other demons and they ran away. He took my hand and said "This is only the beginning. Would you kill or be killed?" Ever since then, I have lived my life believing that it doesn't matter which side you fight for. It is the weak that die, and the strong that live." Aire took a deep breath. After a pause, he smirked.

"Antsos showed me how one's presence is power enough. I grew to like that, and I grew to fight for power. I don't care what I fight for. Just that I am the one standing in the end." Aire explained. Orson smirked.

"Just know: If you fight against Lumus, you won't be standing in the end." Orson started to head south. Aire smirked, but Orson had lowered his gaze as he passed him.

("Watch your back, golden boy.") Aire continued to smirk as he followed him.

Chapter Twenty- Aries, Zodiac of Ariond

Orson and Aire continued on their journey without a word to each other. Cobalt, Orson thought as he looked to the sky. Every so often he would check behind him to see if Aire was keeping pace. He acted like he didn't notice, but each time Orson turned around aggravated him.

Orson passed a sign saying they were entering the Breedlands Region of Virphire. It took him a minute to think of who was sent there, but sure enough, Orson could see Frostear in the distance with Ged.

"It looks like the Frostear and Ged are waiting outside of Virphire. We are not too far off from our destination either it would seem." Orson smiled.

"You know golden boy, I have been thinking. How do we know we are going to the right place? How do we know these beast are even going to show up? How long will we have to wait if they do show up?" Aire's face went red.

"You heard Lumus and Lears. They said these things are coming, so if we are early, we wait. If they don't show, we wait. If we are in the wrong place then we go to the right place." Orson ranted.

Aire smirked at him.

"So calm, so collected. Just looking at you pisses me off." Aire laughed.

"If these beasts are rising from the water near each city then we should set up camp just west of

Ariond. We still have an hour or so to travel, so less complaining and more walking." Orson ordered.

He was happy to bark orders to the opposing team. Somehow it put a smile on his face, but the smile quickly faded as the earth began to shake. The water from the lake to the west started to creep up on land. Orson the edge of the water lapping at his feet, but as he looked down a tornado-like lake funnel of water suddenly shot up.

"Aire get ready! Remember to watch my back and I will watch yours." Orson yelled. Aire watched as the water cleared, but nothing was in front of them. Suddenly he was hit from behind throwing him across the ground toward the water. Orson quickly turned around, but still, nothing was in front of him. Aire picked himself up. He looked at his arm, which had sustained some scratches.

"Aire, are you okay?" Orson asked while glancing back and forth, looking for the next attack.

"Behind you, golden boy!" Air yelled out. Orson didn't think he just turned with his sword blocking his front. A small blast of star energy pushed Orson back a few feet, but he kept his footing and recovered just in time to see above him a creature he had never seen before. It was like pure energy, with tentacles coming from everywhere on its body. A light shot out from each one, dispersing energy. The beast had the zodiac symbol of Aries where its face should be, but there was no face at all. It was roughly nine feet tall, and it loomed over Orson. The more he analyzed the creature, the more he began to fear it. "Careful golden boy, this thing seems faster than a normal demon." Aire brushed himself off. "This is no demon, Aire. This is the Zodiac, Aries. I have a feeling we haven't seen anything yet. Remember this thing was created by the gods to wipe out all living things." Orson announced as he readied his sword.

"Great. How are we going to fight it then?" Aire readied himself with his fist clenched. He grabbed a thick worn-out cloth that he had wrapped around his waist and used it to wrap his fists.

"You plan to use hand-to-hand combat, Aire?" Orson said, surprised.

"Well I usually carry a massive battle axe, but it's in the shop," Aire smirked.

("How did Lumus think we would be a good pair, especially when we have to face one of these?") Orson thought.

Aries reached its arms into the sky, and Orson noticed it was gathering energy from its body. The energy began to form a perfect ball. One of its arms dropped back to its side. The other arm pushed into the ball of energy, pushing it forward in front of its body, and readied itself to attack. Orson blocked the first attack, but he was pushed off balance. Aries turned around after slowing itself down then rammed Orson with the ball of energy once again. This time he held his sword directly in front of his face. He held his sword with one hand on the grip and one hand with his palm holding the sword in place.

"Alright, golden boy, let us try working together!" Aire started running at Aries from behind Orson. He passed Orson and jumped with his arm cocked back. As he drifted through the air he yelled at the top of his lungs. Orson's eyes shifted to him, but Aries didn't seem to notice. Orson could see star energy flow into Aire's fist as he punched Aries on the side of its head. Aries flew through the air like it was nothing. Orson fell forward as Aire passed by him.

"You alright, golden boy? You know the fight isn't over yet. Maybe get on your feet buddy!" Aire taunted with a proud laugh. Orson used his sword to pull himself to his feet.

"You know how to tap into star energy? I didn't think any of Lears' Lords could do that." He blurted out as he took a deep breath.

"Well, it's funny, but none of us have really fought you guys yet. Ged went out against Scarlette and the dragon guy, but I guess you haven't really seen any of us in action. If you guys haven't learned how to really manipulate star energy yet, then you will lose to us for sure." Aire announced. Orson sighed.

"I wouldn't say we can't use star energy, but I guess I was surprised you were able to use such a powerful attack." Orson smiled.

"It's just a drag that I wasn't able to have more up my sleeve. That was my best attack, and it looks like that thing is getting back up." Aire rubbed his hands together.

("I don't think Zelkem can do anything like that attack. Maybe these guys won't be as easy to defeat as I thought.") Orson readied his sword beside Aire.

"Okay, before he attacks, do you have any ideas?" Aire's eyes didn't lose sight of Aries for a minute.

"Yeah, a few things I picked up on. Aries seems to have no hearing at all. It didn't seem to notice you even when you yelled before your attack. Also, it uses that ball of energy to ram its target, but if it misses it takes roughly three seconds to stop and turn around for another attack." Orson pointed out.

"Good, then you draw its attention and I will catch it off guard." Aire moved back a few steps.

("I'm impressed. Aire really seems to have a knack for strategy. It's too bad he never joined the knights.") Orson thought.

"Here it comes, golden boy!" Aire moved out of view of Aries. It rammed the ball of energy forward at Orson. At the last second, it jumped off toward Aire. He quickly jumped and pushed off the ball of energy with one hand. Aries stopped and swung the ball of energy from its front to Aire behind him. Aire put his hands up and caught the energy. The ground at his feet began to crumble, but he was able to hold his footing. Orson ran over, slicing at Aries' arm. Its arm came off and fell to the ground, but it showed no sign of pain. Still, it pushed the ball of energy on Aire. Its other arm faded into little bits of energy and rose to the sky until it faded entirely. Orson swung again, but this time the tentacles from its body caught the sword. "Golden boy! I don't think I can hold this off much longer." The earth below Aire began to push further down. Orson couldn't pull his sword up or down. After a second of thinking, Orson decided to pull the sword toward himself. The tentacles were cut off as he dragged the sword away. He swung the sword around right after cutting Aries in two. He fell to one knee in exhaustion, with his sword still held up. Aries's head pointed up to the sky. The zodiac symbol on its face began to shake. With the last of his strength, Orson thrust his sword as hard as he could into its head. The zodiac symbol on its face turned to stone, then after a moment the star energy that made up its body slowly petrified as well. Aire pushed the ball of energy up and jumped out of the crater just before it fully petrified.

Orson began to laugh. Aire was panting on the other side of the crater.

"What exactly is so funny?" Aire said out of breath.

"I was just thinking. It's a good thing you were able to push Aries' energy out of the way in time. You could have been trapped with that giant stone ball over you. You would have had to dig your way out." Orson continued to laugh. Aire frowned. Then he started to laugh with him.

Chapter Twenty-One-
Taurus, Zodiac of Taurald

Antsos stood at the top of the waterfall overlooking Lake Twilight, his arms crossed and an angry look in his eyes. Zynx sat on a rock just a few feet behind him with his legs crossed, and his eyes closed. Antsos began to pace, still gazing down below.

"I am beginning to think this is a waste of time. I don't see why we would make a good pair. I have my claws and you a spear. What are we going to poke and scratch our way to victory?" Antsos looked to Zynx for a reply. He shrugged when he realized Zynx wouldn't answer.

"On top of everything, they pair me with a cat that can't even speak. Can you speak? Do you even understand what I'm saying to you?" He yelled.

Zynx opened one eye to look at Antsos. "Useless house cat… This is beginning to irritate me." Zynx opened his eyes and hopped off the rock with his spear ready. He turned west toward the mouth of the river leading to the waterfall. Antsos didn't bother looking.

"Sensitive little cat… calm yourself. There is nothing back there. I can hear just as well as you." Antsos continued to stare below. Suddenly the water upriver began to bubble. Slowly, a creature of pure energy swam to shore. Zynx watched as it stood up on land. Antsos turned hearing the water sizzle on its body. It stood with energy flowing out like tentacles. Antsos threw his cloak to the ground. He was topless with just baggy black pants and a black sash holding them up.

"Look, it's the Taurus symbol on its head. This thing doesn't even have ears or a face. Interesting. Then it won't see me coming!" Antsos ran with his claws out. He jumped in the air and swiped downward. Taurus raised an arm, and slapped him aside, flinging him hard against a tree.

"Ah… It was able to see me after all. Fine, let me try this again. No one makes a fool of the great demon Antsos!" He yelled out in rage.

He charged once more with his arms out and claws ready. Just as he got in front of Taurus he leaped in the air landing just behind it. He quickly clawed at Taurus, but it turned so quickly that he was spooked. His tail puffed up as he looked at the Zodiac symbol on its head as if it was staring right at him. Taurus grabbed Antsos' wrists. The tentacles from its arms wrapped around his forearms. He cried out in pain as the tentacles began to burn his arms.

He cried out, but Taurus' tentacles just tightened. His mouth opened wide revealing his fangs. His first thought was to bite its arm, but he realized that it would just cause him more pain. Antsos looked at the zodiac symbol on its face once again.

"You will not beat me! I am Antsos, Demon Lord of Twilight!" Suddenly its head pushed forward toward Antsos with a small tip of steel pushing through the creature's head. Antsos looked with confusion and realized that Zynx's spear had pierced it from behind. Taurus began to turn to stone Antsos tried to shake free, but its grip didn't loosen even as its body began to petrify. Zynx pulled his spear from its head and slowly walked to Antsos. He looked at Antsos' wrists and then raised his spear. His spear came crashing down against the petrified Taurus breaking the hands off its body.

"Great, now look at this. How do you suppose I break myself free from this?" Antsos said in frustration. Zynx made a grunt then started to walk away. Antsos walked over to the rock Zynx was sitting on before the fight. He mashed the stone against the rock to break free from Taurus' stone grip.

"Since you don't speak, you won't mind I tell the others that I was the one that defeated Taurus?" Antsos said with a laugh, but Zynx didn't bother reacting as he continued south toward Sagnet. ("I don't think that fight was supposed to be as easy as it was. It is strange, but Taurus didn't even acknowledge Zynx during the fight. It was as it couldn't hear him come up from behind. I imagine whatever made these Zodiac creatures didn't account for... Unless they don't see or hear, but perhaps they can feel star energy? My claws don't require star energy, but I raised my speed using my star energy. Maybe the Zodiac can feel the power we emit? Interesting...") Antsos thought to himself. He rubbed his wrists as he followed behind Zynx.

Chapter Twenty-Two-
Gemini, Zodiac of Geminite

Zelkem and Jol were waiting by Geminite Pond in between the two Geminite cities. Zelkem and Jol sat on opposite sides of the pond. Zelkem was picking blades of grass, using them to spell the word 'bored'. Once he finished he looked around to see if he could find something else to occupy his time. He ended up looking over to Jol. She was a small, delicate-looking girl. Zelkem thought she was about thirteen or maybe fourteen years old. The thought bounced around his head for a bit until she noticed him looking at her. He quickly looked away pretending he wasn't looking at her.
"What were you looking at?" Jol protested.
"Honestly, I was thinking about how old you were. What are you, like twelve years old?" He said with a laugh. He laid back on the grass. She stood up with an angry look.
"You incompetent fool. I may look young, but I am nineteen years old!" Jol yelled. She turned around crossing her arms in anger. Zelkem shot up after he realized what she said.
"No way, you are a little liar! You can't be nineteen. You look like you are still a kid." He announced as if he knew better. He laid back down, confident she was lying.
"You pompous jerk! Its people like you that made me fight for Lears!" Jol sat down with a furious look in her eyes.

"What do you mean?" He asked. She had caught his interest.

"I have been told so many times that I can't do things because of what my physical appearance is. Just because I look like a child doesn't mean I am. The knights turned me down because of that same reason. Those jerks even laughed at me. I couldn't find any work after my parents died in the Dragon Wars because everyone thought I was lying about my age." She said, close to tears. Zelkem sat up again. This time he put his arms back for support.

"Hey, I'm sorry. I didn't mean to piss you off. I kinda understand how you feel. My parents died in the Dragon Wars too. I was left with only my brother, but he ended up leaving me to join the knights. I was too young to go with him. I was left in an empty house all alone, but because I was a child the city took the house and tried to put me in a group home for kids that were orphaned in the war. I ended up living on the streets. So yeah, I can relate." He explained.

Jol picked up a stone from the side of the pond and stood up.

"It would seem we are similar in a way. Don't think your sob story will get me to leave Lears though." She contested. Zelkem laughed.

"I don't care what you do. If we are enemies, then we are enemies. Fight for what you believe in. I get it. I wanted to confront my brother for years for leaving me, but in truth, he didn't know our home would be taken. I realized he joined the knights to make money. He doesn't know this, but I went back to our home years later and found out that Orson had been sending money to help me the whole time. I was able to claim the money and live a good life for a while. I owe him for that. There are a few reasons I fight on their side, but that would be near the top of the list. Who knows, if I didn't go back and find that money maybe my hatred for my brother would have made me end up joining Lears to just to spite my brother." He said with a grin. Jol smiled.

"I guess you aren't as much of a jerk as I thought." Jol laughed. Zelkem laid down once again. "Glad to hear it." He said with a smile.

Jol closed her eyes, clenching the stone in her hand. After a moment she opened her eyes and threw the stone into the pond. She continued to smile. Suddenly the stone she threw flew out of the pond landing near Zelkem. He sat up looking at the stone with a puzzled look.

"I heard the stone hit the water, so that's weird. What happened?" He asked. Without warning a creature burst through the calm surface of the pond throwing both of them off their feet. They both saw its face bearing the zodiac symbol of Gemini. The nearby knights stationed at the city watched in fear.

"Wow, it's pure energy. Look at this thing!" Zelkem said as he climbed to his feet.

"What are those things waving on its body?" Jol said as she grabbed her daggers from her belt. "I don't know, but I wouldn't get too close." He answered quickly.

"Gemini, the zodiac of Geminite. Careful Jol, if the legends are true then this thing is meant to kill everything. I can only imagine what kind of power it has." He added.

Gemini stood on the water in the middle of the once-calm pond. Water came down over the pond as if it was raining. Gemini turned west toward the city of Virphire and began to walk just as the water stopped falling.

"It doesn't even care we are here? Come on big guy aren't we gonna see what you got?" Zelkem called out. Gemini didn't seem to notice him at all.

"It's leaving. Why doesn't it fight us?" Jol ran along the river toward the north. Zelkem kept up with her speed on the other side of the river.

"Gemini isn't moving fast, but it is starting to head toward the water over toward Virphire. I'll follow it, Jol. Cross the bridge up ahead and catch up with us." He commanded. He turned toward the west. He was just behind Gemini, but still, it wasn't paying attention to him.

"Alright, big guy. Time to get your attention!" Zelkem brought his fists together as he ran. Slowly he pulled them toward his chest.

"This move was meant for Orson before everything happened, but at least I can see how it holds up in a real battle" He called out. His fists began to glow against his chest. Star energy encased his body as he ran. He looked up at Gemini. He noticed the moment he began to focus his star energy into his fists Gemini's head turned toward him. He jumped into the air toward

Gemini thrusting his right fist toward it, but it made a fist and punched back, slamming its full force into his fist. There was a pause as they collided until a flash sent Zelkem flying backward. He slammed into the ground, landing flat on his back.

"Ugh. Damn that hurt. Hey Jol, I got its attention…" Jol ran past him with such speed that he didn't see her, but he felt the wind along his face.

Jol yelled as she came to an abrupt halt then jumped straight up. Her two daggers lit up with a glow. She made the motions of throwing her daggers but didn't actually let them go. Instead, copies of the daggers flew through the air at Gemini. The beast shook and split into two separate Gemini, making all of Jol's attacks fly right past it. The two Gemini rushed her. One ran and dove to the ground, sliding into position below Jol who was still hovering in the air. Once it was directly under her, it kicked both its feet straight up catching her chest. As she was momentarily suspended in the air, the other Gemini clenched its fists together in the air above her and slammed her hard toward the ground.

"JOL!" Zelkem yelled out as he got back on his feet.

"You bastards!" Zelkem squeezed his fists tight. His eyes opened wide as he put his head down. His fists began to glow. Once they were completely engulfed he slapped his palms on his chest. The two Gemini turned their attention back to him, but they didn't pause. They rushed him as he stood still glowing.

Zelkem began spinning on the spot and picked up so much speed that he became a blur. The two Gemini stopped in their tracks. Zelkem's star energy was channelled into his fists, pummeling the two Gemini Zodiacs. Though they were pure star energy, he was stronger than the both of them. The energy in their bodies began to pulse. The attacks struck the faces of the two Gemini simultaneously. Zelkem continued to spin, launching attack after attack. Even though he continued, Gemini started to turn to stone. As it turned to stone, the attacks chipped away the body of Gemini until it had crumbled to pieces.

Zelkem started to slow down until he eventually stopped. He was woozy from the spinning and fell to the ground when tried to take a step forward. Jol crawled toward him as he laid flat on his back.

"Zelkem that was the craziest thing I have ever seen. Are you okay?" Jol said as she tried to smile.

"I have never done that before, and I promise I never will again. Ugh... I feel like I'm gonna throw up. I can't move at all and everything is still spinning..." Zelkem kept his eyes closed to try to keep himself from spinning.

"That was incredible! The way you put your own spin on...." Zelkem put his hand over his mouth.

"Ugh don't say spin..." He quickly interrupted.

The Knights of Geminite rushed over as the dust settled. Jol was helped to her feet, while Zelkem was carried off on a makeshift stretcher.

("I hope the others are having better luck than us… I'm sorry Lumus, but it doesn't look like we are going to be able to help anyone like this.") Zelkem thought.

He was rushed into Geminite with Jol at his side passing out from fatigue on the way through the city gates.

Chapter Twenty Three-
Cancer, Zodiac of Canby

Dyne stood with a smile on his face as he looked out at the Canby Delta. Levitz just stared at him. Dyne raised his arms with his palms up, and he closed his eyes.
"It's beautiful here. A little muddy, but such a beautiful view. Wouldn't you agree Levitz?" Dyne blurted out. He opened his eyes to see if Levitz was paying attention.
"Your optimism makes me sick. You do know we could very well die here, right?" Levitz said in a deep tone. Dyne put his arms down.
"I don't see a problem with living in the moment. You should pull that stick out of your ass and enjoy life a little more." Dyne added. Levitz stepped forward with a fist raised at him.
"What did you say!?" Levitz said as he got angry. Dyne laughed.
"For a guy that wears a pink vest and all pink clothes, you don't see to be very happy…" Dyne laughed. Levitz took another step forward.
"What are you implying!?" He quickly replied. Dyne sat on the beach close to the shoreline.
"You should calm down. Get angry when the monster of legend we all grew with comes to kill us." He said with a laugh. Levitz put his fists down.
"I don't know how your friends keep you around. I'm shocked they haven't hung you yet…" Levitz added. Dyne laughed again.

"Well... Usually, Zynx is with me. Maybe they haven't killed me yet because they don't want to fight their way through him."

"You mean that big cat? It's funny that we have a giant cat on our team too." Levitz calmed down. "When I was a child I would have thought seeing a giant cat walking around Twilight would be a drunken story or something, but now look at things. Gods, star energy, plant creatures, demons, and the list goes on." Levitz said with a faint grin. He joined Dyne on the beach.

"Yeah, I agree with you. When Zynx was a little kitten that was when things were simple. The moment he turned into a seven-foot cat... That is when everything just went all strange. The day I heard demons attacked Capaz knights in the Aster Mountains was almost like it was expected. I remember thinking that this is just the beginning. That's why I picked up this rapier at the local blacksmith. Zynx made a spear out of junk he found and boom! We were ready for disaster." Dyne laughed.

"Once you get past the stupidity. You aren't that bad." Levitz declared.

"You know, I have heard that before. On more than one occasion. Honestly though, Twilight, Dystopia, gods, and planet cores. None of this interests me. The only reason I fight is because of Zynx drags me with him." Dyne picked up a twig floating in the water and used it to draw in the mud.

"Why fight at all then? If the cat wants to fight then let him go with Lumus and just live your life." Levitz asked.

"It's funny. We are supposed to be enemies, but here we are talking about quitting the game. Truth be told, Zynx is my only friend. Before I met him I was just a kid alone in a world of orphans from the Dragon Wars. I act like he follows me, but it's me that follows him. It's because I am afraid he will die out there all alone. He kept me from dying alone in a river, so I will fight till my last breath so that he won't die alone either." Dyne explained. Levitz smiled. He found a twig and began to draw in the mud too.

"The day Lumus came into this world, my wife died. She was killed by demons near Aquoise. I used to work as a fisherman out near Scorpial. These pink clothes were made by her, and she made them as a joke for me because I was such an ass. I was home one night, sleeping, and she threw all of my clothes away. All I had to wear were pink pants, a shirt, these gloves and this vest." Levitz explained. Dyne looked up at him.

"I'm sorry I said what I did. If I had known I wouldn't have been so heartless." Dyne apologized.

"You know, if we weren't enemies because of who we follow I'm sure we would have been friends," Levitz added.

"Maybe, we are both asses, so we have that in common. When it comes to the final battle between Lumus and Lears I'll avoid you on the battlefield." Dyne said with a grin. Levitz laughed. "I guess I'll extend the same courtesy. We will just kill each other's friends on the battlefield." Levitz added, grinning. Dyne stood up and took a step forward toward the water.

"That's a bit grim, but yeah, either way, you look at it. Things don't end well between us."

"Dyne look!" Levitz jumped to his feet.

"In the middle of the Canby Delta!" He added.

The Cancer Zodiac emerged from the depths in the distance with a monstrous roar.

"Well, I'm about to fight a legend I grew up drawing pictures of. I use to dream about…"

Levitz put his hand over Dynes' mouth.

"Please shut up Dyne. We should back up and draw it to a better terrain. There is too much mud here, and it could cause problems during battle." Levitz didn't wait for a response. He turned and ran up the beach toward the forest north of Canby.

"I guess we are doing your thing then, good. I didn't have any suggestions…" Dyne took one more look out toward the water.

("Well if I die here, I hope you live a good life Zynx.") Dyne thought with a grin.

Dyne ran up the beach behind Levitz. Cancer made its way across the water with increasing speed. Levitz reached the small forest. Dyne couldn't help but notice Levitz crawling on the ground.

"What are you doing?" Dyne shouted.

"Focus on the enemy Dyne. Also, don't enter the forest through this path. Run around." Levitz whispered.

"What?" He wondered. He checked behind him. Cancer had made it to land.

"Great…" Dyne ran up the side of the forest. He came to the edge of the sand and scoped some up as he ran by.

"Okay, here goes." Levitz walked backward holding a rope he tied to two trees creating a slingshot. When he released the rope, a small black container flew through the air hitting Cancer's chest. When it made contact it exploded. The smoke cleared quickly in the ocean breeze. When Dyne was able to see Cancer again, he couldn't believe his eyes. The monster's head was gone and part of its chest was missing.

"No way! You did it, Levitz. All of that panic and secret meetings for that? Some legend. Cancer went down with one attack…Wait, what?" The head was scurrying across the sand like a small crab made of star energy.

"Great, looks like this isn't going to be as easy as I thought. Tell me you have another bomb, Levitz." Dyne added.

"I do, but the rope snapped. You are going to have to buy me some time to fashion another." Levitz pleaded.

"Yeah sure, I'll go fight a zodiac of legend with a rapier sword. Good call…" He laughed sarcastically.

"Dyne go stall it! We don't have much time to make this work. Just go!" Levitz yelled.

Dyne looked at Cancer then Levitz. He turned back to Cancer and started to walk toward it.

"I swear Levitz, if you blow me up with that bomb I will haunt you until the day you die," Dyne yelled.

He started running at Cancer, its head returning to its body and using star energy it reattached itself. Dyne thrust forward while throwing the sand he picked up earlier in its face. His rapier pierced its chest, but it didn't flinch.

"Oh shit, it has no eyes. LEVITZ, IT DOESN'T HAVE A FACE, MAN!" Dyne yelled out. Cancer grabbed him by the throat. It held him up in the air and began to squeeze tighter as he cried out in pain.

"Dyne you need to get out of the way!" Levitz shouted.

("If I could I would...") Dyne thought. Cancer threw him backwards into the delta. As he hit the water Levitz released the bomb. This time it hit Cancer on the head. The explosion blew its head to pieces, causing the rest of its body to immediately turn to stone.

"Stone? I guess that one did it. Two bombs though? Lumus spoke of these things like they were unstoppable killing machines... Dyne where did he go?" Levitz jumped from the woods onto the beach, but he couldn't see him anywhere. As he ran down the beach toward the delta; Dyne burst through the surface of the water.

"Ah. Well, that sucked… Hey, Levitz, have you seen my rapier?" Dyne swam back to the shore as Levitz dropped to his knees. They burst into laughter.

"Yeah, I saw it on my way down. You might need to buy another one though." He replied.

"What? What do you mean? Did you blow it up?" Levitz continued to laugh as Dyne crawled up the beach. He looked up at Cancer now turned to stone with his rapier sticking out of its chest.

"Great, it figures. Story of my life." Dyne added with a sigh. Levitz rose to his feet and offered a hand to him.

"It could be worst right?" Levitz shrugged.

"Yeah, I guess so. Maybe it's time I upgraded anyway." Dyne laughed as he sat on the beach.

Chapter Twenty Four- Leo Zodiac of Leodot

Brinx sat on the branch of a tree high in the sky with his legs stretched out along a narrowing branch. He didn't pay much attention to Hedree pacing down below. Hedree walked back and forth impatiently. There are few trees in the area, Brinx thought. North of Leodot is mostly mountains with the odd tree placed alone like the one he sat in.

("I won't be able to use the trees to my advantage here. Only one tree in all of this area except the one on the other side of this reservoir. That is too far for even me to jump though. Hedree hasn't spoken a word in our whole time together. A brute of a man he is, and almost as big as Frostear. It would be wise to go over our skills to see if we complement each other, but on the other hand, he doesn't look like he wants to chat at all. The dark looks he keeps throwing my way give me the creeps.") Brinx thought.

He looked down to Hedree once again. He had stopped pacing and was now watching the fish in the reservoir. He had his arms at his side and made no other movements other than his eyes back and forth as the fish moved.

("Strange, but he doesn't seem to have a thought in his head. The man seems distracted by anything that moves. Can I really rely on him to work together if it comes to that? Maybe I should try speaking with him?") Brinx thought. He climbed down the tree and walked up behind him.

"Hedree, may I have a word with you?" Brinx asked, but he didn't turn around. Instead, he scratched the back of his neck like he didn't hear him at all. Brinx walked around him to face Hedree.

"I understand, Hedree. Under normal circumstances, we would be enemies, but being in this situation maybe we can work together just for now?" Brinx suggested. Hedree finally made eye contact with him.

"I don't care for idle chit-chat. Keep your distance, and mind your tongue in my presence." He explained. He walked around Brinx and continued to look at the fish in the reservoir.

("Not the friendliest of people. Blunt, and to the point too. Very well. I will leave him be.") Brinx thought as he went to turn back to the tree. He paused for a moment.

"Is something the matter?" Brinx looked Hedree in the eyes as he asked him.

"I just wondered why you were green with purple eyes. The one we found was black with red eyes." Hedree seemed confused. Brinx paused with hesitation.

"What do you mean the 'one you found'?" Brinx asked. Hedree turned back to the reservoir. "Never mind, I don't need to know." He replied. Brinx took a few steps closer to him.

"Please Hedree, I need to know. Where did you find another Grenton?" Brinx urged. Hedree turned to face him once more.

"Lord Lears found a creature that looks just like you. He said it will be of great importance one day. It doesn't move. It doesn't breath. It just is." He explained and walked away from Brinx.

("Another Grenton... Could he be telling the truth? I don't know much about my kind. I'm still too young to know the full extent of the Grenton race... my kind. With no one to teach me, I just learn what I can as I go... but to have another Grenton on Twilight. I must find it.") Brinx thought.

Hedree took his large axe off his back. Brinx looked over and noticed the fish had fled down the river.

"It comes!" Hedree shouted. The water burst like a volcano. Brinx shielded his torso and face with his vines.

"Careful Hedree, back up quickly!" Brinx could see perfectly through the water was coming down still. Hedree had blocked his view with his axe.

"This is it: Leo, Zodiac of Leodot. I can't feel its power at all, but it is clearly pure star energy. If only I had rooted on Twilight I would be able to feel what we are up against." Brinx didn't hesitate. He shot thorns from his palms as he ran at Leo. Hedree ran from the right toward Leo with his axe above his head. The symbol on its head flashed, sending a shockwave at Hedree as he approached. He flew over Brinx, crashing hard into the ground.

"A head-on attack doesn't seem to work!" Brinx shouted as he stopped his advance.

"I will bind Leo with my vines, and it should allow you to strike," Brinx yelled out. Hedree nodded. Vines flew at lightning speed through the air. One latched on Leo's left wrist and the other on its right leg.

"Go Hedree! Now is your chance." Brinx yelled out. Hedree looked at him briefly, then advanced at Leo with his axe above his head once more. He jumped into the air as he got close to Leo. His axe began to glow, and as it began to glow Leo's attention followed. Brinx's vines held tight, but he could see them about to tear. Suddenly they burned off just as Hedree came crashing down. Leo leaped up, catching him by his throat. While in the air Leo brought his arm out with Hedree in its hand. Leo arched its arm then threw him with all of its strength to the ground. Brinx quickly launched vines from his body and wrapped them around a tree on the other side of Hedree. The vines caught his fall, but pulled Brinx closer to him, dragging his feet along the hard earth. Brinx detached the vines and got his footing back once he saw Hedree make his way to his feet.

"Hedree are you okay?" Brinx called out. Hedree rose to his feet.

"Thank you for catching me." He replied. Brinx smiled. Leo landed softly near Brinx, but it was like it didn't notice him at all. Leo's symbol on its face began to glow again, but Brinx ran in front of Hedree. As he did a shockwave came from Leo once again. Brinx took the whole attack head-on. The energy tore his green protective shell off his body. He stood still for a moment with his arms still up.

"Is that all you can..." Brinx fainted, and he fell face first onto the ground. Hedree rushed to his side.

"Brinx, you saved me. Even after I spoke to you the way I did? Why?" He pleaded. Leo charged another shockwave from its head.

"This thing is too powerful. You need to get out of here! Save yourself." Brinx whispered. Hedree clenched his fists.

"Not for me! Not for me!!!" He yelled out. Brinx watched as his rage grew more and more. Brinx began bleeding on the ground, his blood was an oozy green liquid.

"Hedree, you don't have to fight. You can't win head on, don't do this..." Hedree stood up. His pupils were pure white with rage. He gripped his heavy axe with only his right hand and he threw it with all of his strength. Leo moved its head, following it until the glow faded. When it looked back Hedree was already charging at him. Leo quickly released its shockwave. Hedree staggered for a moment, but the sheer force of his determination and rage pushed him forward. As he got close he reached out to Leo's head. He grabbed Leo's Zodiac symbol and squeezed it until it shattered.

Leo dropped to its knees and slowly turned to stone. Hedree stood panting as he watched Leo petrify before his eyes.

"Brinx!" Hedree turned as fast as he could then ran to his aid.

"Brinx, wake up. Wake up, Grenton!" Hedree continued to shout for several minutes before he finally realized. Brinx had begun to wither where he laid. Hedree picked him up in his arms and started walking southeast toward Capaz. He walked until he reached halfway from Leodot to Capaz.

"This is Dornet region, Brinx. The land of Aquoise. I heard some time ago that it has the best soil of all the regions." Hedree explained, his voice quaking. He set Brinx down gently and began to dig with his bare hands.

"This will be your resting place, my friend. I wasn't the best person to be partnered with. I ignored you most of the time, but you saved my life regardless of how I treated you. I will forever respect you, and I am honored to have fought together with you in battle." He said as he cleared the tears from his face with his forearm.

He picked Brinx up and set him in the hole. He stared at him for a moment with a sad looking grin on his face. He slowly covered him with dirt as he sang a song from his childhood.

"A melody of the spirit a song of strength, peace fight with me to keep the beast restrained. Warrior of people, fighter of legend. Let the life protected now protect you." Hedree continued to hum as he stood up.

"Goodbye Brinx." He said with a soft tone. He walked toward Capaz with his axe over his shoulder and a tear rolling down his cheek.

Chapter Twenty Five-
Virgo, Zodiac of Virphire

Frostear waited alone just south of Virphire. He traveled in the front, leaving Ged far behind. When he arrived at his destination to wait for the Virgo Zodiac, he noticed Ged wasn't with him. It was strange to him, but even with his dragon senses, he couldn't feel Ged's presence.
("I knew better than to trust a pawn of Lears. I guess I will have to face this thing alone. If it even exists. It is laughable to think Ged would have come along anyway. That bastard thought I would fall for his tricks last time we met. Making shadow copies of Aire and Levitz to face me. Though it was impressive to make them seem so much like the originals and to even trick my senses to think they were real...") Frostear laughed.
"Maybe I scared Ged away with how brutally I took down his shadow copies." Frostear continued to laugh.
"Don't get too cocky, dragon. My copies were weak. The real Aire and Levitz would have torn you apart." Ged announced. His eyes glared at Frostear as he peered out from Frostear's shadow.
"If you think I'm scared of my shadow then you are sadly mistaken. I am surprised I couldn't sense you in my own shadow." Frostear laughed.
Ged's eyes shone brightly from the shadow, while the rest of him remained hidden under the shadows as if he under water.

"It's funny, I was going to tell you to watch your back too." Ged slipped away within Frostear's shadow.

"Don't get too comfortable Ged. If you stay too long I may have to charge you rent." Frostear laughed to himself, but Ged didn't reappear. Frostear waited with his arms crossed. Time feels like it is slowing down, he thought. He sat down after a while and started to look out toward Virphire Cove to the southeast, wondering if he was in the right spot.

"Ged are you still there?" Ged didn't answer him. "Ged we need to move. If these things come up through the water then maybe the cove would be a better location. I doubt Virgo would come through a river. It's just too shallow here." Frostear said.

"For once I agree. Hold on." Ged's arms emerged from Frostear's back like large dragon wings.

"Whoa! Ged what's going on!?" Frostear shouted as they flew into the air.

"Once I'm in a shadow I can move within it and produce what I choose to, and don't worry about me dropping you. I have attached your shadow to my shadow realm. It is bound until I choose to release it, and even if light hits me, the attachment will still stick since it is linked with my shadow realm." Ged explained.

Frostear's eyes lit up with excitement. He could feel the air flow through his hair once again. He had forgotten how much he missed that feeling. Ged flapped the shadow wings across the sky as Frostear gazed down at everything around him.

("I can't see Zelkem or Jol at Geminite. I thought they would have been waiting there by now? I didn't really get a chance to say goodbye to Zephry before we all departed. I hope she is okay. Everyone just kind of scattered. She is strong though, with a kind heart like no other I have met.") He thought.

"Frostear, ready yourself to land. Don't want to snap your legs as we fall toward land." Ged laughed from inside the shadow. Frostear readied himself for impact, but even still they hit the ground harder than Frostear thought they would.

"Are you crazy, Ged!?" Frostear yelled out.

"We both know you are a Drayhelm. A fall like that wouldn't harm you at all." Ged retracted his wings back into the shadows.

"That's true, but another fact about Drayhelms is to not make them angry." Frostear smiled as he walked around to survey the new area, although Ged couldn't see his face.

The water began to bubble in front of Frostear. He took a step back.

"Ged, it seems we are ready to begin," Frostear added. Ged pushed out of the shadow realm from Frostear's back.

"Perfect timing. Allow me to take this one." Ged's face split into a sinister grin as shadows poured out of Frostear's back onto the ground. Without giving Frostear a second to react, the shadows wrapped around his body encasing him completely in shadows. After a pause, the shadows burst like an eruption causing them to expand to a thin layer of black shadow. They formed into wings as the rest formed a body like a dragon around Frostear's body. The water from Virphire cove calmed as the shadow dragon stared at Virgo, the Zodiac of Virphire.

Ged was in complete control. Frostear couldn't move at all inside. He flapped the shadowy wings to levitate for a moment. After a devious glare, Ged swooped in and grappled Virgo. He flapped his wings harder to build altitude. Once he was high enough, Ged released Virgo to free-fall toward the ground. He opened the mouth of the shadow dragon and shot out a steady stream of shadows. Virgo was pushed with such might that it burst when it hit the ground. Virgo's head spun across the dirt. As it came to a stop Ged landed on the ground nearby. The head shook and the energy started pouring out forming it a new body.

"This thing is able to regenerate? It can't be immortal! I'll show you my full power Virgo!" Ged forced the shadows to shoot out like Brinx's vines. The shadows wrapped around Virgo's newly formed body, neck and arms. His shadow dragon stood still with its monstrous mouth open wide, pulling Virgo closer and closer. Virgo was right in front of the mouth of the shadowy dragon but was able to stop itself. Virgo grabbed the shadows on its arms with its hands and started pulling back. Suddenly Frostear's large red sword pierced through the shadows and pierced the head of Virgo. Virgo immediately turned to stone. Frostear pulled his sword back into the shadows, and Ged retracted back into Frostear's shadow, but as Frostear finally opened his eyes as himself again he fell to his hands and knees.

"Ah. Why do I feel so weak? Frostear gasped for air as he raised his right hand from the dirt to his chest. He unstrapped the harness that held his sword to his back as he coughed.

"I didn't have enough star energy to generate that many shadows. I simply borrowed your power." Ged smirked as he fell back into the shadow realm.

"Bastard! To be used by such a thing. When I get my strength back I will kill you for this Ged…" Frostear promised. His vision began to blur. For a moment he tried to stand up but fell back to the ground falling unconscious.

Chapter Twenty-Six- Libra Zodiac of Librine

Zephry followed quite a way behind Coldblood. They hadn't spoken a word at all since partnering up in Capaz. Coldblood didn't even look back once. He just kept his hand on the hilt of his sword as he walked. When they came to the point between Librine to the south and Librine Delta to the north, Coldblood stopped. Zephry caught up with him but was too worried to say anything. She waited several minutes until she couldn't hold her tongue any longer.

"Why did we stop? Is something wrong? Did you hear something?" Zephry took a few steps forward with her sword drawn.

("Stupid girl, she is starting to irritate me. I wonder if I killed her here would anyone really care. I could say the Zodiac got her... There was nothing I could do, I could tell them.") He thought with a smile on his face.

"You look like your father, you know? After meeting your mother, I can see you have her eyes too." Zephry smiled. He turned away to hide his face.

"Stupid girl. What do you know?" He replied. Zephry shrugged.

"Your father acts like that when he is embarrassed too. Maybe it's a Drayhelm trait. Anyway, shouldn't we continue to Librine?" Zephry sheathed her sword as Coldblood looked back to the Librine Delta.

"I suggest we split up. You go just south of Librine, and I'll go to the Delta." Zephry looked at him in confusion.

"What is a Delta?" She asked. He shook his head. "Really? It is the mouth of a river. It's where a river opens up to a larger body of water." He explained. She smiled awkwardly.

"Oh, I see. Well if I head south then how would I be able to let you know if I run into the Zodiac?" She wondered.

"I guess we will see how it works out." He started walking north. Zephry didn't understand what he meant.

("See how it works out? What does that even mean? I won't even be able to see him from that far away. I guess I'll just head to Librine. Although I'm a little concerned if I end up fighting the Zodiac alone, but I'm stronger now. I can fight any monster that dares to take me on!") She thought. She walked off toward Librine alone with a skip in her step; Coldblood looked back occasionally, but not to see if she was okay. He just wanted to make sure she had left his sight.

("That woman is intolerable. I barely spoke, but the moment she started… She just gave me a headache. I don't think I have ever met someone so annoying since Antsos. Ridiculous creature never shuts up about how much power he has, when in fact he may very well be the weakest of us all. I was surprised to see mother in Capaz of all

places, come to think of it. It has been years since I have seen her face. Though I hate her I was still happy... Why? She cares more about the humans than her own race. A traitor to her own kind. Mother or not, that is unforgivable, but look at me. A hypocrite as well! I too have left my kind to fight with Lears. It doesn't matter, though. In the end, Lears will wipe them all out, and I will rule Scorpial the way it should be. With no forgiveness and no mercy for those that even speak of betrayal.") He smiled as he thought to himself. He arrived at the cove north of Librine. The weather seemed oddly calm, even the wild animals gave no sign that they were scared.
("I thought a river ran from this cove. I suppose this isn't a delta after all. Ah well, that girl wouldn't know the difference anyway. Even after I explained it to her just looked at me with that blank stare.") He laughed. The water in Librine cove started to bubble as he thought to himself. The Libra Zodiac burst from the water, landing just a few feet away from him. Without looking he drew his sword and sliced at its head. Libra turned to stone as he continued to think to himself.
("I find it odd she would show so much interest in my father, and it seemed mother glared at Zephry when she saw her in Capaz. My father wouldn't sink as low as partnering with a human girl would he?") He wiped his sword, completely unfazed by the danger he had just been in, and put it back in his sheath.

He continued to think to himself as he walked away from Libra. He made his way to Capaz, leaving the fully petrified monster behind him. Zephry sat cross-legged on the riverbank just outside Librine.

("Oh Frostear, I miss you but I'm not worried about you. You are a Drayhelm, and I know you will be just fine. Lady Concy didn't seem too happy to see me though. It was almost like she was angry I was part of the meeting outside of Capaz. Strange though, I don't think I have ever actually talked to her. Maybe she is mad because she is friends with Scarlette, but she and I have barely said hello? When I get back to Capaz I will ask her to join me for a drink. That might be the icebreaker we need!") She smiled with a simple look on her face.

She continued to wait alone on the river bank, picking grass and tossing it into the wind. She still lingered on thoughts of Frostear and Concy. Coldblood silently walked by her. He stopped and shook his head as he gazed at her, then he continued back toward Capaz.

Chapter Twenty Seven-
Scorpio, Zodiac of Scorpial

Concy and Doxas waited just south of the city of Scorpial. The city was empty with the exception of the Scorpial knights. Concy watched as Doxas paced back and forth in front of her.

"Are you nervous, Doxas?" She asked with concern in her voice.

"No...it's not anything like that. It's just that I'm worried we may be too late. You were smart to turn around and head back to Capaz. The tunnel from Neutral City was very efficient. Without that shortcut, I fear we would still be traveling by foot." Doxas explained. She smiled.

"Yes, you are right. The plains can be a troublesome place if you are ill-prepared, but I wanted to find out how you know Orson from our earlier chat in Capaz. You don't wear the mark of any city, and you carry a unique weapon set that I have never seen before." Concy looked down at Doxas' shield blades.

"These are called shield blades. They are weapons Orson helped me design and build. A normal looking shield crafted with knife-like edges. I wear them like gauntlets, but they are actually offensive and defensive weapons." He explained.

"I see, so you and Orson are old friends then?" She asked. He looked at his shield blades.

"Yes, you could say that. They are called "Steel Rampart." Orson named them for me. He saved my sister, myself and two others from a fire. Well, the story is that we lived in an orphanage in south Twilight when Orson stopped for shelter one day. A woman named Rose took care of us there. Over time, Rose and Orson fell in love and were married, and together they watched over us like their own. One day Orson took four of us to a city in the south for supplies. When we returned the orphanage was engulfed in flames. Everyone was trapped inside… Rose too. We lost everyone". He paused lost in thought.

"Orson took us to a city called Dongaro. We stayed at an Inn for weeks, but Orson never stayed with us. After some time he came back and took us north, and there it was: A new home Orson had built by himself. Days went by, then weeks. Eventually, years. Orson taught us to fish, grow crops, fight, and build. One day he said he had to go find someone, but being naïve I didn't ask many questions or try to stop him." Doxas took a deep breath.

"What is your sister's name?" Concy asked. Doxas looked down at his feet.

"Her name was Zana." He replied in a whisper. Concy put her hand in front of her mouth embarrassed.

"Doxas I am sorry. I didn't know." Doxas looked up with a smile on his face and a tear in his eye. He wiped his face then looked at Concy.

"It's okay I wouldn't expect you to know. We just met after all." He said with an optimistic smile.

"We can talk about something else if you prefer," Concy added.

"No, I haven't been able to say any of this out loud. I have been alone for some time now. It makes me happy to be able to just vent you know?" He sighed in relief and Concy smiled in return.

"Then please continue with your story, Doxas." She said.

"Well, after Orson had left, life was great for a while. Zana, Saxsus, Noah and I all lived a peaceful life in that little house. Noah and I added more rooms to the house. Saxsus tended the garden, Zana fished almost every day. The problem started when men came from Dongaro one day. Unbeknownst to us, the east and west areas of south Twilight had been at war with each other. Noah and Saxsus agreed to join their ranks. Zana...well she wanted to help bring the two nations back together. She talked me into joining too. After all, I couldn't leave my family alone out there. The war went on for years, and the four of us were promoted quickly through the ranks. I didn't know at the time, but Don was the cause of the orphanage burning down. He wanted to build a reinforced knight outpost there since it was the only way by land to get to Dongaro. We followed a false savior. We killed for him. We lied for him. In the end, we were ordered to assassinate the leader of the east. The four of us went together under the cover of night. Zana froze when she found the mark. I still to this day don't know why. Saxsus entered after her to finish the job, but he turned on Zana. She killed him and fled the building.

Together we ran with Noah through the night…" Doxas began to tear up.

"Doxas you can stop if you want to." Concy blurted out. He wiped his tears.

"It's okay. I'll finish. My sister…Zana was hit with an arrow in front of me as we ran across the fields. I picked her up and I carried her. Noah had left us behind. I ran with her in my arms until I took an arrow in the back of the bridge. Zana and I fell down the slope to the riverside. I crawled to her side, but she was dead. To save my life I rolled into the river and let the current drag me away. That was the last time I saw Zana. I was found and nursed back to health by some fishermen down the river. When I was able I returned to Dongaro and found that Noah had denounced me as a traitor to save his position as Don's lapdog. He told them I sided with the east. I sent word to Orson of Zana's death, and we met up in Geminite. I was quite harsh to him there, but he wasn't angry with me. I planned on returning to south Twilight, but I overheard the Geminite knights talking about Orson and something big happening in Capaz. I had already lost my sister. I couldn't lose him too. That's when I ran into you in Capaz." He explained.

Doxas sat down with his back against the wall of Scorpial City. Concy looked at him long and hard before she walked over to him and sat down beside him.

"Everyone has a story, Doxas. It only matters how you use the past to build the future and determine who you will become. Many people don't think about that. I suggest you take that anger, that sadness, and that inner agony, and convert it into something your sister would be proud of. Let Zana guide you now." Concy stood up with a smile. She walked a few steps forward to hide her face as a tear rolled down her cheek.

("Such a hard life for such a young man. I never knew south Twilight was such a cruel place. Then again, they would surely put on a good show for their guests. As a councillor I wouldn't see such things. If we survive this ordeal then I shall go back to south Twilight and see it for myself.") Concy had her head down. Doxas looked at her with a smile. He knew she was saddened by his story. He decided to let her have a moment alone. Just as things began to calm down, the water south of Scorpial began to swirl like a whirlpool. They watched as the vortex grew in size.

"We are not in the right place. I thought the Zodiacs were supposed to appear near the cities." Doxas called out.

"Yes, but maybe we can force it to meet us." Concy closed her eyes. Doxas looked at her with confusion. Suddenly her eyes opened wide with a solid red glow. Doxas backed up in fear as she began to transform. Her arms formed scales while her head and back began to grow in size. Doxas fell backward staring as she fully transformed into a Dragon right before his eyes.

"Lady Concy!?" Doxas cried out.

"She can't respond to you in her dragon state. She can only hear what you say. But don't fret; Lady Concy has the most control over her dragon form than anyone else ever did." Doxas turned his attention to the voice.

"Who are you?" Doxas asked as he got back on his feet. A man in emerald green armor came from the shadows by the city gates.

"I am Joffree. Captain of Scorpial knights." Joffree had a serious look in his eyes.

"If she is one of the Drayhelm of Legend, does that mean you and those knights are also Drayhelm?" He asked. Joffree laughed.

"No, the Dragon Wars wiped all but a few from Twilight. There are but a handful left. I couldn't say how many, but we as Scorpial knights know the secrets of the Drayhelm. No one outside of Scorpial knows of Concy and her ties to the Drayhelm." Joffree explained.

"I too will protect her secret. Lady Concy is a great person, and I will see no harm come to her." He added. Joffree put his hand on Doxas' shoulder.

"She has monstrous power, but the kindness of a princess. Now watch her unleash her might." He said with a smile as he watched Concy roar.

She bellowed a roar as Scorpio raced toward her. Concy flapped her wings, but Scorpio didn't stagger. It jumped into the air and slammed its fists of energy hard on her back. She spun around in the air grabbing Scorpio as she spun upright. She squeezed Scorpio tight, but its tentacles of energy stabbed through her hands. She let go and landed as Scorpio did. Scorpio formed a tail of energy from its lower back that looked like a scorpion's stinger. Concy flapped her wings in rage but didn't take to the air. Doxas noticed the tip of the stinger on Scorpio turn purple.

"Lady Concy!" Doxas raced across the battlefield. Joffree reached out to stop him but just missed him. Scorpio shot the stinger at lightning speed, but Doxas was able to reach her in time. He jumped into the air and took the attack just above his heart with such speed and strength that he flew back, crashing into Concy. He rolled off her chest onto the ground and lay there without moving. Concy's eyes lit up with rage. She gripped her claws deep in the dirt below and shot off with a flap of her wings at Scorpio. The monster couldn't react. She clawed at Scorpio and scratched the Zodiac symbol right off its face. Her rage took over. Even as Scorpio began to petrify, she continued to claw away until Scorpio was just rubble. Her rage subsided and she began to transform back into her human form. Joffree raced to her side with a blanket to cover her. He looked up to the guards at the gate.

"Clothes! Now!" He yelled out.

"Joffree. Is Doxas okay?" Concy couldn't see over his shoulder. He turned to look at Doxas. He turned back to her with a frown.

"I am sorry my lady." Joffree shook his head.

"No...NO! He can't be! Not him!" Concy pulled herself up enough to see over his shoulder. Doxas had turned to stone. Tears overflowed Concy's eyes as she buried her head in Joffree's chest.

Chapter Twenty Eight-
Sagittarius, Zodiac of Sagnet

("Lake of the Archer; Sagnet's own little river of dreams. This world has grown into quite the paradise. West Zin must be proud of what it has become. I can already sense the Zodiac coming toward the surface. They were created to protect this planet, but the people here on Twilight have now become the protectors. I see now why she needed my help with all of this. Her time is almost up. My child will soon come to pass, but her successor seems like a fitting replacement for her side of the galaxy. Our Scarlette Rose. She also concerns me though. She has an inner power like nothing I have ever felt. West Zin must have felt that power in her too. It seems I will have to trust in my child's wishes in choosing a mortal to take the place of a god.") Kontaminate thought.

He waited patiently as he thought to himself. The water began to bubble at the surface, but he didn't flinch. As the Zodiac shot out of the water and onto the land, Kontaminate just glanced at Sagittarius of Sagnet. Sagittarius didn't move once it faced him. He walked over to Sagittarius and placed his hand on its Zodiac symbol on its face. "You have done well, I shall release you now." He said calmly. The star energy flowed from the zodiac symbol on its face into the air. As the energy came out from its body Sagittarius began to slowly turn to stone but in the shape of a man holding a bow.

"I am sorry, you have done everything right but we have no need for the guardians anymore." He whispered.

He stepped back to look at the Zodiac once it was fully petrified. He raised his hand and opened a portal.

("Now that I have met you and your companions, Lumus, I feel like allowing this course of life to bloom as fate would will it. Good luck") He thought. His smiled as he entered the portal, leaving Sagittarius petrified in front of Lake Archer as a reminder to the people that they are in good hands.

Chapter Twenty Nine-
Capricorn, Zodiac of Capaz

Scarlette sat beside Lumus in a patch of grass enclosed by the small forest that overlooked Lake Twilight, with the waterfall in front of them. She had her hand resting on her pocket with thoughts of the hourglass in mind. They didn't speak to one another. They just sat in silence. She finally took the hourglass out from her pocket.
"I can feel their powers, you know. The god somewhere up there. I can feel the West Zin's power. I can also feel the others, but they are faint." He blurted out. Scarlette smiled.
"You never told me you knew of them. That makes this much easier." She said. Lumus stood up.
"I have to tell you something, Lumus. I have to leave Twilight soon, and I just… I just want you to know I will miss you!" She blurted out. Lumus looked at her for a while before answering.
"Leave Twilight? What do you mean? Are you planning on going back to Dystopia?" He asked. Scarlette shrugged.
"You know already that you were born from the positive energy of Twilights core. "Twilight's core is blue, and it represents the positive energy of the west side of the galaxy. Dystopia's core is red, and it represents negative energy for the west side of the galaxy. These two planets are the only planets on the west side, though Twilight stands alone in our solar system. Dystopia is in a mirror realm we call the second dimension. When you were born

the mass amount of positive energy used by the core to create you had drained the core's energy, and because of this, it caused Twilight's core to turn red. With both cores on the west side negative the whole west side became unbalanced. Demons made their way down the Aster Mountain caves, and this is when I was killed. When I lived in the realm of the dead the West Zin took care of me and I was taught things about the planets, and a little about how the universe works. I was given the chance to come back to help you. I told you that already, but what I didn't tell you was this." Scarlette held her hourglass up for him to see.

"I was given a whole other life to live, but my time will be up soon, and I just wanted you to break the news to everyone for me." She smiled. He hugged her, but as he tightened his hold on her two large splashes of water shot from Lake Twilight. Lumus turned and powered up his star energy. Scarlette pulled her bow off her back and readied an arrow.

"Scarlette, be careful. I cannot feel their power anymore." He said.

"I know. They are but shells of their former selves. I imagine that the others are not having as much trouble as I thought they would." Lumus looked over at her.

"How could you know that?" He asked. Scarlette loosened the grip on her bow.

"I suppose I won't be needing this anymore." Scarlette dropped her bow to the ground. Lumus stepped back from her as she began to levitate. Her hair blew up in the wind as her power radiated around her body in a faint pink glow.

"My power is almost full. West Zin has almost fully transferred her power to me. Lumus please stand back. Capricorn of Capaz is mine. You take the other zodiac." She demanded. Lumus was surprised to feel so much power hidden inside of her.

("Scarlette, what is happening to you? I will have to lure the other away from her. If I can fight Pisces of Piscyst alone then we won't be in each other's way.") Lumus began to generate star energy as quickly as he could. His power quickly exceeded Scarlette's. Both of the Zodiacs turned their attention to Lumus.

("Too much power. They are attracted to star energy. I need to drop my power down.") He thought. He took a deep breath, and some of his power drifted into the sky. He looked at Scarlette, but she didn't flinch. Her power continued to grow. Lumus turned his attention over to Pisces.

("Okay big guy, time for us to go.") Lumus shot off at incredible speed, striking Pisces in the centre of its chest, then he started running through the forest and south of Capaz. Pisces followed without hesitation.

("Lumus, I was hoping we could fight them together. As our last moments together I wanted to stand beside you as an equal. Don't forget me, okay?") Scarlette's eyes lit up with a solid pink glow. She was levitating as she drew in star energy. Capricorn waited patiently as her power grew. When she was finally ready to fight, her hair slowly floated back to her shoulders. Capricorn shot across the surface of the water. Scarlette rivaled its speed as she also shot across the water at Capricorn. As the two collided it created large explosions of energy around them. It seemed like a stalemate until Scarlette let out a scream. The pink energy around her exploded and engulfed Capricorn completely. After a moment Capricorn flew out of the energy and skipped across the water like a rock skipping the surface of a calm lake. Capricorn flew into the waterfall as it slowed down. Scarlette began to fly higher into the air. ("This power is incredible. I can fly too, this is amazing. The power of the West Zin has almost fully taken over. I have truly become a goddess of the west galaxy.") She smiled. Her hair blew in the wind as she gazed at her hands. She didn't notice Capricorn slowly exit the waterfall. It raised its hands to her. With a flash, it launched a barrage of horn-shaped energy attacks. She raised one hand and the star energy shot from Capricorn broke apart and faded into the sky.

("This will be my final gift to you all. Lumus, I am sorry for everything you have gone through. I hope I will see you again. Goodbye, my friends.") She thought while closing her eyes.

She raised her hands and formed two balls of star energy. The left was red and the right was blue. As they finished collecting energy she pushed them together to form one large purple ball of energy. She dropped her arms out in front of herself and clapped her hands together, releasing a shockwave that pushed the energy at an incredible speed. Capricorn took the attack head-on but tried to stop it with its hands. The energy slowly erased its body. Scarlette smiled as a portal opened behind her.

"Seems my time is up. Since the portal has opened, that means West Zin has already faded away, and I am now the West Zin. It is time to go then. Goodbye, Twilight. I will be watching over you from now on. Lumus, take good care of Twilight while I am gone." She announced as she backed into the portal.

She turned with a smile and a small tear in her eye as she turned into the portal. Her tear rolled off her cheek and fell into Lake Twilight. The tear hardened into a small condensed ball of star energy, then sank into the depths of Lake Twilight.

Chapter Thirty- Aquarius, Zodiac of Aquoise

Lears stood on the edge of the mountains overlooking Aquoise. From high on the mountaintop, he was able to see all of the ocean east of Aquoise. He waited with his arms crossed. A smile struck his face as his eyes opened.
"I can feel the Zodiac's power. It's faint, but it is there." He jumped down from the mountaintop and slid down the dirt on the side of the mountain. As he raced down, he noticed the Aquoise soldiers mobilizing in the city below.
("Insects scurrying below. Those fools think they would be able to stop me if I tried to kill them. Cute. Hahaha.") Lears reached the bottom of the mountain. He came to an abrupt stop as he felt something strange in the distance.
("That power. It is overwhelming. Is that Lumus? No. It can't be. That is someone else. It almost feels familiar to me.") He thought. He turned toward Capaz.
("A second power? Wait, the second power is Lumus without a doubt. It seems he is starting to get serious.") Lears smiled.
"He is growing more powerful, but he isn't reaching his full potential, but why? Maybe these Zodiac creatures are not as strong as we anticipated.") He thought. He let out an ominous laugh as he turned back to Aquoise.

The guards of Aquoise had their eyes on Lears. He approached with a smile, but the guards backed away in fear as he passed the gates to look upon the ocean. He watched the surface beginning to bubble.

"So it begins. The power of this creature is weak. I can barely feel its star energy. I will make short work of this. I see now why Lumus is holding back." He said. He laughed as the Zodiac Aquarius of Aquoise emerged from the ocean surface. Aquarius flew through the air and landed on the shoreline in front of Lears. The monster reached out and grabbed him by the shoulders. Its tentacles of star energy pointed toward him, then went to strike him. Lears laughed as he generated a barrier of dark energy around his body. Aquarius tried to force its attack through his barrier, but it just caused Lears to laugh even louder.

"I was hoping you would be stronger. I was planning on unleashing my full power on you. Though I suppose I still could. You are but star energy, and killing you won't matter, now will it."

Lears continued to laugh as his barrier expanded, causing Aquarius to let go of him and stagger backward. He extended his arms out on each side of his body as the barrier grew in size. He let out a roar as the energy rolled off of him like a shockwave. Aquarius flew back into the water, but Lears continued to generate power. He ran up to the edge of the water then jumped straight up into the air, and held his arm up with his hand extended towards Aquarius. Lears opened his hand and shot a huge ball of black transparent star energy at the water. Aquarius jumped from the water just to take the attack head-on. It broke apart as it took the attack. Bit by bit the star energy that formed its body dissolved into nothing but the emblem of the Zodiac Aquarius from its head. The emblem fell to the shallow shore in front of Lears. He stood panting on the shore looking down at the emblem.

"I guess going all out really does drain my power. This is the first time I was able to use everything I had in one attack." Lears raised his leg and slammed his foot hard on the Aquarius emblem, shattering it into pieces.

("Odd. The shattered parts are turning to stone. What a waste of power. This thing couldn't even give me a decent fight. Lumus will be expecting me to turn on him right about now. I will give the order once we meet back at Capaz.") He thought. He turned to the guards in Aquoise. He gave them a sinister grin as he walked past them.

("I can feel Lumus powering down. He must be returning to Capaz soon. Then I shall meet him for our final fight.") He laughed as he thought about the fight to come.

He walked southwest with excitement. There was a sinister grin still on his face as he made his way toward Capaz.

Chapter Thirty-One- Pisces, Zodiac of Piscyst

Lumus raced along the Torson region home of Capaz, He led the Zodiac Pisces of Piscyst across Torson plains. The Zodiac was able to keep pace with him. He found it interesting that it was so easily manipulated into following him from Lake Twilight.

("This should be far enough away from Scarlette. I just didn't want to have her in the way if things got out of hand, but Scarlette should be able to handle herself now that she has become a goddess. That is a strange thought...A goddess of the west galaxy. Someone I have known almost my whole life becoming something I thought... well, I never really gave gods much thought. I don't really know what to think of all of this. Then again I was once a mortal boy on a farm. All of this is new, and I suppose anything can happen at this point. I don't even know what I am. A god? An abomination? A mistake created through a child's wish? People call me Prince, or savior, but what am I really?") He thought to himself.

Lumus came to a sudden stop. Pisces overshot him by a few feet but turned around with a sharp twist. Lumus had his head down in deep thought.

("What am I really? I can't stop thinking about this. Why now? How come I never had these thoughts before? I just don't know what I am. Everyone just called me the prince and the savior..., but I haven't saved anyone. I haven't done anything for Twilight. Lears, Kontaminate, and the Zodiacs... I have brought nothing but pain to them. Why do they care for me when all I do is bring more grief?") He shook his head in frustration. Pisces ran at him at an alarming speed, but Lumus didn't react. His head was still down and his mind raced with thoughts of his life. Pieces threw its right fist forward hitting Lumus on his left cheek, but he didn't even move an inch. His eyes lit up with a bright white glow. He raised his hands to hold his head as he continued to shake his head in frustration.

("I don't know who I am, and I just don't know what I am doing! WHO AM I?") Lumus' body began to emit mass amounts of star energy that formed like waves in all directions like layers of energy forming a disk of energy around him. The power began to cause him to levitate into the air. Pisces paused as it waited for Lumus to make a move. The star energy from him confused Pisces. It couldn't understand what to attack.

("I have to fix everything! I have to save this world, but not from Lears. I need to save this world from me!") He screamed out as he thought to himself.

The power from Lumus pulled back into his body with a flash. He dropped to the ground, and as he landed on his feet he jumped toward Pisces and grabbed his zodiac symbol off of its face He crushed it like it was nothing. Pisces began to petrify, but Lumus had already begun walking back to Capaz.

("I need to find Scarlette. I have so many questions that I need to ask her. I need to know what I truly am. I can't feel the power of the Zodiacs anymore, and that tells me they have all been defeated. Kontaminate has left too, but Scarlette… I can't feel her power anymore either. Her energy is completely gone.") He cringed to think he wouldn't see her again, but he knew she was gone. No matter how many ways he tried to convince himself. He knew he wouldn't see her back at Capaz with the others. He stopped, and he looked up to the sky. He smiled as he gazed into the red moon, the Scarlet Moon.

"She really is gone...... I thought we would have had more time. I never had a chance to say goodbye, nor will I get the answers I seek." He whispered to himself. He felt something behind him. Like pulses of energy appearing and disappearing.

"I'm sorry Lumus. I didn't mean to leave so suddenly." Scarlette said softly. Lumus turned around with a surprised look in his eyes. It was Scarlette in a white robe stretching down to her ankles. Her hood covered her eyes, but he recognized her voice and her smile.

"Scarlette? But I thought you had already gone to the realm of the dead?" He cried out. Scarlette pushed her hood off to reveal her face.

"I'm the goddess of this planet now Lumus. I can go where I please, but I can't stay long. Coming to this world drains my star energy." She explained. "Well, I am happy that I at least get to properly say goodbye to you. I have been trying to think of what I might say, but I just couldn't find the right words…" He said embarrassed. Scarlette stepped forward and grabbed him by the shirt. She pulled him close and kissed him. She held him tight like she never wanted to let him go. At first, his eyes were open, but after a few seconds he closed his eyes and wrapped his arms around her. After a moment he opened his eyes, but she was gone. He looked up to the sky and smiled once again. "Thank you, Scarlette. That was one of the questions I didn't know how to ask you." He said with a big smile on his face as he made his way back to Capaz.

Chapter Thirty-Two- Goddess of Twilight

Twilight seemed silent as Lumus stood on the bridge that connected the Dornet region of Aquoise and Torson region of Capaz. The air was still, the animals were nowhere in sight, and time seemed to be moving slower than normal. He felt uneasy as he waited for everyone to return. He wondered how everyone was. He knew it was going to be difficult to explain what had happened to Scarlette. As he waited, he stared at the sky. His thoughts were clouded with doubt and confusion but he tried to stay optimistic.

("Scarlette. How do I explain what happened to you? Do I just tell them the truth? Do I just explain that you agreed to become a goddess? How do you tell people something like that?") He thought. As he lowered his head he noticed Hedree coming from the north. Lady Concy and Coldblood came from the south. As they got closer he noticed Frostear, Ged, Dyne, and Levitz. He smiled until he noticed Concy, Coldblood and Hedree were alone. Zelkem had Jol on his back. Zynx carried Antsos in his arms. Orson and Aire were barely visible in the distance, but he smiled when he realized they looked okay.

("There are a few people missing. Lears isn't here yet either.") He thought. He crossed his arms to wait for everyone to arrive before jumping to conclusions.

"Lumus!" Orson called out. He opened his eyes to see Orson right in front of him.
("I only shut my eyes for a moment...Zero? What just happened?") Lumus shook his head.
"Lumus are you okay?" Orson had put his hand on his shoulder, but Lumus didn't have any memory of him doing so.
"Yes, I'm fine. I must have been daydreaming. What's going on? Is everyone back?" Orson pulled his arm away from Lumus.
"We have four people missing. Doxas, Brinx, Zephry, and Scarlette. You were with Scarlette, so where is she?" Orson asked eagerly. Lumus couldn't help but notice the sadness in his eyes.
"I will tell you about Scarlette later, please don't worry she is fine. What do we know of the others?" Lumus asked. He looked over his shoulder and saw Lears with all of his people standing together on the northern part of the bridge. Lumus looked at him to see Zelkem Zynx, Dyne, and Lady Concy.
"Your friend Brinx gave his life to save mine while we fought against the Zodiac. After the battle, I buried him in the centre of Dornet region. I am sorry for your loss." Hedree said, his eyes lowered.
"He died?" Zelkem blurted out.
"He was a brave warrior, and I wish I could have saved him. I truly am sorry." Hedree turned and made his way back to Lears and the others. Lears he looked up at him. He dropped his axe then continued to walk north.

"You dare quit my ranks, Hedree?" Lears shouted out. He picked up his axe, and threw his arm back, but Lumus ran over and grabbed the tip of the axe. "No harm will come to Hedree. I will make sure of that." Lumus demanded. Lears let go of the axe. He knew he didn't have the strength to fight Lumus as he was.

"Have it your way. He isn't worth my time anymore anyway." Lears shouted. Lumus turned away from him and gave his attention to Coldblood.

"Where is Zephry?" Lumus asked. Coldblood smirked at him.

"The girl? I sent that fool to Librine. I fought Libra on my own. She is probably still waiting for the Zodiac to arrive." Coldblood announced. Lumus clenched his fist.

"You left her?" He replied.

"You travel with her right? Then you know how useless she really is." Coldblood laughed.

Frostear ran up and punched him in the face.

"Watch your mouth boy!" Frostear yelled out. Coldblood wiped the blood from his mouth as he rolled onto his back.

"Ah yes, father has a thing for the girl. A human? Really? You always were a disappointment." He said. Frostear reached down to him and picked him up by his throat with one hand.

"Another word, and I won't hesitate to kill you." Frostear's eyes had a dim glow of red.

"Frostear!" Concy yelled out. Frostear turned his head to look over his shoulder. He looked back at Coldblood.

"Know your place, boy." Frostear heaved him through the air. He slammed hard against the ground. He staggered as he tried to stand, but once he stood up he was silent and brushed himself off. Frostear walked back across the bridge but didn't stop. He made his way toward Librine. No one said a word to him as he passed them.

"Concy, what of Doxas?" Orson finally said to break the dead air. She looked back at him with dread.

"Scorpio turned him to stone. He was moved to Scorpial throne room, and is under protection by my knights." She hesitated to say. Orson dropped to both knees.

("Doxas... No! Another one of our kids I couldn't protect...") Orson thought to himself as tears filled his eyes. Concy walked onto the bridge, but Zelkem stopped her from going further.

"Just leave him, Lady Concy. Let him deal with the loss." Zelkem suggested. She backed up from the bridge. Tears filled her eyes.

"Is there a cure for petrification? Can he be helped?" Orson said with panic in his voice. Concy moved forward, pushing Zelkem aside.

"If there is I will find it. You have my word. Concy turned to Capaz and ran as fast as she could. Lumus offered Orson a hand. He reached out, and let him pull him to his feet.

"He isn't lost yet. We will help him, Orson." Lumus smiled.

"I don't mean to interrupt your sad moment of loss, but I think we will be leaving now." Lears blurted out. He turned toward Aster Mountains. He started to walk, but only Ged, Antsos and Coldblood followed him. He noticed after a few steps and turned to look at the others.

"What are you fools waiting for?" He asked. Aire, Levitz, and Jol didn't move. Finally, Aire turned to Levitz.

"Hey Levitz, you were telling me about your hometown of Canby a while back. You know in all the time we spent travelling I don't think I have ever been there." Levitz smiled.

"You're right. How about we take Jol to Canby. I could show her around too. Would you like to come too, Jol?" Jol smiled.

"Yes, I think I would. I heard it is a peaceful city." She quickly replied. They started to walk past Lumus on the bridge. Jol turned to Lears with no expression on her face. Just a stare, then she followed behind Aire and Levitz. Lears turned back to Aster Mountains without a word.

"Looks like Lears is losing control of his people," Zelkem said with a smile.

"Don't forget: we have also lost friends today. We should go back to Capaz." Lumus walked past Orson.

"Lumus... What about Scarlette?" Orson asked once again.

"Maybe we can leave that until everyone has time to get themselves together. We can all meet in Neutral City when the council sends everyone back." Lumus didn't wait for a response. He just walked by Orson with a sad look on his face.
"Zelkem, Dyne, and Zynx. You all did great today. Let's go back to Capaz for now." Lumus shouted back.
Zynx and Dyne followed behind him. Zelkem looked at Aster Mountains as he joined Orson on the bridge.
"He is right brother. If something happened to Scarlette, then I'm sure he just wants to tell us when we are all together. Don't let it get to you, and if it was something terrible then he wouldn't be as composed as he seems right now." Zelkem said. Orson leaned on the railing of the bridge. We suffered many losses today, Zelkem. I am thankful you are alright." He smiled.
"Just a few cuts and bruises. Seems I'm tougher than a few god-made legends." Zelkem said with a laugh.
"Let's go back to Capaz. I would like some answers. I would also like to join Lady Concy in her search for a cure for Doxas." He put one hand on Zelkem's back and gave him a pat.
"Let's go little brother." They were last to walk back to Capaz. Lears looked back from the distance with anger.
"Lumus!" Zephry called out.

"I heard from Frostear. Brinx and Doxas... I can't believe it! Brinx was..." She blurted out. Lumus' face went red.

"I know Zephry...Brinx was the first one to show me humans and demons can work together. He was also a great friend, and he is unreplaceable. But remember: He will always be in our hearts. I didn't know Doxas, but Orson is taking the news hard. It would seem they knew each other from before I met him." He explained.

"I didn't get a chance to meet him either, and even though he didn't know us... He fought with us. I wish I would have known him better." She added.

"Zephry, can I ask you to do something for me?" He asked.

"What can I do for you, Lumus?" She tried to hold back her tears, but a few slipped down her cheek as she thought about Brinx and Doxas.

"Let the council know that it is over. The people can return to their homes." He added. She nodded.

"Yes, sir." She said with a serious face as she ran toward Penelope's shop.

Orson and Zelkem came walking up to the gate. Lumus looked back at them and then waved them over.

"Frostear? I thought you would have been long gone to Librine. Was that Zephry I saw run off into Capaz?" Orson scratched his chin as he approached him.

"Well, she had already been waiting here when I was on my way to Librine. She said she was looking for Coldblood, but when she couldn't find him she returned to Capaz." He explained.

"We have some time before the people clear from Neutral City. How about we take a walk, Frostear?" Orson suggested. Frostear seemed confused.

"Sure Orson." He agreed.

"We won't be gone long, Lumus," Orson shouted back.

Orson led him east to the bridge connecting Nuran region to Librine, towards the Torson region of Capaz. It was much closer than the bridge connecting Torson and Dornet regions.

"So I wanted to ask you about Drayhelms," Orson asked. Frostear fixed his sword on his back. It had been bugging him since they left Capaz.

"Is that so? Why bring me all the way out here for a question about the dragons? Is now really the time for a history lesson?" Frostear asked.

"Truthfully, I just wanted to know if Concy will actually be able to find a cure for my friend Doxas, or would it even be possible. I have never heard of petrification cases on Twilight before, so I'm a little skeptical. I understand she felt responsible for what happened. That is clear, but I just want to know if she is giving me false hope or not. I don't want to give up on Doxas, but I need to know I'm not chasing fairy tales." He explained.

Frostear leaned on the railing, looking toward the south.

"I see. Then let me tell you a story: When I was a soldier for Scorpial, Concy was a medic for our kind. No, I shouldn't say medic, because of her father she was not allowed to fight in the Dragon Wars. Instead, her father sent her here to Capaz. At the beginning of the war, she did tend to the wounded, but she had no training as a real medic. So I don't know for sure what she does or doesn't know about such things. However, I do know that medicine was an interest to her. What she studied while we were separated, I couldn't say." Frostear added.

"So it wasn't a ruse to spare my feelings?" Orson asked.

"I wouldn't be able to tell you for sure. That woman has a way of surprising people though. She came to Capaz and made her way into the council. True, it was in the works for some time, but when she gained power she fought to stop the war. Everyone called her a traitor... Even me. I didn't find out until years after the war was over what the truth really was. Concy fought tooth and nail. In the end, it didn't matter. My kind was nearly wiped out. Only a few survived, and the rest scattered like animals. Even after the war, we were hunted. When Geare was elected to be a councillor of Aquoise the hunting stopped. I don't know the whole story of that man, but something about him doesn't seem right to me. In any case, Concy may know something we don't. Don't give up on her or your friend." Frostear said with a reassuring smile. Orson noticed him looking at something in the distance, but he couldn't see it himself.

"What are you looking at Frostear?" He asked.
"Don't worry. I was just daydreaming. I have a lot on my mind these days. A lot has happened to us since we all came together. It is almost hard to believe. Before I met you all, I didn't care for anything. I just kept to myself and searched for something." Frostear added.
"What were you searching for?" Frostear turned to Orson and patted his back as he started to walk back to Capaz.
"I don't know. Maybe I was just looking for a reason to put one foot in front of the other. Now that I have joined all of you, I have felt like I am needed once again, but losing Brinx angers me most of all. He was a force for good, with the ability to help others and still be strong. I haven't told anyone this before, but I looked up to him. He was learning how to be human, and I was learning how to be human from him. Funny isn't it?"
Frostear walked off toward Capaz, but Orson stayed behind.
("I think we were all searching for the same thing. Just that none of us knew it.")
He looked back to Capaz. Frostear was well ahead of him though. He started to walk back too. He thought about his comrades a lot on the way back. He thought about Doxas, and he thought that Concy still might have a way to save him. It made him happy again to think that he may be able to help him. He thought of Brinx, and how they didn't see eye to eye, but in the end, he knew Brinx had become something else: A friend.

Orson arrived at Capaz, but he saw Frostear walking into town alone. Lumus wasn't waiting at the gate. He assumed he would be there when they got back.

("We weren't gone that long. Lumus couldn't have gone far.") He thought. He turned to the north. He noticed someone in the distance.

"Lumus? Where is he going?" He looked into Capaz but decided to go see if the person in the distance really was Lumus.

("Where is he going? We were all supposed to meet in Neutral City. Dornet region is... Oh, Hedree did say he had buried Brinx out in the middle of Dornet region, so maybe Lumus went to see for himself.") Orson concluded.

He continued to follow him. As he got closer he noticed Lumus had stopped and was looking toward the ground. He joined Lumus, but they didn't speak at first. They both just looked down at a small sprout growing over the newly turned soil.

"Orson, does it seem odd to you that a sprout has grown to this stage already?" Lumus asked. He didn't actually notice at first, though he was looking right at it.

"You were a farmer, right? You would know better than me, but as far as I know, this shouldn't be as big as it is within a few hours." Orson said.

"I thought the same thing. I just wanted to be sure." Lumus added. Orson saw a smile on his face.

"What are you thinking Lumus?" He asked.

"I was thinking that we should protect this area." He suggested.

"I'm confused. I know Brinx is buried here, and we will have a proper grave built around Brinx, but…" Orson's eyes opened wide. Then he looked at Lumus.

"Brinx is going to need a lot of space if what I think is right," Lumus said as he began walking back to Capaz with a smile, and his eyes closed. ("That massive tree Brinx told us about on Dystopia. Could that be what this little sprout is?") Orson thought. He looked at the sprout once more, then he started to smile.

Capaz was full of life once again. People filled the streets with life as Lumus and Orson made their way to Penelope's shop. Penelope was standing outside with Brunius. Orson found it odd that they were without guards.

"Councillor Brunius, it is good to see you," Orson said as he shook hands with Brunius. Lumus nodded to Penelope with a smile.

"Sir Orson I am glad to see you looking well after the battle. I have been talking with Penelope for some time about something she brought to my attention." Brunius smiled as he looked at Penelope.

"Is it something I can help with?" Lumus gave a quick response.

"No that is quite alright. Your friend Captain Nex has already been kind enough to take the job." Brunius added. Orson smiled awkwardly.

"What exactly are we talking about?" Orson asked.

"Yes Sir Orson, I suppose some context would help. Penelope has offered to relocate her general store to another location in town. She had the idea to tear her shop down. We will then build a stronger structure around it, and that will be linked underground to our palace." Orson gave Penelope a nod.

"That will make access to Neutral City more secure from our end. Thank you, Penelope. But where would you put your shop?" Lumus asked.

"I was thinking Neutral City. I can set up shop there for anyone that may need supplies. Those paths to each city are long and tiring. For example, it could take many hours to make it from Scorpial to Canby. I was hoping, Lumus… would you allow me to set up a shop and an Inn for those passing through?" She asked.

"I think that is a great idea, but there may not be as much traveling through as you think. Neutral City is supposed to be a secret, and so you may not have the business you make here." He added.

"Lumus we just had everyone from every city in North Twilight in Neutral City at once. I would imagine that Neutral City is no longer a secret." Brunius blurted out.

"I guess he has you there Lumus. Look, the tunnels are great, and since the secret is out of the bag: The council has already agreed to build structures around the entrances in each city. We will be charging people to use the tunnels after this year's Zodiac Awakening." Brunius explained.

"What did you say? Zodiac Awakening? Also, I never agreed to allow you to charge the people for use of the tunnels." Lumus took a step toward Brunius.

"I'm sorry Lumus, but we voted on it. All cities agreed to enforce a fee for travelers, but we would obviously grant free travel in times of crisis." Brunius was slightly scared of Lumus when he moved closer to him.

"So I have no say in the matter?" Lumus cried out. Orson put his hand on his shoulder.

"The cities are in need, and will all benefit from this. When money is collected from people leaving the cities they can use it to build and restore the city, and purchase supplies and people will still be granted safe passage in times of need. It will work for everyone." Orson explained.

"Neutral City was created by us, Councillor Brunius, and the council shouldn't have the right to change things. As owners, I grant Penelope the city, and all cities will give twenty-five percent of all money collected to Penelope. She will decide how to use it to benefit Neutral City. Do you agree?" Lumus suggested. Brunius was taken aback for a moment.

"I will have to talk to the rest of the council, but I do agree to your terms. It is fair that Neutral City sees some of the money for its own growth. I will send word to the rest of the council immediately." He agreed. He bowed politely then made his way to Capaz palace. Penelope was silent with a surprised look on her face.

"Penelope, do you agree to all of this? I'm sorry I didn't give you more of a warning, but it just kind of came to me." Lumus apologized. Penelope smiled, her eyes shining.

"Thank you Lumus. Thank you so much! I will do everything I possibly can to make Neutral City a welcoming place for everyone. But what should I do? I mean where do I start?" She said with panic creeping into her voice. Lumus and Orson looked at each other. Orson took a step toward Penelope.

"First, you should talk to Captain Nex. He has been building for us since the beginning. He would be able to help you build what you need to make the city prosperous. We are going to have to add some more shops to Neutral City too." Orson explained. Penelope turned to look at her sign from her shop.

"More shops? I will need to find someone to run my general store and someone for the inn too. Will I need to have a deli or food stands? Maybe a blacksmith, and a tavern too." Penelope began to rant to herself.

"You got it, Penelope. We will leave Neutral City in your hands." Orson gave Penelope a pat on the back then made his way into her shop.

"Lumus, why wouldn't you and your friends run the city? Am I really the one you want to do this?" Penelope asked. Lumus smiled.

"I have a few reasons. With Lears still out there, I don't know if I could run a city, and I was a farmer once upon a time. Something like this doesn't suit my expertise. The other thing is that Neutral City was built for the people. Who better to run it than the people? I am happy that everyone will have a better life because of Neutral City, and they will need a leader among them to guide them. I won't always be there for them, so I leave that to you." Lumus walked past her into her shop.

("A shop owner to a town leader. I don't even know how to take this in.") Penelope sat down and against her shop to cry tears of joy.

Lumus found Orson waiting for him at the bottom of the ladder to the tunnels. He stood with his arms crossed staring down the tunnels toward Neutral City.

"Well, you made her day Lumus. I'm surprised you gave her control over the entire city." He said.

"We don't have time to run cities. Neutral City was meant to help the people. Now they can use the tools we gave them to help themselves." Lumus added. Orson laughed.

"Give someone a fish, feed them for a day. Teach them to fish, feed them for life right?" Orson said.

"Yes exactly." He added.

"That really is kind of you, Lumus." He pointed out.

"We have bigger things to deal with. We need to find a cure for Doxas, and protect the sprout in Dornet region. More importantly, we need to talk about Scarlette" Lumus explained.

"Let us meet with the others. I would like to know what happened to Scarlette as I'm sure everyone else does too." Orson said as he adjusted his sword in its sheath.

"No, Orson I mean you and I need to talk before we confront the others." Lumus interrupted. Orson paused.

"Is she…dead?" Orson said in a whisper.

"You know as well as I do that Scarlette died in the caves of Aster Mountains when I was born. Her time with us was borrowed, and she was never meant to have come back at all. We should be thankful for the time we did have with her. I know I am, and I would have never met Scarlette if she had stayed in the realm of the dead. I didn't realize it until I came to meet you and our friends that Scarlette has guided me through everything. I owe her everything." He said sadly. Lumus leaned on the cave wall out of the reach of the torches light.

"What are you saying Lumus?" Orson said as he turned his full attention to him.

"Scarlette's time ran out. During our fight with the Zodiac… She started to become a goddess, and she was beautiful Orson. She became the goddess of the west side of the galaxy. West Zin passed away during our fight, and Scarlette had no choice but to leave. She isn't dead, but she won't be coming back to us either. It was all pre-arranged, even before I met her on Dystopia." He said softly. He tilted his head down and went silent. Orson put an arm up to catch himself from falling. He began to cry but tried to hold it in.

"No… Scarlette. Is she gone? Why? How come she didn't tell us anything? How could she just leave? If she became a goddess, then why couldn't she come back to us? She is a goddess after all…" He cried out. He broke down, causing him to fall to the ground in tears. He called out her name, then stood to his feet in rage. He drew his sword and began slashing at the wall with all his strength. Lumus continued to lean against the tunnel wall and waited while Orson let it all out.

"It's not fair, she was my responsibility. I should have known... I could have protected her if only she..." He dropped his sword and fell to his knees once again.

"Orson, she isn't gone forever. I have seen some things... I can't go into detail just yet, but someone sent me to a faraway place, and there I learned that everything will work out. That is how I was able to stay so calm through all of this. Though I am of course sad, and very angry with the way things worked out, remember that everything will be okay." Lumus explained. He took a step toward Orson. Lumus walked a bit closer to the light to reveal a smile, but his white hair had become brown, and his eyes weren't glowing.

"Lumus?" Orson stood up with a panic.

"I have learned how to revert back to this human form, but my point is that everything can become what it once was. You just have to find a way." Lumus stood as he once did as a human when he was on Dystopia, living with Orson's familiar Rozell.

"How is this possible?" Orson's surprise caused him to walk closer to Lumus to gaze upon his face.

"I can't say where, but with this ability, I can blend into the mix of people to go unseen. Plus while in this form I store Star energy, so when I become me again I can fight with far more power. Scarlette will come back to us, time will help us find a way. Don't worry Orson." Lumus powered up once again. His light lit up the caves. Orson was inspired to see Lumus transform like the first time they met all over again.

"Let's get to Neutral City Orson, and please don't let the others know I told you first. I just wanted you to know so that you and I could help the others through this." Orson nodded with a revived sense of clarity. They started to walk down the tunnels together.

Dyne, Frostear, Zephry, Zynx, and Zelkem stood in a semi-circle near the entrance to Capaz tunnels. As soon as Lumus emerged from the doorway they all looked up at him. Orson left his side and joined the others.

"Okay, I understand. You all are worried about Scarlette. I'm not sure exactly how to explain her situation." Lumus admitted.

"Just tell us what happened to her. Where is she? Is she okay?" Zephry said in a fit of rage with a stomp of her foot.

"Okay, here goes: Scarlette was slowly turning into a goddess to take over for the West Zin. She is in the realm of the dead, and she is fine. As Orson suspected, she did, in fact, die the day I came into this world. She waited in the realm of the dead for almost ten years. When I was about ten years old she appeared in Dystopia, and we grew up together. She and I met once in a while during the ten years I spent in Dystopia. I learned very little about her, but she knew who I was the whole time. I didn't find out until I came to Twilight that she was really there to watch over me. A little while ago here on Twilight, she showed me an hourglass that was given to her by the West Zin. It was a timer that counted down her time left until she had to return to the realm of the dead. She was slowly becoming a goddess the whole time she was in Dystopia and while she was travelling with us." Lumus explained.

"That explains why she always seemed to recover so quickly from her injuries, like the time she fought Ged. She should have been out for days, but she was fine within a few hours. At the time I didn't really notice. Now it all makes sense." Zelkem blurted out. Orson took a deep breath then turned away from the others.

"Is she coming back Lumus?" Zephry asked with fear in her eyes. Lumus hesitated to answer.

"No... She will remain in the realm of the dead as the goddess of our side of the galaxy. She says to always do your best, and to always watch over each other." He added.

"What does that mean? She told you that before she left?" Frostear asked with confusion.

"She is talking to me as we speak. This is how I know so much. I only knew some of the things she is telling me. Some of this is new to me too." Everyone gasped. Orson turned back to him with a surprised look in his eyes...

"You are speaking to her now? Tell her we will find a way to bring her back!" Orson yelled out. "I can't, Orson. She is talking to me but I can't speak back. I was able to speak to her last time, but I think it was because she was still tied to Twilight. The more she speaks the quieter she becomes. Soon I won't be able to hear her at all." Lumus closed his eyes to focus.

Zephry ran over to him and grabbed his wrists. She fell to her knees with tears in her eyes.

"Then tell us what she is saying! Please!" Lumus tried to smile when he looked down at her, but he couldn't.

"She wants everyone to work together. She says we are stronger when we are together. 'Don't give up' she says… The path of fate has brought us all together, and together will not only change Twilight but the universe." He repeated Scarlette's words in his head. Zephry's grip tightened on Lumus. His eyes widened like he had just realized something.

"What else Lumus? What else!?" Lumus turned his head away from everyone.

"I can't hear her anymore." He whispered. He shook Zephry off of him and turned back to the tunnels leading to Capaz. He walked to the doorway then stopped for a moment. His head turned as if he was about to say something, but he didn't. He continued to walk back to Capaz alone, leaving everyone behind.

Chapter Thirty-Three- Serpentarius

Lumus made his way outside Neutral City tunnels into Capaz. He passed the people in the streets as they called out his name with excitement. He ignored everyone though. He was so deep in thought that he couldn't care less about their compliments. He walked until he got to the North Gates overlooking Dornet Region. He paused for a moment and thought about what he wanted to do until he remembered Brinx. He ventured into Dornet region past the North Capaz Bridge but was shocked to see the sprout was now a six-foot tree.
("No tree I have ever seen has grown this fast. It seems Brinx will be okay after all.") He thought as he rested his hand on the bark of the tree and closed his eyes.
("I can feel Brinx' life force. It is good to have you back Brinx, but I have to say things are a mess right now. We have lost Scarlette and you. Orson's friend was petrified by the Zodiacs too. I'm not sure what our next move is, but I have a feeling things will work out. Everyone is completely exhausted and lost. Especially me. They wouldn't admit it, but I can tell from looking at them that the battles with the Zodiacs have left them drained physically, and the losses we took drained them mentally. Maybe we should all just take a break for a while. It would be best for them I think.") He

thought to himself as he opened his eyes... He felt like his head was shaking from the inside.

"Ah what is this feeling?" He cried out.

"You have just felt the power of something far more powerful than you have ever faced." A voice said from behind the tree.

"Who's there!?" Lumus began to emit a faint light around his body with his fists clenched.

Lears came walking from the other side of the tree. "So that power I felt during the fights was that girl after all, and this tree is that plant creature that you dragged back from Dystopia. Interesting..." Lears smiled, but he wasn't looking at Lumus. His focus was on the tree.

"Why are you here, Lears? (How did I not sense his energy so close to me?)" Lears walked cautiously to Lumus' side.

"It is simple. That headache you are having is some power that I haven't felt for some time now." Lears described.

"Lears, all of the twelve Zodiacs have been defeated. Whatever this power is it can't be them right?" Lumus asked.

"Are you so sure? Have you not heard the legend of the thirteenth Zodiac?" Lears said. Lumus powered down to give him a chance to answer.

"Okay Lears, I'll bite. What is the legend of the thirteenth Zodiac?" He asked. Lears didn't do his sinister laugh as he usually did. Instead, he was serious and stared off into the distance as he thought how he wanted to answer.

"Ophiuchus… The hidden Zodiac of the snake. The legend says that it is hidden because of the other twelve Zodiacs. Serpentarius…, or Ophiuchus, however you perceive it, is the strongest of the twelve. It is said that it stays hidden because it can only be taken down by the twelve Zodiacs if they were to combine their power against it." Lears explained.

"How do you know all of this?" Lumus asked.

"I read, Lumus. Am I not allowed hobbies?" He replied. Lumus smiled.

"You said you felt this power before?" Lumus asked.

"Yes. When I was still young, I felt it above me. It felt like it flew through the clouds so fast that I didn't really know what had happened, but then I felt it again a few years later. I saw it the second time though… It was like a surge of energy in the shape of a snake going through the clouds. I would imagine a normal person wouldn't be able to have felt it, or even see it, but I did. Its power was incredible. So much so that I was even trembling." Lears said while clenching his fists. Lumus turned his attention to the clouds above.

"Look, as much as it pisses me off to work with you. We will need to combine our strength to fight this thing." Lears finally whispered.

"If it just passed by last time, why would it come down now?" Lumus asked.

"Were you not listening to me at all? It only feared the twelve Zodiacs. Without them here anymore it will no longer have anything to fear." Lears yelled out.

"I suppose you are right. Then we just let it come to us?" Lumus asked.

"Exactly. We will have to draw it to us. If I'm right then it is drawn to star energy just like the other Zodiacs. All we have to do is generate enough power to lure it to us." Lears pointed out as he watched the skies.

"Agreed," Lumus added.

"Let's head to a more open area first, we can go north of Aquoise. The plains there are open enough for us to fight this thing, but remember that after this we are enemies again. I won't hesitate to kill you, Lumus." Lears reminded him.

"I'm glad we are going to be working together. It's too bad I don't trust you at all though. I was hoping while working with you and your followers that we could live peacefully afterward." Lumus said with a grin.

"You are living in a dream, Lumus. I have every intention of killing you after this, but we both know that even at our max, this won't be an easy fight." Lears quickly replied.

"How do we know this thing wants to fight? Maybe it just wants to live a peaceful life. All the stories you told me are just stories of legend." Lumus added. Lears laughed even more than normal.

"Concentrate on the power Serpentarius emits. It has more evil within it than I do, and I'm pretty evil… In any case, this thing has the desire to destroy, and anger built up over centuries based on the legends I have read. I would imagine this thing is ready to show its true colors." Lears explained.

Lumus pondered the idea for a moment. He couldn't help but feel like this creature is misunderstood, or maybe it just wanted to live its life, and he still hasn't explained why he left the others in Neutral City the way he did. He felt like he had to talk to them. He knew he was being selfish, but the news of Serpentarius bothered him too much. He knew this could be his only opportunity to stop it before it attacked.

("Maybe I should tell the others about the god of time, Zero, and how he took me to another planet… I felt like I was gone for weeks, but time only passed a few minutes here… I saw Orson in the distance, but then he was in front of me with his hand on my shoulder. I still have questions about Damen and Rel… Will they be okay? Zero told me I wasn't supposed to tell the others about their world, or what I did there… Maybe I should focus on Serpentarius for now… This creature was created from the energy dispersed over time by the other Zodiacs; if the books that I have read are true… I feel like we are the same. Created by something else with no mentor or path shown to us. We are the same where neither I nor Serpentarius knows what we are supposed to do. It has been alone all this time, and I think Lears is right. Serpentarius didn't understand why the other Zodiacs stopped it from coming to the surface. I don't know if I can bring myself to fight this creature.") Lumus thought to himself while Lears stared into the clouds.

"We have no choice but to leave now, Lumus. If this creature lands it will go for star energy just as the other Zodiacs did during our fights with them. My Lords have told me information from their battles, and they explained that these things are drawn to star energy. I believe that Serpentarius will go for something worth devouring." Lears explained. Lumus walked a few steps toward Aquoise.

"What do you mean?" He asked.

"Think about it, you fool. Why do you think it would risk its life by exposing itself like that?" Lears yelled frantically. Lumus turned his head to him.

"I don't know." He said.

"Think about it. The other Zodiacs never had to feed. They are creatures of star energy made by the West Zin, but they live at the bottom of the ocean. I would guess that their legend was passed down by the people that saw them descend from the skies in the first place. They must be feeding off the star energy from fallen stars right? So if that is true, Serpentarius must have descended from the skies to feed. That is the only thing that would make sense to me." Lears continued to stare at the sky as he yelled.

("I'm impressed by his theory. It does make sense. The other Zodiacs didn't speak, so reasoning would be out of the question, but fallen stars? I would guess they fed off the energy from the planet's core, but telling Lears that would probably only anger him further.") Lumus thought. Lears turned to him and grabbed him by the shoulders.

"This thing will eventually find the core of the planet, Lumus. Think about it: we have no choice but to stop it." Lears yelled out. Lumus finally agreed with a nod.

"Okay, I am convinced there is no other way. We need to stop this thing from getting to the core of Twilight." He agreed.

"Finally you come to your senses. Keep up!" Lears turned and began running toward the North to Aquoise. Lumus hesitated for a moment and looked up to the sky.

"Scarlette please, if you think this is the right thing to do… Help me understand…"He muttered. He started running behind Lears. The two raced across the open plains with their attention toward the skies.

Lumus couldn't help but notice a purple tinge in the clouds above. Lears wasn't paying attention to the color, but his eyes were scanning for any movement from Serpentarius.

"Lumus, try to generate some star energy. We need to start luring Serpentarius now!" Lears demanded as he began to emit an eerie dark shade from his entire body. Lumus followed with him, though he found it a little more difficult to emit star energy while running.

("I haven't tried to bring out my power while running for some time now. Maybe I should have trained more. Sometimes I think Lears could very well be better trained at things like this.") He thought.

"Fool! you are slowing down. Pick up the pace." Lears shouted back. Lumus pushed himself to generate more power, finally, he was able to pull enough power to generate a dim white light surrounding his body.

"Look, Lumus! Serpentarius is there in the sky to the north! It is descending to the surface." He shouted again. Lumus had finally seen Serpentarius. He found it hard to see it at first, because it was a solid white star energy. It was well hidden in the clouds.

"Lears, it's coming straight down to us!" He shouted.

"Keep running, Lumus. I would prefer an open area to fight, and we just have a bit farther to reach the edge of Aquoise." He suggested as he watched the skies.

They sprinted as fast as they could as Serpentarius came crashing down into the surface. They focused on dodging as much as they could, but Serpentarius didn't let up. It burrowed through the dirt and came up through the ground, trying to catch either of them in its mouth, but its oversized body was so long that they had to jump over its body while trying to dodge its large mouth chasing close behind. Finally, they made it to the edge of Aquoise, and Serpentarius spiraled up into the sky and stared down at them. After a pause in the air, Serpentarius lit up like an explosion of bright white lights. When Lumus was able to open his eyes he couldn't see Serpentarius anywhere. He looked to his right, and Lears was also frantically looking around for Serpentarius, but they both saw nothing.

"Lears?" Lumus said with concern.

"Underground?" Lears replied. Suddenly a bright sphere came from the clouds landing only a few feet away from them. They couldn't see what it was, but Lumus braced himself in case of an attack. He shielded his face enough to see past his arms and put one leg back a bit to strengthen his stance.

"So you two are trying to keep me from what is mine too?" A voice said from inside the light.

"Serpentarius?" Lumus asked.

"Ophiuchus, but you can call me Rasel in this form." Rasel walked from the sphere of light as a woman. She was wearing a suit of light armour resembling snakeskin, and a pure green dress also with the snake pattern. She put her hand out in front of her with her hand open to reveal her palm. A small circle of light formed on her palm, then she reached her other hand into the light. She pulled a large snake from the light by its tail. The snake fully left the portal from her palm and hit the ground. She snapped the snake like a whip turning it into an emerald green steel polearm. The snake's mouth opened to its widest, the handle all the way to the snakes head was covered in green steel in a snakeskin pattern. The tongue of the snake stretched out before turning to emerald colored steel and formed a sharp flat blade.

"Do you like my polearm? I suppose I should give it a name. How about Snake Bite?" Rasel giggled.

"Don't laugh yet, you still have me to deal with!" Lears began to emit a dark aura around his body. Lumus didn't notice before, but Lears wasn't carrying a weapon. He hadn't been using his sword for some time now, he thought. He left his sword that Scarlette gave him in Capaz Palace, he quickly remembered.

Lumus shouted as Lears ran at Rasel. Lears leaped into the air. He yelled as he pointed both of his palms at her. He began to shoot small spheres of dark star energy at her. She smiled as she raised her polearm, and began to spin it as fast as she could. The dark star energy was easily deflected all over the fields of Aquoise.

"You expect to fight me without a weapon in hand? Foolish man." She jumped into the air at him as he was coming back down to the ground. She spun her polearm, hitting him in the gut with the bottom of her weapon, then flung him through the air. He rolled along the ground without any means of stopping himself. Lumus clenched his fists, helpless to aid him.

"Lears!" He shouted. He powered up with a light aura around his body and ran at Rasel.

"You will suffer the same fate!" She yelled out. After she had spoken she had to look at Lumus a second time. The second look at his face caused her to flinch. He threw his right fist as hard as he could but stopped before hitting her. The sheer force of his punch threw her across the ground just as Lears had suffered.

"Why didn't you follow through, Lumus? You could have ended her with that attack." Lears said as he made his way to his feet.

"No matter. My enemy is still a woman, and I cannot hit her." Lumus straighten his stance and took a deep breath. Lears just stared at him.

"Are you kidding me!? That is no woman. She is an It. A creature and nothing more. It just appears to be a woman." He shouted at Lumus. He expressed nothing but anger as he yelled at him.

"Even so. I...I just can't." He put his head down. With a flash, Rasel appeared in front of him and delivered a devastating strike to his neck. The energy around his body faded.

"Never let your guard down, human! I will not take any mercy on those that seek to stop me from my goals." She screamed. Lumus fell to his knees as she pulled her polearm back. Lumus laid upon his knees with his head down.

"Lumus... Lumus wake up! I need you to wake up Lumus!" A familiar voice spoke to him inside his head.

"Scarlette? Is that you Scarlette?" Lumus could hear a gentle laugh that seemed to echo in his head.

("Yes, it's me Lumus. I seem to have a better connection with you now. It would seem... Well I can't seem to tell you.") Scarlette's faint giggle seemed to get louder.

("What are you talking about, Scarlette?") He answered her just by thinking.

("It doesn't matter, you will learn in time. As a goddess, I am bound by laws of the gods. I couldn't tell you if I wanted to, but you need to listen now. This creature that you fight may look like a woman, but she is just another demon. If you don't beat this thing then it will consume the core of Twilight. You need to stop that from happening. Not only would everyone on Twilight perish, but the entire universe could be at stake. This monster is not a creation of the West Zin. It is all of the negative leftover star energy from the Zodiacs since they were created. Lumus, please destroy this creature. Not just for me or you, but for everyone.") Scarlette begged. Rasel watched him closely.

"I know you still have some fight in you. I won't turn my back to fight the other one until I know I have finished with you. So get up and let us finish this!" Lumus' eyes opened suddenly, causing Rasel to gasp. He grabbed her wrist with the hand that held her polearm.

"Ah, you filthy human! Get your hands off of me!" She yelled out. Lumus stood up then looked down at her.

"I am Prince Lumus, protector of this world. I will never allow a monster like you to harm my friends, my family, or my home!" He snarled. He began to glow brighter than ever before. Lears backed away slowly to watch.

("I have never seen such a power. This is something else entirely. How can he tap into so much power? Where is this all coming from? This is far stranger than that girl.") Lears stumbled backward but didn't even blink when he hit the ground. He just continued to stare at Lumus and he began to tremble.

"Don't think you have won yet! My star energy is from the beginning of this planet's time. I have been storing power from the day I was chased away by the Zodiacs." She said, then laughed. Lumus squeezed her wrist tighter, then pulled her close. He threw his head forward, hitting her with a hard headbutt. He turned his body to face the South with his hand still gripping her wrist. He arched his arm forward and threw her up in the air, and slammed her back down into the ground. She laid on the ground and spit up blood onto her chest. She suddenly began to glow, then a flash blinded Lumus as she turned back into the giant serpent of star energy. The massive body only began to appear as she started to slither through the air. Lumus was pushed aside with ease. Lears rose to his feet and jumped out of the way as Serpentarius' head came charging at him with its fangs pointed directly at him.

("So she can turn back into her snake form at will. This will make things far more difficult.") Lears thought. He waited for a chance to jump on its back. Just as the head turned around to attack once more. He jumped up over its head and onto its back. Quickly he turned and ran toward its head upon its back. Lumus watched from the ground. Lears charged his hands with star energy as he made its way up its back as fast as he could. He jumped again when the head turned back to attack, but he dodged it. This time he slapped his hands together sending a shockwave at the back of Serpentarius' head. Serpentarius halted its movement to look at him with a glare. A flash blinded his sight for a moment, but Serpentarius turned back into its human form.

"Two on one, my snake form isn't going to be of use here." She muttered to herself. She drew her polearm from her palm once more. Lumus smiled. "So you will fight us in that form then?" He suggested. Rasel swung her polearm a bit to analyze its weight.

"I find it entertaining that you try to mock me, but I have been around since the beginning. My dear human, I do not fear you, and I only choose this form because I know that the serpent is too slow. I feel as though you are not entirely human either. You both have the same face as well. I find that odd. I have been watching from the skies all of my life, and I don't recall seeing either of you with such power until recently. If I was to fight a human I wouldn't have to resort to this, but I will in your case." She explained. She flicked her long green hair from her face.

"You have it right about us Rasel. Lumus and I are not what you would call normal. We are something else entirely. Similar to how you came to be actually…" Lears bragged.

"I don't care. Neither of you matter to me. I will take the core of this planet and ascend to space for my next meal. I will become a goddess, and I will rule this universe as I see fit." She protested. Lears laughed with a sinister grin on his face.

"Why? What makes you think you can be a god? You were created as a result of the scraps of beings created by a goddess. You are just the garbage left over that we have been stuck cleaning up." He added.

"How dare you, you filthy abomination! I will enjoy killing you both! Before, I was going to just kill you because you were in my way. Now I will take joy in it!" She explained.

Lumus' power rose. Lears noticed his power jump significantly.

"I guess I have no choice. If Lumus wants to max out then I will do the same." Lears said to himself. He began to yell out as he tried to boost his power too. His faint dark aura became solid. Lumus could only see past parts of the aura, and Lears just smiled as he clenched his fist in a furious rage.

"I will show you the power of darkness!" He shouted. He continued to emit so much power that the dark aura built up around him completely. The leftover dark energy started to seep out in a perfect circle around him. The farther the dark energy got from him the more it faded until it disappeared entirely.

("What is he doing? If he generates too much power who knows what will happen. That kind of power could kill him. Only a god would dare generate so much at once.") Lumus thought. He blocked his face with his arms to stop the heavy winds from hitting his eyes.

"You may want to take some shelter Lumus, I wouldn't want you to die from this before I get a chance to kill you on equal ground." Lears smiled at him with a sinister grin then turned his attention back to Rasel.

"You two are not companions, yet you fight me together. Interesting. Whatever it takes to save your world I suppose. It is too bad that you don't stand a chance. I will kill you both and take the core of this planet. You cannot stop me." Rasel looked at Lears, but her body faced Lumus.

"You might want to focus on me, Rasel! I'm the one that is about to kill you!" Lears shouted.

"Please. You both bore me. This little light show is pathetic. You two must be proud that you defeated the Zodiacs, but you have no idea that I have been sapping their star energy from them for centuries. Did either of you think at all about it? Why do you think the weak humans were even able to defeat them? If they had their true power they would have destroyed every living thing on this planet in seconds." Rasel smiled.

("Rasel is right. They were oddly weak, but we had such a hard time with them, and not all of us made it back from that. Is it possible she is hiding far more star energy then we know?") Lumus continued to think to himself as he backed away from Rasel and Lears.

Lears finally stopped. His muscles had grown a bit more toned, but his face still carried his sinister smile. He unclenched his fists and took a deep breath.

"You should be worried, Rasel. I will show you the true power of darkness." He announced.

"I'm not worried Lears because you are but an insect under my foot." Lears chuckled to himself.

"Rasel, Serpentarius, Ophiuchus. Whatever your name, is it doesn't matter. You are just another pawn this world put before me to knock down." Lears starred at her with a serious look in his eyes.

This time she turned her full attention to him. "Okay, insect. Go ahead! I'll give you the first strike." She announced.

"Very generous of you Rasel, but I believe the lady shall have the first strike," Lears argued.

"Very well, but when I send you to the realm of the dead don't feel bad that a woman killed you." Rasel declared with a smile.

She began to run at him with all of her might. He smiled then matched her speed as he ran at her. The two met in the middle of Aquoise fields with a huge flash. Lumus watched from the edge of Dornet region only a few steps from Zangus region of Piscyst to the west. A massive shockwave blew by him, but this time he didn't block his face. This time he watched without a blink at all. Rasel and Lears clashed blow after blow, but he could only hear them. The flash of light didn't disperse. The energy around them was so powerful that the light didn't fade because of their power clashing again and again.

("Lears has learned too. He has taken control of the star energy inside of himself completely. This will complicate things later when he turns on me.") Lumus pondered to himself.

The ball of light in the middle of Aquoise fields slowly moved. Lumus assumed Lears and Rasel were shifting the tide within the fight. He could see a crater as the energy from their fight dragged across the land. With a flash, the blinding ball of light that encased the fight faded slowly. Lears and Rasel stood on opposite sides of the crater panting.

"I didn't expect so much trouble from the life forms on the surface. I have been watching for so long, but your power is far stronger than anything I could have imagined." She worried.

"I told you I would show you the darkness. Now you want to run away?" Lears warned her. She looked at the sky quickly, then back at Lears.

"Don't bother Rasel. The moment you try to flee as that snake I will blast you with everything I have." Lears argued.

("He is right, even if I try, I am too weakened to flee, and the other one doesn't have a scratch on him yet. I have no choice but to try to kill Lears, and then flee before Lumus makes it to the battlefield, or I could…) I won't flee, Lears. You have suffered too many injuries, and as you stated before you want your friend over there dead. I am going to assume he will not interfere, and that will allow me the time I need to kill you." Rasel continued to struggle for air after talking to Lears. "Enough talk, Rasel! Make a move while we are young." Lears demanded.

Rasel flung her hair from in front of her face. She hesitated for a moment then dropped to one knee. She put her polearm on the ground in front of her with her palms facing each end. The light came from her palms, and with a flash, her weapon changed back to a living snake. She pet the snake then stood up straight and pointed toward Lears. The large snake slithered quickly toward him. At first, he thought of the snake as just a distraction until it got closer. The snake began to split the closer it got. By the time the snakes closed in on him; there were hundreds of them. He put his arms up and straightened his fingers with his palms up. Then he coated just his hands with his dark star energy, but this time even Lumus on the other side of the battlefield could see that his power was fading. The snakes began to strike, but he used the energy on his hands like sharp daggers to slice the snakes to pieces.

"Are you afraid of snakes, Lears?" Rasel burst out into laughter as she took one knee once again. Lears didn't have time to respond with all of the snakes striking him at once. He continued to walk backward and kill all that he could. He knew that he couldn't keep up with the little star energy he had left. Rasel laughed hysterically as he tried so hard not to allow the snakes too close to him. He began to show panic in his eyes until they just stopped. The snakes just rotted away on the ground. The star energy on his hands faded as he fell to his knees. He looked over to Rasel expecting her to be on her way toward him to finish him off but to his surprise, she had her eyes open wide. Lumus stood behind her on a bit of an angled stance with his hand on the center of her back.

"What are you doing? Don't you want Lears dead too?" She said in fear.

"Maybe, but If he dies it will not be like this. I will return you to the planet, Rasel. No more fighting, no more anger, no more fear. You want to get the core to become something that threatens everyone I love. I cannot allow that, but I also cannot kill someone that was just born differently. You don't deserve such a fate. You and I are similar where we both have been accidentally created by means out of our control. Out of anyone's control. I will bring you back to Twilight's core and give you a second chance." He assured her.

"I see. I suppose I wouldn't have been able to beat you both in the end. I accept your offer Lumus. Return me to the planet I won't stop you." Rasel giggled.

"Goodbye Rasel. I hope we meet again someday." Lumus added.

"You can count on it Lumus." Rasel glared at Lears with a sinister looking smile on her face. Lumus' hand began to glow on Rasel's back. She closed her eyes and tilted her head back. Slowly her entire body turned to star energy, and she gently rose into the air then faded away. Lumus staggered then fell to the ground.

"She can return to the planet's core now and have a chance to redeem herself in the realm of the dead. Lears laid upon the ground across the battlefield. He raised his head in confusion. ("What did he just do? How did he do that? Whatever he did just drain him completely. He was able to defeat Serpentarius just by resting his hand on her back. After everything, I threw at her, but I suppose now is my chance to finish him off.") Lears started crawling toward Lumus as the wind swept across the devastated Aquoise fields.

Chapter Thirty-Four- Chaos

Aquoise fields had been laid to waste. The once lush open fields of long grass and flowers had become an uneven devastation of craters. Lumus lay face-down in the dirt, struggling to take in a breath. Lears crawled on the other side of the craters toward Lumus with blood rolling down his face from the battle with Rasel. Lears tried with all of his strength to pull himself across the rough terrain to Lumus. He couldn't help but think over and over what had just happened.

("What did he do? I couldn't see exactly what happened from so far away, but it looked as if Lumus just touched Rasel, and then she turned into star energy. I have never seen anything like that before. I suppose it won't matter as long as I can make it to him before he gets his strength back. I can end him now, then take my place as this planet's ruler once and for all." Lears wheezed as he pulled himself along the rocky terrain.

("Lumus? Lumus can you hear me?") Lumus laid with his face against the dirt with his eyes closed.

("Scarlette? I recognized your voice. I'm glad I get to talk to you again.") Lumus confided.

("I'm sorry Lumus… It turns out that I need to ask permission to speak to someone on Twilight this way. I am still learning their ways and how things work here.") Scarlette muttered with a tone.

("Permission? You are a goddess, right? Why would you need permission Scarlette?") He asked as he coughed.

("We don't have a lot of time to chat, Lumus. Let's just say 'higher powers' get very upset when I intervene with the people's fate. You seem to have confused a few of the gods here with that ability to revert Serpentarius to star energy. It would seem she is trying to break free from the Realm of the Dead Core, but Omega has her contained for the time being. I don't know how you did that, but I wouldn't recommend you ever do that again. The other Zins tell me that that ability was something only the gods know, and I should tell you that it was a one-time thing. Even the gods can only send one willing soul back to the core once every few hundred years. I too don't know how you did that Lumus.") Scarlette went quiet for a moment.

("I don't know. It was like a voice in my head was walking me through the steps of how to perform the transfer of star energy. It nearly killed me though.") Lumus replied.

("It scared me Lumus. Somehow I felt your life force immediately begin to fade, but I feel the others coming to my world. I have spoken to you too long. Please Lumus, open your eyes! Now!") She shouted. Lumus felt like his head shook from Scarlette's voice echoing in her head.

He felt a small shock in his chest too, enough to physically shake his body. He opened his eyes wide then squinted from the light. As he focused his blurred vision he noticed Lears' eyes as he crawled toward him, but using the ability to return star energy to Twilight caused him to feel completely drained of energy.

("Scarlette... I won't die here...") Lumus thought. He tried to lean on his forearms, but it took everything he had to even lift his head up.

"Lears, you are as worn out as I am. Are you sure you want to fight now?" Lumus coughed.

"Lumus it doesn't matter if we are one hundred percent or one percent of our power. I will always be better than you, and I will end you to take this world as mine, as it should be!" Lears boasted as he continued to crawl toward him. He used every ounce of strength to make it to one knee. He continued to wheeze as he drew in each breath. Lears pulled himself up to one knee matching his stance.

"So you really want to do this now, Lears?" Lumus asked.

"Like I said to Rasel; I will show you the darkness!" Lears struggled to raise an arm and opened his fist. He aimed his palm at Lumus, matching his movements.

"Okay, Lears. Have it your way." Lumus continued to struggle for each breath.

There were thirty feet between the two warriors. They began to emit what star energy they could. They formed a concentrated sphere of star energy in front of their palms.

"Now you die, Lumus!" Lears announced with rage in his eyes. Their energies shot at each other and collided in between them. A flash of white and black energy sparked a massive reaction of energy that tore up the already devastated terrain. They both yelled as the attacks continued to collide. Their power slowly sapped their strength, but they managed to stay up on one knee. A flash blew a shockwave, sending both warriors flying in opposite directions across the ground. Both warriors fell unconscious where they landed. The wind had settled, but something wasn't right. The entire planet began to shake and the ground around them began to crack. A large dimensional hole opened in the sky above them with a clear view of Dystopia from Twilight's surface. A beam of blue light suddenly blew a hole through the ground at Aster Mountains, and up into the sky. Another beam of light from Dystopia came from the dimensional hole, but it was a solid red light. When the two lights collided just outside Twilights atmosphere, the lights spiraled higher into space. Another dimensional hole appeared in the far reaches of space, and the lights caused an enormous flash visible even from the surface of Dystopia.

The light faded to reveal a large red sphere. The dimensional hole leading to Dystopia shut, and shortly after the dimensional hole leading to the new mysterious red planet also shut. Neither Lumus nor Lears was conscious to witness the event, but people all over Twilight were able to see everything. The two warriors laid almost lifeless on the battlefield as the world in front of them had unknowingly changed forever.

Made in the USA
Columbia, SC
12 June 2018